BABES
in the
WOOD

Mark Stay got a part-time Christmas job at Waterstone's in the nineties (back when it still had an apostrophe) and somehow ended up working in publishing for over 25 years. He would write in his spare time and (he can admit this now) on company time, and sometimes those writings would get turned into books and films. Mark is also co-presenter of the Bestseller Experiment podcast, which has inspired writers all over the world to finish and publish their books. Born in London, he lives in Kent with YouTube gardener Claire Burgess and a declining assortment of retired chickens.

@markstay
markstaywrites.com
witchesofwoodville.com

Also by Mark Stay

Robot Overlords
Back to Reality (with Mark Oliver)
The End of Magic

The Witches of Woodville series

The Crow Folk

BABES
in the
WOOD

The Witches of Woodville II

Mark Stay

**SIMON &
SCHUSTER**

London · New York · Sydney · Toronto · New Delhi

First published in Great Britain by Simon & Schuster UK Ltd, 2021

Copyright © Unusually Tall Stories, Ltd 2021

1 3 5 7 9 10 8 6 4 2

Simon & Schuster UK Ltd
1st Floor
222 Gray's Inn Road
London WC1X 8HB

Simon & Schuster Australia, Sydney
Simon & Schuster India, New Delhi

www.simonandschuster.co.uk
www.simonandschuster.com.au
www.simonandschuster.co.in

A CIP catalogue record for this book
is available from the British Library

Paperback ISBN: 978-1-4711-9799-4
eBook ISBN: 978-1-4711-9800-7
Audio ISBN: 978-1-3985-0718-0

Typeset in Sabon by M Rules

Printed and bound by CPI Group (UK) Ltd, Croydon, CR0 4YY

MIX
Paper from
responsible sources
FSC® C020471

This book was written in lockdown, and my gratitude goes out to all frontline workers. My family had need of you more than once, and you never let us down.

July, 1940

The Battle of Britain has begun.

After a crushing retreat at Dunkirk, the remaining Allied Forces gather in Britain and prepare for invasion. From their bases in France, the Luftwaffe attack targets on the English coast and shipping convoys in the Channel, with the aim of devastating British air defences and supply lines. In the skies above a small village in Kent, RAF Spitfires and Hurricanes do battle with Luftwaffe fighters and bombers. But there are other dangers here, too. Ones of a magical kind ...

THE MANY MERITS OF GEORGE FORMBY

Faye and Bertie were chatting on the bus home when a plane dropped out of the sky.

They had spent the day in Canterbury. Any other year and this would have been the Saint Irene's Bell-Ringers' Tower summer outing. A jolly old time visiting bell towers all over Kent, ringing their bells, trying new methods and, most importantly, quaffing local beers and ciders and scoffing homemade scones and cake. Alas, since the government's ban on bell-ringing in June, their plans were scotched. It had been suggested by Mr Hodgson, the tower captain, that they still visit the towers, but ring handbells instead. This was greeted with much grizzling, not least from Faye.

'Handbells ain't proper ringing,' she had said, with many murmurs of agreement from the rest of the tower band. 'It's like asking someone to play a concert on a grand piano and then handing them a bleedin' accordion. It's not the same.'

Mr Hodgson then suggested ringing tied bells – where the clapper is tied up so that it doesn't make a sound – which they tried for a couple of practices at Saint Irene's, but to pull on a rope and not even get the satisfaction of a bell actually ringing was deemed completely pointless by all concerned.

When it also transpired that there would be no beer, cider, cake or scones at the bell towers on the itinerary it was clear that the district outing needed a rethink.

Ideas were put into a hat, then put to a vote, and then ignored and argued over until a compromise was reached whereby Mr Hodgson pouted until he got his own way and they all went to Canterbury for the day. Mr Hodgson arranged for a tour of the bells of the cathedral, and he promised that the city would have plenty of beer, cider, cake and scones in its pubs and bakeries.

The day had been a success, topped off with the glamour of the silver screen when they all went to see the new George Formby flick, *Let George Do It!*, at the Friars Cinema. For Bertie – possibly the world's biggest fan of the banjolele-playing comedy croonster – this was the cherry on top, and he didn't stop jabbering about it all the way home.

'I think my favourite part was the bit at the end when he went flying out of the torpedo tube,' Bertie said, snorting a laugh. He and Faye were sitting in their favourite seats on the bus. Top deck, right at the front. Before the war they would sit here to enjoy the view, though these days all the windows on the bus were

covered with anti-blast netting, a mesh that would protect any passenger from shards of glass if a Luftwaffe
bomb dropped nearby. The only view passengers got
now was one through a net curtain, though some of the
netting had a clear little diamond shape in the centre
for nosy parkers to peer through.

The bus was dotted with shoppers. Mr Hodgson
and the other ringers were flopped around them. The
Roberts twins were still polishing off slices of sponge
cake, Mrs Pritchett snored like a blocked drain, and
Miss Burgess and Miss Gordon were both knitting
what looked like two ends of the same scarf. Faye was
the only one paying attention to Bertie.

'Or, no, no, it was the bit when he sang "Mr Wu's a
Window Cleaner Now", that's my favourite. No, no,
it was the bit when he had that dream and knocked
Hitler's block off. That, now *that* was funny.' Bertie
gave a little sigh of satisfaction. 'You ever have a day
you wish could last for ever?'

Faye had, but she kept it to herself. Not long ago,
she'd used magic to speak to her late mother. Well, she
was fairly sure it was her mum. Just a simple candle
ritual at the hollow oak in the woods. The birds
around Faye replied with a giddy cacophony of chirps
and whistles that came to her as words of love and
reassurance.

It only worked that once. She tried it again the next
day, and the day after, but the birds did not reply. Birds
were quieter in July anyway, she told herself. Many
of them were moulting, making flight cumbersome,

and singing would only draw them to the attention of sparrow-hawks.

Besides, she had been warned about using magic unsupervised. Mrs Teach and Miss Charlotte were overseeing her magical tuition now, and the witches wouldn't stand for any nonsense, so Faye put aside any thoughts of trying again. She told herself she was being greedy and to be happy with what she had. At least she was given the chance to say goodbye and to tell her mother that she loved her. Few folk got that, especially these days.

'I think I'll go and see it again,' Bertie said, bouncing in his seat. 'I ain't never seen a flick twice, but I could watch this one over and over. I've never laughed so much in my life.'

Faye was happy to see Bertie so animated. He'd been less lively since the events of last month, when the village was besieged by the crow folk, a band of walking, talking scarecrows. Thanks to Vera Fivetrees' obeah magic, no one could quite recall what happened with their leader Kefapepo, the demon scarecrow with a pumpkin for a head, but some remembered more than others. Faye reckoned that Bertie – who had been instrumental in helping the witches defeat Kefapepo – retained more memories than most. She remembered the shell-shocked look in the poor lad's eyes when it was all over. He might not know exactly what he remembered, but the darkness of it haunted him like a bad dream. A bit of George Formby's tomfoolery was just what he needed.

Faye had the tune of 'Mr Wu's a Window Cleaner Now' in her head and began tapping out its rhythm on her thighs.

Then she started to whistle.

Then she started to sing.

Bertie smiled as he joined in, as did the Roberts twins, Miss Burgess and Miss Gordon. It wasn't long before everyone on the bus was singing along.

Almost everyone. Mrs Pritchett was still asleep and Mr Hodgson – who compared Formby's singing to a trip to the dentist – refused to come out from behind his newspaper, his fingers tightly gripping its edges.

The sun was dipping below the rooftops as the bus turned onto the Wode Road. They would be home soon. As the double-decker chugged slowly around a tight bend, Faye spotted something through the anti-blast netting covering the bus window. She peered through the diamond-shaped gap in the fabric to read a poster on a village notice board:

WOODVILLE VILLAGE SUMMER FAIR
For the benefit of our wounded boys

Tops for attractions, including . . .

Cake of the Year
Tin Can Alley
Sack Race
Punch & Judy
Morris Dancers

Miss Woodville, 1940
Horticultural displays and much, much more!

Hayward Lodge, Saturday 20th
July from noon till dusk.

'That's this Saturday.' Faye nudged Bertie, who took a break from singing to catch a glimpse of the poster. 'Are you going?'

Bertie looked from the receding poster to Faye to the poster then to Faye again. He sputtered a series of vowels, 'Oh, eh, I, oh,' before nodding. 'Will you be there?'

'Dad's running the beer tent,' Faye said. 'I'll be helping out, but when I take a break we can have a go on the stalls. Mr Paine is running the coconut shy and he says he's putting little Hitler moustaches on them. Good for morale, he said. You fancy that?'

'Oh.' Bertie nodded and blushed. 'I do, very much.'

Why was he blushing?

'In fact,' Bertie continued, 'I was thinking that you and me could, y'know, p'raps go together and ...'

As he burbled on, his whole face flushed red. Something fluttered in Faye's belly as she realised something that had been in front of her all this time.

Bertie was soft on her.

But they were friends. You didn't get all mushy and romantic with your friends. And Faye had never thought of him in that way. To be honest, she didn't think much of courting or romance generally. She skimmed those bits in books and pulled a face when actors got all smoochy in films, and she'd seen how daft girls like Milly Baxter behaved around boys and wanted nothing to do with it, thank you very much. And besides, there was a war on. All the lads were away fighting.

Except Bertie, with his one leg shorter than the other. He wanted to fight and had been first in the queue to volunteer, but they'd turned him away. He joined the Local Defence Volunteers instead. Doing his bit with the older chaps to defend the land.

'What do you think?'

Faye blinked and noticed that Bertie had stopped talking and was looking at her with his big puppy eyes and waiting for an answer to a question she hadn't quite heard.

'Think?' She played for time.

'About us.' Bertie was faltering. Having summoned the courage to ask Faye out once had all but exhausted him and she wasn't sure he had it in him to do it again. 'Going to the village fair.'

Faye had no idea what to tell him. If she said no, she would break his heart and never forgive herself. If she said yes . . . She knew how fast gossip travelled around the village and in the blink of an eye she'd be married with a little one on the way, and she definitely did not want that. She just needed a little time to think.

'Well, er, it's like this, Bertie—'

A shadow overhead blotted out the sun. Faye caught

sight of black smoke, a flash of light reflected off glass and red flames boiling as a burning mass of engine, propeller, wings and tail rammed down onto Mr Allen's garage on the corner of Unthank Road.

A FLAMING HURRICANE

'What the blimmin' 'eck is that?' Faye managed to cry before the bus driver hit the brakes, hurling every passenger into the one in front. Faye and Bertie both butted their heads on the glass of the top-deck window then were thrown back in their seats, all thoughts of romance gone in an instant.

'Looks like a Hurricane Mark One with a two-blade Watts prop and Browning machine guns,' Bertie said, shaking his head clear.

Faye pushed her specs back into place and squinted at him. 'How do you know this stuff?'

'It's in my scrapbook,' Bertie said, pointing at the flaming wreckage sticking out of the garage roof. 'And you can tell by the shape of the wing, and the wood-and-canvas structure of the fuselage. The interesting thing about the Hurricane—'

'Later, Bertie, eh?' Faye had already been well briefed by Bertie on his aircraft scrapbook and didn't need a refresher now. She patted him on the shoulder, got to her feet and looked back along the length of the bus. The deck was full of dazed passengers. As well as Faye's fellow bell-ringers, there were several folk in uniform, others in civvies and a few children wailing in fright. 'Anybody hurt?' Faye called.

Mr Hodgson shook his head, though he was wide-eyed, white as milk and his newspaper was scrunched into a tiny ball. The Roberts twins clung to one another tightly, and Miss Burgess and Miss Gordon were draped in loose knitting wool.

Mrs Pritchett snorted herself awake. 'We there yet?' Her eyes bulged when she saw the flames and black smoke. 'What did I miss?'

'A plane crashed on Mr Allen's garage,' Faye told her. 'Let's all exit the bus calmly and—'

She was cut off by Mr Allen's garage exploding.

A fiery combination of aircraft fuel and burning wreckage all piled onto a petrol station forecourt will do that.

Every window shattered as the double-decker shook. The anti-blast netting saved Faye and the passengers from being lacerated with broken glass, but even so, countless tiny shards spun through the air and Faye instinctively snapped her eyes shut.

The blast wave tipped the bus over to one side. Faye's ears rang as all around her the passengers joined in a terrifying chorus of 'Whoooaaah!' as the double-decker teetered at a perilous angle for what felt like for ever. Just as Faye was sure they would slam onto the road below, the bus righted itself, thumping all of its wheels on the ground, flinging the passengers about and sending splinters of glass sliding across the deck.

Black smoke billowed in through the empty window frames and heat pressed on Faye's skin. She fumbled for the cardboard gas mask box that hung from a string over her shoulder. People were required to take these everywhere they went. Faye rarely bothered in the village, but you didn't want to be caught without one on a trip to town, though she never suspected she would actually use the blooming thing.

Mr Hodgson was already leading the other passengers down to the lower deck. A few people had cuts from the glass, and one of the Roberts twins had a sizeable shard poking out of the top of his head like a wafer in an ice cream, though he looked quite oblivious to it.

'I'll see if anyone's hurt,' Bertie said, wriggling his own mask on. His first aid training with the Local Defence Volunteers had only seen him practising on his reluctant colleagues with fake wounds. Now he was about to put it to the test.

Faye made for the stairwell to the lower deck.

'Where are you going?' Bertie said, his voice muffled by the mask.

'I'm going to put that fire out.'

Just last month, Faye had helped put out a barn fire, but that was in very different and very strange circumstances. For a moment, she almost wished for some of the demon Pumpkinhead's magic that allowed him to extinguish fires with the clap of his hands. Any magic would do, but she didn't know anything that could tackle a blaze like this. She looked around for Mrs Teach or Miss Charlotte, hoping to catch sight of them passing through the village, but they were nowhere to be seen. This would have to be done the old-fashioned way. On Monday, she had been training with Mr Paine as part of her Air Raid Precautions duties. Captain Marshall from the Local Defence Volunteers had shown them how to point a hose at a fire around a corner by threading it through a length of wood with a couple of holes drilled in it. Faye had asked what if there was a fire and she didn't happen to have a length of wood with a couple of holes drilled in it? Or a hose? She was told to stop being so impertinent.

Faye's specs and the gas mask's goggles were misting over as she dashed from the bus across the road to where the street's fire party volunteers were gathering, responding to whistles blown by those on watch. The garage wasn't big, with only one pump station, which had already exploded, and a mechanic's repair bay where Mr Allen did most of his work. It was obscured by black smoke and Faye hoped he was safe but didn't think anyone could have survived this.

A stocky man with mutton-chops came running from the smoke-filled garage. It wasn't Mr Allen, but Mr Baxter who lived opposite. He wore a grandfather shirt and red braces held up his trousers.

'Mr Baxter.' She hurried to his side, patting his back as he leaned forwards to cough the smoke from his lungs. 'Did you see him? Mr Allen? Is he in there?'

'Can't see a thing,' Mr Baxter said between wheezes. 'Poor bugger must've bought it.'

Faye's heart sank. Poor Mr Allen. She wondered if he had seen it coming. The skies had been streaked with planes dogfighting since what Mr Churchill called the Battle of Britain had begun. It was only a matter of time before one of them fell on some poor soul minding their own business. Mr Allen was a peculiar fellow. He talked to all the cars that came through his doors like they were people and always reassured them that everything would be fine. Now he was gone, Faye wondered with a pang of sadness who would reassure the villagers' cars in the future.

'That you, Faye Bright?' Mr Baxter peered at her. 'Take that mask off, it won't do you any good here. Go and help Dotty with the stirrup pump.'

Dotty was Mr Baxter's youngest daughter. A little younger than Faye, she dashed by with a pump and a length of hose.

'You pump, I'll point,' she said to Faye, placing the pump and coiled hose on the pavement.

Faye took off her gas mask, happy to be free of its rubbery aroma, though she flinched as her cheeks and nose tingled from the heat of the flames. It didn't seem to bother Dotty, who was a cheerful, big-toothed mess of freckles and blonde curls.

'Jolly exciting, isn't it?' Dotty beamed as they both unravelled the hose.

'Dotty, we're going to need water at some point,' Faye pointed out.

'Right behind us,' Dotty said, glancing over her shoulder. Faye angled her head to see Dotty's older brothers Timothy and Simon carrying a tin bath under the railway bridge towards them. Dotty's older sister Milly was nowhere to be seen. Faye recalled she had volunteered for the Women's Auxiliary Air Force in the hope of meeting dashing airmen. 'Daddy has been insisting we keep our bathwater every night for just such an occasion. He's secretly delighted.' Dotty added this last bit in a whisper as her brothers lowered the tin bath onto the pavement with a metallic scraping noise. It was three-quarters full and a toy submarine sloshed about in its water. 'Keep it coming, boys,' Dotty told them as they ran off for more.

Faye plunged the stirrup pump into the water and began pushing and lifting the pump's handle. It was hard work to get going, but soon Dotty had water coughing from her end of the hose.

'That's it, girls,' Mr Baxter called. 'Keep attacking it, don't let it spread. The fire brigade will be here soon.'

Faye's arms were aching already, but she gritted her teeth and kept pumping as Dotty pointed the hose at the garage office wearing a grin of determination.

'Help, help!' A girl's voice came from beyond the flames.

Faye looked up from the pump. 'Did you hear that? There's someone in there.' Dotty was too focused on aiming the hose and Mr Baxter was busy giving orders to the other fireguard volunteers.

'Help, help us!' the voice came again. A break in

the smoke and Faye caught sight of a black Austin 10 motor car tipped on its side in the garage. It was hidden again before she could blink, but she was sure she saw movement inside.

'Oh, blimey,' she muttered to herself, looking around for someone who could help. Bertie came limping around the front of the bus, ushering an elderly lady to the other side of the road where she could rest. 'Bertie!' she cried, and he looked up. 'Come and help with this pump, quickly.' Faye regretted the last word, as *quickly* wasn't something that came to Bertie as easy as others. Faye watched as her plucky friend limped across the road as fast as he could.

'Want me to take over?' he asked, reaching out.

'Please.' Faye guided his hands to the pump. For a moment they both pushed and pulled up and down without losing the rhythm, then once he had the hang of it Faye let go and started putting her gas mask back on.

'W-what are you doing?' Bertie asked, and from his expression Faye knew that he wasn't going to like the answer.

'Do not stop pumping, do you understand?' Faye commanded from inside the mask.

'Faye, no, don't do this.'

'There's someone in there,' she said, before dashing into the black smoke.

A Funny Turn at an
Awkward Moment

Faye's goggles misted over as she stumbled blindly through the curtain of smoke. Her shoes kicked tools strewn across the ground, and she bumped into one of the iron girders propping the garage up.

'Ow, bugger it.' She staggered back, lost in the smoke and feeling the heat on her skin. Every instinct was telling her to turn back and run to safety. She wriggled a finger under her mask and wiped the goggles clear, finding herself perilously close to the wreckage of the Hurricane. Black and flaming, it had crashed through the garage roof, its nose crumpled, propellers bent, wings broken. It lurched to one side, sending countless orange embers spiralling into the shimmering air and Faye pitied any pilot who met such a hellish fate.

She backed away from it and turned to find the car she'd glimpsed tipped over on one side. She looked through the smashed windscreen to see a jumble of kicking limbs. Three children, piled on top of one another in the back seat, and an unconscious driver, blood trickling from a wound in his scalp.

'Help!' the girl's voice cried again from inside the car.

'I'm here, help is here,' Faye called as she tried to clamber onto the bonnet. 'Ow, double-bugger it.' The car's metal shell was too hot to touch. She looked around the garage and found a couple of oily rags on a worktop that she wrapped around her hands for protection. She scrambled back onto the car and grasped the rear passenger door handle. The frame was buckled and would only move a quarter of an inch. She pulled and pulled and it juddered back and forth, but simply would not open. Through the cracked window she could see three terrified faces, wide eyes willing her to open the door, little fingers grasping up at her.

The door handle snapped off in her grip.

'Oh, fffff-fiddlesticks.' She scowled at it before tossing it away. 'Clamber across,' she hollered, waving them to the front of the car.

The skeletal wreckage of the plane groaned as it shifted again. Faye glanced back to see the fuselage slowly tipping towards them. Any second now the car might be consumed in its fire.

'Quickly, quickly!' she cried, catching a glimpse of her masked face in the wing mirror and wondering what scared the children more: her or the fire.

She grasped the front passenger door handle and swung it open.

Faye reached down and took the hand of the closest child – the eldest – who pushed herself off the steering wheel, clambered out of the car and jumped onto the deck of the garage.

'That way.' Faye pointed through the smoke to the street beyond. 'Deep breath and run.'

The girl did as she was told and vanished through the black curtain of smoke. Next was the older boy, who vaulted out of the car and followed the girl. The final child, a little blond lad, froze like a rabbit in headlights. Surrounded by shards of glass, he shook his head and wrapped his arms around his knees, curling into a ball.

Behind Faye, the Hurricane moaned in its death throes. There was a crash as part of the tail tumbled to the floor, fanning the flames around it.

'Please.' Faye leaned into the car to grab him, but he inched into the farthest corner, still shaking his head. 'What's your name, sonny?'

'*Nein, ich habe Angst,*' he said.

'W-wot?' Faye stammered. That sounded a lot like German. She didn't know much, other than what she'd seen in newsreels and films, but this little chap wasn't local, that was for sure.

'*Lass es verschwinden,*' the boy wailed, ducking his head down and kicking his feet.

Definitely German, Faye thought, and absolutely terrified. She didn't blame him. The crackle of the flames was getting louder and the asbestos roof above started to pop. This whole place could come tumbling down any minute.

'Hey, mister.' She shook the unconscious driver. 'Wake up, hey, wake up!' He rocked back and forth and his eyelids flickered. He needed a little something to jolt him awake. Faye jabbed the heel of her shoe on the Austin's horn. It honked over and over and the driver's eyes bulged open. He gasped a breath, his head darting around as he tried to make sense of his topsy-turvy world.

'*Was ist passiert?*' he said.

'Oh, blimey, it's like a Nuremberg Rally in here,' Faye muttered to herself. 'It's a fire, mate. Fire. Do you understand?'

'Yes, yes,' he said, then reached back to the frightened little boy. '*Rudolf, komm her.*'

The boy, Rudolf, shook his head.

'*Bitte, Rudolf!*'

The boy threw his head back and began to howl.

'*Verdammt,*' the driver cursed and, with a groan, reached behind his seat, grabbed the wailing boy by the scruff of his neck and hauled him up to Faye, who took the lad's hand.

The world swam around her.

A body lies among trees. The sun shines down through the canopy. It had rained, and the air was sweet.

Faye shook her head clear, but the garage tilted to one side.

The little boy stands over the body, shaking it, calling out a name over and over. 'Klaus, Klaus!'

22

'What are you doing?' the driver's accented voice cut through Faye's vision. She was standing over the upturned car's door, holding the little boy who wriggled in her grip.

'Sorry, yes,' Faye said, all but hurling the boy away from the car and onto the deck of the garage. He landed on his sandalled feet and, hearing cries of, 'Rudolf, Rudolf!' from his siblings, he ran like a whippet after them.

Faye leapt off the car and the driver clambered out, clutching his bleeding head, just as the wreckage of the plane came crashing down on the car.

'Mr Allen! Mr Allen!' Faye yelled as she took a quick last look around the garage, hoping to see the garage owner safely huddled in a corner, but the place was a hellish inferno.

'This way.' Faye waved the driver towards the street and they both staggered, coughing and wheezing, into the sunshine. Faye yanked the gas mask off and filled her lungs with fresh air.

She cleaned the lenses of her specs on her blouse, then pushed them back in place to find the three shivering children huddled together. The girl looked about eleven, her dark hair neatly tied in a clip. The middle lad was a year or so younger, also dark-haired and bespectacled, and the little blond boy had the mucky chops and scruffy hair of six-year-olds the world over. They gathered close to the driver, a tall chap who Faye was surprised to see was about her age.

Beyond them was the double-decker bus with all

its windows blown out and shocked passengers being attended to by Bertie and other first-aiders, all in the shadow of a burning garage and RAF Hurricane. A gleaming fire engine had arrived and the firemen were aiming their powerful hoses at the shrinking flames.

A shadow flitted over the street and everyone looked up, gasping and half-expecting another aircraft to drop on them, but this was something altogether slower. A parachute drifted in an arc over the rooftops. An RAF pilot in a wool-lined leather jacket gripped the lines of the chute as it became snagged on the railway bridge. He dangled there, swinging back and forth like the pendulum of a clock.

'Ah, hello,' he said with a little wave. 'Awfully sorry. Got caught short by Jerry and had to bail out. No choice, I'm afraid.' He grimaced when he looked at the burning garage. 'Oh, gosh. I do hope nobody was hurt.'

'Dougie,' Mr Baxter said, rushing to where Faye was coughing her lungs free of smoke. 'Did you see Dougie?'

Faye could only cough, but gave Mr Baxter a look that said, *Who the hell's Dougie?*

'Mr Allen, it's his garage. Did you see him?'

Still coughing, Faye fell to her knees and shook her head. Poor Mr Allen. She could only hope that he hadn't suffered.

'What the bloody hell is this?' a Glaswegian voice cried.

Every head turned to see Mr Allen standing under the railway bridge. He held in one hand a half-eaten sausage roll. Faye was sure it was from Mrs Yorke's bakery on the Wode Road.

'I was only gone five minutes,' Mr Allen said, baffled even further by the relieved cheers from the gathered crowd.

Faye saw the little blond boy tug at the driver's sleeve. The lad sniffed, wiped a tear away, pointed at Mr Allen and asked a question in very loud German.

The cheering stopped and every head now turned to the little boy. The driver rested a hand on the boy's shoulder in an attempt to gently silence him.

'*Klaus?*' the little boy persisted. '*Klaus? Was ist los?*'

Faye shivered. Klaus. The body in her vision.

'I say,' the pilot said from his harness. 'Is that little chap a Hun?'

A harrumph of indignation swept through the crowd.

'Krauts!' someone shouted.

'Narzees!' yelled another.

The harrumph became a rumble of discontent. People started rolling up sleeves in anticipation of a fight. Cries of 'Spies!' and 'Go back to Germany!' followed.

The children clung together in a frightened huddle. The young man, Klaus, stood before them, shielding them from the patriotic anger, saying the same words over and over, '*Kindertransport, Kindertransport, Juden, Juden.*'

Somewhere in Faye's mind a penny dropped as she recalled a newsreel she had seen before the war. She positioned herself between the simmering mob and Klaus and the children. She raised her hands for calm but got none.

'They're not Nazis,' she said. 'They're Jewish.'

The crowd rippled, unsure if this was a good thing or a bad thing. Prejudice has a long and muddled memory.

'They're on our side. They're being persecuted by the Nazis and have come here to—'

More villagers arrived, knowing only that some German speakers had shown up and there was a war on, fuelling the patriotic anger of the crowd.

'Listen to me, you daft berks, just because they speak German—'

Faye ducked as an empty milk bottle was hurled over the crowd and smashed on the street by her feet. Another followed fast and smashed on a dustbin lid held by Bertie, who had rushed to her side, wielding the lid like a knight of old.

'Thanks, Bertie,' Faye said, and he flashed a smile. She gestured to the children to take cover behind him. They cried out and squeezed even closer together.

'I reckon we can leg it to the pub,' Faye told Bertie. 'Dad can let us in and—'

'Right, what's going on here, then?' Constable Muldoon's booming voice announced his arrival, but even that wasn't enough to quell the mob. Fortunately, the constable had a whistle. If there was anything the great British public understood, it was to obey the shrill call of an Acme Model 15 Metropolitan Police whistle. He blew it three times and the crowd fell silent.

'That's more like it.' Constable Muldoon's scrubbing-brush eyebrows shifted closer as he held up the whistle like a cowboy with his revolver. 'If I have to blow it again, names will go in my notebook.'

That settled it. No one in the village wanted their name in Constable Muldoon's notebook. It was a life sentence with no chance of parole.

He turned to Klaus and the children. 'Morning, folks, let's have a shufty at your papers, shall we?'

'*Mein Herr*,' Klaus said, handing the constable his identity papers. 'I am Klaus Schneider.'

The police officer took a moment to read them, his moustache bobbing as he moved his lips.

'Very good,' Constable Muldoon said, handing the card back to Klaus, then turned to address the waiting crowd. 'These children are guests in this country as part of the Kindertransport organisation, and this young man is their guardian. They're here to stay with Lord and Lady Aston up at Hayward Lodge. We are to show them every courtesy. So, if you don't have any business here, I suggest you move along before my boot makes short and sharp contact with your rear end.'

There were nods and murmurs of understanding from the crowd, which began to disperse.

Faye stood, hands on hips, quite baffled. 'That is exactly what I was just tellin' 'em, and they never took a blind bit of notice.'

Constable Muldoon gave her a wink. 'Ah, but did you have a whistle?'

'No, but I might have to get one,' Faye said.

'Impersonating a police officer is a crime,' Constable Muldoon said, patting her on the shoulder. 'Might I suggest a kazoo instead?' He turned to Klaus. 'Now, young lad. Why don't you lot come to the station and we'll give her ladyship a call.'

Klaus took the officer's hand and shook it till it blurred, thanking him over and over. His big blue eyes bright, his skin dotted with acne, the lad grasped Faye's hand next, thanking her, too.

Once more, Faye's world swirled around her.

Tree trunks reach up to blue skies dotted with little white clouds, then tumble away. A limp arm flops to the ground. The little blond boy weeps on his knees. 'Klaus, Klaus!'

Faye snatched her hand back and the vision was gone. Klaus took a step back, probably wondering what he had done wrong.

'Sorry,' Faye told him. 'I need . . . I need to have a bit of a sit down.'

And that's when everything went black.

MAX

Max just wanted to play chess. It was after dark and they were still at the police station, speaking to the officer with the big moustache who wrote everything down. Lots of phone calls and checking documents. Their cousin Klaus did all the talking for them. He was the only one with good enough English. Magda spoke a little – she knew enough to call for help, thank goodness – but she had said nothing since they were rescued from the burning garage. Rudolf would be fine for a short while, then he would burst into tears and call for Mama.

But Max just wanted a game of chess.

He loved chess. Once he was inside a game, he never wanted to come out again. Everything about it made sense. There were rules. Good rules established thousands of years ago. If you followed those rules, it made the game more exciting. You had to think harder. You had to think ahead. There was a sweet logic to the rules that made Max happy.

Now there were no rules. Not in real life, anyway.

Everyone in real life cheated. Everyone did what was best for them. There was no thinking ahead, no one cared about other people, they just did what was easy here and now and the hell with the future. It started with the Nazis. They cheated. They lied. Max's cousin Klaus was old enough to remember when it started. When the Nazis said that we took jobs from others, that we hoarded our money, that we were greedy.

Max remembered the day when the other children changed. Former friends now told lies. Max used to play chess with a boy called Walter. He was a little older than Max and a good player, they were evenly matched. One day at school, Walter told the others that Max was a dirty little Jew, and that all Jews were devils, lazy and that they drank the blood of Christian children. Their classmates gasped and called him names, and Max wondered how they could be so stupid as to believe such lies. He got into a fight with Walter. They were not evenly matched. Max got a bloody nose and was sent home, but not until his teacher, Herr Schmidt, humiliated him in front of the class. Herr Schmidt used a word to describe him that Max did not know. Subhuman. Max had to ask his parents what it meant, and it made Mama cry.

Not long after, the Nazis came to their home. The storm troopers kicked in the door and smashed their windows. They were allowed to take one bag. Mama said they were going on a big adventure to see friends in Munich where they would be safe, but they had to leave right now. There was no room for Max's chess pieces.

Since then, they'd hardly stopped moving and some days even one bag felt like too many.

All Max ever wanted to do was play chess with his father. He could never beat him. He had come close a few times, but even in his dreams Max would always be outfoxed by Papa. When Papa won, he always explained how he did it. Every time Max lost, he learned something new. That was another thing he loved about chess. No two games were exactly the same, because no two players were alike. The way someone played told you all you needed to know about them, and Max knew that his father was kind and wise and patient. The thought of never playing with his father again stoked a furnace in Max, and he knew that if he let his anger out it might never stop. And so he kept silent. If he had something to say, he would whisper it in Magda's ear and she would speak for him.

The police officer was typing something now, and the clatter of the typewriter made Max's ears hurt. Rudolf began to cry. Again. Klaus kept telling them they were safe. He had been saying that since Rotterdam. He said it when they pulled into the garage, just before a plane fell from the sky in a ball of flame.

Even now, he kept saying it. They were going to stay with a friend of Mama's. Lady Aston. Klaus said she had a big house and they would stay there until it was safe to go home again. But Max knew the truth. She would be like all the others. For months they had gone from friend to friend to friend. At first, they were welcomed with smiles and open arms and friendship, but when they heard the howl of the Stukas, the rumble of the Panzers, they told them to leave. For your own safety, they always said. Lady Aston would be like all the others. War would come here soon. It hunted them like a wolf. And Rudolf, Magda, Klaus and Max would have to pack their bags again, cursed to walk the Earth for ever, like the Wandering Jew, never finding anywhere to call home.

Max didn't care. All he wanted was to play chess.

CLOGS

Faye woke in her room. She was still dressed in the dungarees she had worn to Canterbury and was lying on top of her sheets. It was dark, the steady tock of the longcase clock downstairs the only sound. Her father Terrence slumped asleep in an armchair close to the bed, his hands clasped across his belly which gently rose and fell with each snore. His face, wrinkly when he was awake and alert, folded in on itself like a bulldog's when he was asleep.

A lit candle, Faye's glasses and a mug of tea sat on the drawers by the bed. Faye's mouth was dry, and just the sight of a cuppa set off all kinds of excitement which was dashed the moment she placed her hands around it to find it cold.

'Buggeration.'

Faye put her specs on as the clock chimed the three-quarter hour. Quite which three-quarter hour, Faye couldn't be sure, but if Dad was here then it was after closing time. Tuition started at midnight and there was

33

a strong possibility she was late, and that wouldn't go down well with Miss Charlotte or Mrs Teach. Faye swung her legs off the bed and placed her toes oh-so-gently on the floorboards.

Faye and her father lived above the Green Man pub, an establishment that had stood in the village since 1360. The building didn't have a single straight edge within its walls and every door, hinge, handle and floorboard creaked like a galleon in a storm. The board that Faye trod on was no exception.

'Ah, good, you're awake.' Terrence's eyes blinked open, circled around in their sockets as they focused and then fixed on his daughter. 'How are you, girl?'

'Just had the best kip ever,' she said, and it was true. She felt bright and refreshed. She stood and stretched, making an odd squeaky noise at the back of her throat as she did so, then found her boots at the foot of the bed. She loosened the laces and wriggled her feet in.

'You gave us all a bit of a fright,' Terrence said.

Memories of the afternoon's excitement came flooding back. The plane, the fire, the children, the terrifying portent of doom. 'Sorry, must've been the smoke.' She had seen a vision and it had snuffed her out like a candle, completely knocking her for six. She'd had them before, but never as powerful as this.

Faye wasn't sure how much her father remembered of last month's little adventure, so she kept this disturbing development to herself. Though he was privy to the family's magic streak and not so easily fooled, telling him now that she was having grim visions of death would only make him worry all the more.

'The Hurricane pilot was in here earlier, the one whose plane crashed. Him and few others told me you saved those nippers.' Terrence's lips drew into a small smile. 'I'm proud of you, Faye, but—'

'Oh, it weren't nothing. I was closest, that's all. Anyone else would've done—'

'No, let me finish.' Terrence raised a finger. 'I'm proud of you, but don't you ever do anything so stupid again.'

'What do you expect me to do? Stand there like a lemon as they burned to death?'

'The fire brigade were on their way.'

'That's as maybe, but it couldn't wait. Anyways, I told you, it weren't no fuss. I was in and out.'

'And then you fainted.'

'I'm awake now, ain't I?' Faye pulled on her bootlaces and tied them tight. 'Blimey, you'd think I'd set meself alight or something.'

'Lor', you don't half sound like your mother,' Terrence said, softly shaking his head.

'I'll take that as a compliment.'

'It was.' Terrence heaved himself out of the armchair, scruffing his receding white hair into a curly halo. 'I know we haven't really talked about what happened with you and that thing in the graveyard.'

'Not much to say, is there?' Faye replied with a sinking feeling in her belly. At least now she knew that he remembered something. She wondered just how much he recalled of their fight against the Pumpkin-headed demon Kefapepo. Whenever she thought of that thing bearing down on her, it gave her the shakes. 'What's done is done.'

Terrence nodded. 'That's true enough. But I was with your mother when she was about your age, and she would have these little funny turns. Sometimes . . . she had visions.'

Faye tensed, but kept tying her bootlaces.

'Reckoned she could see the future,' Terrence continued. 'Not that much of it made sense. She always said she never understood what she'd seen till it was happening or had already passed. She would feel guilty if she couldn't help folk, and when a vision turned out to be true and something bad happened and she missed it . . . It weighed on her.'

Faye felt a chill as the memory of the vision returned. The little boy weeping over the body of the older lad, Klaus.

'There's a war on, Faye,' Terrence said. 'Bad things happen every day and I don't want you thinking that you – with all the things that you can do – should be the one to fix everyone's problems. You'll go half-barmy if you do.'

Faye slipped on a cardigan, buttoning up the front. 'I know I can't fix the world's problems, Dad, but I will do what I can. If someone needs help and they're right in front of me, I ain't gonna ignore them.'

'Yup,' Terrence said, 'as I thought, just like your mother.'

'I'm off out.'

'Where? It's nearly midnight.'

'It's Tuesday. You know where I go on Tuesdays at midnight.'

'Oh.' Just one word, but coming from Terrence it was saddled with all kinds of disapproval.

'Don't be like that.'

'How's it going? They teaching you anything useful?'

Faye grinned and raised a finger. 'Watch this.' She moved across the room to her wardrobe and opened the door, revealing a half-length mirror inside. Leaving the door ajar, she took the candle from the bedside drawer and walked across the room. She took off her specs, holding them up to the candlelight and angling them at her own face like a make-up mirror.

'What are you—?'

'Look over at the mirror,' Faye told her father.

'Bloody hell,' he said, taking a step back. 'How'd you do that?'

Faye's face appeared in the wardrobe mirror. A floating apparition trapped in glass, wreathed in the glow of candlelight, it grinned at her father.

'A bit of candle magic,' the apparition said.

'Blimey.'

'Just don't tell anyone,' Faye said, her voice a whisper. 'I'm not supposed to do this unsupervised, and if Mrs Teach and Miss Charlotte knew, they'd have a fit. But it's good, innit?'

'What use is it?' he asked.

'No idea.' Faye lowered her glass and the candle. Her face vanished from the mirror. 'But it's something.'

'Yeah, it's something all right,' Terrence said with a grumble. 'I know this is all fun and games to you, but you don't have to do this. You could have a perfectly quiet life here, learning a trade. When I pop me clogs, this pub could be yours.'

'I don't want you to pop your clogs.'

'I have no intention of popping me clogs any time soon, but when I do—'

'Don't be so morbid.' Faye hurried over to her father and pecked him on the cheek. 'And stop talking nonsense. I'm off. I'll see you in the morning. Get some rest and keep your clogs on.'

Magical Puberty

'Next thing I knew, I woke up in my room. Dad had made me a cuppa, but it was cold.' Faye finished her story, brushing away nettles as she moved through the wood.

'And you would describe it as a vision?' Mrs Teach followed Miss Charlotte who led them along the path. The amber glow of a waxing gibbous moon could be seen through the canopy. 'What sort of vision?'

'I've had them before,' Faye said, trying to keep up with the two older women as they navigated a steep path. It had rained in the afternoon and the moisture hung in the air with a scent of honeysuckle. White moths fluttered around and mozzies buzzed in to nip the bare skin on Faye's arms. She slapped them away, though she was already bitten to buggery as she scratched at fresh bumps on her elbows.

'You never mentioned them,' Charlotte said, turning her head, her long white hair glowing as it caught the moonlight.

'It never came up,' Faye said. The ferns they trudged through grew thicker and tugged at her shins. 'Besides, I didn't think anything of it at the time, just a funny turn, that's all.'

'Describe it to us,' Mrs Teach said between puffs. She was not a woman predisposed to midnight hikes. Though her pear-shaped body moved swiftly and daintily through the wood, she had made it clear several times that she preferred flat surfaces and slingbacks to slippy hills and sensible shoes. 'When did you first have one?'

'Last month, when ...' Faye hesitated. They hadn't really talked about the strange events of June, when a group of scarecrows came to town led by a demon in disguise. The three of them had all made mistakes and none wanted to dwell on how it had almost gone horribly wrong. 'Y'know, all that business when Mr Craddock went missing? Me and Bertie went looking for him. And I found Craddock's boots and when I touched them, well, I don't know how else to say it, but the world went all topsy-turvy and I saw what happened to him. In me 'ead. Like a vision.'

'And it happened again at the garage?' Charlotte asked.

'Twice,' Faye said. 'When I took the boy's hand, and then his guardian's. I saw the guardian, Klaus, dead. And he was surrounded by trees. I have no idea where he was, but I reckon it's here in the wood.'

'It's a big wood,' Charlotte said.

'Exactly.' Faye threw her hands wide. 'What am I supposed to do?'

'Do-o?' Mrs Teach broke the word into two sylla-
bles, rising in pitch. 'Young lady, you do nothing.'

'What?'

'Visions like that are next to useless,' Mrs Teach
continued. 'You could try and warn him, but what
would that achieve? Spook the poor fellow into a state
of agitation that might well cause the very calamity
that you want to avoid. No, I should ignore the thing
if I were you. What will be, will be.'

'I can't ignore it. He might die.'

'He *will* die,' Charlotte said with her usual level of
cheer. 'We all do. Eventually.'

'And what happens when he does? How am I supposed to live with that?'

'If you didn't kill him, you have nothing to worry
about,' Charlotte replied. 'They're someone else's
problem now.'

'What she's trying to say in her own perverse
manner,' Mrs Teach said, 'is the children are in good
hands. They're at Hayward Lodge now, yes?'

'I suppose so. I was planning to pop over there in the
morning to see how they're doing.'

'Hayward Lodge? Lord and Lady Aston. Really?'
Charlotte turned to Faye, an eyebrow raised.

'That's what Constable Muldoon told us.' Faye
shrugged. 'Why the eyebrow?'

'Was Lord Aston there with the children? How
did he look?'

'Did you miss the bit of the story where I blacked out?'
Faye couldn't recall the last time she had seen Lord

Aston. Lady Aston was always galloping about on her horses, or cutting the ribbon at some charity do, but Lord Aston rarely left the grounds of Hayward Lodge.

'When you do see him, tell me how he looked,' Charlotte said.

'Well, he's a stout fella, isn't he?' Faye shrugged. 'Huge mutton-chops and very shiny boots from what I can recall.'

'Not what he looks *like*,' Charlotte said, 'but how he *looks* – is he fit and healthy?'

'Why, what do you care?'

Mrs Teach made a saucy 'Oo-oh' noise, then said to Charlotte, 'Do you have a thing for his lordship, then?'

'Certainly not,' Charlotte snapped.

'Then why the sudden concern for his health?'

Charlotte ignored her. 'We're here,' she said.

Faye tingled with excitement. Tonight was her first visit to the standing stones with the witches. They had promised to show her the power of the stones for some time, and Faye had imagined mighty granite dolmens draped in ivy, basking in the mystic glow of moonlight, a secret and ancient place where magical folk had congressed since the dawn of time.

A ragged circle of rocky stumps stood in a clearing. Most were barely knee-high, worn and eroded. One lay flat in the centre, surrounded by nettles.

'Hardly Stonehenge, is it?' Faye muttered, though she had to concede that it made a nice change from Mrs Teach's living room, which had ambitions to be the world's first chintz doily museum.

The clearing was on a rise in the wood and in the day you could see the village of Woodville from here, but in the wartime blackout there were only shadows on shadows. Somewhere in the distance a train chuffed to a far-off destination.

'Stonehenge is for tourists.' Charlotte moved to the head of the flat stone and looked up at the not-quite-full moon as if taking some measurement. 'And these were here first.'

'What are we doing tonight, then?' Faye clapped her hands together in anticipation.

'Tonight, we will discuss the importance of the moon,' Mrs Teach said. 'But first, we need a little privacy.'

Charlotte looked from the night sky to Faye. 'Please stand at the other end of the slaughter stone.'

'The, er, what?' Faye shuddered, wondering where this was going.

Mrs Teach took her elbow and guided her to the long, flat stone in the centre. 'This one, dear.'

'Did she say "slaughter stone"?'

'It's just a name,' Mrs Teach said with a smile.

'Yes, one with the word "slaughter" in it. If this is going to involve sacrificing adorable little animals or dancing around in the nuddy, then I'm not interested.'

Mrs Teach tutted. 'Certainly not. No animals will be harmed if I have anything to do with it, and if a ritual requires any form of nudity, you can guarantee it was devised by men. Usually ones in loose-fitting robes, with long, scruffy beards and ghastly sandals. It's the men who draw silly pentagrams, it's the men who have a perverse obsession with animal entrails and virgins. We will have nothing to do with that nonsense, thank you very much.'

'Yes, you can keep your clothes on tonight,' Charlotte said. 'Witness the power of the stones in conjunction with our closest heavenly body.' She raised her hand, palm flat, and swiped it across the moon. It vanished and everything outside the circle of stones went black.

'Blinkin' flip!' Faye blurted into the void. 'What happened?'

'Patience.' Charlotte's voice sounded distant, yet it tickled Faye's ear.

'How did you do that?' Faye found herself whispering.

'It's called magic, Faye,' Mrs Teach said. 'We're witches, it's what we do.'

'Here we go,' Charlotte said as the stones began to glow with the same amber hue as the moon. The three of them stood around the slaughter stone, which shone brightest of all. Outside of the stone circle was a great, endless nothing.

Faye didn't feel scared, more off-kilter. Like she was on a ship in a storm. The ground ebbed and flowed under her feet and it was becoming increasingly difficult to tell up from down.

'Where are we?' She was whispering again.

'We haven't gone anywhere.' Charlotte sat cross-legged at the head of the slaughter stone. She produced tobacco and a clay pipe from within her coat and began stuffing one into the other.

'We can come here when the moon is fat,' Mrs Teach said, laying down a picnic blanket. 'This is one of the ways we can get away from it all. A marching band could stomp through here and they would never see us nor hear us.' She reclined on the blanket and patted at a spot next to her. 'Sit down before you fall down, girl, you'll find it's easier on your constitution.'

Faye did as she was told. Mrs Teach was right, the ground felt firmer with her bottom on it.

'It's like a magical bubble,' Faye ventured. 'You come here to hide.'

'We do not hide.' Charlotte scratched a match into flame and lit her pipe.

'We exist in plain sight,' Mrs Teach added, 'but most folk see only what they want to see. No, this is a special place. We use it to practise away from prying eyes.'

That sounded like hiding to Faye, but she knew better than to say so.

'How did you do that?' she asked, swiping her hand as Charlotte had. 'With the moon?'

'I'm not sure you're ready for that quite yet,' Charlotte said, dragging on her pipe.

'And if you were, you shouldn't do it on your own,' Mrs Teach said.

'And only on a night like tonight,' Charlotte said.

'Oh, goodness, yes. Try this with a crescent moon and the effects would be quite devastating. We would be cleaning up the mess for days.'

'What if I go outside the circle?' Faye asked, peering between the stones to the darkness beyond.

45

'Definitely do *not* do that,' Mrs Teach said, bulging her eyes at Charlotte. 'She's an inquisitive one, this one, isn't she?'

'That's cos you won't let me do anything.' Faye raised her hands then slapped them on her thighs. 'All I've had since you two promised to show me magic is *don't do this* and *don't do that*.'

Mrs Teach bristled. 'We've shown you mirror magic, candle magic.'

'Only after I nagged all night.'

Charlotte grimaced at the memory.

'Let me have a go,' Faye persisted. 'Why won't you let me try, at least?'

'Fine, just be quiet. Your voice hurts my ears when you get like this.' Charlotte got to her feet, reached up and moved her hand to one side, revealing the moon. The stars returned along with a warm night breeze whistling through the trees.

'We're ... we're doing this now?' Faye asked.

'Stand here,' Charlotte said, pointing to a spot on the ground next to her.

Faye hesitated.

'Do you want to try this or not?' Charlotte raised an eyebrow.

Faye hurried to her side, noticing that Mrs Teach was watching with a wry smile on her face, clearly expecting her to fail.

'The moon is key to our magic,' Miss Charlotte said. 'Our year is not dictated by the Gregorian calendar, but by the four sabbaths, the solstices and equinoxes.

The moon is never late. As a young woman, you will know this.'

Faye nodded and grimaced.

'In time, you will learn of its true power. Of drawing down the moon. Of its twenty-eight mansions. Of the Goddess and the sacred feminine.' Charlotte looked to the moon as one might look upon a cathedral. Then she sniffed and clapped her hands together. 'Let's have at you. Face the moon.'

Faye did as she was told.

'Reach up,' Charlotte said, and Faye obeyed. 'Close your eyes. Can you feel the light of the moon on the palm of your hand?'

Faye was about to tell her to stop being ridiculous, but then she felt it. The same power that moved tides was pulsing in the centre of her hand. It tickled, like someone was stroking their finger on her palm.

'Take that light and gently push it to one side,' Charlotte said.

Faye swiped her hand, but the feeling of the light did not come with it.

'Try again,' Charlotte said. 'Gently, now.'

Faye raised her hand, moving it about, trying to find that sensation again. She heard Charlotte huffing impatiently behind her and could sense Mrs Teach's smug *I-told-you-so* expression becoming all the smugger.

'I . . . I can't find it,' Faye said.

'Take your time,' Charlotte said, though her voice became tighter.

47

Faye moved her hand faster, desperately trying to locate that elusive feeling once more.

Mrs Teach cleared her throat with the same tone as someone who has a bus to catch.

Faye swept her hand back and forth, but it just wasn't there.

'That's enough,' Charlotte said. 'Open your eyes.'

'But I had it,' Faye protested. 'I just need—'

'You're getting flustered and distracted,' Charlotte said. 'We'll try another night when you're prepared and calm.'

Faye opened her eyes and was about to give her a mouthful, but she realised Charlotte was right. She hadn't been thinking straight.

'Try again in five minutes?' Faye suggested.

'No, this needs preparation and a clear head,' Charlotte said, casually reaching up to the moon, swiping her hand and making it vanish effortlessly in a way that had Faye grinding her teeth. 'Another night.'

'Sorry,' Faye said. 'I just want to do magic that's useful.'

'You want to be useful?'

'Yes.'

'Then shut up and listen.' Charlotte pointed her pipe at Faye. 'Your visions are the beginning of your magical kindling. A similar thing happened to me at your age. Little lumps and bumps of your mind are awakening, lumps and bumps that most people never use. If we could scoop out your brain and put it under a microscope, it would be lit up like Doctor Frankenstein's laboratory. Sparks will fire inside your noggin and will continue to do so as you adjust to the change. You will see things, have visions, experience strangeness every day.'

'Think of it as a kind of magical puberty, dear,' Mrs Teach said.

'Over time you will learn to control your mind. We will teach you how. Until then you will have to ride the storm. It gets better, I promise.'

Faye raised a finger like a child in class. 'Maybe I could keep a journal? That might help make sense of—'

'What have we said about writing things down?' Mrs Teach sat upright. 'We already had to burn your mother's book, we don't want to destroy any more. It's very upsetting.'

'Not as much for you as it was for me,' Faye grumbled.

'Written records are strictly forbidden by the Council of Witches,' Charlotte said, an evasive look in her eye making Faye wonder if she had a secret stash of books hidden away somewhere. 'Your mother knew that, and she knew the consequences.'

Not for the first time, Faye wished her mother was teaching her instead of these two. The book that Kathryn Wynter created before she died was full of magical instruction, ritual, sketches and advice. If it hadn't been for the book, they would not have defeated the demon they encountered last month. But the order from Vera Fivetrees, Head of the UK Council of Witches and High Witch of the British Empire, was to destroy it and so they had. It had broken Faye's heart.

The last connection with her mother was gone. Well, most of it. She had kept back a page, but these two didn't need to know that.

'What about this fella, Klaus?' Faye asked. 'Am I supposed to just let him die?'

'We've already discussed this, Faye,' Mrs Teach said, glancing to Charlotte who puffed on her pipe before answering.

'Faye, there is a whole world out there, full of misery, death and sadness. More so today than ever before. If we were to try and use our magic to solve every person's sorrow, it would only lead to more misery, death and sadness.'

Faye bristled. 'Dad said I would go half-barmy if I tried to solve all the world's problems. He said it used to upset me mum.'

'He is correct,' Mrs Teach said. 'It is our burden.'

Charlotte exhaled smoke through her nostrils. 'We use our magic to resolve magical problems,' she said. 'We keep supernatural evil at bay. The rest of the world can clean up its own messes.'

Mrs Teach scrunched her nose and her voice rose in pitch. 'Does that make sense, poppet?' Faye realised she was getting a lesson tonight. One in being patronised.

'I do,' Faye replied, knowing full well that the first opportunity she got, she was going to find out more about Klaus and the Kindertransport children.

HAYWARD LODGE AND ITS MANY KNICK-KNACKS

Hayward Lodge was a mile and a half from Woodville Village off Edge Road, hidden down a long, winding drive lined with silver birch trees.

Faye yawned as she pedalled her Pashley Model A bicycle along the drive, tyres scrunching on the gravel. She had managed to get a few hours' kip after last night's meeting at the standing stones, but the dawn chorus woke her at first light, and she couldn't stop thinking about Klaus and the children. Straight after breakfast, she got on her bike.

Beyond the trees, a doe started and bounded away into the morning mist. As Faye rounded a bend, Hayward Lodge came into view.

Bits of it dated from the sixteenth century, but the big mock-castle extension was originally built in 1817 after the First Lord Aston returned from Waterloo and decided what he really wanted was a house with turrets and crenellations, but without the rather draughty disadvantages of an actual castle.

Topping it off was a more recent addition of a small tower with a glass dome. The Third Lord Aston's observatory. Mr Paine of the local Air Raid Precautions committee had asked Lord Aston if they could use the dome to keep watch at nights. Lord Aston had declined them the use of the observatory but offered any of the other turrets around the house. Faye had done a shift here just a few weeks ago and the view over the wood with the full moon shining down upon trees gently swaying in the breeze was pretty breathtaking.

Faye leaned her bicycle against the impressive stone fountain bowl that sat before the main steps of the house. The fountain had been dry since the start of the war to preserve water and there were a few pennies at the bottom of the bowl where wishes had been made.

She was just wondering which of the house's four doors she should knock on when Lord and Lady Aston themselves strode out of a pair of glass French doors on the left.

The Third Lord Aston filled out a tweed jacket, hands clasped behind his back, the face behind those mutton-chops as serious as ever. Lady Aston was in her jodhpurs and bowler hat with a riding crop tucked under her arm. Whenever Faye encountered Lady Aston she was either on a horse, getting off one or about to get on one again.

'Faye Bright, the hero of the hour,' Lady Aston trilled. 'How delightful.'

Faye wasn't entirely sure of the protocol when you met a lord and lady out in the open like this. Did you curtsey? Bow? Get down on one knee? In the end, she went with a jolly wave. 'Morning, folks,' she said. 'I was just wanting to check on the Kindertransport kiddies. They must've had a hell of a shock yesterday and all.'

'Oh, Faye, you are sweet,' Lady Aston said. 'From what I hear, they may owe their lives to you.'

'I dunno about that. I just did whatever anyone else would.'

'Tish and nonsense.' Lady Aston patted Faye on the shoulder with the riding crop. 'Those are the children of a dear friend and we are indebted to you, young lady.'

'Elizabeth, darling, I should get back to work.' Lord Aston's voice was deep and soft.

It occurred to Faye that she had never heard him talk before. He leaned in and took her hand, gripping it gently and giving it one precise shake. 'Faye Bright, your bravery is an example to us all. We thank you.'

'Ah, weren't nothin',' Faye said, feeling her cheeks blush. She was reminded of Miss Charlotte's curiosity about how he looked. He was a handsome fellow with bright green eyes. He somehow looked younger than his wife. Faye had it in her head that he was much older, but his skin was smooth and tight with only the suggestion of crow's feet around the eyes. Faye would report back to Charlotte that he looked fine and dandy.

'Nevertheless, you are always welcome here,' he said, flashing a grin of white teeth. 'Do please excuse me. I'm afraid I have some work to attend to.'

'Yes, off you pop.' Lady Aston pecked him on the cheek and he walked around the side of the house, hands still clasped behind his back.

'Come through, come through.' Lady Aston waved Faye towards the French doors. 'I'm delighted you're here as it saves me the bother of seeking you out. The children have a little something for you.'

'For me? That's nice, but they didn't have to—'

'And yet they did. Follow me.'

Lady Aston strode through a different set of doors – big oak ones that cried like a giant redwood felled by a lumberjack as they opened – into an entrance hall with a grand marble staircase that split off in a Y-shape. There was a nook with a chair and telephone, and large canvases with paintings of stags staring at mountains for no apparent reason.

Faye had never been inside Hayward Lodge before, and as the sound of their heels clacking on the polished wooden floor echoed around them, she wondered why anyone should want a gaff this big. She was about to comment that it must be a bugger to dust when she glimpsed a maid down a hallway dabbing a feather duster on the bust of some Roman-looking bloke.

They entered a grand hall that you could fit the Green Man's saloon bar into twice over. Chandeliers hung from the ceiling and tapestries adorned the walls, much as Faye expected. She knew that the halls were being used as a hospital, but she still wasn't prepared for the twenty or so beds lined up along each side of the hall. A wounded soldier lay in every one of them, with doctors and nurses attending to their injuries.

'Morning, all,' Lady Aston called as she strode through. A few patients murmured replies, but most were too weak, wrapped in bandages or trapped in plaster casts.

Faye hurried to keep up. 'Good of you to open your house up as an 'ospital.'

'The requisition order arrived the day after war was declared,' Lady Aston said as they entered another hall, this one lined with tall windows. Bright, sunny rectangles shone on more beds. These patients looked a little less ravaged. A few on crutches were smiling. 'But it was after Dunkirk that the place really filled up. Poor chaps took something of a hammering. Ah, Pinder.' She called after a man coming the other way dressed in the black suit and tie of a butler. He was bald on top with tufts of startled white hair erupting from behind his ears, which made Faye think of her father. Pinder's expression brightened at her ladyship's approach.

'Have you seen the children?' Lady Aston asked.

'Last observed in the garden, m'lady,' he replied, swinging open yet another set of doors. 'I set them to harvesting more of the gooseberries.'

'My gardener ran off and joined the Navy of all things,' Lady Aston told Faye. 'I said to him, Royston, what exactly do you expect to grow on a destroyer?'

They didn't break stride as they barrelled through more doors and marched into a private study lined with the heads of lions, tigers, bears, deer of every kind and a startled rhino.

'Ghastly, aren't they?' Lady Aston said, weaving between dusty armchairs and antique tables. 'Most came to a grisly end thanks to my husband, though a few of the smaller ones are courtesy of our son, Harry. I've told him to stop, but he's keen on completing the collection with an elephant. Can you imagine?'

'My dad once had a stuffed owl that he won in a raffle and displayed at the end of the bar, then one of Mrs Pritchett's dogs got hold of it and tried to mate with it. It ended up in the bin after that.'

'Best place for it,' Lady Aston agreed.

Most of the animal heads had some kind of explanatory note beneath it, engraved in brass as you might find in a museum, though these had somewhat pithier declarations: 'Bagged in the Hindu Kush, March 1882'; 'Got this blighter in Rhodesia, June 1890'; 'This bugger almost had my leg, August 1892'.

Beneath them was a table dotted with framed photographs. Faye glanced at a daguerreotype of a group of hunters standing under a tree. There was no slain beast, which was unusual, and no triumphant remark. Simply, 'Tien Shan foothills, Kazakhstan, July 22nd, 1885'. Front and centre of the group was the Second Lord Aston looking remarkably smug with his puffed-out chest and lantern jaw. He sported the same mutton-chops as his son.

'Blimey, don't he look like his dad?' Faye said, holding up the frame for Lady Aston to see.

'Beg pardon?' Her ladyship's left eye gave a little twitch when she saw the photo.

'Lord Aston. This is his old man in the photo, right?' Faye said. 'They don't half look alike.'

'Yes, the resemblance is remarkable.' Lady Aston tapped her foot, impatient to move on. 'Good breeding,' she added, unable to look directly at the daguerreotype, as if doing so would turn her to stone.

Faye recalled the late Mr Craddock going off on one in the pub about how toffs all looked alike because they married their cousins or something, and Faye reckoned that was what Lady Aston was embarrassed about.

'Come along, girl!' Lady Aston crashed through the study doors and into another hallway without looking back.

Faye was about to put the daguerreotype back on the table where she found it when she saw something in it that made her gasp.

The Second Lord Aston was posed with a retinue made up of Kazakh trackers and guns-for-hire, all furry hats and bandoliers, but at the back, with snow-capped mountains rising behind her, stood a tall, elegant woman with long white hair. There was no mistake. It was definitely her, and she hadn't aged a day since the picture was taken.

'Charlotte bloody Southill,' Faye whispered to herself.

WHEN LIFE GIVES YOU
GOOSEBERRIES

'Faye!' Lady Aston's voice echoed from the hall.

Faye took one last look at the photograph. If it wasn't Charlotte, it was her dead spit. She had the same default expression of disdain on her face, and there was a clay pipe clenched between her teeth.

'Do come along!'

Faye replaced the photo and hurried after her ladyship.

Lady Aston burst through two more sets of doors before entering something she called an orangery, which wasn't orange at all, but long and narrow and bright and dotted with small orange trees in pots. Tall windows looked out over the rolling grounds of the Aston estate, and a glass ceiling made the air as muggy as a greenhouse.

Faye puzzled over how Miss Charlotte was in a photo from nearly sixty years ago looking exactly the same as she did now. The questions that Faye had for her fellow witches began to pile up in her head.

Chandeliers hung from the glass ceiling and Lady Aston's boots clack-clacked on the black and white tiles. There were no animal heads hung on the walls here, and no photographs or paintings.

Here, there was only one work of art. It was at the very end of the orangery, by the door to the kitchens. Set in a frame that was as tall as Faye, it was unlike any other piece of art she had ever seen.

'Who did that?' Faye asked.

'Oh, do you like it? It's my favourite.' They stopped to admire the picture. 'I picked it up in Cologne before the war. It's a Hannah Höch. Do you know her work?'

Faye shook her head. Lady Aston's hands flapped about in excitement.

'Photomontage. She creates these wonderful collages from photographs. Taking the old to create something new and exciting. I find her simply fascinating. *They say she's bisexual,*' she added in a scandalised whisper. Faye's befuddled expression betrayed her ignorance. 'It means she has a fondness for ladies as well as chaps,' Lady Aston clarified and Faye nodded in approval, wondering if that explained the funny feeling she got in her tum whenever she saw a photo of Greta Garbo.

The artwork was centred on a man with an axe. He was hand-drawn like something from a book of fairy tales, as were the two children who lay either asleep or dead at his feet. All around them were trees snipped from old photos. In the trees were cut-outs of eyes. Faye tried to imagine hanging this in the pub where the stuffed owl had been and what her dad might say.

'Höch disowned it,' Lady Aston continued. 'Said it was cursed. She was about to throw it out when I got it for a steal. An absolute bargain.'

'Cursed? How's it cursed?'

'I think Höch was having some sort of torrid affair at the time and the work reminded her of the break-up.'

'What's it called?' Faye asked.

'"*Kinder im Wald*",' Lady Aston said, before translating. '"Babes in the Wood." Harry says it will frighten the children, but a few nightmares never hurt anyone, I say. Shall we?'

They were on the move again, passing through the kitchens before finding themselves out in the garden.

This wasn't like the postage stamp that most folk had in their back yard. This was about five football pitches of rolling lawn dotted with raised beds full of fruit and vegetables growing in the sun.

'Aren't they splendid?' Lady Aston said when she noticed Faye admiring the beds. 'Dig for Victory and all that. We've already had some early potatoes and asparagus. Doreen in the kitchen is over the moon at the prospect of more fresh veg. Of course, when we have the Summer Fair here on Saturday, I suspect some of the less salubrious types might try and pinch my calabrese et cetera, but I trust most villagers are honest types, and don't forget we have a house full of His Majesty's armed forces at hand. Even when recuperating, they are a force to be reckoned with and will show no mercy to any light-fingered black marketeers.'

More soldiers in hospital gowns lay in beds in the

shade of the house. A few sat in wheelchairs, reading or snoozing in the sun.

Around them darted the two boys, laughing and chasing a little black and white dog between the raised beds. Watching them from the steps leading down to the garden was the older girl, her arms wrapped around her legs, chin on her knees.

'Magda, darling,' Lady Aston said, and the girl jumped to her feet with the lightning reactions of someone living on their nerves.

'*Ja*, Lady Aston,' the girl replied, eyes darting to Faye.

'Could you gather the boys and ...' Lady Aston gave Magda a wink as she rested her hands on Faye's shoulders.

The girl understood this prearranged signal and hurried off towards another wing of the house, calling for the boys to follow her. They stopped chasing the dog to look at Lady Aston and Faye and then ran after their sister.

The dog's head darted from the children to Lady Aston, uncertain which way to go.

Lady Aston clapped her hands together and crouched down. 'Nelson, come on, boy.'

The dog came bounding over and Lady Aston scruffed his neck making his tail wag like a Spitfire's propeller. Faye joined in the scruffing and Nelson started licking her face.

'Blah, cheers, matey,' she said, pulling away and tickling him under the chin instead. That's when she noticed. 'Oh, he's only got one eye. Is that why ...?'

'Nelson, yes.' Lady Aston nodded. 'I heard about him from a friend and took him in. Our son Harry objected, but then he always complains about the waifs and strays that I bring home, but Nelson is rather special – aren't you, boy? Yes! – not least because I think young Rudolf is a puppy in human form and the two of them wear each other out.'

'Rudolf?'

'The little blond moppet. Youngest of the three. Magda, Max and Rudolf. He barely understands what's happening, poor little tyke. Especially why he can't go home and see his mother and father again, tears before bedtime and all that.'

'Will he see them again?' Faye asked. Like most people, she read the papers and saw the newsreels and knew that Jewish folk were being persecuted by the Nazis, but like most people she didn't want to dwell too long on what that actually meant. Once you were thrown out of your home, or had your business taken from you, where did you go? What could be so bad that you had to send your children to another country to stay with strangers? A dark part of Faye's mind had some idea of the answers, but she wasn't sure she was ready to face them yet.

Lady Aston changed the subject. 'Ah, here they come,' she said as the children hurried across the patio.

Magda sorted them into a neat line, pointing out Max's untied shoelace and wiping Rudolf's glistening nose clean with a hankie. Magda carried a pie, Max a jar of something green and Rudolf clutched a crumpled sheet of paper to his chest. At Magda's command they spoke something German in unison and bowed.

Faye looked to Lady Aston who translated. 'They thank you from the bottom of their hearts and have each made you a gift.'

Magda stepped forwards with her pie, handing it to Faye. 'Thank you very much, *Fräulein* Bright.'

'Aw, ta, that's lovely,' Faye replied. 'What sort of pie is it?'

Magda crinkled her lips and looked to Lady Aston. Faye realised the girl's English might have been pre-rehearsed.

'Gooseberry pie,' Lady Aston said.

'What a treat. We'll have that tonight for pudding,' Faye said.

Max shuffled forwards next, peering at Faye over his specs and offering up his jar. '*Danke*,' he muttered.

'Gooseberry jam,' Lady Aston said.

'Well, you can never have too many gooseberries,' Faye said with a smile.

Max looked at Faye, wondering if this was his cue to respond.

Magda whispered, 'Max,' and the boy shuffled back in line.

Rudolf was not as shy and hopped forwards, reeling off a long speech at Faye with intermittent sniffs and breaks to dry his nose on the cuffs of his shirt, finally handing the crumpled sheet of paper to her.

'Er, thank you, Rudy,' Faye said, then looked to Lady Aston. 'What did he say?'

'I didn't quite catch all of it, but he says he thought you were an angel and at first he was frightened, then something about a tree—'

Faye turned the paper over. It was a picture, scribbled in colourful crayon. A row of apple trees. Around them were green sticky fingerprints.

Faye tentatively dabbed her finger in one of the green prints. 'And these are ...?'

'Gooseberries, yes,' Lady Aston confirmed. 'We've been harvesting an awful lot of them.'

'Luckily, I love 'em,' Faye said, then spoke to the children the way every English person speaks to foreigners. Loudly, and in English. *I'm so glad you're all right. If you're ever in the village, come and say hello. I'm usually in the pub –* hang on, that didn't come out right – *I work in the pub, the Green Man, so come and say hello. And I'm sorry some of the people were shouting and threw things. I think they were just scared and, as my dad says, people are smart, but crowds is stupid.*

She looked to Lady Aston who translated for her. The children nodded politely in unison once more.

'*Danke!*' yelled Rudolf.

'Off you go now, children.' Lady Aston dismissed them with a wave and they gave Faye one final nod before hurrying off. 'I trust that satisfies your curiosity, Faye. They're all in fine fettle as you can see.'

'What about the older lad who was with them?' Faye asked.

'Klaus?' Lady Aston looked up across the grounds. 'I think he was helping in the orchard, or possibly picking some runner beans. I can't be sure, but I can tell you he's simply fine.' There was something in her ladyship's voice that made Faye think it was time to go. You could only keep this woman away from her horses for so long.

ℬ

Pinder the butler guided Faye back through the house and past the wounded soldiers in their makeshift hospital, and before long she was arranging the gooseberry pie, jam and sticky painting in her bicycle's basket.

As Faye rode back down the drive she was both relieved and concerned that she hadn't bumped into Klaus again. How could she tell him what she had seen without sounding completely unhinged? And was she wrong not to warn him? The dilemma pinged back and forth in her head with no easy solution.

At least she hadn't experienced another funny turn or terrible vision. The children looked happy and healthy, and they were now safe, even if the poor blighters might never make it home or see their parents—

Faye's train of thought was interrupted by the honking horn of a bright red MG Midget sports car. She looked up to see it haring straight towards her in a cloud of dust and gravel.

Faye twisted her handlebars, missing the car by a whisker and careening off the drive. Her front wheel hit the exposed root of a birch tree and she went flying in a somersault, landing hard on the grass before being knocked unconscious.

HARRY OF HAYWARD LODGE

Faye woke to the eye-watering smell of liniment. She opened her eyes to find a dozen wounded soldiers staring down at her. All wore hospital gowns and bandages, though one chap stood out like a posh thumb in a tweed jacket.

'I'm most dreadfully sorry,' he said, clutching a flat cap. A pair of driving goggles dangled around his neck. 'I was so intent on looking out for one of Mater's horses that I didn't expect to encounter anyone on a bicycle. I—'

'My bike.' Faye sat upright, dreading the thought of losing her only means of getting around the village. The hall swirled as if they were at sea. She blinked and flopped back onto a very comfy pillow.

'The Pashley is perfectly shipshape,' the man said, flashing a grin and revealing a tiny gap between his two front teeth. 'Slightly wonky handlebars, but I took care of that. I left it safe by the fountain out front. The good news is there's nary a scratch on the MG.'

'The what?'

'MG TA Midget. My car.' Harry came over all winsome. 'Quite the love of my life. I'd be lost without her. Oh, I'm afraid the gooseberry pie is a bit flat and the jam is a goner.'

'I'm pretty sure there's more where that came from.' Faye edged herself up on her elbows. She was lying on top of the sheets on a hospital bed in one of the grand halls she and Lady Aston had walked through earlier. Most of the patients were gathered around her bed, fascinated by the new arrival. One of them handed Faye her specs and she pushed them into place. 'How long was I out?' she asked, reaching around the back of her head where she found a tender bump.

'Not long – I brought you straight in and Matron found you a bed. I say,' he said, giving a little snort to announce that he was about to say something funny, 'if you're going to get a bump on the noggin, then this is the place to do it, what?'

'What?'

'Quite.' He brushed back his hair and grinned again. 'I'm Harry, by the way. Lord and Lady Aston's offspring, if you hadn't quite joined the dots.'

'Harry. I'm Faye.' She forced a smile and swung her legs off the bed. 'No harm done, I suppose. I'll get off home if that's all right.'

'What's all this?' Matron's Edinburgh brogue reverberated around the hall. She was half the size of any soldier, though they all trembled at the sound of her voice. She came skittering towards Faye. 'Why are you gentlemen out of bed?' The walking wounded dispersed rapidly as if an air raid siren had gone off. 'And how is our new patient? You're awake, I see.'

'Bit groggy.' Faye eased herself off the bed and onto her feet, happy that she didn't collapse into a heap. 'Believe it or not, this is the second time in the last twenty-fours hours that I've blacked out then woken up in a bed. I think I might be getting used to it.'

'It's certainly not something you should make a habit of, young lady. Think you can walk?'

'Reckon so.'

'Good,' Matron said. 'I need the bed. Any head-aches? Nausea?'

'No.'

'How many fingers am I holding up?'

'Two and one thumb,' Faye replied correctly.

'Say the alphabet backwards.'

'The alphabet backwards.'

Matron smirked. 'You'll be fine. Though I would suggest someone give this young lady a lift home. Cycling is not recommended for the time being.'

'Oh, I'd be happy to,' Harry said. 'It's the least I can do.'

'No need. I'll walk,' Faye said. 'Don't take this the wrong way, but I've seen your driving.'

'Ha! Jolly good. She's got spunk, this one. At least allow me to escort you to your steed.'

Faye thought about fobbing him off, but she had a feeling he wouldn't take no for an answer and together they ambled out to the main entrance where Faye's bicycle leaned against the fountain. The air was sweet after the medicinal fug of the hospital beds.

'Oh, I almost forgot,' Harry said, reaching into the pocket of his tweed jacket. 'This was in your basket. Isn't it delightful?' He unfolded the crumpled picture drawn by Rudolf. 'Who drew this?'

'The little blond chap.' Faye closed one eye as she thought. 'Rudolf. Here, you can ask him what crayons he used if you like.'

The trio of children came hurrying around the side of the house, voices chittering with concern as they surrounded her. She couldn't understand a word, but she got the gist.

'I'm fine, thank you, really, it's just a bump on the head.'

'I say, young man.' Harry crouched down to Rudolf's eye level, displaying the lad's drawing. 'This is jolly good, what? Where did you draw such wonder-ful trees?'

Rudolf took a step back, hiding behind his big sister, his wide eyes peering out from behind her.

'Was it in the orchard, perhaps?' Harry said, then squinted as he thought. 'The, er, *der Obstgarten*?'

The boy nodded and muttered a reply. '*Der Obstgarten.*'

'Splendid,' Harry said, and Faye wondered how he knew the German word for orchard. 'That's lovely. Very colourful. And this tree I like most of all.' He sin-gled out the middle tree in Rudolf's drawing. It looked like all the other apple trees, except Rudolf had added little yellow lines emanating from it, as if it glowed. 'You'll have to show me where you saw this later, hm?'

Rudolf shrugged and said, *'Der Obstgarten,'* again before ducking completely behind his sister.

'Oh, I say, he's turned rather shy,' Harry said, standing upright.

'The little lad's been on the run from the Nazis,' Faye told him. 'That'll make you wary of strangers.'

'I hope we won't be strangers for long, laddie. Perhaps I'll teach you cricket, eh? Bowl a few googlies, hm? How about you?' He prodded Max, the older boy, on the shoulder. 'Cricket? Or football? Have a bit of a kick-about later, yes? No?'

Max whispered in his sister's ear, then she poked Harry and wagged a disapproving finger.

'I don't think he likes being poked,' Faye said.

'Righto, suit yourselves.' Harry threw Faye a little gap-toothed grimace. 'Delighted to meet you, Faye. Hopefully next time under less dramatic circs, hmm? Toodle-pip.' He tipped his cap and started to hop up the stairs to the house.

'Harry,' Faye called after him.

He stopped and gave her a quizzical look.

'The drawing?' She extended her hand. He was still clutching it.

'Goodness me. You must think me the most frightful oaf. Of course, here you are.' As he handed her the drawing, their hands touched and a blackness swirled, filling Faye's vision.

Klaus lies dead among the trees. His parted lips chalk-white, his skin a sickly blue. He looks straight at Faye.

Someone was calling Faye's name over and over. The world was fuzzy as a daydream. She glanced down to see Rudolf staring up at her.

'Sorry, drifted off,' she said.

'You sure you're quite all right?' Harry asked.

'Hmm? Yes, fine,' Faye lied. This vision had been more intense. She could feel the cold evening chill, the grass under her feet. She wanted to run back through the house, find Klaus and warn him. But what could she tell him that wouldn't make her sound like a complete loon? 'I'll ... I'll walk it off,' she told Harry and the children.

'Jolly good.' Harry gave her a wave and ambled over to his red MG. He produced a cloth from his jacket and proceeded to buff the already shiny bonnet of the car.

Faye crouched down, gathered the children around her and spoke in a low voice.

'Does any one of you have a pen? Paper?' She mimed scribbling on her palm.

Max reached into his blazer and produced a little notebook and the nub of a sharpened pencil, handing both to Faye.

'Perfect, thank you.' She began to write instructions. 'Give this to Klaus. Yes? Klaus?' The children nodded. 'I want him to meet me at the Green Man pub tonight at seven. This is the address. It's important.

Understand?' She handed the notebook back to Max. All three children nodded, though she wondered how much they really understood and what on earth she would tell Klaus if he actually came. She would think of something. She wanted to give them all a hug, but the thought of another funny turn or dreadful vision stayed her hand. 'Right, off you go.'

The children ran back the way they came. As they did, Faye caught sight of Harry watching her as he polished his MG Midget. He gave her a little wave and a smile. She waved back and started walking her bike down the drive, certain that if she turned around again he would still be watching her.

Orders from on High

'That's your solution?' Faye was in Mrs Teach's living room, the place where doilies came to retire. There wasn't a single surface left unadorned by some kind of lace or chintz. 'I should stop touching people?'

'That's clearly what's triggering your funny little turns, Faye,' Mrs Teach said as she poured afternoon tea for two. Every Wednesday, Faye popped round at 3pm and Mrs Teach would instruct her in useful herbs and fungi. Essential grounding, she called it. 'Keep your distance and you'll be fine.'

'I can't spend the rest of my life dodging people when they go to shake me 'and. They'll think I'm a loon.'

'You'll grow out of it. Eventually,' Mrs Teach said, dropping two lumps of sugar in her teacup. 'Probably. Until then, consider wearing gloves.'

'Oh, very reassuring.' Faye splashed a little milk in her own tea and stirred vigorously. 'Do you know anyone else who's had this?'

Mrs Teach's teacup was halfway to her lips when she

pursed them in thought. 'Agatha Laine up in Leeds was said to have visions that gave her screaming fits.'

'And what happened to her?'

'She had one at a funeral, fell into the grave and broke her neck.' Mrs Teach slurped her tea. 'Sorry, that's not very useful, is it?'

'No, it's not. And if I'm being honest with you, Mrs Teach, none of this is.' Faye sat back on the armchair's antimacassar cloth, folding her arms. 'All I've been taught so far is how *not* to do things. When will I learn stuff I can use to help people?'

'Help people?' Mrs Teach clinked her cup on a saucer and placed them on the table. 'We keep the supernatural at bay. Spells and the like rarely help people. Our magic should be a last resort. If that lot out there thought we could solve their every problem, we'd never get a minute's peace. This is precisely why the Council of Witches was created. Do you really want a return to the Dark Ages? Doing the bidding of maniacal kings and queens? Only now it wouldn't be scuppering knights on the occasional quest. It would be us fighting tanks and bombers, and I've got enough on with my volunteer work as it is.' Mrs Teach leaned forwards, touching Faye's knee. 'Most of what you've heard about witchcraft is cobblers,' she said. 'We don't fly on broomsticks, we don't eat babies, we don't bestow true love and we certainly don't give folk the evil eye and put hexes on them.'

'Then what *do* we do?'

'We watch. We listen. And we protect. Our concern is with the underworld. That business with the demon last month is precisely the sort of thing we're here to prevent.'

'But we didn't.' Faye glared at Mrs Teach through the steam of her tea. 'If anything, we made it worse.'

'Let's not cry over spilled milk, shall we? Besides, we were somewhat at odds back then. We're working together now and that is all for the good.'

'And what about Klaus?'

'We've gone over this, poppet. Do not interfere. It will only end in tears.'

'She's right,' said a voice by the door.

Faye jolted in shock and her tea splashed on the rug.

Miss Charlotte stood framed by the living-room door, a dubious saint in a stained-glass window.

'You ever heard of knocking?' Mrs Teach asked.

'I have, but no plans to try it soon.' Miss Charlotte handed Mrs Teach a Manila envelope. 'Our orders have come.'

'Orders?' Faye was on her knees, dabbing at the tea spill with a hankie. 'What orders?'

'You won't like it,' Charlotte said, taking a seat opposite Mrs Teach and pouring herself a cup of tea.

'Help yourself, why don't you?' Mrs Teach said as she opened the envelope and took out a sheet of paper. She frowned. 'It's in code,' she said, flipping the paper around for them both to see.

Charlotte had insisted on being the recipient of their only code book. After committing it to memory, she had burned it. 'It's not the only thing they sent,' Charlotte said. 'There's more in the envelope.'

'What orders?' Faye asked again as Mrs Teach peered into the envelope.

Charlotte looked at Faye as if seeing her for the first time. 'Vera Fivetrees is leading the council in occult counter-espionage,' she said, her eyes glinting at the prospect.

Faye was not well disposed to Vera Fivetrees – what with the book burning and all – but she came across as someone who wouldn't take any nonsense and she didn't miss a trick. The day after they defeated the demon Kefapepo, Vera sent them all a copy of the Official Secrets Act to sign. Her number-one priority was to keep any magical activity to a minimum and under wraps.

Charlotte took a sip of tea before speaking. 'Vera has been liaising with the War Office on how we can help, and this is our first mission.'

Mrs Teach found another smaller envelope inside the larger one. She opened it, took a peek and snapped it shut again, a grimace on her face. 'What in Heaven's name is this?'

Charlotte's bright red lips curved into a wicked grin as she took out her pipe and stuffed it with tobacco. 'It's hair.'

'I can see that. Whose hair?'

'Otto Kopp's.'

'He's bald and this is curly.'

'It's not from his head.'

Mrs Teach made a disgusted noise and tossed the envelope at Charlotte who caught it with her thumb and forefinger.

'I'm not going to ask how this came into our possession,' Mrs Teach said.

'I imagine Otto has the needs of men and we have spies in the field prepared to do terrible things in the name of freedom,' Charlotte said, lighting her pipe.

'Excuse me.' Faye was still on her knees from cleaning the tea spill. She raised a hand. 'I am still here, y'know, and it would be nice to have some clue as to what is going on. Who's this Otto Kopp? A friend of yours?'

'He's the leader of the Thule Society,' Mrs Teach said, wrinkling her nose in disapproval.

'*Too-lee* Society?' Faye shrugged. 'Sounds jolly.'

'They're a bunch of overexcited Nazi zealots who think they know about magic and are obsessed with the Aryan super-race.' Mrs Teach pursed her lips to let everyone present know exactly what she thought about that.

'Not so jolly, then?' Faye said.

'No. And Otto is the worst of them. Vile little man.'

'I've encountered him a few times,' Charlotte said, wreathed in pipe smoke, her eyes drifting to the middle distance of memory. 'Otto is a short chap and bald and doesn't look terribly threatening, but he's as powerful as Vera Fivetrees – if not more so – but with none of her redeeming qualities. He's ambitious, fearless and completely committed to making black magic a part of Hitler's armoury.'

Faye shivered. 'So he deserves all he gets?'

Charlotte puffed on her pipe. 'Yes.'

'And what will he be getting?' Mrs Teach asked.

'Our orders are simple.' Charlotte crossed her legs and held up the envelope. 'Use the hair to create a hex to indispose Otto.'

'A hex? Like a curse? Whatever happened to not interfering, eh?' Faye pointed an accusing finger at Mrs Teach who had the decency to cringe as she clutched her teacup.

'A hex, Miss Charlotte,' Mrs Teach said with a grimace. 'It's not really the done thing, is it? Do we really have to—'

'There's a war on.' Charlotte stood and moved to the door, taking the envelope with her. 'We have orders and we have a duty to follow them. We do this at the stones at midnight. Wrap up warm, it might be chilly.'

'What are we going to do?' Faye asked, unsure if she wanted to hear the answer.

'*You* will do as you're told,' Charlotte said. 'We will think of something ... appropriate.'

She made to leave and was halfway out of the living-room door when Faye piped up. 'I saw a photograph of you today, Miss Charlotte.'

Charlotte slowly eased back into the room. Her eyes took aim at Faye. 'There are no photographs of me.'

'Not a photograph as such, no. It was a wajumacallit ...' Faye took a long and noisy slurp of tea as she thought. 'I think it's called a daguerreotype. A really, really, *really* old type of photograph. All brown and faded and wrinkly. And you was in it.'

'You're mistaken.'

'P'raps.' Faye shrugged. 'It was taken in a foreign country. There was mountains and the previous Lord Aston and someone who is the dead spit of you.'

Charlotte pressed her lips together. 'The stones. Midnight. Don't be late.'

She slipped out of sight. Faye didn't hear the front door open or close, but somehow knew she was gone.

'It was definitely her,' Faye told Mrs Teach, nodding so hard she sloshed her tea about. 'She must be a hundred years old, what do you think?'

'If you think I'm going to discuss a colleague's private and personal history while they're still in earshot, you're off your chump.'

'Still in earshot? She's gone.'

'She's still in the village. That's in earshot.' Mrs Teach stood. 'We have orders. I don't like them, either, but that's by the by – we have a duty. I'll see you tonight. Come here after closing time and we'll go up together.'

'Mrs Teach,' Faye began, 'I don't feel right about putting a hex on someone I ain't ever met.'

'Orders are orders, Faye. And take it from me, Otto Kopp is a very bad man indeed. He would do much worse to us, given the opportunity.'

'That's what I mean. What if they were to get a lock of my hair? Or yours?'

'Who cuts your hair, Faye?'

'Me dad. He does it with a bowl on me head and a pair of barber scissors left in the bar one night.'

'Is your dad a Nazi spy?'

'Not bloody likely.'

'Then I reckon you're safe. Midnight tonight. Don't forget.'

Stranger in a Strange Pub

Seven o'clock had come and gone and Klaus had not shown up. Faye would have to find some other way to warn the lad. In the meantime, the Green Man pub was busier than ever. An influx of RAF pilots and crew from nearby Mansfield Airbase meant every night the saloon was packed with chaps in uniform from all over the Commonwealth and Europe. Some were stationed at the base, but most were passing through to another mission, another base, another fight with the Luftwaffe.

Faye liked to play 'Guess the Accent' with them. The South Africans were easy, but she couldn't always tell the difference between the Poles and the Czechs, or the Belgians and the French, who were all equally determined to get revenge on the Nazis. The Canadians and New Zealanders were so friendly and charming that Faye struggled to imagine any of them shooting other aircraft out of the sky. The Aussies drank the most, were by far the loudest and took great delight in winding up the Brits. A few nights ago, they had a pilot from Barbados pop in; they once even had a couple of Yanks pretending to be Canadians in order to join the fight, and tonight there was a trio of Air Transport Auxiliary women pilots playing darts.

Faye and her dad were run ragged with all this new business and so Terrence Bright was forced to do something he swore would never happen. He hired other villagers to help behind the bar. Terrence had always resisted letting any of them see behind the scenes, as there were some things best kept as trade secrets, not least the location of the safe, where the keys to the cellar were to be found, and his knobkerrie's hiding place.

With that in mind, he took on only the most trustworthy folk and tonight was supposed to be Mr Hodgson's shift, but the tower captain had a dodgy tum after a few too many ciders on the bell-ringers' day out. So Dougie Allen – a man with a bit of time on his hands after the destruction of his garage and in need of ready cash – stepped in at the last minute.

There was no denying that Dougie knew how to graft. He was one of the fastest barmen Terrence had ever worked with, which would have been perfect if it wasn't for the running commentary he gave every time he served someone. He talked to the pints the same way he talked to his cars.

'Oh, look at that. The amber glow, no cloudy bits and a perfect head,' he would say in his soft Glaswegian voice. 'You are a perfect pint. That's almost too good to drink, that is. If I put it next to the others ... oh yes. A spectacular round of drinks. Congratulations all round. Five and tuppence, please.'

On the plus side – and to Terrence's delight – Dougie took his wages cash in hand, no questions asked, and knew enough to keep his gob shut about the safe and how Terrence had the combination written in a notepad hidden under a squeaky floorboard.

Tonight, the three of them were serving a group of Canadian, Australian and Brit pilots who all appeared to be having some sort of moustache-growing contest as they swapped banter about missions, aircraft and spin bowling.

Bertie was in his usual spot – being wherever Faye was serving – and trying to be heard over the hubbub.

'My ears are still ringing from Dougie's petrol station going up,' Bertie told her. 'Makes you think how lucky we was. Especially you. I reckon you should get a medal or something.'

'Medals all round, Bertie.' Faye gave him a wink. 'You came to my rescue with a dustbin lid, don't forget.'

'I just did ... well, the lid was there, and we couldn't have anyone getting hurt, could we?'

Bertie's cheeks reddened and he clumsily took a sip from his cider. Faye recalled their conversation on the bus and knew the poor lad was still waiting for an answer from her.

'So, the village Summer Fair,' she started, and the poor lad stiffened, his knuckles turning white as he gripped the pint glass. 'Why not, eh? I'll be working in the beer tent with Dad, but when I get some time off let's have a laugh. The two of us.'

Bertie's face broke into freckled happiness and Faye felt a flush of relief. They were going to have a laugh. A fun time. That's what friends did, and there was no friend as loyal as Bertie.

'A laugh,' he echoed. 'We will indeed have a jolly old time of it.'

'That we will.' Faye smiled back at him, realising how ridiculous her previous fears of stepping out had been. She and Bertie would be friends whatever the weather.

'I was thinking we could start at the coconut shy and—'

'Hold that thought.' Faye raised a finger, silencing blushing Bertie.

Klaus stood in the pub doorway with the lost look of a stranger. He surveyed the pub for a friendly face, no doubt aware that if he started asking for Faye in his own accent, the gathered ranks of the Allied armed forces would turn against him as the villagers had done yesterday.

Faye had all but given up hope of him showing up, but here he was an hour late. She gave Klaus a little wave and he smiled in relief. She gestured to a quiet corner by the fireplace. He nodded and began to make his way through the throng.

'Back in mo', Bertie. Dad, gimme five minutes,' she said, then added before he could complain, 'Lovely, ta.'

As Faye sat opposite Klaus around the little

shove-ha'penny table, she wondered what she would say to him. This had been bugging her all day. Blurting out, 'I've seen you die in a vision!' would understandably come across as just a little bit stark raving bonkers, so she started with small talk.

'Thanks for coming, I hope this isn't a pain, but I wanted to chat and see how you're settling in after all of yesterday's palaver. Are you all right? No injuries or nothing? I'm sorry about the crowd. You understand they were scared, right? People can be quick to—' She stopped when she saw him staring at her in bafflement. 'Oh, blimey, I just realised I don't even know if you speak proper English. Can you even understand a word I'm saying?'

'Yes, yes, I can. Forgive me. You have many questions and I don't know where to begin.'

'Sorry, I'm blabbing. Let's start with how are you?'

'We're ... alive. Thanks to you.' Klaus's eyes brightened. 'I was driving the children to Hayward Lodge and we were lost. I pulled into the garage to ask for directions and then everything went black. The next thing I know there is smoke and screaming and ... and you. I cannot thank you enough.' He leaned forwards on the table and Faye got the feeling that he wanted to take her hand in gratitude. She had anticipated this and deliberately kept her hands on her thighs, hidden away under the table for fear of any contact triggering another funny turn. Also, she could sense Bertie over by the bar and didn't want him thinking there was any peculiar stuff going on between her and Klaus.

'What matters is you're all fine,' she said. 'That is ... you are all fine, aren't you? No one's ...' It was still too soon to bring visions of murder into the conversation. 'Everyone's being nice, are they?'

'Lady Aston is like an angel,' Klaus said, then smiled again. 'An angel with the bowler hat and riding whip, yes? After the journey we have had, this place is a paradise.'

'Where have you come from? If you don't mind me poking my nose in?'

Klaus looked around the room. The Air Transport Auxiliary girls had finished their darts and were enjoying drinks at the next table, chatting merrily. He kept his voice low.

'Berlin,' he said. 'But we left there ...' His brow wrinkled as he remembered. 'A year and a half ago. After *Kristallnacht* everything changed.'

'Crystal-what?'

'It was a pogrom,' he said, but Faye remained baffled. He struggled to explain. 'A ... a mob, led by the *Sturmabteilung*, the Brownshirts, they came for the Jews. They ransacked our homes, our businesses, our synagogues. They took ... they took my father.' Klaus's jaw set and his chest rose and fell. Faye wanted to take his hand but didn't dare. 'He was a tailor. He made suits. He was a good man.' Klaus took a deep breath, then slowly exhaled. 'My mother sent me to stay with my aunt and uncle in Köln, but the same thing happened there, over and over. They put me and my cousins – Magda, Max and Rudolf – on a train organised by the Kindertransport. They told us we were going on a big adventure, they tried to make it sound like a vacation and waved us goodbye, promising to meet us in Rotterdam. Rudolf believed, but Magda and Max ... They're young, but they're not fools. Their parents never came. We waited and waited. The Red Cross gave us letters from our families. They pretended everything was fine, but then the letters stopped. We moved from home to home until it was no longer safe. As the Luftwaffe bombed Rotterdam, we took the last Kindertransport boat to England and stayed at a place called Dovercourt before getting our papers. And here we are.' Klaus shrugged. 'Sitting in a nice English pub, chatting away like there is nothing wrong in the world.'

'You're safe now,' Faye told him.

'I don't want to be safe,' Klaus snapped, his accent drawing a few glances. 'I want to go back.' He was getting louder and attracting disapproving looks from others in the pub. 'I'm eighteen in ten days, and on my birthday, I won't be opening gifts or eating cake. I will march to the nearest conscription office and I will ask for a uniform and a gun, because I want to return to Germany and kill Nazis. I want my country back, I want my home back, I want my mother and my father and—' The words caught in Klaus's throat. He had been shouting. He sniffed and wiped the tears from his eyes.

Faye looked up. They were surrounded by aircrew. Canadians and Aussies, Kiwis and Brits. They held pints and glared down at the boy. They had heard his accent and gathered closer.

Faye was about to warn them to pack it in when one of the Aussies – a regular called Jack who was never backwards in coming forwards – spoke up.

'Terrence,' he called to Faye's dad. 'Get this kid whatever he wants. Anyone who wants to fight the Nazis is a mate of mine.'

A cheer rose throughout the pub and Klaus was bombarded by pilots scruffing his hair and patting his shoulder. Klaus looked stunned as one of the ATA girls dashed over and planted a kiss on his cheek, leaving a red smudge of lipstick.

He looked at Faye, gobsmacked. And she heard him laugh for the first time.

A Moonlit Kiss

Faye pushed her bicycle as she walked with Klaus to the top of the Wode Road by Saint Irene's Church. The waxing moon poked its belly around the bell tower and bats darted between the trees.

Despite complaining that English beer wasn't as good as German beer, Klaus hadn't needed to buy a drink all evening. He threw his arms to the sky and wavered across the road as he continued with the German drinking song he had been teaching the airmen in the Green Man.

'*Ein Prosit, ein Prosit, der Gemütlichkeit!*'

'Klaus, shh!' Faye said, gesturing the lad in the direction of Hayward Lodge. 'You can't sing in German while there's a war on. You're going to get us shot. Let's take you back to your auntie.'

'*Nein, nein, nein,*' he said, wagging a finger at Faye. 'Lady Aston is not our auntie. We call her auntie, but she is a friend of *my* Auntie Greta in Köln. They both like avant-garde art. Dada.'

'Dada?'

'Dada. Crazy stuff. Collage, sticking things together, film, photos. Chaos. Hitler hated it.' Klaus stopped walking and all the joy slid off his face. 'They burned art, you know. Books, also. Nothing was sacred. They claim to be superior, but they are savages.'

Faye wasn't sure she could cope with another outburst this late in the evening. She prodded him with her front tyre to start walking again and changed the subject. 'You knew Lord and Lady Aston before the war, then?'

'Oh, *ja*. Lady Aston used to come to Berlin every autumn to buy art and antiques and drink schnapps. She loves schnapps. My mother knew the best gallery owners. Not the big ones, not the bourgeois rubbish, but the real art. She would find pieces that were unique, special, and Lady Aston loved her for it. They were good friends. Art was their little secret language. Only they really understood it.'

'Expensive hobby, collecting art.'

'They can afford it. Do you know how they got so rich?' Klaus said, leaning closer to Faye. She could smell the beer on his breath as he whispered, 'Lord Aston's father used to steal antiques.'

'What?'

Klaus nodded, eyes flaring. 'When he was in the British Army. My Aunt Greta told me, he would invade some place in Afghanistan or the Crimea and ransack the temples, galleries and museums. He would have his men pack the loot in crates and send them back to Hayward Lodge. They say the basement is like Aladdin's cave.'

'What sort of stuff has he got?' Faye asked, imagining mountains of trinkets stacked to the ceilings.

'I've not seen it myself, but Doreen in the kitchen told me there are statues, religious icons, paintings, tapestries, bronze busts and gold cups.'

'We should melt them down for the war effort.'

'*Nein*, they sell them when they need money. Or they used to. No one's buying now there's a war on.'

'They sell them? I thought she was rich.'

'How do they *stay* rich? They inherit a fortune from a thief and sell off his trinkets. Ach.' Klaus winced and rubbed his forehead. 'I'm being a cynic. They have saved my life. And the lives of my cousins. I'm wrong to complain. I am a fool when I drink. Lady Aston is a good woman. Lord Aston spends all his time in his little glass house on the roof.'

'The observatory,' Faye said. 'Have you been up there yet? What's it like?'

'It is private. Forbidden. People with big houses and money, they're all a little strange. *Ein Prosit, ein Prosit!*'

Faye waved and shushed him into silence. She wanted to slap a hand over his mouth, but she worried that might trigger another vision.

She gripped the handlebars of her bike. Faye was itching to tell him what she had seen. All night she had been thinking of the different ways she could casually slip it into the conversation. '*Did I mention, I have the gift of foresight? Oh yes, I can see the future, and the funny thing is, I think I saw you lying dead in the woods.*' There simply wasn't any way she could fathom of telling him without making herself sound like she was completely off her rocker. There was nothing for it. She would have to risk it.

'Klaus, look, I have something I have to—'

'I'm sorry,' Klaus said, breathless, 'about the singing. It's been a difficult couple of years with so much fear and death and despair and ... and now ... I ... I FEEL SO ALIVE!' He roared this last at the stars, spun on his heels, took Faye's head in his hands and kissed her full on the lips.

The world fell backwards, taking Faye with it.

Klaus lies dead on the ground. A doctor brushes his hands over Klaus's eyes, closing them. Lady Aston stands nearby. Rudolf wails, Magda and Max hold one another tight. A final breath escapes Klaus's lips, a black nothing swallows him up.

'Bloody 'eck!' Faye found herself lying in the middle of the road, her bicycle next to her.

'I am sorry, so sorry, I should have asked. Please, Faye, let me help you.' Klaus offered his hand.

Faye started to take it, then snapped her hand back.

Klaus pouted and narrowed his eyes. Even in his drunken stupor, he knew something wasn't quite right.

'This ... this happened before,' he said, his finger bobbing as he gathered his thoughts. 'After you rescued us. I thought it was the smoke from the fire, but it was the same thing. We touch, and you fall.'

Faye clambered to her feet, still a little woozy as she raised her hands. 'Let me explain—'

'It is fits? Uh, epilepsy?'

'No, it's ... difficult to describe.' Faye pressed her fingers to her temples in a final effort to figure out a sane way to tell him. None came. 'I have visions,' she said with a matter-of-fact shrug. 'Of the future. I think. I have magical powers that I don't know how to control and whenever I touch you, or Rudolf, or Harry, I see the same thing.'

Klaus gaped at her, his mouth a crinkled little 'O'.

'I'm ... a witch,' Faye said.

And instantly regretted it as Klaus collapsed into fits of laughter. There followed a stream of incomprehensible German, some pointing and much slapping of his thighs.

'Klaus, please listen to me, matey, I'm not joking. I see ... I see your death.'

That got him. He stared at her, breath puffing in the night air.

'You see me die?' A little smile crept across his face and he moved closer. Faye took a step back. 'How?' he asked. 'Where?'

'I'm ... I'm not sure,' she said. 'There are trees, like a wood, and the other children are there. Klaus, I'm really worried that you're going to come a cropper.'

Klaus tilted his head from side to side, almost examining her. 'You're serious.' He blinked hard in an effort to sober up. 'Tell me again,' he said, his voice more sombre now. 'What did you see?'

Faye told him all the details she could remember as they walked out of the village and along Edge Road to Hayward Lodge.

'When you take my hand, you see it as if through my eyes?' Klaus asked.

'No, it's like a dream. I'm there, standing and watching. And when it was Rudolf and Harry, I could see you, like you was right in front of me.'

'Harry is there, too?' Klaus put two fingers to his lips as if struck by a thought.

'Why's that got you all excited?'

'What do you think of Harry?' Klaus asked with half a smile.

Faye shrugged. 'Posh. A bit up himself. Drives like a loon, but he seems all right. He likes the littl'uns.'

'Really?'

'Yeah. Especially Rudolf's drawing. He was like a slightly peculiar uncle.'

'He showed kindness to Rudolf?'

'He was nice enough.'

'And to Magda? Max?' Klaus asked, a little more intensely.

'He said he was going to teach 'em cricket. Not sure if that's cruel or kind, but I reckon the intent was a good'un.'

Klaus pursed his lips and shoved his hands in his pockets. 'Perhaps it's just me.'

'What's just you?'

'Harry ... does not like me. Or, should I say, he doesn't like my kind.'

Faye wondered what Klaus meant. As far as she was concerned, he was the funny kind. Slightly odd, but as he said, he had been through the wringer. His eyes were kind. And big. And his face, too. Faye shook her head clear. *Give it a rest, girl.*

Klaus must have noticed her confusion. He leaned closer and whispered, 'I don't think Harry likes Jews.' He smiled then added, 'He calls me *the Little Kike*, but only when his mother's not around. He says it with a smile, makes it a joke, like he's daring me to be offended and tell Lady Aston.'

'You should,' Faye said. They had arrived at the end of the drive to Hayward Lodge. The house was lost in the darkness of the blackout. 'I've got half a mind to march to the door right now, wake up Harry and make the gap-toothed goon apologise.'

'It doesn't matter,' Klaus said, warmed by her concern.

'Yes, it does.'

'Ach, maybe a little, but I don't care.'

'It's not too late. To turn back,' Faye said, glancing the way they had come. 'We can put you up in the pub tonight. Just one night. Just to be safe.'

'Do you know how much death I've seen?' It was getting chilly and Klaus stuck his hands in his pockets. 'How many friends and family I've lost? How many times I never got to say a proper goodbye? I won't live to see the end of this war—'

'Don't say that.'

'I know it to be true. The children are safe, and I have nothing to lose. In ten days I start training for war. I will charge the Nazis without fear. They will see what one Jewish boy can do.'

'But what if you don't get to do that? What if you die tomorrow?'

'If I die tomorrow . . . ?' he mused, looking into Faye's eyes. She was aware of an odd sensation in her belly. Her feet felt like lead weights and she was glad she was gripping the bicycle to prop her up. 'If I die tomorrow, then at least I get to say goodbye to you, Faye Bright.'

He leaned in and gently kissed Faye on the lips.

The world remained defiantly upright, as did Faye.

Faye's heart fluttered, and all sorts of new and strange feelings sparked inside her. Her cheeks warmed, her eyes widened and her mouth was dry.

They broke apart, waiting for something strange that never came.

'There, you see?' Klaus said. 'No vision?'

'No vision,' Faye said, the words coming out more breathy than she would have liked. She coughed and cleared her throat. Why no vision this time? Did that mean he was safe? Faye's heart fluttered with hope.

'I will see you tomorrow, Faye,' Klaus said. '*Gute Nacht, Hexe.*'

'*Hexe?*' The word prodded Faye. Something important. 'What does that mean?'

'Witch.' Klaus winked and hurried up the drive.

Faye watched him fade into the darkness. *Hexe.*

Hex! Tonight was the night she had to meet Mrs Teach and Miss Charlotte. She had no idea what the time was, but it was after closing time and the moon was high, so she was probably late. But for this moment Faye remained rooted to the spot, wondering how she had suddenly acquired a Jewish German boyfriend and what she was going to tell Bertie.

A Hex on Otto Kopp

The ride from Hayward Lodge to the village was along winding country roads, downhill all the way, which helped, but the blackout meant there were no working street lights. The front lamp on Faye's bicycle projected a feeble yellow finger ahead of her; the battery on her rear red lamp had died weeks ago. She had painted her mudguards bright white for what it was worth. Any car coming the other way might have its headlights on if she was lucky, then she recalled that Mr Hodgson had given her a lift in his car a few days ago and he had regulation blackout masks fitted to his headlights, meaning he could only see about six feet in front of him.

The good news was the moon almost full, bright, and the night sky was cloudless. Faye ducked her head down behind the handlebars and pedalled hard, the wind ruffling up her hair and threatening to whip off her specs. She kept her mouth shut tight to avoid inhaling any insects.

A boy had kissed her.

She hadn't asked him to, or even expected it, and he had beer breath and an itchy bit of stubble on his chin.

But a boy had kissed her.

This hadn't happened since Cecil Sutton had tried to plant one on her at the church fete's fruit tart stall back when they were both ten. She had thumped Cecil before he could get his sticky jammy lips anywhere near her and sworn off boys and kissing that very day.

Nevertheless, a boy had kissed her.

And despite the stubble and the beer breath, it had not been the altogether disgusting, slobbering mess that she'd feared it might be. If anything, it gave her a pleasant tingle all through her body.

Faye was seventeen-and-a-bit and had managed to avoid any romantic tanglings with lads so far, and now she had somehow ended up with two fellas vying for her attention. She hadn't asked to be kissed, she didn't want to be kissed, but she was surprised by how it made her feel.

What could she say to Bertie? *Should* she say anything to Bertie?

See, this is why you don't step out with friends, because then you end up keeping secrets from them and Faye never wanted to keep anything from Bertie.

Oh, Bertie, why didn't you keep your big soppy trap shut?

Faye noticed the freshly painted white markings in the middle of the road, which meant she was close to the village. A few trees had white visibility bands painted around their bases and the kerbs on the street corners were also daubed a dazzling white. She sped past Saint Irene's – glancing at the tower clock to see it was already a quarter to midnight – and stopped off at the Green Man to pick up her satchel and the handbell she had borrowed from the tower for tonight.

She hurried out again to find Mrs Teach waiting in front of her terraced home, dressed smartly in her Women's Voluntary Service overcoat and hat.

Faye gladly put aside any thoughts of boys and kissing and came to a breathless stop at Mrs Teach's doorstep.

'You're late.' Mrs Teach tapped on her wrist where a watch might have been. She rarely wore a watch – claiming she could tell the time of day by looking at the sun or the moon – though that didn't stop her from regularly using the tapping-on-the-wrist gesture to admonish others for being tardy.

'I can pop back and get my bike.' Faye nodded towards the pub where her bicycle was parked. 'Want a backie?'

'Certainly not,' Mrs Teach said, appalled. 'We shall proceed à *pied.*'

ɤ

The walk to the standing stones had taken over half an hour last time, but that included a couple of diversions, three dead ends, a tense argument about following badger trails and some occasional mushroom picking by Charlotte. Tonight, Faye and Mrs Teach made faster progress on the uphill journey.

'I wish we did have broomsticks.' Faye puffed as they moved up a narrow path lined with brambles. In the day they had pretty pink flowers. By night they tugged at any bit of loose clothing, like a child desperate for attention. 'It would make this bit a lot easier.'

'And it might help with your timekeeping, young lady.'

'Sorry, I was walking Klaus home.'

'Oh, really?' Mrs Teach all but purred at the prospect of fresh gossip.

'Nothing like that,' Faye half-lied. 'He was a bit worse for wear and I didn't want a German lad getting lost in the middle of the night. That's one surefire way for him to end up dead.'

'Any further visions?'

'Yes ... and no.' Faye wondered how much she should tell Mrs Teach. She didn't want her getting the wrong idea about Faye being kissed, but Faye had also insisted after their last adventure with the pumpkin-headed demon that they shouldn't keep secrets from each other. 'He – and I don't want you jumping to conclusions, Mrs Teach – he kissed me goodnight and I had a funny turn.'

'We've all been there, my love.' Mrs Teach chuckled. 'The same vision?'

'Yes, but then he kissed me again—'

'I say, how forward.'

'—and nothing happened.'

'Perhaps true love's kiss broke the spell, hmm?'

'This ain't a joke. I'm still worried about him. I touch

him and see visions of his death, and then he kisses me and I don't get a vision. What does that mean?'

'Visions are horribly unreliable, Faye. Like dreams and déjà vu, they become muddled by emotion and perspective. It's less about what actually happens in the vision and more about your interpretation of the vision. For example, you feared for the boy's safety when you hardly knew him, but now that you are entangled romantically with him—'

'It was two kisses.'

'In my day, two kisses and the chap would be asking Father for permission to marry. Anyhow, you asked me what it means and that is my professional opinion. It was all to do with the flitter-flutter of young love.'

'No, no, that don't feel right. It weren't like a dream. It was like I was actually there.'

'Whatever it was, we are actually here,' Mrs Teach said as they stepped into the circle of stones. 'Take my advice. Do not get involved. Do not interfere. It only ever ends in tears. Now, let us put aside all thoughts of youthful passion. We have a job to do. Good evening, Miss Charlotte.'

'Ladies.' Charlotte was already waiting for them. She stood at the head of the slaughter stone dressed in tan culottes and a matching waistcoat over a cream blouse, her white hair tied into a bun. Despite the slight nip in the air, her sleeves were rolled up and she was ready to hex. Laid out on the slaughter stone were a candle, a small art knife and a length of string. 'You're late,' she told them.

'My fault,' Faye said, catching her breath again. 'I was—'

'Not interested. Did you bring the bell?'

'Yes.' Faye reached into her satchel for the handbell. She gave it a little ding, but Charlotte raised a finger to her lips to silence her.

'We shall begin.' Charlotte turned to face the moon. She half-closed her eyes, raised her hand, swiped it across the moon and the sky fell dark.

Faye raised a finger. 'Oh, I was hoping I could try that again tonight.'

'We're in rather a hurry,' Charlotte said.

'I think I know what I did wrong last time,' Faye said. 'I need a clear head. No distractions. I can do that.'

Charlotte looked to Mrs Teach, who nodded.

'Very well,' Charlotte said, swiping her hand across the darkness. The moon returned, along with the stars and the burble of the woodland around them.

Faye stood at the head of the slaughter stone. She closed her eyes, focused on her breathing and reached up to find the pulsing energy of the moon.

There it was, gently stroking the palm of her hand.

She did not want to fail this time. The thought of how unbearable these two would be if she did was unthinkable.

Faye moved her hand slowly, sure to keep the energy in the palm as she swiped it across the—

'Bugger.' She lost it. She took a breath, lowered her hand and tried again. She found the moon's energy once more. Good, that was one better than last night. She hoped they noticed that. Oh so slowly – and desperate not to screw up – she moved her hand and—

'Oh, bumcakes.' She lost it again.

'Close,' Charlotte said, patting Faye on the shoulder. 'But no cigar.' She all but shoved Faye out of the way, reached up, swiped and the moon vanished. 'Next time, perhaps? Right now, we have work to do.'

'I was so close,' Faye protested. 'Just give me one more—'

Charlotte raised a finger to her lips. Faye nodded and shut up.

'Mrs Teach, please take the knife and carve the subject's name into the candle.'

'Certainly.' Mrs Teach bent gracefully at the knees to scoop up the two items.

'Faye, take the handbell and ring three times at each compass point. Turn widdershins.'

'Turn what?'

'Anti-clockwise.'

'Righto,' Faye said, gripping the bell by its leather handle. She still didn't think handbells were proper ringing, but it was good to be involved in something she was familiar with. Faye looked in every direction at the blackness around them. 'Er, which way's north?'

'The slaughter stone points north.' Charlotte gestured behind her, her eyes closed.

Faye moved to face north and rang the bell three times. 'What does this actually do?' she asked.

'It's a warning to anyone in the darkness to move their arses and get out of the way lest they be caught up in the hex,' Charlotte said, eyes still closed.

'Who's out there?' Faye asked, peering into the void.

'It's a place where only the most advanced practitioners of magic dare to go. Now please be quiet. I'm trying to concentrate.'

Faye opened her mouth to thank her, then shut up and moved to face west. As she rang the bell, Mrs Teach had a question.

'How many Ps in Kopp?'

'Two, obviously,' Charlotte said.

'Are you quite sure? I don't want to be carving the name of some innocent Otto Kopp into this candle.'

'Very sure.' Charlotte opened her eyes. 'Besides, we have his hair.'

'Is that how it works?' Faye asked, ringing the bell to the south. 'The combination of hair and name? Is that enough to make sure we have the right Otto Kopp?'

'Yesss.' Charlotte drew the last letter of that word out for far too long, and Faye decided not to test her patience any further.

Mrs Teach, on the other hand . . .

'You don't want to double-check?' she asked. 'You're sure it's not one P?'

'Very sure,' Charlotte said.

'And that's his real name, is it?' Faye asked, ringing the bell to the east.

'What?'

'If he's the leader of this top-secret society, that might

mean he's working under a false name. Spies do it all the time. I saw it in that George Formby film.'

Charlotte folded her arms. 'Otto Kopp and I have had a few run-ins in the past. I know him far too well for my liking, and that is definitely his real name. And in any case, it doesn't matter what name he goes under yesterday, today or tomorrow.' She reached into the pocket of her waistcoat and took out a familiar Manila envelope. 'Because we have this.'

She bent her knees and shook the envelope. The curly hairs fell as one tangled clump onto the slaughter stone. Charlotte tossed away the envelope, took the length of string lying on the stone and – trying to touch as little of the hair as possible – bound the curls together in a tiny little bundle.

Mrs Teach placed the candle with the name Otto Kopp – two Ps – carved into its length next to the hairs.

Charlotte outstretched her arms and closed her eyes. Faye put the handbell down and the three women joined hands. Charlotte spoke the same unknowable words three times over.

On the slaughter stone, the hairs flashed into flame and vanished. The light left little green traces on Faye's eyes. She blinked.

'Is that it?' she asked.

Charlotte's blood-red lips widened into a wicked smile. 'Somewhere in Berlin, Otto Kopp is wondering where that burning sensation in his nethers is coming from.'

'How do we know it's worked?' Mrs Teach asked.

'We have people watching,' Charlotte said. 'Most likely the same people who procured the hair. We'll hear from Vera soon enough.'

Faye shoved her hands in her dungaree pockets. 'Don't seem right,' she said. 'It feels ... sneaky.'

Mrs Teach gave her shoulder a squeeze. 'I understand, Faye, though we are working under orders from a top-secret occult organisation, and *sneaky* does somewhat come with the territory.'

Faye couldn't decide if she liked Mrs Teach less when she was haughty or patronising.

'Mr Hodgson says there's rules of war and we should stick to them. We don't win by sinking to their level.'

'Faye, take it from me,' Charlotte said, raising a hand. 'You will never sink to the level of a vicious rodent like Otto Kopp. He's a despicable swine. Just be thankful you'll never meet him.'

Charlotte swept her hand across the blackness. The moon and the stars filled the sky again. This time they were accompanied by the faint droning of aircraft engines. Faye craned her head up, but the aircraft couldn't be seen. She wondered if they were RAF or Luftwaffe. Bertie would know, Faye thought, and felt a tug of guilt.

The three women moved to the edge of the stones, drawn by silent flashes pulsing in the southern sky. They watched as streaks of tracer bullets from anti-aircraft guns took shots at the unseen enemy, the gentle, distant thuds of detonating bombs arriving seconds later.

'Is ... is that happening here? I mean, over England?' Faye asked.

'Too far away. That's over the Channel,' Charlotte said. 'The Luftwaffe are bombing supply convoy ships. They attack them in the Channel because they know our fighters cannot protect them. Still think we're the only ones being sneaky?'

'Fine, though I still don't see how us making one man think he's got the clap is doing much for the war effort.'

'Think of it as a test,' Mrs Teach said. 'If we get this right, then we will be assigned other more important tasks.'

'What, like giving Hitler diarrhoea?' Faye sneered.

'Now that *would* be a challenge.' Charlotte's eyes widened at the prospect. 'I wonder who does his hair.'

THE MYSTERY OF LORD ASTON

First thing after breakfast, Faye dashed over to Saint Irene's to return the handbell she had borrowed for the ritual. She strode through the lychgate, passing the big sycamore tree, its leaves already sticky with honeydew in the morning heat. The fingers of a branch swayed as a squirrel leapt to a nearby cherry tree, sending twigs tumbling to the path.

Faye longed to come back here and ring even the most basic methods with her friends. It was her happy place where everything made sense, but until the war was over there would be no bell-ringing by order of the War Office.

Faye had a key to the tower, but when she came to the bell-ringers' entrance, she found the door was already unlocked. As she hopped up the spiral stone staircase she could hear someone whistling 'Roll Out the Barrel' accompanied by the *swish-swish* of a broom being pushed back and forth over the floorboards. The ringers had all agreed to take turns to keep the tower clean and Faye had completely forgotten that it was Bertie's turn on this week's rota.

'Oh,' Faye said as she squeezed through the narrow entrance to the ringing chamber. 'Wotcha, Bertie.' Her mind turned over as she wondered if she should tell him about Klaus and the kiss and all that nonsense. She had promised herself that she would tell him all in good time in a way that wouldn't upset him, but she hadn't quite fathomed how to do that, yet here he was right now smiling at her.

'Faye,' he said, leaning on his broom, 'what brings you here?'

'Just popping this back,' she said, opening the box of handbells and returning the missing one to its slot.

'I thought you didn't like handbells?' Bertie was standing under the bell ropes, which were up, just as they had left them a few weeks ago when Mr Hodgson, Bertie and the others rang for the last time. 'Ain't proper ringing, you said.'

'It's not.' Faye hadn't exactly asked for permission when she borrowed the handbell, but she knew Bertie was no fool. 'Truth is, I borrowed it for a magic ritual that I performed with two other witches up at the standing stones in the woods last night.'

Bertie mulled this over, shrugged, then returned to his sweeping. 'Fair enough. None of my business.'

Faye closed the latches on the box, then grabbed a dustpan and brush from the storage cupboard and helped Bertie finish cleaning the room. With each passing second, she felt more and more guilty for not telling him what had happened with Klaus. She reasoned that she hadn't actually asked to be kissed, so it wasn't her fault, so who else needed to know? No one. No one needed to know. Least of all Bertie.

'Did that Klaus fella get home all right?' Bertie asked, idly sweeping a corner by the steps to the roof. Faye realised Bertie had seen her leave the Green Man with Klaus. Everyone had. Oh, crumbs. She was going to have to tell him.

'Yes, he did.' Faye's grip on the dustpan and brush tightened and she held them like a sword and shield. 'Bertie, I don't know how to say this, but I reckon you ought to know it, cos you're a mate and I don't like keeping nothing from you, but here's the truth: that fella Klaus kissed me goodnight.'

Bertie stopped sweeping. 'Oh,' he said, frowning like he'd been asked to do algebra in his head. 'Well, they do that, don't they?'

'Do what?'

'Folk on the Continent. They kiss each other all the time. I've seen it in the films. One on each cheek.' Bertie bobbed his head forwards as he mimed kissing someone on the cheeks.

'No, Bertie. This . . . this was on the lips.'

Bertie didn't get angry, he simply looked puzzled, and that made Faye feel all the more rotten.

'I didn't enjoy it,' she told him. Her first lie to Bertie. 'And he'd had a few jars by then, so I reckon he'd have kissed Constable Muldoon if he'd been there, too.' Faye gave a little chuckle to try and lighten the mood.

'Is he . . .' Bertie held the broom handle closer. 'Is he taking you to the Summer Fair, then?'

'Oh, Lordy, no.' Faye wanted to hug the lad now, but she was worried that might confuse things even further. 'That's *our* thing, Bertie. We'll have a jolly old time, right?'

'A jolly old time.' Bertie nodded, biting his lip.

'I just wanted you to know what happened, in case some blabbermouth saw us and started to gossip. Klaus is a stranger and he needs friends. You could be his friend, too.'

Bertie nodded again, less convincingly this time.

'Do you forgive me, Bertie?'

Now he looked really confused. 'There ain't nothing to forgive,' Bertie said. 'Can't be helped when a tipsy German lad plants a smacker on you. Could happen to any of us.'

Faye really did want to hug Bertie now, but she resisted. 'Exactly,' she said. 'It's a common peril. They'll be handing out leaflets about it. *Beware smooching foreigners.*'

They were both chuckling now. Bertie lowered his eyes and started gnawing on his lip again.

'Faye,' he said, 'I think you're smashing.'

Faye felt her heart thump against her chest. How was a girl supposed to reply to that? She should take his hand, that's how. She should hold him tight and tell him he's smashing, too. These thoughts and more raced through her mind, but she was paralysed and flummoxed. Bertie was always just a friend. A really good and loyal friend. The thought of any romantic nonsense had never occurred to her, and now she had peculiar feelings for two fellas and whatever she decided to do would upset either one or both of them. And she really didn't want to upset Bertie. But did she want to step out with him in a romantic fashion? Wouldn't that ruin everything? Or was that what had been right in front of her all this time? Was Bertie the chap for her? As she tried to regain control of her limbs, she decided she would do it. She would take Bertie's hand and—

'Morning, lovebirds!'

Faye jolted like someone had just dropped an electric eel down her dungarees.

Mrs Pritchett sidled into the ringing chamber, wearing a blue housecoat and a fetching yellow headscarf. A smouldering roll-up cigarette was stuck to her bottom lip and she grinned at Faye's and Bertie's attempts to look innocent.

'I ... who? Love? What are you doing here, Mrs Pritchett?' Faye babbled, pleasantly flushed with relief that the interruption would put off what promised to be an awkward and excruciating conversation with Bertie about smoochy stuff.

'Forgot to remind Bertie to check the bells for pigeons.' Mrs Pritchett patted the boy on the shoulder. 'So I reckoned I'd come along and help him with it.'

'Let's all do it together,' Faye suggested. Mrs Pritchett agreed. Bertie could only nod.

Checking the bells for pigeons was the task on the rota that everyone wanted to avoid, but it had to be done at least once a month. The messy buggers were always trying to nest in the bell tower and the last thing the ringers needed was a family of birds leaving their guano everywhere.

Getting to the bells meant climbing up a creaky ladder and clambering through a hatch into darkness. Most folk would have taken one look at Mrs Pritchett's frail frame and suggested she leave them to it. Most folk didn't know that Mrs Pritchett could go ten rounds with Joe Louis and all with a roll-up ciggie on her lip.

The bells were raised, ready for ringers to make them sing again. Faye gave a mournful sigh when she saw them.

'I know, darlin',' Mrs Pritchett said. 'I miss it, too.' She started singing 'We'll ring again' to the tune of 'We'll Meet Again', and Faye and Bertie joined in as they checked each bell for pigeons. There were none and they ended the song with breathless laughter – and it gladdened Faye to see Bertie smile again – but it was short-lived.

'Will we, though?' Bertie asked.

'This war won't last for ever,' Mrs Pritchett told him, 'and despite what you read in the news, I reckon we might be on the winning side.'

'What makes you so sure?'

Mrs Pritchett grinned. 'Let me show you.'

She led Faye and Bertie up to the level above the bells and through another hatch to the roof. They found themselves at the highest point of the village, looking down the Wode Road from the bell tower's crenellations. A summer breeze buffeted them, and Faye's shins tingled the way they did whenever she was high up. She wasn't afraid of heights as such but was aware of some strange urge at the back of her head that she should jump off just to see what would happen.

The village was up and about. There were people standing in line outside the butcher's and baker's. Cars and motorcycles moved up and down the street, and an army truck rattled around the tight bend by Unthank Road. Mr Allen's garage was still a smouldering ruin. The wreckage of the Hurricane was gone, but the place was an ink-blot on an otherwise idyllic street.

'I come up here quite a bit,' Mrs Pritchett said. Her arms were crossed on one of the stone crenellations. She rested her chin on them, and for a moment Faye could imagine the old woman as a child. 'Best view in the village. Lived here all my life. Born in the same house I live in on Gibbet Lane. Went to school here. I was the first woman to work at the bank, y'know? Lived through the last war, of course.'

'That don't mean we'll win this one,' Faye said.

'Maybe we won't.'

'But you said—'

'Look at that lot down there.' Mrs Pritchett raised her chin at the village folk pootling about below, unaware they were being observed. 'Maybe the Nazis will cross the Channel with their tanks and jackboots. Maybe they'll beat us and try and rule over us, but do you think those people down there will put up with it for long? We live in terrible times, Faye, and horrible things will happen, no doubt. But I've seen enough goodness in that rabble below to convince me that we'll make it through. Some days that belief will be tested, girl. But I'm thinking that goodness will win in the end.'

'In the end?' Faye frowned. 'When's the end? Three years? Five? The end of the world?'

'I think what she's saying is there's more good folk than bad,' Bertie said as he joined Mrs Pritchett at the crenellations.

'Zactly.' Mrs Pritchett took a drag on her cigarette. 'What you have to remember is the good stuff don't sell newspapers, so you hardly hear about it. "Cub Scout Helps Little Old Lady Cross Road" is hardly front-page news, now, is it?'

'It's only when things go bad that we're interested,' Bertie agreed.

'Yup, we all love a bit of gossip,' Mrs Pritchett said, flashing a grin.

Faye and Bertie shuffled awkwardly again.

'Speakin' of which …' Mrs Pritchett nodded back towards the Wode Road just as Lord and Lady Aston were stepping out of the florist's.

'You've got gossip on Lady Aston?' Faye said, feeling a shameful tingle of excitement, but happy to veer the subject away from her and Bertie. It wasn't right to enjoy gossip, of course, but the Astons were a private pair and that made any titbits all the more enticing.

'Nah, Lizzie's all right,' Mrs Pritchett said. 'I was thinking about his lordship.'

'What about him?' Faye asked, looking on as they stopped in the street to chat with Reverend Jacobs.

'This is going to sound strange—'

'We live in Woodville, Mrs P,' Faye said. 'Strange is every day for the likes of us.'

Mrs Pritchett snuffed out her roll-up with her finger and thumb before planting it behind her ear. 'What would you say if I told you this Lord Aston – the Third Lord Aston – just sort of . . . turned up out of the blue?'

'What do you mean?' Faye asked.

'S'true,' Bertie said, getting excited and whispering even though they were at the highest point in the village and only curious birds could hear them. 'My dad told me all about this. Lord Aston's old man, the Second Lord Aston, was trampled by an elephant and then came back from the dead . . . or something.' Bertie found both Faye and Mrs Pritchett frowning at him and he shrugged. 'S'what I heard. Is that right?'

'Not quite.' Mrs Pritchett beckoned Faye and Bertie closer to tell the story. 'The Second Lord Aston was a very private fella. You never saw him in the village. Maybe in church at Christmas and Easter. But truth be told he was hardly here, anyway. The man was always off gallivanting around the world – India, Africa especially – shooting anything that walked. Then one day there's a headline in the newspaper: "Lord Aston Trampled by Elephant".'

'Told you!' Bertie said, but Mrs Pritchett waved him into silence before continuing.

'Story goes, he's out there in the jungle and this

mother elephant takes a disliking to him – under-standable as he's probably got half her family's heads mounted on his walls – and she stomps on him till the job is done.'

'Blimey,' Faye said with a gasp. 'What a way to go.'

Mrs Pritchett pursed her lips, tilted her head from side to side and made a noise halfway between agreement and doubt. 'That's if he went in the first place.'

'What do you mean?'

'This is the bit where you're going to think I'm loopy.'

Faye half-opened her mouth to make a flippant comment, but something about the conspiratorial look in Mrs P's eyes made her hold back.

'It was August 2nd 1915. A Monday. I know that cos it was the same day my little brother Ralphie went off to fight in the trenches and it was the last time I ever saw him.' She took a breath. 'That's when his lordship – the Third Lord Aston down there – returns from India with his new missus in tow. No announcement, no fuss. They just set up shop at Hayward Lodge and carry on like nothing's happened. It's almost like they hoped no one would notice.'

'What's wrong with that? The son of a lord usually takes over, don't they?'

'Tell her, Bertie,' Mrs Pritchett prompted the boy.

'The Second Lord Aston didn't have a son,' Bertie said. 'That's what my dad said, anyway.'

'Or if he did,' Mrs Pritchett continued, 'he never told no one.'

'Then who is he?' Faye asked.

122

'You tell me.'

'He has to be his son,' Faye said. 'He's the dead spit of his old man. I saw a photo of him at Hayward Lodge.'

Their conversation was broken by the clanging of a bell as an ambulance came haring up the Wode Road.

'Aye aye,' Mrs Pritchett said. 'Someone's day's been ruined.'

The ambulance screeched to a halt by the Green Man. Faye's heart skipped a beat, worried that something had happened to her father, but then the ambulance crunched into reverse and made its way back to the florist's where Lord and Lady Aston were still chatting with Reverend Jacobs.

The driver leapt out and Bertie recognised her. 'That's Edith Palmer,' he said.

Edith hurried to Lord and Lady Aston, her head bobbing urgently as she spoke. Lady Aston gripped Reverend Jacobs' arm in shock. Edith jumped back into the driver's seat and Lord and Lady Aston dashed to their Bentley parked nearby. They all took off up the road, the ambulance's bell clanging.

'What was all that about?' Bertie wondered.

Faye's feet felt like lead as she darted across the roof of the church to see the ambulance heading up Edge Road towards Hayward Lodge. 'Klaus,' she whispered.

She gave Bertie an apologetic look before rushing for the stairs.

Ambulance Chaser

Mrs Pritchett took a little convincing to loan Faye her motorcycle to catch up with the ambulance.

'I can't explain now, Mrs Pritchett, as I would come over as fruity as a nut cake, but this is a life or death thing, and—'

'Just kick-start it and away you go!' the old woman called after Faye as she hurried down the bell tower's winding stone staircase.

Back when Faye first got her bicycle off Alfie Paine, he had just bought a motorbike and he let her have a go. She recalled something about kicking something and perhaps a button and maybe a key, but Mrs Pritchett's 1925 Douglas only had a kick-starter.

Faye slung her leg over the saddle and put all her weight on the kick-starter, spinning the engine to life. She spotted a gear lever that said 'low' and nudged it into position, then gripped one of the levers on the handlebars. The motorcycle lurched forwards and promptly careened into the church fence by the lychgate with an almighty crash that drew stares from passers-by.

She was righting the motorcycle as Mrs Pritchett and Bertie dashed out of the bell tower.

'I'm ... I'm just getting the hang of it,' Faye said, giving a thumbs-up as she hopped on again. She kicked the starter, but the engine just made a grim clacking noise and black smoke coughed from the exhaust. 'On second thoughts, I'll take me bike.'

⌀

The uphill ride was harder than ever. Legs burning, heart thumping and blood pumping in her ears, all while fending off terrible thoughts of what she might see when she got to Hayward Lodge. Faye turned off Edge Road and sped down the drive to the house, leaning forwards over the handlebars.

As she approached the house, she saw the ambulance, Lord and Lady Aston's Bentley and Harry's shiny red MG parked by the dry fountain.

Edith was leaning against the big red cross on the side of her ambulance. She alternated between smoking a cigarette and biting her nails. When she saw Faye, she put her nibbled fingers behind her back.

'Morning, Faye. What brings you here?'

In all the rush, Faye hadn't expected anyone to ask her that. What could she say that wouldn't make her sound bonkers or the nosiest person in the village? That she came here on a hunch?

'The kids,' Faye said, still gasping for breath. 'I saw

the ambulance and had a bit of a fright. Are the kids all right?'

'I'm just the driver, duck,' Edith said. 'Doc told me to wait here while him and Lord and Lady Aston—'

'Where did they go?'

'Round the side and out the back, I think.'

'Mind me bike, will you? Ta.'

Faye's legs were a little wobbly after the cycle from the village, but she found reserves of energy to pelt around the side of the mansion house, past the orangery and into the garden. A few patients were milling about, reading in wheelchairs or tending to the shrubs, but there was no sign of—

A child's wail came over a wall at the bottom of the garden.

The orchard.

Faye ran to it and entered through the iron gate. Beyond were apple trees in neat rows, bees buzzing between them. The wailing peaked again, and Faye turned to find a small group gathered together. Nelson the one-eyed dog scampered around them, barking for attention, but they were looking down at something on the ground. Faye wished it not to be true, that this was some silly prank played by the children and they would all be laughing about it soon.

She saw Lady Aston dabbing at tears with her handkerchief, Lord Aston holding her, grim-faced and silent.

The doctor crouched by a body lying on the ground. Rudolf next to him, shaking the body, wishing it to wake. Magda and Max holding one another. And, standing back from them all, was Harry clutching his driving hat.

'Klaus, Klaus!' Rudolf sobbed as the doctor made one more check for vital signs.

The doctor looked up at Lady Aston and slowly shook his head.

Faye had arrived in time to see Klaus just as he had been in her vision. His parted lips were chalk-white, his skin a sickly blue. The doctor gently brushed his hands over Klaus's eyes, closing them for ever.

Faye's heart sank through her.

The vision had come true. Only the trees weren't in a wood, they were in an orchard. Why hadn't she realised that sooner? She could have simply told him to keep away from the orchard, but she hadn't and now he was dead. She should have been more insistent that he stay in the pub, or simply go somewhere without trees, but she didn't and now he was dead. Countless *should haves* and *could haves* that might have saved Klaus came rushing at Faye, but now the boy who wanted to fight to get his home back was dead.

'Faye, darling.' Lady Aston sniffed and gave Faye a puzzled look. 'What are you doing here?'

For a moment, Faye couldn't speak. Unable to draw her eyes away from Klaus. She blinked and felt a tear trickle down her cheek.

'I saw the ambulance and ... I wondered if I could help,' she said, feeling it was a lame excuse for crashing in on their grief. 'I'm so sorry,' she added, desperate to

ask how it happened, but worried that it might seem a
bit rude with the lad still lying there.

A numbness hit Faye. Klaus had been unstoppable. He
was a fighter. How could someone so full of life and rage
suddenly be so empty? She recalled the warmth of his lips
when they kissed, the fire in his eyes. The voices around
her faded to a dull mumble, the colours drained from the
grass, the trees and the sky. The sensation of grief and
shock held her in its embrace and she welcomed it.

That's when Faye noticed the axe nearby. It rested
in the long grass under one of the apple trees, Nelson
sniffing at it.

Faye shook her head clear. What had Klaus been
doing with an axe in an orchard? Chopping down an
apple tree? Faye looked to Lady Aston and wondered
if now was a good time to ask, then the doctor stood
and brushed a hand through his hair.

'Lord Aston, Lady Aston, if I may?' he said, glancing at Faye and the children. 'Could we have a word
in private?'

'Of course.' Lady Aston turned to Faye. 'Darling,
would you mind? Take them to the kitchen. There
should be some cordial or something.'

'Er, righto.' Faye thought about suggesting sitting
them in the shade on the other side of the orchard wall.
Somewhere peaceful and within earshot so she could
earwig the doctor's conversation with Lord and Lady
Aston. But she caught Harry looking at her and decided
that doing anything other than Lady Aston's wishes
would be suspicious.

'Here y'go.' Faye extended a hand to the children, but Max and Magda formed a protective cordon around Rudolf and led the sobbing boy away through the orchard. She followed with Nelson panting at her side. She dared to look back only once.

Harry was staring, as if to make sure Faye did as she was asked.

※

They gathered in silence in the kitchen, Nelson napping at their feet. Mr Pinder brought them all lime cordial to drink and they sat in a sorry circle around one of the tables as staff came and went.

Faye's visions had come true, and it made her sick to her stomach. She had been ready to dismiss them – much as Mrs Teach and Miss Charlotte told her to – but the nightmarish déjà vu she had seen in her mind's eye had just played out in reality only moments before. What did this mean? She had half a mind to rush straight to Mrs Teach and Miss Charlotte for help, but they had made it very clear that she shouldn't get involved. They would order her to keep away and leave these poor children alone. Faye wasn't about to abandon Magda, Max and Rudolf, not when they needed comfort more than ever. She was desperate to ask the children what had happened, but it didn't feel right. Not yet, anyway.

'Rudolf, I almost forgot.' Faye reached into one of the pockets of her dungarees, unfolding a sheet of paper. 'I still have your drawing. Look.' She spread it flat on the table. 'It's ever so lovely, I take it with me everywhere I go.'

'*Der Baum*,' Rudolf said, bopping up and down in his seat and jabbing a sticky finger on the drawing.

'Der ... der what?' Faye looked to Magda and Max for help.

'*Der Baum, der Baum*,' Rudolf continued, followed by a stream of German that Faye hadn't a hope of following.

Max pushed his specs back and whispered in his sister's ear.

Magda nodded, looked to Faye and said, 'Tree.'

Rudolf continued to prod the same tree again and again. It was the one he had drawn with little rays of light emanating from it.

'This tree?' Faye asked with an encouraging nod and got a further stream of German. One word stood out. *Klaus*. 'This is the tree where Klaus ...' She faltered, unsure how to put it other than via a pained expression.

Rudolf shook his head.

'Then what's so special about this tree, Rudolf?'

The boy looked from her to Max and Magda. None of them understood.

'Faye.' Lady Aston peeked around one of the doors into the kitchen. She smiled and beckoned Faye to join her.

'Hold that thought,' Faye told the children, and stepped out to the orangery with Lady Aston.

They stood close to the Höch photomontage. Faye winced a little at the image of the man with the axe and the children dead in the woods.

131

'How are you, Lady A?'

'After all they've been through, and now this.' Lady Aston shook her head and lit a cigarette. She took a drag and exhaled a cloud that made Faye's eyes water.

'What happened?'

'The doctor thinks it might be a bee-sting. Allergic reaction.'

'Oh no.' Faye deflated at such a horrid, random thing to happen. Though she couldn't shake a niggling suspicion at the back of her mind that something wasn't quite right. Just what had Klaus been doing in the orchard with an axe?

'The head girl at my old school went the same way,' Lady Aston said, taking another drag on her cigarette. 'There's a swarm on the orchard wall. I've been meaning to get a chap in to take care of it all week, but what with one thing and another—'

Faye noticed her hands were trembling.

'This ain't your fault,' Faye told her.

'Such a lovely lad. Troubled in all sorts of ways, of course. Who wouldn't be after what they've been through? I promised his mother he would be safe. Lord knows if she's still alive. Even if she is, this might finish the poor woman off. Damn this war and all who started it.'

Faye hummed in agreement.

'And he was so good with the children. Oh, Lord.' A thought occurred to Lady Aston and she took a step back. 'I shall have to get a nanny.'

'I can help,' Faye said, immediately wondering how

she would square this with her dad who needed her at the pub.

'Oh, you're a darling. Would you? Just for a few days, until the real thing comes along?'

'Love to. What will I need to do?'

'Keep them occupied. Games and such. I simply need someone to watch over them while I engage a proper nanny and a tutor. Make sure they don't, well, get stung by bees or end up like them.' She glanced at the Höch photomontage with the dead children in the wood.

Faye sank a little under the sudden weight of responsibility. 'I reckon I can do that,' she said with a confidence that wasn't entirely genuine. 'I need to let me dad know. He'll have to get someone to cover at the pub.'

'Oh, yes indeed. I'll pay you for your trouble, of course. Marvellous, simply marvellous. Can you start tomorrow?'

SEEN AND NOT HEARD

Faye found her bike where she'd left it by the dry fountain. Edith was closing the rear doors of the ambulance with the doctor and Klaus's body inside. Edith gave Faye a sad smile as the ambulance pulled away. The dust cleared, revealing Harry still clutching his hat.

'I say, dashed awful business,' he said to Faye as he ambled over to her side to watch the departing ambulance. 'The little ones will be devastated. Still. Death, eh? Lot of it about. I suppose that in these times of war we need to get used to such tragedy.' He contorted his face into a half-smile, half-grimace.

'It was a bee-sting,' Faye said. 'Unless the bee was a secret Nazi spy on a suicide mission, it didn't have nothing to do with the war.'

Harry became a fluster of blinks. 'Yes, that's true. A tragedy all the same. Hey-ho.' He began to back away towards the house.

'Who found him?' Faye asked.

Harry's feet crunched on the gravel. 'I'm afraid it was

the little chap. Rudolf. Went off like an air raid siren, poor blighter.'

'What was Klaus doing in the orchard?'

'I say, you're coming across as something of a young Miss Marple.' Harry smiled, revealing the gap in his teeth. 'Do you suspect foul play?'

He was perfectly chummy, but Faye caught an edge to his voice. She trod carefully.

'No, nothing like that. Just wondering what he was doing in the orchard with an axe. Was he going to chop a tree down?'

'Not bloody likely,' Harry said. 'Mater's orchard is sacred territory. No, though there is some knotweed at the bottom of the orchard. Perhaps that was his target? *I, Hercule Poirot, shall apply zee little grey cells to discover zee truth, hm?*' This last was delivered in a terrible Belgian accent, topped off with a honking laugh.

Faye didn't join in with his laughter. She was distracted by a head popping out from around the corner of the house, then popping back again. It was either Magda or Max. It was there and gone too quick for her to be sure.

'It's from Agatha Christie,' Harry said, miffed that she hadn't found his joke funny. He mimed opening the pages of a book. 'She writes mystery novels.'

'I know Agatha Christie,' Faye snapped. 'Books ain't just for toffs, y'know.'

Harry took a step back. 'Hm. Indeed. Speaking of grey cells, how's the noggin?'

'Much better, thanks,' Faye said, cross at herself for

snapping at him and wishing he would go away. 'No harm done.'

More heads popped around the corner of the house again. Magda, followed by Max, then Nelson the dog scurried out and was called back again. The noise distracted Harry, who glanced in their direction, but they were gone.

'Jolly good,' he said, clasping his hands and cap behind his back. He didn't move, and Faye got the feeling he wanted her to leave.

She didn't much fancy staying here any longer, either. She swung a leg over her bike and was about to pedal off when a child's hand waved at her from the corner of the house. Harry saw it, too.

Faye nodded in the direction of the children. 'Er, I think they want to speak to me. In private.' She got off her bike and started towards the children.

Harry pasted a grin back on his face, his fists clenching and unclenching.

'Of course, of course,' he said. 'Poor little tykes. Don't start them off with the wailing again, will you? I don't fancy being the one who has to console them.'

'I think that's my job now,' Faye said, enjoying the confusion on Harry's face.

'Beg pardon?'

'Her ladyship just asked me to look after the children. Only for a few days till a proper nanny turns up. I start tomorrow.'

Harry's forced grin was bigger than ever. 'How ... marvellous. Wonderful news. Phew, for a moment there

I thought Mother was going to unload them on poor old me. What a relief.'

'Don't you like children?'

'I'm not sure anyone in the Aston clan does, Faye. Let's just say my arrival was something of an inconvenience to my darling parents.' For a moment, his strained jollity faded. 'Children are to be tolerated, not loved.'

'If they don't like children, then why's she taking in these German kids?'

'Oh, other people's are fine. They can be handed back or passed on to the likes of you. Mother and Father are lumbered with me.'

The French doors behind Harry opened and Lord Aston stepped out, a meaty fist gripping the door handle. Faye recalled what Mrs Pritchett had told her about his sudden appearance in 1915. The man before her barely looked forty, so was he a child when he became lord? But he couldn't have been if he was married to Lady Aston. Just how old were they both?

'Harry,' Lord Aston said, his voice almost rattling the glass in the windows. 'A word.'

Harry's grin wavered. 'Certainly, Father. Just chatting with Faye and I'll be right with you, lickety-split.'

'Be sure that you are. I'll be in the observatory,' Lord Aston boomed before marching inside.

'Right,' Faye said, jabbing a thumb towards where the children were hiding. 'I'd better go and reassure the littl'uns.'

'Yes, yes, you do that.'

Faye stood her ground, and waited as Harry

marched inside to meet his father. Once he was gone, she rounded the corner of the house to find Magda, Max, Rudolf and Nelson all waiting for her. Their eyes were still red from crying and they continued to huddle together for safety.

'Blimey, look at you lot,' Faye muttered. 'You ain't had an easy ride of it, have you?'

Max whispered in Magda's ear again.

The girl nodded and spoke, her voice barely a whisper. 'Tree?'

Max moved his fingers as if drawing and Faye understood. She reached into her dungarees and unfolded the picture that Rudolf had given her.

'Let's pick up where we left off, eh?' she said, recalling their interrupted conversation in the kitchen. 'There's something special about this tree, is there?'

The children chattered among themselves in German, came to a decision and hurried off towards the garden.

Magda beckoned her to follow. '*Komm. Komm mit uns.*'

Faye did as she was asked, though she was worried they were heading back to where Klaus's body had been found in the orchard. She was surprised when they took a swerve for the orangery. They slipped in through one of the glass doors and gathered around the Höch photomontage. Rudolf was particularly agitated, pointing at the trees in the picture and hopping up and down.

Faye looked to Magda and Max. 'What's he on about?'

'Tree, uh ...' She glanced at Max as she tried to think of the word.

Max snapped his fingers and pointed at one of the orangery's light fittings.

Magda was making a flashing gesture with her hands.

'The tree lit up?' Faye ventured, and the children nodded. 'Like this?' She pointed at Rudolf's drawing and they nodded even harder. 'So you're telling me that a tree in that picture lit up and Rudolf drew it?'

Faye curled a lip, unsure what this had to do with anything. The children were now standing still with blank faces. They had reached the edge of their understanding.

'Faye, you're still here, darling?' Lady Aston strode through the doors at the end of the orangery in her riding gear, her bowler hat and riding crop tucked under her arm.

'You speak German, don't you?' Faye asked her. 'They're getting all excited about something to do with this picture and a tree and I can't make head nor tail of it.'

'I have a dash of German,' Lady Aston said, flexing her riding crop. 'I can ask for directions or order a meal, just don't call on me to negotiate a peace treaty or anything too tricky or we might come a cropper.'

Faye nodded to the kids. 'Tell her ladyship what you told me.'

There followed a burble of overlapping voices in German, with Lady Aston occasionally asking questions, which created more excitement from the children.

It ended with her ladyship nodding. 'Aah, I see. Jolly good.'

'What? What did they say?'

'I haven't the first clue,' Lady Aston said, maintaining her smile for the benefit of the children. 'Something about a tree glowing on the Höch or some such. You'll have to get used to this, I'm afraid. These three have quite vivid imaginations.'

'I wonder ...' Faye bit her lip. What she wanted to say might make her sound crackers, but she reflected that if she had been a bit more forthright with Klaus, the lad might still be alive. 'I wonder if this had something to do with Klaus's death?'

'In what way?'

'You said the Höch was cursed—'

'Oh, Faye, really?' Lady Aston grimaced. 'You're not going wet on me, are you?'

'No, but they seem very excited about the tree in the picture, and—'

'Indulge their little fantasies to an extent, but don't let them drive you potty. Harry was the same whenever he came home from boarding school. My advice is to let them wear themselves out. Jolly good. I'm off for a ride. What a simply awful day.' She popped her bowler hat on, then marched out of the orangery doors towards the stables.

Magda looked with disbelief at Lady Aston as she turned the corner out of sight. The girl didn't need a translation to know that the children's concerns had been dismissed by their horse-obsessed guardian.

'I think that's all we're going to get out of her ladyship.' Faye shrugged.

Magda was fuming. She ranted red-faced and

actually stamped her foot. Max tried to calm her down and Rudolf began bawling again. Even Nelson started to howl, and Faye began to wonder just what the bloody hell she was letting herself in for.

'Hey, hush now, it's all right.' She crouched down and extended her arms, beckoning them in for a hug. Rudolf slammed into her, a sticky hot mess. Magda and Max were next, their arms wrapped around Faye.

The world tilted on its axis and Faye realised too late her mistake in hugging the children.

Moonlight. A full moon.

Faye shook her head clear. This vision was as strong as the others, though she remained upright and conscious. It was almost as if she was getting used to—

The children lie among the leaves of the wood. Huddled together. Eyes closed.

Faye couldn't pass out now. The children had been traumatised enough for one day.

Their skin is pale as the moon. Their bodies still. There is no question about it. Max, Magda and Rudolf are dead.

Faye held on tight to the children. This could not happen. She had to protect them. She would not fail them the way she had failed Klaus.

Two Sherries
and a Gossip

Through a series of elaborate mimes and repeated promises of the internationally recognised 'Cross my heart and hope to die' gesture, Faye managed to convince the children to let her cycle home. She didn't want to – not after a vision of them lying dead in the wood had chilled her to the bone – but she left them safe in their room and a long way from the woods. Faye had a more immediate problem. She had to convince her dad to let her play nanny for a few days.

ॐ

'You did what?' Terrence Bright was not a man given to anger. Surrendering to the baser instincts was not good business for a publican. By all means, allow the punter to lose their rag and then politely bar them or toss them into the street, but never, ever get angry yourself. Today, however, Faye was testing this long-standing serenity to its limits.

'It's only for a few days,' Faye said as she swept the floor. 'I think.'

'You *think*?'

'Dad, I'm the only person who can do this.'

'Says who?'

Faye set her jaw. She could tell him that she reckoned the visions were warnings that had given her the feeling that someone or some*thing* was behind Klaus's death, but she didn't think that would wash with her father. She barely believed it herself, but as far as Faye was concerned, she was the only person who knew what kind of danger those children were in, and she was the only one who could keep them safe.

'They like me,' she said. 'They trust me. It's just till her ladyship gets a new nanny.'

'Oh, well, as long as her ladyship is all right. And what am I supposed to do without you helping me?'

'Dougie Allen could do a few more shifts?'

Terrence made a grumbling noise.

'What's wrong?' Faye asked. 'Is Dougie not working out?'

'Dougie's all right – I mean, he never shuts up about bleedin' cars, but he can pull a pint and he's a grafter – but … He ain't you, Faye.'

'I should think that was obvious, Dad. He don't wear specs for a start.'

'What I mean is, I like the way we work together as a team. Father and daughter. Did you think any more about what I said?'

'About you popping your clogs?'

144

'No. About running the pub one day.'

'After you've popped your clogs?'

'You can start any time you like, girl. I'll show you the ropes right now. You could practically run this pub on your own already, anyway.'

Faye placed a chair on the floor and sat on it. 'I dunno, Dad,' she said. 'The pub is all well and good, but I ain't rightly figured out what I want to do with my life yet.'

'Sounds like you want to be a nanny more than a publican.'

'No, Lor' no. I don't plan on bein' a nanny for good. It's just, in a funny way, I feel responsible for them.'

'Because you saved them?'

'Not exactly.' Faye pushed her specs up her nose as she wondered how she could justify her plan without mentioning her visions. 'When they arrived, they were nearly killed, and then people threw stuff at them just because they're German. They need to see a friendly face.'

'And that has to be you, does it?'

'Yes.'

'Hang on.' Terrence raised his chin. 'Is this ... witchy stuff?'

'No, it's just a bit of nannying, Dad. I won't be turning them into frogs.'

'Cos if it is, you should get that pair to sort it out for you.'

'Don't call them that.'

That pair had become shorthand for Mrs Teach and Miss Charlotte, and Terrence always grimaced when

145

he said it. 'Don't get me wrong, Faye, I like both Mrs Teach and Miss Charlotte. But there's something about the two of them together that reminds me of when they knew your mother, and seeing them side by side always makes me teeth itch.'

'It's not witchy stuff, Dad. Besides, they're busy enough.' Faye had thought about contacting Mrs Teach and Miss Charlotte, but they'd been so dismissive of the visions the first time around, she knew this was something she had to sort for herself. 'Please, Dad. These littl'uns trust me. I have to be the one.'

Terrence was gifted with the wrinkled complexion of a cowboy's well-worn saddlebag. The smallest expression would create all-new rifts on his mug, and a big smile, like the one creasing his face right now, had more lines than a map of the Highlands. He cackled and shook his head.

'Just like your mother,' he said. 'What you did the other day, girl ... Exactly the sort of daft thing she would've done. She'd be proud of you. Just don't make a habit of it, eh? My nerves are bad enough as it is. To think, what could've happened—'

'This won't be nothing like that, will it?' she insisted. 'I'll just be looking after a few kids.'

'Yeah, I s'pose so. I'll talk to Dougie. I know he could do with the work.'

'Thanks, Dad.' Faye wanted to give him a hug, but he was already at the pub's door, about to open up for the lunchtime rush.

His hands rested on the door's lock and handle. 'Just promise me one thing,' he said.

'Anything.'

'Don't let them get you all hoity-toity.'

'No chance of that, Pa. I shall proudly be droppin' me aitches as a matter of principle.'

'Nah, I don't mean your Ps and Qs. I mean, don't fall for all the airs and graces. Toffs are your best friend when they need something from you, but once they're done with you they'll toss you out like yesterday's newspaper. They'll make you think you're one of the family, but don't fall for it.'

Faye wanted to ask how her dad had discovered this for himself, but he'd unlocked the door to find a group of thirsty Australian airmen waiting impatiently.

❧

Faye worked in the pub all afternoon and through to the evening. The pub was packed. Though something wasn't right. Bertie wasn't in his usual spot.

'Is Bertie on patrol tonight?' Faye asked her dad. Both he and Bertie were Local Defence Volunteers and took turns to go on night patrols along the coast to spot U-boats and enemy aircraft.

'Don't think so,' Terrence said, distracted by a smudge on the pint glass he was drying. He held it up to the light. 'Not on a Thursday. Why do you ask?'

'I dunno.' She shrugged. 'It's Bertie, isn't it? He's like part of the furniture.'

'I'm sure he'd be delighted to be compared to a bar-stool.'

'You know what I mean. I hope he's all right.'

Terrence lowered the glass and looked at Faye. 'Why wouldn't he be?'

Because Faye had run off and left him to check on the welfare of a strange German lad she hardly knew but had kissed the night before?

'No reason,' she said.

'I reckon he's soft on you,' Terrence said, finally satisfied with the pint glass and putting it in place above the bar with the others.

Faye made a series of scoffing noises.

'You sound like a train pulling out of a station,' Terrence told her. 'Am I right or am I wrong? I've seen how he looks at you with those big doe eyes.'

'He's a mate. We like to chat, that's all. He's a good listener.'

'If I know you, that means he never gets a word in. Be nice to the lad. If you don't fancy him, let him down gently.'

'Oh, wonderful. Now my own father is poking his nose into my—' Faye stopped herself. She very nearly said *love life*. 'Personal life,' she said. The thing with Bertie definitely wasn't love. Though Faye found herself wanting to be around Bertie more. Nothing mushy. She just liked to chat with him. She also wanted to talk to him to make sure he wasn't upset at her for running off after Klaus's ambulance. Would she have bothered with such a gesture a few days ago? It's funny how a few words between friends can change things. Had she upset him? Was that why he wasn't here tonight?

'This is why you don't step out with mates,' she muttered.

'Whassat?' her dad asked.

'Nothing.' Faye marched out from behind the bar to collect the empty glasses, mumbling to herself and cursing the whole idea of romance as a very bad thing.

⌀

Dougie turned up for the eight-till-ten shift and Faye took a quick break.

She had noticed Mr Gilbert sitting in his usual spot with his business partner Mr Brewer. They both lived above their antiques shop on the corner of the Wode Road and Rood Lane, and would regularly pop over for a snifter or two. A thought had occurred to Faye, and she hoped they might be able to help her with it.

Faye sidled through the crowd to their little round table.

'Hello, gents, mind if I join you for a few minutes?' she asked.

Mr Gilbert had the most impressive Roman nose that was propped up by permanently pursed lips. Always immaculately dressed in Savile Row suits, he had the air of someone who might be condescending – or even 'hoity-toity' – but he was known for being one of the most gracious proprietors in town.

'My darling Faye, you may join us for as many minutes, hours or days as you wish,' he said in his nasal voice. 'Just don't spoil the view.'

Faye wondered what he meant, then followed his

gaze to find a cluster of handsome pilots standing behind her.

'Oh, don't be so crude,' Mr Brewer piped up. He was considerably shorter than Mr Gilbert, though just as smartly dressed and the possessor of two huge owl-like eyes, made even bigger by the thick lenses on his spectacles. He raised his half-pint of Guinness before addressing Faye. 'Forgive him, Faye. Two sherries and he becomes a monster.'

Faye chuckled. Everyone knew that Mr Gilbert and Mr Brewer had a relationship that was more than busi-nesslike, but what with *that-sort-of-thing* being illegal and so on, no one ever spoke of it. In the village of Woodville, you could be whatever you wanted so long as no one ever said it out loud.

'Ms Bright, have you come to brighten our evening?' Mr Gilbert asked, relishing the weak pun. 'You have the look of Alice about you, Faye. Curiouser and curiouser.'

'I do have a few questions.'

'Ask away, darling.'

'You gents know about art and all that stuff.'

'Art and all that stuff?' Mr Brewer looked mildly offended. 'Yes, I suppose we did study relentlessly and toil for many years in the greatest schools and galleries to master the mysteries of "art and all that stuff".'

'Don't mind him,' Mr Gilbert interjected. 'Half a Guinness and *he* becomes a miserable old so-and-so. Art and all that stuff, Faye? Yes, that's us. How can we help?'

'Have you ever heard of Hannah Höch?' Faye asked.

Both men made impressed noises, sharing a look and a nod.

'You have modern tastes, Faye,' Mr Brewer said. 'Dada, photomontage, political discourse. Kudos to you, young lady, kudos.'

'We are great admirers of the woman,' Mr Gilbert said. 'Even if she is considered one of the enemy now, along with Beethoven, Goethe and Dürer. Such a shame.'

'Her work was always very critical of the powers-that-be,' Mr Brewer said. 'The Nazis called her a degenerate.'

'Which is good enough for us.'

Mr Gilbert leaned forward. 'Did you ever see her most important piece – "Cut with the Kitchen Knife Dada through the Last Weimar Beer-Belly Cultural Epoch in Germany"?'

'Er, no,' Faye said. 'Is that what it's actually called?'

'It is, it is. Simply remarkable.' Mr Gilbert pressed a hand to his heart. 'The woman is a genius.'

'Do you have a favourite piece of hers, Faye?' Mr Brewer asked, taking a sip of his Guinness.

'I only know one,' Faye said. 'It's the one up at Hayward Lodge. Lady Aston has it hanging in the orangery. It's called "Babes in the Wood".'

Mr Gilbert gasped. Mr Brewer choked on his Guinness.

'What?' Faye looked at both men, who were still agog.

'Faye, my darling,' Mr Gilbert said, patting the still panting Mr Brewer on the back to clear his blockage, 'where does one start? That piece is thought to be lost. Many believe it to have been destroyed.'

'Nope. Seen it with me own two peepers.'

'We have to view it.' Mr Brewer got his voice back and gripped his partner's forearm.

'For valuation purposes if nothing else,' Mr Gilbert agreed.

'You know all about this one, then?' Faye asked.

'As much as can be known about a lost piece of art,' Mr Gilbert said.

'Do you ...' Faye started, then raised a finger. 'This is going to sound silly, but do you know anything about it ... glowing?'

Both men's faces contorted in confusion.

'That's a no, then?' Faye concluded.

'Glowing, how?' Mr Brewer asked.

'Rudolf, the littlest of the kiddies staying with Lord and Lady Aston, he said one of the trees on the montage was glowing. He was getting really excited about it and I'm trying to make sense of what he said.'

'We definitely have to see it now,' Mr Gilbert said.

'And soon,' Mr Brewer said, then added in a sardonic tone, 'before Harry realises what it's worth and flogs it.'

'Why would he do that?'

Mr Brewer leaned closer to Faye. 'Have you met his young lordship, Harry?'

'Yes.'

'What do you make of him?'

'He nearly ran me over.'

'There you are.'

'He was very apologetic.'

'He always is, after the fact,' Mr Brewer said.

'Does he make a habit of running people over, then?' Faye asked.

'Harry is a perfectly nice chap,' Mr Gilbert said, his tone considerably more forgiving than Mr Brewer's. 'Just don't lend him any money.'

'You'll never see it again,' Mr Brewer snapped, sounding like he had personal experience of such an exchange.

'He fell in with the wrong sorts at Eton.'

'Then Oxford.'

'Then the Home Office,' Mr Gilbert said. 'He runs up the most dreadful gambling debts and has to come home cap-in-hand to Mummy and Daddy when the well dries up. He is something of a wastrel.'

'Can't have been easy,' Faye said. 'Being packed off to boarding school by his parents and all.'

'I went to boarding school,' Mr Brewer said, raising his chin, 'but you don't see me lording it over people.'

'Not much,' muttered Mr Gilbert, then continued, 'Harry simply lacks direction. He has no passions other than gambling.'

'And his car,' Faye added.

'Indeed. I'm sure he just needs a guiding hand. Someone to steer him in the right direction and find some purpose in life.'

'Faye!' Terrence called over the hubbub of the crowd. Her break was over. Mr Gilbert took her hand. She started a little at his touch, but no visions of doom were forthcoming.

'Speak to Lady Aston,' Mr Gilbert said, 'see if you might arrange a viewing. We can assess it and value it for insurance purposes. She'll want to know what it's worth, and then we can help you with this glowing mystery.'

Faye stood, leaning close and lowering her voice. 'I'm helping out with the children at Hayward Lodge tomorrow. Why don't you pop by then?'

'Perhaps once we shut up shop?' Mr Brewer looked to Mr Gilbert.

'How does little after six sound, Faye?' Mr Gilbert asked.

'Perfect,' Faye said. 'The kids'll be having their tea and I'll meet you out front. You can have a quick gander and no harm done.'

'A clandestine viewing?' Mr Brewer said. 'Can we sanction such thing?'

'It's simply a viewing,' Mr Gilbert replied. 'We shall see you there, Faye.'

'Thank you, gents,' Faye said, but Mr Brewer still looked agitated.

'Are you sure about this?' he asked.

'We shall look, but not touch,' Mr Gilbert said, then lowered his voice. 'Though if it's worth a few bob, we can try and convince her ladyship to auction it via us. The commission alone will be a king's ransom. I'll cut you in for a percentage, Faye.'

'What did I tell you?' Mr Brewer pouted. 'Two sherries and I'm ashamed to know him.'

MAGDA

Magda needed to learn more English. They all did. This was their home now. For how long, she couldn't be sure – maybe for the rest of their lives – but this place felt more like a home than anywhere else since they left Berlin. But until they could be understood by Lady Aston, by Faye, they would remain strangers here.

Magda's mind was in pieces and she could not sleep. She sat cross-legged on her bed as her brothers snored. She watched the silver clouds slide before the full moon. She thought of her cousin Klaus and how he would have spoken for them. A too-familiar sadness twisted inside her. He had taken them so far, and to be felled by a bee-sting was the cruellest joke. And for poor Rudolf to have found him made it all the sadder. They had done all they could to shelter her youngest brother from the horrors of the war on their journey. A hand over the eyes and ears had preserved his innocence when windows were smashed on *Kristallnacht*, when guns were fired in Munich, when bombs were dropped

155

on Rotterdam, so for him to first encounter death in an English orchard was another wicked prank by God.

Magda wasn't sure she believed in God any more. Her family had not been the most faithful Jews. They observed Shabbat when they remembered, which wasn't often. She couldn't remember the last time they went to the synagogue or ate kosher food.

As they fled from Munich, Mama said none of this would have happened if they had been better Jews. Papa said the Nazis were rounding up *all* Jews. They weren't checking how strong their faith was. Mama scolded him and said that God had abandoned them because there were too many bad Jews. They had argued into the night. In Rotterdam they had stayed with a Christian family and the mother there had told Magda how God would return in the form of Jesus Christ in our darkest hour. Magda nodded meekly at the time, but she wanted to tell the woman that they had been thrown into the streets by Nazi storm troopers with guns and those who disobeyed were shot. After that they were hounded out of Germany altogether. How much darker could it get? And why was God leaving it so late to come back? And then she realised he might not be coming at all because, well, he might not be real. She didn't dare mention this to anyone. Papa sometimes talked about something called a 'crisis of faith' and it always started arguments with Mama. Magda had no time for shouting. She was the eldest now that Klaus was gone and she had a duty to protect her brothers.

Not that either of them was making her life easy.

Rudolf had bad dreams every night, and he often wet the bed, and since yesterday he would not shut up about seeing the tree glow on that scary picture in the orangery. Magda had hoped that Faye or Lady Aston would tell him it was a reflection or a trick of the light, but Lady Aston didn't seem interested and when Faye gave them a hug she looked like she was going to pass out again. That only made Rudolf all the more convinced that there was some strange magic behind it.

He had roused Magda and Max late last night to show them the strange picture of the man with the axe and the dead children. He said he had been woken by a noise from the garden and he and Nelson had gone to investigate, and that's when he had noticed the strange light in the picture. He was buzzing with excitement and wouldn't go back to sleep until they had all seen it, so they sneaked downstairs in their pyjamas to the orangery.

Rudolf was right. The tallest tree in the picture did seem to glow. Rudolf was convinced it was some kind of magic. Magda thought it was a reflection, though there were no lights on in the orangery. Max didn't care and complained about the cold.

That's when they heard Klaus singing, '*Ein Prosit, Ein Prosit!*' Magda had heard him sing that once before in Rotterdam. Klaus and her father had downed too many beers and then sung old drinking songs. It sounded like it was coming from the orchard, but Magda told the boys they had to get back to bed before Klaus found them, otherwise he would be very cross.

They never saw Klaus alive again.

Rudolf took Nelson for a walk after breakfast. The dog had led him to the orchard where they found their cousin's body.

Rudolf was convinced the glowing tree in the picture had something to do with Klaus's death, and it had taken all of Magda's patience to calm him down. He moped about for the rest of the day, but she had no time for that, either. This was their home now. No more running, no more hiding. Rudolf must learn to stop crying and Max to stop sulking. They had to make themselves useful. But first, Magda needed to learn more English.

JUST NOT CRICKET

Faye arrived at Hayward Lodge a little after seven the next morning. Mr Pinder welcomed her and led her through the first hall of recuperating soldiers. A few of them were sitting up already, reading newspapers or books, though most were too badly wounded to move. Nurses bustled about, and the disappointing aroma of slightly stewed tea drifted from a forgotten tea-trolley in one corner.

'Hang on a mo', will you?' Faye asked Pinder as she stopped in the middle of the room. 'Morning, gents,' she said, raising her voice so all could hear. 'Now, this will sound like a funny question ... but I don't suppose any of you lot speak German, do you?'

'Are you having a laugh?' was the first angry reply, followed by jeering and boos.

'No, I'm not—'

'Get out of it!'

'It's just I need to speak to the children and—' Faye ducked as someone tossed a bedpan at her. 'There's no need to be like that, I was only asking a question.'

Matron stood before them and pointed to the far door. 'Out!' she commanded and Pinder shielded Faye from more jeering and projectiles as they hurried from the hall.

The door slammed behind them and Pinder glowered at Faye as they caught their breath in a hallway.

'Sorry,' she said. 'I didn't mean nothing by it.'

'I'm sure you didn't,' the old man said. 'But you must understand what these chaps have been through. Few of them talk of what happened in Dunkirk, but many wake up at night most perturbed.'

Faye had noticed this with the soldiers and sailors who had come back to the village on leave. You couldn't shut them up before they left, but they were silent on their return. Pilots were different, though. In the pub, they all shared stories of near misses and close shaves. It was more like a game for them.

'Gotcha. Sorry again.' Faye stuck her hands in her pockets. 'Blimey, I haven't even been here five minutes and I've already goofed.'

'Think nothing of it,' Pinder said. 'They are, it must be said, a rowdy bunch. Trained to kill, we can't expect them to return to their meek old selves overnight. Rest assured, I shall make *discreet* enquiries to see if we have a German speaker in the building.'

'Thanks, Pinder.' Faye smiled, though Mr Pinder's reminder that she was in a building full of hardened troops prompted an uncharitable thought. Could any of these men have killed Klaus? None of them had any love for the enemy. And Klaus had made little effort to hide where he came from.

'This way.' Mr Pinder's voice swept Faye's thought from her mind. He gestured to the grand staircase.

Faye followed him to the children's bedroom on the second floor.

She heard them first. Three voices in close harmony, singing the German version of 'Ring-a-Ring o' Roses', though instead of repeating 'Atishoo' they sang 'Hush-hush-hush'.

Pinder opened the door to reveal three beds under three tall windows overlooking the garden. There was a washbasin and a wardrobe and a hint of sticky polish on the wooden floorboards. There were no toys, but a small pile of books and comics were piled on a table.

Rudolf was chasing Nelson about the room as he sang. Magda was dressed and making her bed and Max sat in his pyjamas, a discarded copy of *The Beano* by his side. As Faye walked in, they all sang 'Hush-hush-hush' then fell silent and stared at her.

Faye felt her heart tripping about in her chest. She hadn't slept much last night. Not only was she haunted by dreams of dead children, but she'd also spent far too long pushing aside any nagging doubts that she could do this. She had looked after children before – most village families had entrusted her to mind their littl'uns at some point – though never for more than a few hours. Here were three children who had about a dozen words of English between them, all traumatised by their journey, mourning their late cousin, missing their parents who were most likely in a ghetto or worse, and facing an uncertain future in a strange country that might well be invaded by the very armies that had been chasing them across Europe.

Faye's plan of a few ball games followed by jam sandwiches was looking a bit thin.

Pinder cleared his throat, a signal for the children who hurried to stand at the ends of their beds like soldiers awaiting inspection. Nelson just panted and wagged his tail, wondering what was going on.

'You've got 'em well trained already,' Faye told Pinder. 'You don't need me, I reckon.'

'I have other duties to attend to, I'm sure you understand,' Pinder said, unfolding a handwritten note. 'Her ladyship is out with the Woodville Mounted Patrol for much of the day, and when she returns she will be busy with preparations for Saturday's Summer Fair. She asked me to pass on these instructions.' He held it at arm's length, squinting as he read. 'Dearest Faye, let them play all day and wear them out, just make sure they don't kill themselves.'

Faye grimaced as her heart tightened. She sincerely hoped that Lady Aston's little joke wouldn't turn out to be prophetic.

'Sincerely yours, Lady Aston,' Mr Pinder concluded as he folded the paper away.

'Sounds simple enough,' Faye said. 'Easier said than done, though.'

'I might also add that a gentleman is coming to take away the swarm of bees this afternoon, so please keep them away from the orchard until he is done.'

'No orchard. Gotcha.'

'They're all yours.' Pinder gave her an encouraging smile as he closed the door. 'Good luck.'

⌀

Faye got Max and Rudolf washed and dressed with little fuss, though Rudolf needed reminding to wash his hands after popping to the loo. The sky was blue and the sun was shining, so they gathered up some sports equipment and Faye led them out to the huge lawn at the back of the house.

They started with football and a friendly kick-about, using the raised vegetable beds as goals. Max and Magda weren't that interested, and Nelson eventually bit down on the ball with a little too much enthusiasm and the match had to be abandoned.

They tried rounders next, but none of them could hit the ball with the tiny bat and Max decided to sulk.

Faye set up the cricket stumps with little hope, but the bigger cricket bat turned out to be much easier for the children and Magda sent one ball flying for a six. She and her brothers stood there watching it, wondering what to do next. Faye ran back and forth between the stumps, though they couldn't quite understand the point of that. But they liked the bowling and batting and continued to do that, with Magda demonstrating not only a good defensive stroke, but also surprising Max with her spin-bowling.

It soon became apparent that Max couldn't catch for toffee. Faye tried to recall what her dad had told her when she was Max's age.

'Put your hands like this,' she said, her palms up and cupped. Max did the same. 'Have your pinkie fingers touching. That's it. Now, when I throw you the ball, bring your hands towards your belly, like this.'

She gently threw the ball. He fumbled and dropped it. Magda tutted.

'Don't be like that, Magda. Just takes a little practice. Max, throw the ball to me.' He did, and she caught the ball as demonstrated. She tossed it back to Max.

He dropped it and stomped his feet.

'Keep your hair on, son,' Faye said, her voice calm. She stood before him, almost nose to nose. 'Hold your hands out.' She demonstrated, and he copied her. She threw the ball all of two inches into his hands. He threw it back. They moved a little further apart and did it again and again until they were ten feet apart and tossing the ball back and forth. The smile on Max's face made Faye tingle.

'I reckon that's the first time I've seen you smile, Max,' she said, throwing him another. Distracted by her words, he looked up and completely missed the ball. Rudolf laughed. Nelson farted. Magda joined in the laughter and Max did, too.

It turned out that Max was even worse at batting than fielding, but he was learning, and they were all having fun.

As Faye prepared for Max's last bowl of the over, she heard a rhythmic creak behind her. She turned to find one of the soldiers hobbling over on crutches.

'Oi, stop that,' he said, pointing a crutch at Max as he raised an arm to bowl.

164

After this morning's bungled request for German speakers, Faye was wary of another bad run-in with the walking wounded, but she stood herself between the soldier and the children.

'What's the problem?' she asked.

'It's bad enough the Australians and Indians beat us at the game without the bloody Germans getting in on the act, too. Pack it in.'

'They're just children,' Faye said. 'And I've finally got them smiling, so leave 'em be, eh?'

'They ain't just children.' The soldier leaned forwards on his crutches and got in Faye's face. She shivered to think again that a soldier like this – wounded in mind as well as body – might have taken out his aggression on Klaus. On the children behind her now. 'They're *Kraut* children,' he said, his eyes glistening with rage.

Faye was about to give him an earful when they were distracted by the drone of engines from above.

A dogfight. Bright white contrails spiralling against the blue sky, a dozen tiny dots, too far away to make out who was who. Faye reflected on the oddity of seeing such life-and-death duels from the relative safety of an English country garden.

More soldiers, nurses and doctors came to view the battle, shielding their eyes from the sun. Others gathered around windows on the upper floors of the house.

One of the dots flashed in flame and its white contrail became a smudge of black. It dropped out of the sky, plummeting over the horizon and out of sight. A few seconds later came the distant thud of impact.

'Was that ... was that one of ours or one of theirs?' she asked no one in particular. Bertie would know. He would be able to tell by the shape of the wings.

The soldier who had complained caught her eye and looked bashful now. His gaze fell to the ground. He turned and slowly made his way back to the house on his crutches.

Faye looked to the children, thinking of their first encounter. A plane falling out of the sky. An adventure where through sheer luck no one had been hurt. They huddled together again. For a moment, they had all been smiling and laughing, but the moment was already melting away like the vapour trails above.

She looked at the bats and balls scattered on the lawn, then to the men sitting in wheelchairs and hobbling about on crutches.

'Magda, Max, Rudolf.' She picked up a cricket bat. 'We should tidy this stuff away,' she said. 'Then, let's make ourselves useful, shall we?'

LANGUAGE LESSONS

Faye sought out Mr Pinder who was happy to put them on mid-morning tea-trolley duty. All they had to do was go from bed to bed offering tea and biscuits.

Max, Magda and Rudolf pushed the tea-trolley from the kitchen down the corridor to the first great hall. Nelson followed behind, panting with his tongue lolling about. A hot urn sat on the trolley like the funnel of a steam train, and mugs were piled high, rattling nervously as they moved. Mr Pinder led the way, and Faye briefed the children as they walked.

'This lot gave me a load of grief this morning when I asked if anyone spoke German, so you'll need to learn a few bits of the King's English to spare your blushes.'

Max looked to Magda. She shrugged.

'Stop the trolley, stop the trolley.' Faye waved them to a halt by the door to the hall. 'Pinder, hold on a mo',' she said, then picked up a mug from the trolley. 'Max, Magda, Rudolf, eyes on me, right?' She held up the mug. 'Let's pretend that Mr Pinder here is one of the lads in there.' She offered the mug to Mr Pinder. 'Cuppa tea, guv'nor?' she said in a chirpy voice. 'Now you do it.'

Faye handed the mug to Max. He looked to Magda with wide eyes.

Faye prompted him. 'Cuppa tea, guv'nor?'

Max shook his head. Rudolf snatched the cup from his hand and stepped forward.

'Gubba dee, guv'nor!' he declared.

'Good lad,' said Faye, giving him a little round of applause. 'Magda?'

Magda looked at the mug, then at Faye. 'Cuppa tea ...?'

'Guv'nor?'

'Guv'nor.'

'Once more: Cuppa tea, guv'nor?'

Rudolf and Magda replied, 'Cuppa tea, guv'nor?'

'Good. Max, if you don't want to speak, fine, just keep it zipped. No German – *nein Deutsche* – understand?'

Max, biting his nails, nodded.

'They'll probably want milk and sugar, too,' Faye said, 'but that's advanced stuff, so leave that to me. Right, here we go. Ready, Pinder?'

'As one will ever be, Miss Faye,' Mr Pinder said, pushing the doors to the great hall open, revealing rows of beds filled with wounded soldiers.

The mid-morning sun shone through the tall windows and the walls shimmered with the refracted light of the chandeliers. Matron sat making notes at a desk at the far end. A gramophone played classical music.

Faye wasn't sure what the tune was, but the violin made her think of a bird's wings fluttering as it took to the skies, climbing higher and higher.

It felt like church, or a library, so Faye kept her voice low as they came to the first bed. Pinder poured steaming hot tea into a mug and gave it to Faye.

'Rudy, you're up,' she said, handing the boy the mug and steering him towards the first bed.

The lad in the bed wasn't much older than Faye. Lost in donated pyjamas that were two sizes too big for him, he stared into space, unaware of their presence.

She was about to suggest to Mr Pinder that perhaps they should start somewhere else, when Rudolf stood before the lad and bellowed at the top of his voice, 'GUBBA DEE, GUV'NOR?'

The lad jolted out of his daze and shifted in bed. Faye saw only one leg moving under the sheets.

'GUBBA DEE, GUV'NOR?' Rudolf yelled again, and Faye shushed him, spotting Matron looking up at them from the other end of the hall.

'What ... what did he say?' The lad blinked and looked around as if wondering how he had come to be here.

'Tea?' Faye clarified.

'Oh, ta very much,' the lad said, taking the mug from Rudolf.

'*Bitte*,' Rudolf blurted.

'Wot?'

'Milk and sugar?' Faye asked hurriedly, placing herself between the two of them.

'Oh, ta,' the lad said. 'Two sugars and nice and milky, please.'

Magda was next, and she offered the tea at the right volume with very good diction and no German. Max followed her in silence, and the transaction worked just as well. They moved in that manner from bed to bed. Nelson wagging his tail, Magda quiet and polite, Max mute and Rudolf hollering, 'GUBBA DEE, GUV'NOR?'

He caused such a stir that by the time they were halfway round he was getting requests. 'I say, can I be served by the little chap?'

The second hall was just as full, though more of the men were moving about here. Those in bed read books or newspapers. A jazzy dance number played on a gramophone and the sun's haze glowed a little brighter.

As Faye poured tea for a chap with a bandage wrapped around his head, she spotted Harry hunched over a small table. He was playing chess with the grumpy soldier who had berated them for playing cricket earlier. Faye was just making a mental note to serve the grump herself to spare the children any unpleasantness when Max broke away from their little group and wandered over to where Harry and the soldier were playing.

'You gonna stand there gawping all day, or do I have to pour it myself?' the chap with the bandaged head said.

'Sorry, miles away,' Faye said, pouring him his tea. When she was done, she looked back to see Max closely observing the game between Harry and the soldier. Harry took a pawn. At least, she thought it was a pawn. Faye knew a little chess, though all the pieces in this set looked like tiny Vikings, but if the scowl on the soldier's face was anything to go by, Harry was winning.

Magda and Rudolf moved to the next bed with the tea-trolley as Faye continued to watch.

Max tapped the soldier on the shoulder, pressed a hand to his chest, then gestured to the chessboard. He wanted to play.

The soldier narrowed his eyes at the boy and Faye held her breath, hoping he wasn't about to give Max another earful.

'Why not?' he said, sitting back and folding his arms. 'You can't do any worse than me.'

Max made his first move. He slid his knight towards Harry's king.

Harry took the knight immediately and grinned like a gap-toothed fox.

'Oh, no,' Faye muttered under her breath.

Max didn't look worried. He moved his rook. Harry made short work of that, too, taking it with his king.

'I do believe you were wrong,' Harry told the soldier. 'He *can* do worse than—'

Max moved his queen, stood back and smiled.

Harry's grin vanished.

'Bloody hell.' The soldier's eyes darted across the board as he tried to make sense of what he was seeing.

'Language!' one of the nurses cried from the other end of the hall.

'Sorry, but ... blimey.' He slapped a meaty hand on the boy's shoulder. 'That's ... that's checkmate. Checkmate in three moves. I've never seen anything like it.' He scruffed Max's hair. 'Well done, son. What's your name?'

'Max.' The boy smiled, and the man shook his hand.

'I'm Ron, but my friends call me Bingo – don't ask – and you, Max, are welcome to play any time.'

'*Danke.*' Max beamed and shook his hand again. Ron twitched a little at the German language but grinned all the same.

The boy turned to Harry and held out a hand for shaking. Harry hesitated before taking it and muttering half-hearted congratulations. He made his excuses and shuffled away wearing an insincere smile.

'Harry, don't be a bad sport,' Bingo called after him.

'Just remember who had you on the ropes, Bingo,' Harry said before sulking out of the hall.

'Don't be like him,' Bingo told Max. 'Here, can you teach me how you did that?'

Max's smile shone like the sun, and it warmed Faye's heart.

'GUBBA DEE, GUV'NOR?' Rudolf hollered from the next bed. 'MILK *UND ZUCKER*?'

❧

The rest of the day passed in a happy idyll. After lunch, they played hide and seek, catch with Nelson, more cricket, hopscotch and statues. When it got too hot, Max and Bingo played chess while Faye, Magda and

Rudolf helped Mr Pinder water the raised beds until it was time for tea.

ɸ

'Fork. Fork. This ... is a fork.'

Faye pointed at the fork and showed it to each child. They were in the kitchen, sat on high stools around a table, nibbling on cold mutton sandwiches. Their legs swung idly as they looked from the fork to Faye and back again. Under the table, Nelson wrestled with a bone.

'A fork,' Faye said, eyes wide with a fixed grin.

Max whispered in Magda's ear.

'Uh, *die Gabel*?' Magda pointed at the fork.

'*Die Gabel*?' Faye ventured. 'That's German for fork, is it? Good, right. We all know what a fork is, we're on our way. At this rate, I reckon the war'll be over by the time we can have a proper conversation, but we won't let that put us off, will we? No. Ugh.' Faye buried her head in her hands. 'Sorry. I ain't thinking straight. Why are we waffling on about forks? You lot need to be able to talk to a pair of art experts about a cursed bit of Dada art, and we're witterin' on about bleedin' forks. My poor noggin has turned to mush. I've been like this since they made us stop bell-ringing. It keeps the cogs turning. That's why my brain's been gone weird ... See, I can't even put together a proper wossname ... sentence.'

Magda, Max and Rudolf shared worried looks.

'I know. You must think I'm crazy, but I need to

know what you mean by glowing trees. I think it has something to do with the visions I've had, and I don't want you to come to any harm and ... and ... you still haven't got a clue what I'm on about, do you?'

Three pleasant, though still confused, faces looked back at her.

'Fork,' Rudolf said, picking up a fork.

'Well done.' Faye found herself chuckling. She glanced at the kitchen clock. Ten past six. 'Oh, blimey, we're late. Children, come and meet Mr Gilbert and Mr Brewer. Rudolf, I need your help especially,' she told the boy. He smiled at her blankly. 'Come and show these gents which of the trees was glowing.'

ART APPRECIATION

Faye, Nelson and the children made their way around the side of the house so as not to draw any unwanted attention from Mr Pinder or Harry. She pondered the rights and wrongs of inviting Mr Gilbert and Mr Brewer to the house without asking permission, but the place was chock-full of strangers anyway, so what difference would another two make? Besides, if she didn't get to the bottom of what Rudolf had seen she wouldn't be able to sleep at night. She knew it had something to do with her visions and she would do whatever it took to discover what really happened to Klaus and to keep the children safe.

'Hello, Faye, have you seen Harry?' Lord Aston was coming the other way, fists bunched as he marched.

'He was playing chess in one of the halls this morning,' she said, hoping he wouldn't ask where she was taking the children. 'But he left, and I haven't seen him since.'

'If you do, tell him I'm looking for him, will you?'

'Wilco,' Faye said, taking another opportunity to get a good close-up look at the man.

'Everything all right?' Lord Aston was frowning at Faye, and she realised she must have been staring.

'Hmm? Yes, sorry. If I see Harry, I'll point him in your direction,' she said, giving him a little salute as he marched away, calling Harry's name over and over.

Faye led the children like ducks in a row to the gravel drive to find Mr Gilbert and Mr Brewer already there. They had arrived in a motorcycle and sidecar combination and were dressed in tan riding leathers, helmets and goggles. Mr Gilbert peered through the viewer of a camera. He pointed the lens at Faye and waved at her.

'Faye, darling, good evening.' Mr Gilbert lowered the camera and shielded his eyes from the sun as he inspected the facade of the house. 'One has to wonder what sort of man insists on turrets and crenellations on his home. One imagines him pouring boiling oil on unwanted visitors.'

'Don't start,' Mr Brewer warned. 'We're here as Faye's guests. Best behaviour, if you please.'

'Of course, of course.' Mr Gilbert tossed his helmet and goggles in the sidecar. 'Faye, we can't tell you how thrilled we are at this opportunity. Thank you so much and— Ah, and these must be the Kindertransport children. *Guten Tag* to you all.'

He smiled, and the children gave polite smiles back, clearly wondering who these leather-clad men were.

'This is Magda, Max and Rudolf.' Faye gestured to

each child as she spoke, careful not to touch them for fear of setting off any unwanted visions. 'And that's Nelson,' she added as Mr Brewer crouched to scratch the dog behind his ears. 'Children, this is Mr Gilbert and Mr Brewer. They're going to look at Rudolf's glowing tree.'

'*Der Baum?*' Rudolf perked up.

'Yes,' Faye said. 'Lead the way.'

※

'Simply magnificent,' Mr Gilbert said as they stood before the Höch. It hung adjacent to the door to the kitchens, almost as big as the door itself. Faye was used to seeing pictures in ornate frames around the house, but this was under glass like a pressed flower, with a brushed-steel frame that looked too modern and industrial for its woodland scene.

'So much of her work is political, about the now,' Mr Gilbert continued, taking photographs as he spoke, 'but this has a Grimms' fairy tale quality to it. The huntsman with the axe, the children dead at his feet . . .'

Faye shuddered as flashes of her vision returned. She shook the thought away.

'I disagree. This *is* political.' Mr Brewer gestured at the trees. 'Those aren't tree trunks, they're factory chimneys. Look closer.'

Mr Gilbert did so and made appreciative noises.

'It's surely a commentary on how modern industry will be the death of us all,' Mr Brewer said.

'How children will pay the price for the mechanisation of war.'

'Oh, you do take the joy out of everything,' Mr Gilbert said with a theatrical sigh.

'Rudolf.' Faye crouched by the boy. 'Which of the trees was glowing?'

Rudolf wiped his nose on the back of his hand before pointing at the tallest tree next to the huntsman. '*Dieser hier.*'

Faye stood and pointed to one of the trees. 'This one?'

Rudolf nodded, then hugged Magda. She and Max nodded, too.

'Ah, fascinating,' said Mr Brewer. 'Look closer. These are all apple trees, but this big one could represent the Ur-Tree.'

'The er-what?' Faye asked.

'Ur,' Mr Brewer said. '*Yoo-Arr.* Ur, meaning original. The Ur-Tree is the oldest apple tree in the world.'

'The first apple tree,' Mr Gilbert said, taking more close-up photos.

'What? Like in the Garden of Eden?' Faye asked.

'That was the Tree of Knowledge, if you believe in that sort of thing. No, there are many who believe the Ur-Tree to be real, and there are myths about apples from the Ur-Tree keeping one forever young. I wonder why it glows? Perhaps Höch added some phosphorescent paint and it radiates in the dark?'

'I wouldn't put it past her,' Mr Gilbert said.

'Clever minx.' Mr Brewer nodded in appreciation.

'Faye, darling.' Mr Gilbert rested a hand on Faye's shoulder. 'We thank you for sharing this treasure. It's absolutely fascinating.'

'We shall have to do some digging,' Mr Brewer added.

'Where did this come from? How did it get here?' Mr Gilbert said, spreading his arms wide. 'Often the journey of a work of art is as intriguing as the piece itself.'

'We'll be sure to let you know what we discover,' Mr Brewer assured Faye.

'I say, hello, chaps.' Harry's voice echoed from the far end of the orangery.

Faye bristled, wondering if she was in trouble, but Harry was smiling his usual gap-toothed grin. Nevertheless, the children huddled together. Max looked particularly tense, perhaps anticipating a demand for a rematch.

Harry ignored him. He made a beeline for the art experts.

'If it isn't Woodville's very own connoisseurs of arts and crafts,' Harry said. 'What a treat.'

Mr Brewer muttered some curse under his breath.

Mr Gilbert was more magnanimous than his partner. 'Harry, how delightful to see you.'

'Your dad was looking for you,' Faye told Harry.

'Was he, indeed?'

'Sounded quite urgent.'

'That's the thing with Father, it's always urgent.' He turned his attention to Mr Gilbert and Mr Brewer. 'What brings you two here?' Harry asked, his eye flitting to the Höch. 'Ah, is Mater finally having it evaluated?'

'We are here in an unofficial capacity,' Mr Brewer said, doing his best not to answer the question.

'I asked them,' Faye said, feeling her feet get heavy when she saw a tiny flash of irritation from Harry.

'Did you, indeed?' he said, grinning wider. 'May I ask why?'

'Rudolf said . . .' Faye trailed off, wondering just how much she should tell Harry. He could be brusque at times, but that hardly made him a killer. Besides, she had started now, and he was looking at her like a pup that had been promised a bone. 'Rudolf said he saw one of the trees on the picture glowing at night and I thought these gentlemen might be able to tell me why.'

'Glowing?' Harry briefly went bucktoothed in thought. 'I must have walked by this monstrosity a thousand times and I've never seen it so much as twinkle. Trick of the light, perhaps, what?'

'Maybe, though Rudolf won't stop going on about it,' Faye said. 'The lad knows what he saw.'

'Ah, well, who's to argue with such an observant little chap, eh? If he says it glows, that's good enough for me.' Harry ruffled Rudolf's hair. The boy recoiled.

'We were wondering if Höch used some sort of phosphorescent paint,' Mr Brewer said.

'How jolly clever,' Harry said. 'Though one wonders why she bothered. It's not like the galleries are open at night, what?' He snorted a laugh.

'*Magie*,' Rudolf said quietly.

'Pardon, Rudy?' Faye asked.

'*Magie*.' Magda waggled her fingers like a conjuror.

'*Magie* is magic, yes?' Faye did the same, and the children all smiled. 'So, the glowing tree ... the tree?'

'*Der Baum*,' said Magda.

Faye crouched down to meet Rudolf's eyes. '*Der Baum* is *Magie*? The tree is magic?'

'*Ja!*' Rudolf nodded. Harry snickered, but the little boy ignored him and went off on a long and excited discourse in German on magical trees.

'Slow down, slow down.' Faye gently waved her hands at him. 'How is, er, *der Baum Magie*?'

Magda blew air from her lips. '*Rudolf ist ein Dummkopf.*'

Faye didn't need a translator for that. Rudolf's cheeks went the colour of beetroot and he stamped his feet, unleashed an impressive chain of incomprehensible insults at Magda, then marched to the door of the orangery with Nelson yapping after him.

'Rudolf!' Faye called after him.

The boy opened one of the glass doors and dashed outside.

'Oh, blimmin' 'eck, he's heading for the orchard,' Faye said, then turned to Mr Gilbert and Mr Brewer. 'Gents, I'm sorry, I have to stop him before he gets there.'

'Oh, we're all done here, Faye,' Mr Gilbert said. 'We can't thank you enough for the opportunity.'

'Yes, simply marvellous,' Mr Brewer added. 'We know our way out.'

'No, no,' Harry said, gesturing back along the orangery. 'Let me escort you.'

'How gallant,' Mr Brewer said, trying not to sneer.

'See you, gents,' Faye said, then took chase. 'Rudolf, come back.'

HEXE

Faye dashed outside in time to catch sight of Rudolf wrestling with the iron gate to the orchard.

'No, Rudolf, you're not supposed to go in there,' Faye yelled, chasing after him. 'You'll get me sacked on my first day ... and there are bees!'

Rudolf and Nelson ignored her. Faye was about to follow when she realised she wasn't alone. Magda and Max were right behind her. She stopped, holding up a halting hand.

'No,' she said. 'Do you understand? I'm under orders and you might, y'know ...' Faye made a buzzing noise. 'Like Klaus.'

Nelson barked urgently on the other side of the orchard wall.

'Wait there,' she told Magda and Max. 'I'll be back in a jiffy.'

ℰ

Faye hurried through the orchard, calling Rudolf's name. She'd found Klaus's death so harrowing that she hadn't taken much notice of the orchard itself. It was much bigger than she'd realised, with row upon row of trees neatly spaced. Cherry trees bearing their dark red fruits, Victoria plums not quite ripe, fledgling Bramley apples, Red Devils and more. Hundreds of them.

The early evening sun was still unforgiving and there was little shade. Trickles of sweat formed on Faye's back. Nelson barked again. The sound came from behind Faye, so she doubled-back and spotted the boy between the trees.

'Rudolf!'

He slowed, moving from tree to tree as if looking for something. Faye huffed over to him.

'Come on, Rudolf,' she said, extending a hand but hoping he wouldn't take it. The last thing she needed now was another vision. Nelson hurried to her and she scratched his ears.

Rudolf's forehead crinkled in concentration as he inspected each tree.

'What are you looking for?' Faye asked him. 'A special tree? A ... a magic tree?'

He stopped and nodded.

She crouched by his side. 'Which one is it? That one?'

He shook his head.

'That one?'

Again, he shook no.

'To be honest, Rudy, they all look alike to me. Was it an apple, cherry or—'

He ran to one where an axe still lay on the ground. The axe that had been next to Klaus's body.

Rudolf fell to his knees and burst into tears.

Faye desperately wanted to hug the boy and reassure him, but if she had a vision and passed out again, the poor lad would surely be traumatised for life.

'I know, I know. I miss him, too,' she said, kneeling beside him. 'I have a horrible feeling this is something we're going to have to learn to cope with in this rotten war. Meeting wonderful people who then get snatched away. I see it with the airmen who come into the pub. Any given night, there'll be one less of 'em, and I'll ask where's that fella gone with the ginger hair, and they'll say something like, "He bought it over the Solent," and then they'll never mention him again.'

Rudolf looked up at her as he brushed his tears away and cuffed his runny nose.

'You haven't got the first clue what I'm going on about, do you, Rudy? That's all right. But I promise you this, we won't forget Klaus. We could plant him a tree. Would you like that? A tree for Klaus? Whatchacallit? *Der Baum* for Klaus?'

'*Ein magischer Baum.*' Rudolf nodded.

'A magic tree. We're back to that, are we?'

Rudolf pouted and crossed his arms.

'No, no, I believe you,' Faye said. 'About the glowing tree in the picture being magic, I really do.'

Unconvinced, the lad hung his head.

Faye leaned closer to him and lowered her voice to a whisper. 'I know about magic, believe it or not.

I'll let you into a little secret, and one that might be able to help you. I'm a ...' What was the word? She thought back to her last conversation with Klaus. 'I'm a *Hexe*. A witch.'

Rudolf's eyes bulged. '*Du bist eine Hexe?*'

Faye could see the terror on his face and realised too late that she had said the wrong thing. She also realised her hesitation only confirmed his fears.

'Yeah, no, er, I'm a good witch. Good witch.'

'*Sie ist eine Hexe!*' he yelled at the top of his voice and ran away, his hands flailing in fright.

'Nice one, Faye,' she told herself as he disappeared among the rows of trees. 'You're an idiot.'

✗

Fortunately for Faye, Rudolf made such a clanging racket as he exited through the orchard's iron gate that she knew exactly where he had gone. It also helped that Nelson kept coming back for her, barking for her to follow him. She wiped the sweat from her brow and trudged out of the orchard, making sure that the iron gate was properly closed.

The children were nowhere to be seen.

'Oh, blinking flip.'

Nelson pressed his nose to the grass and then took off again, following Rudolf's scent. Faye puffed her cheeks and jogged after the pup. He took her around the house, past the now empty orangery – Harry, Mr Gilbert and Mr Brewer were gone – and out to the front drive.

Magda, Max and Rudolf were standing with two women by the dry fountain. One was unmistakably Lady Aston, returned from her patrol. The children were stroking her horse and Rudolf had made a partial recovery from Faye's traumatic confession. He was still pouting, and he hid behind Max when he saw Faye.

'Ah, Faye, you're just in time,' Lady Aston said, looking her up and down. 'Gracious, they really have done a number on you, haven't they? You look utterly jiggered, girl.'

Faye started to explain but discovered she didn't have quite enough breath to actually talk.

Lady Aston continued, 'The good news is you won't have to endure another day of this exhausting trio. I should like you to meet the new nanny.' She gestured to the other woman and Faye wondered if her specs were misting over as she couldn't quite make out the woman's face.

'Forgive me,' Lady Aston continued, 'what was your name again?'

The woman stepped forwards as if she was emerging from a fog. She wore a long, smart coat and a wide-brimmed hat, skewered in place with bejewelled hatpins. Under the hat, her distinctive white hair was tied into a bun.

'Blanc,' Miss Charlotte said in a French accent. 'Mademoiselle Blanc.'

THE LEGEND
OF THE UR-TREE

Charlotte's sharp expression almost dared Faye to blurt out something that would blow her cover, but Faye managed a feeble hello and the white-haired witch continued her conversation with Lady Aston. Her face went all foggy again and Faye blinked to clear her eyes, but Charlotte's features remained smudged.

'If it pleases you, *madame*,' Charlotte said, showing a deference that Faye hadn't thought the witch capable of, 'I should like to take a moment with young Faye here to discuss today's activities with the children and how I might build on them.'

'Hmm, certainly,' Lady Aston said, then waggled her riding crop at Faye. 'Faye, take Mademoiselle Blanc to the kitchens and bring her up to speed over a pot of tea, will you? And you three . . .' She directed her crop at the three children. 'Wash and scrub today's grime off yourselves and prepare for bed.'

The children looked at her blankly and she tutted

and repeated herself in broken German, but this only resulted in more puzzled frowns from the children.

Mademoiselle Blanc spoke to them in fluent German in a tone that suggested that if they weren't clean in five minutes they would be sent to the Russian Front.

The children nodded obediently to Charlotte and gave Faye one last troubled glance before hurrying inside.

As they did, a truck chugged up the drive, coming to a halt by the fountain.

'Ah, perfect timing, this must be my bee chap,' Lady Aston said. 'Faye, as you and Mademoiselle Blanc are already headed that way, could you point him towards the orchard, please? He knows the drill.'

The person who descended from the truck was dressed in a white protective jacket, complete with hat and veil, and carried a clattering bag of beekeeping bits and bobs, including a hive smoker. The person was tall, pear-shaped and spoke with Mrs Teach's telephone voice.

'Good h-afternoon, your ladyship.'

Faye looked to Charlotte: *What the hell is going on?*

Charlotte simply smiled and blinked and yet somehow conveyed: *Keep quiet, all will be explained in a moment.*

'Where's the usual chap?' Lady Aston asked.

'Unavoidably detained, your ladyship,' Mrs Teach replied, her face going all fuzzy like Charlotte's. 'There's a hive at a school over in Herne Bay that's been creating all sorts of havoc. He sends his sincere apologies, but I assure you that I am highly experienced in the field of bee management, and I am delighted to be serving you, your ladyship, on this fine evening, and might I add what an honour it is to—'

'Oh, right, fine.' Lady Aston waved her into silence, then looked to Faye. 'If you need me, find Pinder and he'll hunt me down.'

'Wilco.' Faye gave a little salute, and Lady Aston skipped back inside the house.

The three witches were alone on the drive.

'What the bloomin' 'eck is going on?' Faye asked. 'And why do your faces keep going fuzzy?'

'Her ladyship knows us from the village,' Mrs Teach said, 'so we're in disguise.'

'A glamour,' Miss Charlotte said, her clipped English accent returning.

'She sees faces, but not ours. You see something fuzzy because you're one of us.'

'Glamours are less effective on the magical,' Charlotte added.

'Can you turn it off?' Faye asked as their faces shifted in and out of focus. 'It's giving me the willies.'

'No. Show me where the boy died,' Charlotte said, all but shoving Faye around the side of the house.

'You know about that?' Faye said, leading the way.

'A lot has happened today, young lady,' Mrs Teach said, bringing up the rear with all the beekeeping gear.

'And here,' Faye said, lowering her voice. 'Can you two now admit that I was right with my vision?'

'Don't gloat, Faye,' Mrs Teach said. 'It's unbecoming in a young woman.'

'I'm not gloating. I saw the poor lad die, and you two told me to do nothing.'

'Did you listen to our advice?' Charlotte asked.

Faye hesitated. 'No.'

'And yet he died anyway. What does that tell you?'

'You're a heartless cow?'

Charlotte let the insult slide, but Faye could tell from her sideways glance that she was filing it away for later. 'It should tell you that nothing can be done to prevent these visions from coming true. They are for your insight only.'

'Yeah, well, I have some new insight for you. I had another vision, and it was—' Faye glanced around, then lowered her voice. 'It was of the children. All three of them, and . . .' She trailed off, unable to say it out loud.

'Like Klaus?' Mrs Teach came to a clattering halt as they found themselves huddled in a quiet nook by the door to the boiler room.

Faye nodded. 'In the woods, at night.'

'How exactly did young Klaus die?' Mrs Teach asked.

'A bee-sting, so they reckon,' said Faye.

Charlotte looked at her. 'You're not convinced.'

'One lad dies and that's tragic and all,' Faye said, 'but if my vision is true and the same thing happens to the other children—'

'A conspiracy.' Mrs Teach nodded. 'But who would be so vile as to kill children? Do you have any suspects?'

Faye gestured at the house. 'This is an 'orrible thought, but this place is full of men trained to kill Germans. Men who just got humiliated at the hands of

192

those Germans, so it could be any one of them looking for revenge. And there's Lord Aston –' Faye glanced at Miss Charlotte '– who looks as fit as a fiddle, by the way, but he's a big fella who might have a temper on him. And then there's Harry. That boy ain't as friendly as he makes out, if you ask me.' Faye turned back to Mrs Teach. 'How many suspects do you want?'

'In your vision,' Charlotte asked, 'did you see the shape of the moon?'

'What's that got to do with—?'

'It might tell us how long we have.'

'A full moon.'

'We've a full moon tonight and tomorrow night,' Mrs Teach said.

Faye allowed herself to get excited. 'Then we can stop it?'

'No,' Charlotte said, and for a long moment no one spoke. 'But that doesn't mean we shouldn't try,' she added.

Faye tingled with hope. 'Good, good. How do we do it?'

'Calm down,' Charlotte said. 'We have another pressing problem, and I have a nagging suspicion the two are connected.'

'What? What problem?'

'Otto is coming,' Charlotte said.

'Otto? Otto Kopp, the man we put a hex on?'

Charlotte and Mrs Teach flapped their hands and shushed Faye as they glanced at the house. A maid rattled past an open window with a tea-tray.

193

'Let's keep moving,' said Mrs Teach.

Charlotte nodded, and they walked in a line around the house.

'The bloke who's as powerful as Vera Fivetrees?' Faye whispered. 'Who wants to give Hitler the power of black magic? That Otto Kopp?'

'Otto somehow traced the hex back to us,' Charlotte said.

'I knew it. I told you it was a bad idea,' Faye said.

'Your delight in our misfortune is a most unlikeable trait, Faye,' Mrs Teach said.

Faye ignored her. 'How do you know he's coming?' she asked Charlotte.

'I received a message from him this morning,' Charlotte continued. 'He appeared to me as a flaming ball and said he recognised my work and was coming for us.'

'That's not quite the language he used, though, was it, Miss Charlotte?' Mrs Teach circled a hand in the air as she recalled. 'What did he say? Clumsy? Hackneyed? Amateurish was one word he—'

'Your delight in *my* misfortune is a most unlikeable trait, Mrs Teach,' Charlotte said pointedly. 'Regardless, he is coming.'

'What for?' Faye asked. 'Revenge?'

'That's just the icing on the cake for Otto,' Charlotte said. They turned a corner to find a dozen or so walking wounded dotted around the lawn playing croquet. 'What he really wants is the Ur-Tree.' Charlotte gave the croquet players a smile and said to Faye under her breath, 'We have orders to protect it. Take me to the orchard, I'll explain there.'

'The Ur-Tree?' Faye said. 'How do you know about that?'

'How do *you* know about that?' Charlotte replied.

Faye shrugged nonchalantly. 'It's the original apple tree. Not the Tree of Knowledge from the Garden of Eden – that's a common enough mistake – but the oldest apple tree in the world that's said to bestow eternal life on anyone who scrumps one of its apples. If you believe in that sorta thing, of course.'

Faye enjoyed the looks of bafflement on the faces of Miss Charlotte and Mrs Teach.

'There's a representation of the old Ur-Tree on a pho-tomontage by Hannah Höch hanging in the orangery,' she added. 'There are those that reckon it's cursed. Little Rudolf said he saw it glowing.'

'Glowing how?' Mrs Teach asked.

'I've not seen it meself, but the little lad sounds sure of it,' Faye said.

'Who told you about the Ur-Tree?' Charlotte asked.

'Who's to say I didn't know about it anyways?'

'I do,' Charlotte said, then half-closed her eyes. 'Mr Gilbert and Mr Brewer. They told you.'

'Oi. I've warned you about mind-reading. It's my brain and I'll thank you to keep out of it.'

'Your brain is safe. I saw them leaving on their motorcycle and sidecar.' Charlotte smiled. 'And it's eternal youth, not eternal life.'

'Eh?'

'If you eat an apple from the Ur-Tree you stay young, but you won't necessarily live for ever.'

'Is that how you stay looking so youthful, Miss Charlotte?' Faye asked with a curious squint. 'Magic apples?'

'I won't dignify that with an answer,' Miss Charlotte said, leading the way. 'I'll explain more once we're inside the orchard. Shall we?'

The three of them wound their way around the croquet players until they came to the orchard's iron gate. They stepped through into tranquillity.

'This place is bigger than I remember,' Charlotte said, looking at the array of trees stretching off to the far wall.

'Been here before, then?' asked Faye. 'When was that?'

Charlotte glanced at Faye but didn't answer.

'This is going to take all night.' Mrs Teach raised the veil on her bee hat.

'What does the Ur-Tree look like?' Faye asked.

'Like all the others,' Mrs Teach said. 'It's a tree that doesn't want to be found.'

'How did it get here, then?'

'Ask that one.' Mrs Teach nodded towards Charlotte.

'I found it once before,' Charlotte said. 'A long time ago. Hopefully, I can do so again.'

'So that *was* you in the photo!' Faye prodded a finger at Charlotte, then turned to Mrs Teach. 'I told you. There's a photo in the house of Charlotte in Khazi-whatever—'

'Kazakhstan,' Charlotte corrected.

'That's it. And his lordship is there, and there's mountains, the Ten-something mountains.'

'The Tien Shan mountains.'

'Yes, and a tree and Charlotte, and she looks exactly the same now as she did then.' Faye took a breath. 'Oh! You ate one of the apples?'

'Certainly not,' Charlotte said. 'Only a fool wants eternal youth.'

'How old *are* you?'

'We haven't got time for *that* particular story,' Mrs Teach said. 'Show us where you found the boy. That might give us a clue.'

Faye looked from tree to tree. 'Keep your eye out for an axe,' she said as they spread out, moving between the trees. 'Rudolf found it earlier. That's where they found Klaus.'

'Here.' Charlotte hurried towards a tree with the axe laying in the grass.

'Y'know, I'm not sure this is the same tree,' Faye said. 'This orchard ... it's like the trees are play-ing a game. You turn your back on them and they move around.'

'I told you it didn't want to be found,' Mrs Teach said. 'Anything?'

Charlotte rested her hands on the tree, her eyes closed. She shook her head.

'We should ask the little'uns,' Faye said.

'You two go ahead,' Mrs Teach said. 'I'll stay here and get rid of the bees.'

197

'We'll start with Rudolf,' Faye said. 'He definitely knows something. He kept going on about a glowing tree, but we need someone who can speak German.'

'Take me to them,' Charlotte said.

What Rudolf Saw

'*Hexe. Hexe!*'

Rudolf ducked behind his bed in terror as Faye and Charlotte stepped into the children's bedroom. Magda was applying soap to her face and Max was towelling his hair dry when they saw Faye and they, too, dashed behind their beds.

'Our reputation precedes us.' Charlotte raised her chin. 'How do they know that word?'

Faye chewed a lip, thrust her hands in her pockets and pivoted a foot on the floorboards. 'I, well, I *might* have told the little one that I was a witch.'

Charlotte's glare of disapproval could have melted butter.

'He kept banging on about magic trees and I thought it would help.' Faye threw her hands up then let them slap against her legs. 'I tried to tell him I was a good witch.' Faye addressed the children directly, pressing a hand to her chest. 'I'm a good witch. Good, er, *hexe*. Like, uhm, Glinda in *The Wizard of Oz*?'

'They're German, Faye. Their concept of witches does not come from Hollywood, but the Brothers Grimm. Witches fatten children up before shoving them in the oven for dinner. As far as they're concerned, there's no such thing as a good witch.'

'Then we should teach 'em otherwise,' Faye said.

'Leave this to me.' Charlotte stepped forwards and addressed the children in their own language.

They emerged from their hiding places and listened closely to every word, with the occasional disparaging glance at Faye. By the time Charlotte had finished, they were holding hands and remained completely calm.

'That did the trick. What did you tell them?' Faye asked Charlotte.

'That you were being silly and trying to play a game and something was lost in translation.'

'Good one, thanks. I was worried you were telling them I was an idiot or something.'

'I did.'

'Oh.'

'Rudolf.' Miss Charlotte beckoned the youngest child and he stepped forward. 'I'm going to ask him about the glowing tree,' she said as an aside to Faye before asking the boy a question in German.

Rudolf began his story hesitantly, pausing only to wipe his nose on his sleeves. As he spoke, Charlotte quietly translated for Faye.

'He could not sleep. He kept thinking of his mother and father and how he could not remember what their faces looked like or what their voices sounded like. There are lots of noises in the night here. Sometimes soldiers call for their mothers and Rudolf wonders if they have forgotten what they look like, too. He heard Klaus singing in the garden. It was after the clock downstairs chimed midnight. Rudolf woke Nelson. Who's Nelson?'

'The dog,' Faye said.

'They sneaked out together. They found Klaus in the ... I'm not sure what he means – the long room with the scary picture.'

'The orangery,' Faye said. 'And the scary picture is that long-lost Hannah Höch photomontage I was telling you about.'

Charlotte had to hurry to catch up with Rudolf who hadn't stopped speaking. 'Rudolf says the long room was dark and Klaus was sitting underneath the scary picture and he stank of beer. He hugged Rudolf tight and told him he loved him, and they were finally safe, and everything would be all right.'

Rudolf began to sniff. Fat tears lined up on his bottom eyelashes. Charlotte crouched, took his hand and gave it a gentle squeeze, but the boy shuddered into a cascade of tears and snot. Faye dropped to her knees, drew a hankie and cleaned up the mess the best she could, but Rudolf pushed her away, stepped forwards to Charlotte and said the same thing over and over. The only word Faye could make out was 'Klaus' and each time Rudolf said the name it triggered another cry that jolted his whole body.

Magda and Max hurried to their brother and held him tight as he dissolved into tears.

Faye looked to Charlotte for a translation.

'He keeps saying he wants him back,' Charlotte said. 'All Rudolf wants is his cousin back.'

℘

Faye and Charlotte helped the children get ready for supper and left them slurping cabbage and potato soup in the kitchens. They met Mrs Teach in the orangery and inspected the Höch photomontage.

'I don't know much about art, but I know what I like,' said Mrs Teach. 'And I do not like this.'

'I think it's really good,' Faye said, nudging her specs up her nose and leaning forwards for a closer look. 'So many little details. I could stare at it for hours.'

'The little lad said one of the trees was glowing?' Mrs Teach shrugged and shook her head. 'There's nothing glowing that I can see.'

'Maybe it glows at night?' Faye ventured.

Charlotte angled her head at each corner of the picture, as if trying to catch a scent. 'Which is the glowing one?'

'This one here,' Faye said, pointing to the tallest tree next to the huntsman. 'Rudolf showed us. He was dead sure.'

'He was upset.' Charlotte stood back from the Höch for one last look. 'No, I'm not getting anything.'

'Mr Gilbert and Mr Brewer reckon it might glow because of some phosphorescent paint,' Faye said.

Charlotte shook her head. 'There's nothing magical here. We have a bigger priority. We must find the Ur-Tree as soon as possible and protect it from Otto Kopp.'

'We could come back at night and—'

'No,' Charlotte said with such bluntness that Faye blushed into silence. Charlotte turned to Mrs Teach. 'Is the orchard clear of bees and people?'

'It is indeed,' Mrs Teach confirmed.

'You really know about beekeeping and all that?' Faye asked.

'Goodness, no,' Mrs Teach said. 'We had a long conversation, and I convinced them to move on.'

'You *talked* to bees?'

'I congressed with the hive,' Mrs Teach said. 'Talking to bees individually would be silly and would take far too long. Now they're gone, we have the orchard to ourselves.'

Faye skipped through her thoughts. 'We've already looked once, and poor Rudolf's too upset to be any help, and you told me it's a tree that don't want to be found. So how do we—?' She snapped her fingers. 'Ooh. A finding ritual.'

'Go on,' Mrs Teach said, mildly impressed.

Faye's mind raced. This was exactly the sort of thing they had been drumming into her these last few weeks. There was a pattern to these kinds of rituals and she was finally getting the hang of them.

'Right, we're looking for something in an enclosed space, an orchard, so that helps,' Faye began. 'We need the essence of the space, so ... we take one of every fruit that grows in the orchard and a branch from each kind of tree. Use the wood to start a fire and boil the fruits, adding any oil or honey on the land to the mix, simmer, drink – which will be the hardest part, cos so few of the fruits are ripe – and the tree will be revealed.' Faye beamed, feeling very happy with herself. She even did a little curtsey.

'Not bad,' Charlotte said. 'You also need the dew from the leaf of each kind of tree.'

'How was I supposed to know that?' Faye protested.

'You weren't. It comes with experience,' Charlotte said.

'And it will all need to be done before sunrise,' Mrs Teach added.

'Let's get started,' Charlotte said, marching back along the orangery. Faye and Mrs Teach followed. 'Did you bring the cauldron?'

'In the van,' Mrs Teach said.

Faye buzzed with excitement. Finally, some proper magic. 'What shall I do?' she asked.

'Yours is the most important task of all,' Charlotte said.

'Oh.' Faye tingled at the prospect of such magical responsibility. 'What's that?'

'Look after the children,' Charlotte said.

'What? Why can't I help with the ritual?'

'This is important, Faye, and we don't have time to be ...' Charlotte waved a hand as she thought of the word. 'Childminders.'

'Tutors,' Mrs Teach said at the same time. The two

women shared a look. Charlotte rolled her eyes as they stepped out of the orangery into the early-evening light.

'Oh, I get it.' Faye stopped in her tracks. 'I'm like one of the kids to you, aren't I? Well, weren't I the one who told you about poor old Klaus? When are you two going to learn to listen to me?'

Charlotte and Mrs Teach had not stopped walking and were already around the corner and out of sight.

SPOTTED DICK AND SHABBAT

Quietly fuming, Faye stomped to the kitchen where she had left the children. While the cook chopped onions, they were polishing off a plate of spotted dick and custard.

When Faye crashed through the door, the children took one look at her and ducked under the table.

'What's up with them?' the cook asked. Of Chinese descent with a strong cockney accent, she finished chopping the onions, the blade of her knife a shining blur.

'I told them I was a witch and now they're scared of me,' Faye said, having decided that simply telling the truth to strangers was so much easier than making something up.

'That'll do it, girl,' the woman said, scraping the onions onto a frying pan. 'Help yourself to some leftover spotted dick and custard.' She nodded to the plate the children had abandoned on the table in their haste to get away from Faye.

'Don't mind if I do. Thank you . . . ?'

'Doreen.'

'Doreen. Lovely. I'm Faye.' Faye scooped up the plate and a fork and jabbed it into the fruity suet pudding, making appreciative noises as she took a bite. 'Thiff iff fanfastic,' she said with a full mouth.

'Thank you very much,' Doreen said. 'Made it myself.'

'Just what I needed, thank you,' Faye said, ducking under the table to join the children. She sat cross-legged on the floor, polishing off the spotted dick. The children scurried back, holding each other tight, but it was Nelson who came to her rescue, licking crumbs off her fingers. She stroked his back and he nuzzled up to her. If Nelson liked Faye, she couldn't be all bad.

The children stopped holding themselves quite so tightly. Rudolf's tears were gone, though Magda and Max still squinted at Faye with suspicion.

'Do you know what it's like to be completely ignored?' Faye asked, her fork scraping on the plate.

The children stared back at her.

''Course you do. This is what we've all got in common. No one takes a blind bit of notice of us. What can you do, eh?'

The children shared puzzled glances.

'You can sit and moan about it, which won't do no good, and I know that's what I'm doing now to be fair, and I'm not one for feeling sorry for myself, but you can only take so much. I try to be useful, I really do, but they think I'm not ready. I'm ready.'

'You wanna be useful?' Doreen's voice came from above. 'Come and dry these bloody dishes.'

'Right.' Faye clapped her hands together. 'We will. Come on, you three, no such thing as free spotted dick. We've got work to do.'

They cleared up their plates, handed them to Doreen to be washed and started to dry the huge pile of crockery from the soldiers' supper. Faye put any thought of magic to the back of her mind and was just happy to be doing something. Faye often sang when she washed dishes, and she started humming 'Run Rabbit Run', and it wasn't long before Doreen joined in. Eventually, Magda, Max and Rudolf learned the words, though Faye's attempt to explain what they meant – by miming a rabbit being shot – only threatened to add to their trauma.

And that's what they did for the rest of the evening. Washed dishes and sang songs. They did Gracie Fields' 'Sing as We Go', and Mr Pinder popped by and taught them the words to George Formby's 'Mr Wu's a Window Cleaner Now', though Doreen objected to the 'Chinese Wifey' referred to in the lyrics.

'And what sort of woman tears up silk stockings?'

They were interrupted by Harry crashing through the door. His presence drained the room of all its joy in an instant.

'Ah, Pinder, there you are,' he said, flashing his gaptoothed grin. 'Message from Father. No supper tonight. He's feeling off. Bit of a dicky tum and all that.'

'Oh dear,' Pinder said, rightly concerned. 'Shall I call for the doctor?'

'Oh, no, nothing as serious as all that. Poor chap

just needs a good night's sleep. Best not to disturb till further notice, what?'

'Indeed. If there's anything his lordship needs, any remedies or—'

'Splendid, good chap,' Harry said, ducking out of sight.

Faye, Pinder and Doreen shared a look.

'That boy ain't right if you ask me,' Faye said.

Pinder stiffened. 'Young lady, I should be grateful if you could keep such opinions to yourself when in the employ of this household. Now, I believe there are more dishes to be done,' he said, raising his chin, turning on his heel and leaving the kitchen.

Doreen shrugged. 'You heard the man. Back to work.'

℘

It took them nearly an hour to clear the pile of plates, and after that Mr Pinder asked if they could help with the bedtime Ovaltine for the wounded men.

They did the rounds of the two halls as before, the trolley laden with tins of Ovaltine this time, and Rudolf's vocabulary stretching to, 'Gubba Obaldeen, guv'nor?'

They received a much warmer welcome this time. Nelson in particular was a big hit. His wagging tail made many smile, despite Matron's disapproval at his presence.

As they moved to the second hall, Faye caught a glimpse of Harry pushing a bed with a patient at the far end of the corridor. He didn't strike her as the sort to play porter and wondered where he was going so quickly, but he was out of sight before she could call out to him.

As they entered the second hall, Max made straight for Bingo. He was sat in bed, doing the *Daily Mirror* crossword. His chessboard was nowhere to be seen.

'Sorry, son, he took it,' Bingo said.

'Who did?' Faye asked.

'Harry. Said he needed it for something.' Bingo leaned forwards and lowered his voice. 'I reckon he's just a sore loser. A shame, as I was looking forward to this one kicking him in the pants again.'

Bingo smiled, but Max looked crestfallen.

'Don't worry, Max,' Faye said. 'I'm sure my dad's got a chess set locked away somewhere. I'll bring it tomorrow.' She knew he couldn't understand the words, but hoped he got the sentiment.

They wheeled the trolley back to the kitchen. It was nearly nine and Faye wondered how Mrs Teach and Miss Charlotte were getting on with their ritual. She had put them out of her mind while having fun with the children, but she felt a familiar sting of anger when she thought of how she was being left out of the real magic.

'I am most thankful for your help this evening, children,' Mr Pinder said, opening a biscuit tin. 'Do please help yourselves, and you are more than welcome to return tomorrow.'

'Ta very much, young man,' Rudolf said as he took a biscuit, using a new phrase learned from the grateful soldiers this evening.

'What time do you lot all go to bed?' Faye asked.

Magda's face was blank.

'Oh, er, sleepy time? When?' Faye briefly closed her eyes, pressed her hands together and rested her head on them. 'Beddy-byes?'

Magda shook her head. '*Nein*.'

'Nine? Off to bed with you then!' She tried herding them to the door with the same waving arms farmers used to move animals around. The children stood their ground.

'*Nein*.' Magda folded her arms.

'Oh, I see. *Nein*. Doreen, any more dishes for this lot?'

'All done, thank you.' Doreen towelled her hands dry and nodded at the children. 'Shabbat for you lot,' she said.

'Whassat?' Faye asked.

'It's Friday night, sun's gone down and that's when Jewish folk start their Shabbat. The children need to light a couple of candles and say a few prayers, then they're done for the day. They're not allowed to do any work all of Saturday till the sun goes down.'

'No one told me about this.'

'Well, her ladyship wouldn't know, would she?' Doreen said, searching through cupboards and taking out a couple of candlesticks. 'She was astonished to discover I spoke English.'

Mr Pinder cleared his throat in disapproval.

'Mr Pinder doesn't like any dissent in the ranks.' Doreen smiled as she twisted two fresh candles into the candlesticks then lit their wicks. 'I admire Lady Aston, I do, but she's not half as cultured as she thinks she is.' Doreen placed the candles in the centre of the kitchen table, their flames stretching and tapering into yellow teardrops. 'Here you go, children. It might not be what you're used to, but these days you take what you get, don't you?'

'I don't know what to do,' Faye said.

'They will,' Doreen reassured her.

Mr Pinder switched off the kitchen light, but the children just stood there. Max nudged Magda who shrugged.

'Or maybe they don't,' Doreen said, hands on hips. 'Magda.' Doreen gestured to the eldest child, placed her hands before her face, lowered them again and nodded to the candles. 'Prayers?'

Magda hesitated. She was the eldest and in charge now, whether she liked it or not. Faye recognised the look of fear in the girl's eyes as she weighed the responsibility.

Magda took a breath, gingerly stepped in front of the candles and, glowing in their buttery light, she placed her hands over her face and began to sing and pray. Moments later, Max joined in. Rudolf stayed where he was and looked on with wide-eyed curiosity as he picked his nose.

As Magda and Max prayed, Doreen warmed up a supper of chicken soup on the stove.

'No idea if this is what you call kosher, but my old Jewish neighbours loved a bit of chicken loop-the-loop.'

The children finished their prayers. When their eyes opened, they looked calmer, if a little lost. They would normally have some sort of grown-up telling them what to do next, and Faye realised that the grown-up in this situation was her and she didn't have the first clue what to do. In the end, Rudolf made their minds up for them. He threw his arms wide and they all held one another, eyes closed.

Soon after, Doreen served the soup and the children lapped it up, and it filled Faye's heart to see them all smiling.

'There are some biscuits in the tin if you want some,' Doreen said. 'My shift is over, but you're all welcome back tomorrow once Shabbat ends. No more work till then. Understood? Goodnight, all.' Doreen then added sweetly, 'Good night, Mr Pinder.'

'G-goodnight, Doreen,' Mr Pinder said, and Faye wondered if she detected a little smidge of longing in the man's voice as he watched Doreen leave. He caught Faye looking at him and flashed her a smile.

'Leave the plates,' he said. 'I'll tidy up. Thank you all for your hard work this evening.'

It was after ten when Faye bustled the children out of the kitchen and into the orangery. The door closed behind her and they found themselves in darkness.

Almost. There was some light.

'*Der Baum, der Baum!*' Rudolf hopped, pointing at the Höch.

One of its trees was glowing.

OF COURSE, A SECRET DOOR

It was the tallest tree, the one next to the huntsman, just as Rudolf had told her. He was hopping with excitement around Magda and Max, making *See, I told you so!* gestures and noises.

What he had not mentioned was the glow around the photomontage's frame.

'Rudy, Rudy, calm down,' Faye said, peering more closely at the picture. 'There's a light coming from behind this thing.' She ran her fingers up and down the edge of the frame. 'I can feel a breeze. Come, look.'

Faye gestured for the children to do the same. The only one bold enough was Magda. She gasped and drew her hand back, then told Max and Rudolf what she had felt. As the boys copied her, the wind whistled through the gap and they retreated.

'I read mystery books,' Faye told the children, 'and in lots of them there's a secret passage or a hidden door. There's usually a candle-holder or a book on a shelf that's a disguised lever, but ...' She took a few steps back, inspecting the area around the picture. It was a plain wall, painted egg-white. 'There's nothing like that here.'

Faye moved her fingers up and down the frame again, more firmly this time. 'Maybe there's a hidden lock, or a ...?' The picture frame juddered at her touch. 'I wonder ...?' Faye leaned her weight against it and there was a click as something released. Faye let go and the entire photomontage swung open towards her like a door.

'Oh, my good gravy.'

A dank aroma of wet stone and mould washed over them. Behind the picture frame was a red-brick arch, beyond which spiral steps led down into darkness.

A single bare light bulb shone, dangling from a cord fixed to the ceiling. Faye noticed that a small, round hole had been cut in the back of the picture frame. The same spot where the picture had 'glowed'. A spyhole for anyone on the other side who wanted to be sure the coast was clear before stepping out.

Faye wanted to rush in and explore, but she had the children to consider, and then she thought about Miss Charlotte and Mrs Teach. She had half a mind to go and tell them what she'd found, but didn't want to leave the children alone, and nor did she want to take them into the orchard for fear of making her terrible vision come true.

It was the noise of a tea-trolley on the other side of the kitchen that made up Faye's mind for her.

'In! Go! *Schnell, schnell!*' She herded the kids through the stone arch, hopping up behind them and oh-so-gently pulling the picture frame towards her until it was almost flush with the wall. She didn't dare lock it in case there was no other way out. She peeped through the spyhole to see Mr Pinder chatting in whispers with Doreen as he pushed a tea-trolley down the orangery. She wondered if they knew about this, but it didn't feel like the right time to ask.

Two children looked at Faye, eyes wide in the gloom.

'Where's Rudolf?' Faye asked, and got her answer immediately as the lad's voice echoed up the spiral steps.

'Faye!' he cried. '*Was ist das?*'

Faye bustled Magda and Max down the steps. These weren't as worn as the steps up to the bell tower, but they were small and slippy and there was no handrail. Round and down they went, hands pressed against the wall to stay steady. Faye was just starting to feel giddy when they found themselves in an old wine cellar. Any bottles had long since been removed.

The cellar was vast, stretching beneath the whole house, with brick arches propping up the high ceiling as they faded into the darkness.

A radio transmitter and receiver sat on a desk cluttered with scraps of paper. A map of France and Britain hung on the wall, with pins stuck in locations around Kent, including a big red one in Woodville.

This part of the cellar was lit by thirteen tall candles. These were arranged in a circle around a pentagram as wide as Faye was tall.

'*Hexe, hexe!*' Rudolf said, gesturing at the five-pointed star on the floor.

'I see it, Rudy, keep back. Everyone, keep back.'

The light from the candles blurred the air above the pentagram.

'A glamour,' Faye said to herself.

There was something in the centre, but however Faye turned her head, she couldn't quite focus on it, though it had a clear shape.

It was a tree.

Most likely an apple tree.

Quite possibly the first ever apple tree.

'Dip me in chocolate and call me a Mars Bar,' Faye whispered. 'I reckon this is the Ur-Tree.'

She felt Rudolf hiding behind her.

'It's all right, Rudy. I don't think this can hurt us,' she said, barely convincing herself, let alone the boy. Faye thought back to Mrs Teach dismissing pentagrams as silly nonsense, but this one with its candles gave off an evil aura, shimmering the air around it.

'This is a pentagram,' she told the children, perfectly aware that they hardly understood a word she said, but she knew that if she spoke in a calm voice it might take the look of abject terror from their faces. 'My mum wrote about these in her book. This is a protective thing. You can stand inside that and be safe from any danger outside of it. Or ... you could trap or hide something in it.'

Gingerly, Faye reached for one of the candles. As she did so, she imagined what Mrs Teach and Miss Charlotte would say about her impetuousness, but Faye knew that if you broke a magic circle, then it lost its power. And if the Ur-Tree was in here, then it was her duty as a witch to nab it.

All thirteen candles stood in silver holders and looked fairly ordinary, like the kind of thing you might have at a posh dinner table or, as she had just discovered, at a Shabbat table. Faye grasped the closest candle-holder. The air crackled and there was a flash of blue light as a jolt of electricity shot up her arm.

'Ow!' Faye snapped her hand back, falling down on her bottom and flexing her fingers. 'That's ... strong magic,' she said, panting to get her breath back.

A question popped into her head and she was sure she wasn't going to like the answer.

'Who here can do this kind of magic?' she asked aloud, then wondered to herself when they might return. Faye didn't much fancy lingering, and she was about to herd the children back up the stairs when she glanced at the desk with the radio transmitter and saw something that made her skin crawl.

Nestled in the scraps of paper – all scribbled with what looked like some sort of code – was a tiny enamel badge, the kind you might pin on your lapel.

A badge emblazoned with a swastika.

She was so hypnotised by the symbol – one she had only ever seen on newsreels or photos – that she hadn't noticed Max's hands reaching for the dials on the radio.

It crackled into life, the white noise of the airwaves filling the room.

'Hey, what did you do? Turn it off.' Faye looked for the dial to shut it down, but this had a lot more knobs than the average wireless.

'Hallo, hallo?' an impatient voice came over the speaker. '*Wer ist das?*'

'*Das ist Deutsch,*' Magda whispered.

'No kidding,' Faye said, turning more dials.

'*Wer ist das?*' the voice repeated more insistently.

'Oh, be quiet.' Faye twiddled a knob and heard her own voice through the speaker. 'Whistle while you work,' she sang. 'Hitler is a berk. He's half-barmy, so's his army, whistle while you work.'

The voice at the other end of the line became enraged and spewed all kinds of angry German at her. 'Up yer bum!' Faye cackled as she finally found the off dial. 'That was fun,' she said. 'Now let's—'

A noise came from the darkness at the far end of the wine cellar. A mournful moan reverberated off the walls, riddled with pain and fury, a wordless cry that was barely human.

Nelson farted and ran.

The children were already out of sight and halfway up the spiral steps before Faye could turn on her heels. She ran on legs of jelly, vaulting three steps at a time before catching up with them and tumbling out of the stone arch. She scurried back and shut the picture frame with a click.

They sat on the floor, legs splayed as they caught their breath. Nelson wagged his tail and ran in little circles.

Faye's mind was scrambled with too many questions. What the hell was that creature? Who had the magical ability to create such a powerful pentagram? What did they want, and what were they hiding?

Lullabies for
Frightened Children

'The. Green. Man. Pub. How. Can. I. Help. You?' Terrence answered with his best telephone voice, which was to bark each word individually as if the volume and effort he put into them would help the words get down the line.

'Dad, you don't have to shout like that. I can hear you fine,' Faye replied from the little nook off the main entrance hall where Lady Aston kept her telephone.

Faye's dad had always been iffy about installing a telephone in the pub. Many of the punters were similarly wary. The pub was a refuge from the world outside, not least spouses, debtors and children. To have a telephone was an invitation to scrutiny, and the ring of its bells would stiffen the backs of many pub patrons. Terrence had arranged a system with many of them whereby he'd catch their eye, point at them and reply down the phone, 'No, I think he left a few minutes ago.' This would be the drinker's cue to quickly down their pint and head back to whatever fate awaited them.

When the pub was busy, Terrence let the phone ring off, so Faye was surprised when he answered first time.

'Faye, where are you, girl?'

'I'm still at Hayward Lodge,' she said. 'Dad, the, er, the kids are still having nightmares. I'm going to stop over and look after them. Is that all right? Can you cope?'

''Course I can cope.' He bristled at the suggestion. 'Besides, I've got Dougie helping me out tonight and he says he can do tomorrow, too.'

'How's he getting on?'

Terrence glanced over to where Dougie had half-pulled a pint but was now sketching something mechanical on a napkin for a Canadian soldier.

'He's fine, though he'd probably get more done if he stopped giving out car maintenance advice to every other punter.'

'He can't help it. It's in his ...' Faye broke off to yawn long and loud. 'It's in his nature.'

'You all right?'

'Fine. Completely fine. Just very tired. Long day.'

'Kids wearing you out?'

'Completely cream-crackered.'

'And how's the lords and ladies?'

Faye wondered how much she should tell him. 'They're fine. Fine and dandy. No problems. All tickety-boo. Oh, Dad, one more thing – how's Bertie? Has he been in?'

222

'He came in for a quick half before going out on patrol tonight.'

'How was he?'

'Not his usual chipper self, but then he's on night patrol along the cliffs tonight, and that can be a long old slog. None of us in the LDV enjoy that shift, I can tell you.'

'Did he . . . ?' Faye hesitated. She felt odd asking, but she had to know. 'Did he mention me at all?'

'Funnily enough, he was curious how you were getting on up at the lodge. I told him I had no idea cos you never bothered to call and you'd probably gone all hoity-toity on me.'

'Dad! You didn't?'

'I may be paraphrasing.'

'Look, if you see Bertie, tell him . . . chin up. Tell him we're still on for the village fair.'

'I hadn't realised I was your personal secretary now.'

'Can you just tell him, please?'

'Yes, milady. And you're sure everything's all right where you are?'

'Of course,' Faye snapped a little too quickly. 'Why d'you keep going on about it?'

'Y'know, your mother thought I had a bit of psychic power. Did I ever tell you that?'

'No. What made her think that?'

'I know people, Faye, and I know when they're either lying or not telling the whole story.'

Faye stiffened, gripping the phone receiver.

'Of course, that's all part and parcel of being a

publican. You see all sorts here. No psychic powers required.'

'Just a bit of mental arithmetic and a good pint-pulling arm.'

'That's right. Your mother never kept anything from me.'

'Bully for her,' Faye said, wondering when this little dance would end.

'The magic stuff concerned me, naturally,' Terrence said, lowering his voice. 'But I knew it was best that I didn't get in the way. All I could do was offer to help if anything ever went wrong.'

'That's ... lovely. Thanks, Dad.'

'So, everything's all tickety-boo?'

'My boo couldn't be more tickety if it tried.'

'Lovely. I have to ring off now as Dougie is lecturing a pint of Guinness and the customer is losing patience. Take care and I'll see ya tomorrow. Night, Faye.'

'Night, Dad.' Faye hung up with a heavy heart. She didn't like keeping the truth from her own father, but careless talk cost lives and careless talk about magic and pentagrams could do all kinds of damage.

Magda, Max, Rudolf and Nelson all huddled around Faye in the telephone nook, and she was grateful for what little privacy it provided. They looked like she felt. Glassy eyes, downturned mouths and sloping shoulders.

'Time for bed,' she said, resting her head on her closed hands and making a snoring noise. The children nodded.

She led them up the main staircase to their room. As they brushed their teeth, Faye closed the curtains. She could see the orchard from here and she wondered how Charlotte and Mrs Teach were getting on. As soon as the children were asleep, she would go to the orchard and tell the witches what she had discovered. Faye didn't want to leave the children on their own for too long. She was wondering if she should lock them in for their own safety when she felt a tug on her sleeve.

Rudolf had returned from the toilet.

'Have you washed your hands, Rudy?' Faye asked, miming the same.

Rudolf nodded, then wiped his nose on the cuff of his pyjamas and asked a question. She was sure she heard the word 'sing'.

'Oh, blimey. You want a lullaby? I'm warning you, I ain't much of a singer. And what can we sing? What do we all know?'

Faye sat next to Rudolf on his bed. Magda and Max were already tucked up in theirs. Nelson lay by the door. They started with 'Ring-a-Ring o' Roses', first in English, then in German, then a strange bilingual version. Then they ran through the songs that Doreen and Mr Pinder had taught them in the kitchen.

The children's voices blended in a slightly off-pitch harmony that made them all forget the world outside.

Faye tried 'We'll Meet Again' with them. It took a few goes to learn the chorus, but they liked it so much they sang it over and over and begged for more.

'I've had my fill of that,' Faye said, spotting a few

books on a shelf by the dresser. 'How about a story before bedtime, eh?' She hopped off the bed, took a book at random and flipped it open. '*Babes in the Wood*. Same as the Höch montage, but this looks much nicer.' She opened the book to find an illustration of two adorable children holding hands in a dense wood. Scrawled above them were the words:

Merry Christmas Harry
Regards,
Mother and Father

'I know you won't understand what I'm on about, but Dad said that Mum would read to me when I was a baby and I couldn't understand her, either, but the words and gentle voice were enough to send me to sleep. So, let's have a go, shall we?'

Faye snuggled up to Rudolf on his bed and turned to chapter one, which began with the parents of the titular babes dying on the first page.

'Bit of an unhappy start, but let's keep going.'

Faye read on as the babes were betrayed by their uncle who wanted their money and sent them into the wood to be murdered by two ruthless assassins.

'Oh, blimey, but I'm sure these ruffians will have a change of heart and . . .' She flicked through the pages. 'No. One murders the other. Righto. Oh, and now he's promising to get the children bread. And he's left them alone in the wood. Why didn't he take them with him? I don't think he's coming back.' Faye flipped to the last page. 'Bloody hell,' she said, reading the last verse out loud.

> *'Thus wandered these two prettye babes*
> *Till death did end their grief;*
> *In one another's armes they dyed,*
> *As babes wanting relief.'*

'They die,' she said. 'They just die. Their bodies are covered with leaves by a robin and that's it. Crikey, no wonder Harry thinks his parents hate him.' She slapped the book shut. Magda, Max and Rudolf were still wide awake and none the wiser. 'Another sing-song?' Faye suggested.

After a few more rounds of 'We'll Meet Again', Faye's own eyelids were feeling heavy. She wondered where she would find the energy to dash to Mrs Teach and Miss Charlotte. She needed some fresh air, that's all. Just one more verse, put the kids to sleep, and then she could find . . .

ɤ

Faye woke to chimes at midnight.

'Oh, buggeration.'

She was still on Rudolf's bed, her arm stuck underneath the boy's pillow. Faye gently wriggled her arm free and, trying not to make the bedsprings creak, lowered her feet to the floor and stood up.

Max's eyes were open. He looked like he was about to cry. Faye put a finger to her lips.

'Nelson,' she called to the dog busy scratching his ear by the door. 'Nelson, c'mere.' The dog dashed over and up onto the bed, licking Max's face. 'Keep guard, boy.' Faye stroked Nelson's fur. 'I'll be back soon,' she said. 'I promise.'

⌀

The house was quiet with a few nurses milling about. There was no sign of Mr Pinder, Lady Aston or Harry. Faye hurried out into the chill of the moonlit night. She opened the iron gate to the orchard, which squeaked so loudly she was sure it would wake everyone in the village. She found Miss Charlotte and Mrs Teach standing around a simmering cauldron in the middle of the orchard. Their faces were no longer fuzzy, but with the grim expressions they both wore, Faye half-wished they were.

'Evenin',' Faye said as she jogged up to them. 'Any luck?'

The two women pointedly did not look at one another.

'What did I say about gloating?' Mrs Teach said.

'Not a sausage, then? Or an apple?'

'We've barely begun, Faye. This sort of ritual requires patience,' Charlotte said, allowing herself a quick glance at Mrs Teach for some kind of solidarity. 'Patience and resolve.'

'Yes, indeed,' Mrs Teach said, nodding emphatically. 'And that can take years of practice.'

'Righto,' Faye said. 'Does that mean you won't be

interested to know that I *have* found something, and I think it's what we're looking for and that it'll blow your socks off?' Faye enjoyed the baffled looks on their faces. 'That was me gloating. Just so you know.'

ɞ

She led them across the lawn, explaining everything to them as they moved. The secret door, the steps, the radio, the pentagram. Her heart was thumping with excitement as they slipped into the orangery. She had finally proven herself to them. After this, maybe they would take her a little bit more seriously. Perhaps they would start showing her some proper magic.

As they gathered by the Höch, the sound of friendly chatter drifted in from the kitchen. Faye couldn't be sure, but it sounded like Mr Pinder and Doreen were flirting.

'We'll have to be quick,' Faye said, leaning on the picture frame as before until it clicked and swung open. 'We can't let anyone see us go in or out, or we'll ... Oh, what the blimmin' 'eck?'

The arch was there as before, but it had been bricked up.

In a Dark and Scary Cellar

'It was here. I swear it was,' Faye said. 'There was a light bulb and steps going down and it stank like mouldy old farts—'

Miss Charlotte's boot kicked into the bricks and most of them fell away, revealing the light from the bulb, the spiral steps and a smell like mouldy old farts.

'Bricks, but no mortar,' Charlotte said, waving dust away from her face before kicking more bricks.

'Do you think you could make more of a racket?' Faye asked, darting her head about.

'Almost certainly,' Charlotte replied with little concern. 'This was done in the last few hours. They only had time to pile them up.'

'Someone is trying to make you look a fool,' Mrs Teach said.

'I do a pretty good job of that myself.' Faye grinned.

'No one makes any of us look foolish and gets away with it,' Mrs Teach said, gesturing to the hole in the wall that Charlotte had created. 'Lay on, Macduff.'

Faye clambered through, then turned to help Mrs Teach. Charlotte was last and took care to close the picture-frame door behind them.

'Watch your step,' Faye said. 'It's a bit slippy, but it ain't far down.'

As they descended to the cellar, Faye felt a sickening inevitability that if the door had been bricked up, then everything else she had discovered would be gone, too.

She was relieved to find she was wrong.

The circle of thirteen flickering candles and the pentagram remained, with their light still distorting the air and protecting the Ur-Tree inside.

'Well, well.' Charlotte smiled, standing before the pentagram.

The radio was still there, though it was silent, but all the papers and maps had been taken.

'There was maps on the wall,' Faye said, 'but they've gone. And paper everywhere, but they've taken that. I think they were planning to meet someone. And there was a Swastika badge.' Faye opened a drawer. There were a few pencils and notepads, but the pages had been ripped out. In another drawer she found a small wooden box. She opened it. 'Knock me down with a feather,' she whispered. Inside was a folded chessboard and all the pieces. 'I wonder if that's ... ?' She took a rook out and inspected it. It looked like a little Viking on a horse. This was the same set that Harry and Max had played with.

'Strong glamour,' Mrs Teach said, joining Charlotte. Faye put the chess piece back into the drawer and looked to where Charlotte and Mrs Teach were inspecting the ring of candles. The Ur-Tree inside was still nothing but a thin and spindly shadow.

'Can we break it?' Faye asked.

'Not without knowing who put this here in the first place,' Mrs Teach said. 'Even then, we would need a vial of their blood or saliva—'

'Or a lock of hair.' Charlotte leaned over and slowly reached into the circle.

Faye waved a warning. 'Ooh, no, don't do that!'

As Charlotte's hand dipped below the candles, there was a flash of blue light. Charlotte cursed and snatched her hand back, shaking the pain away.

'*Very* strong glamour,' Mrs Teach said, impressed. 'They really don't want us having a peek, do they?'

'How long will those candles burn for, do you reckon?' Faye asked.

'Beeswax candles,' Mrs Teach said. 'Don't try to wait them out, you'll be here all week.'

'Whoever it is,' Charlotte said, flexing her fingers, 'they'll be coming back for it soon. We should be patient.'

'It's Harry, isn't it?' Faye said. 'Come on, we're all thinking it. There's something not quite right about that fella. Klaus didn't trust him and said Harry called him anti-Jewish names, Mr Gilbert and Mr Brewer said he's a wrong'un with gambling debts, and he understands the kids when they speak German and ... and ... well, the lazy brickwork. That's a classic Harry half-arsed job.' She moved to the radio desk and showed them the box with the Viking chess pieces. 'This is his, too. All that's missing is his name on the door. He's a wrong'un and ...' Faye faltered, a horrible thought clouding her mind. 'And when I shook Harry's hand I had a vision of Klaus's death. Not when Klaus was found, but when he actually died. Harry must have been there when Klaus died. Bugger it, why didn't I think of that earlier? I'm such a—'

Faye was cut off by a mournful groan that came from the shadows deeper in the cellar.

'Ah, yes, sorry. There's something in the dark making scary noises. Probably should've mentioned that earlier.'

Mrs Teach and Charlotte shook their heads and rolled their eyes.

'What?' Faye shrugged. 'There's a lot to take in at the moment what with secret passages, Nazi spies and black magic, so excuse me for forgetting whatever that is groaning in the dark.'

Moans echoed off the brick walls and ceiling of the cellar. Wordless and agonised, they rose and fell like the drone of a siren.

Mrs Teach found a light switch and clicked it a few times, but the darkness remained.

'One moment,' Charlotte said as she produced her clay pipe and tobacco pouch from her pockets. It took a few seconds for her to select a particular blend, stuff it in the pipe and light it. Once it glowed, she gently blew on the embers and the murky depths of the cellar were revealed in a magical amber light.

Brick alcoves stretched away in a maze of columns. Some of the alcoves were stacked with crates stencilled with the names of faraway places – India, Ceylon, Afghanistan. A few were like dungeon cells with iron bars and locks. Inside were more crates, unmarked and padlocked shut.

'Klaus said there was stolen treasure down here,' Faye whispered as the three of them moved deeper into the cellar. 'Do groaning people count as treasure?'

'You're assuming it's people,' Mrs Teach said, sweetly.

'What's in the crates?' Faye asked, changing the subject.

'The spoils of campaigns in the Great Game,' Charlotte said.

'The Great Game?' Faye asked.

'A war over trade routes between the British Empire and the Russians that lasted decades.'

Faye sneered. 'And they called it a game?'

'Not at the time, but Kipling put it in a book and the name stuck,' Charlotte said. 'As the final treaties were signed, Lord Aston plundered every church, temple and mosque he came across. Most of it he sold to museums, but he kept his favourite pieces for himself. Called it his pension. He planned on living a very long life, you see. Once he found the Ur-Tree.'

'How do you know all this?'

'She helped him find it,' Mrs Teach said.

The cellar fell dark again. Charlotte sucked on her pipe, then blew on the embers and the cellar was filled with light once more.

'It's a long story,' Charlotte said. 'I'm not proud of what I did, but I needed the money and Lord Aston had no shortage of gold. Oh. Here we are.'

They arrived at the darkest cell in the murkiest corner of the cellar, and the moaning was coming from behind the bars. The smell from within – a foetid combination of rotting flesh, faeces and urine – made Faye's stomach turn. Mrs Teach held a handkerchief over her mouth and nose.

It didn't deter Charlotte, who moved closer to the cell. The light moved with her.

A man was manacled to the wall.

Dressed in rags, his hair was thin and rank, his feet bare and swollen. Liver-spotted skin hung off his bony arms like wet towels on a washing line. His eyes were hollow and dark as a well. His moaning intensified as Charlotte's light drew closer.

The iron door to the cell was unlocked. Charlotte opened it with a rusty creak and stepped inside.

'Who is it?' Faye's voice was a whisper. The mutton-chops on the man's face looked familiar. Those dim green eyes surely once shone bright.

Charlotte didn't answer for the longest time. Her chest rose and fell as her breathing quickened. 'It's him,' she said. 'It's Lord Aston.'

GREEDY

'Thomas, it's me, Charlotte.'

Faye watched as Charlotte crouched down by the emaciated form of Lord Aston. The man could barely move, his cracked lips opening and closing wordlessly.

'Hang on a mo'.' Faye crinkled her forehead. 'Which Lord Aston? This can't be our one. I only saw him this morning.'

'He needs water,' Charlotte said. 'Quickly.'

'Water? Yes,' Faye said. 'There's a sink back where the radio was.' She dashed through the cellar towards the glow of the room where they came in. There was a tin mug on the desk with a little cold tea in the bottom. Faye poured that down the sink, then turned on the cold tap. It juddered into life, spurting water into the mug.

By the time she got back, she found Mrs Teach lighting candles in sconces on either side of the cell's entrance.

'He's had a visitor,' Mrs Teach said. 'There's a box of candles here.'

Faye ducked inside, trying not to recoil from the stench of decay coming off the man. She handed the cup to Charlotte who gently held it to Lord Aston's mouth.

He moaned in pain with each gulp, but one eye came into focus.

He took a breath before he spoke, his voice ghostly. 'Charlotte? Charlotte Southill?'

She nodded. 'Thomas Bowes Aston, what bloody trouble have you got yourself into now? I thought you were dead.'

'I wish I were,' he said, the words coming slowly.

'What are you doing down here, Thomas?' Charlotte asked, brushing the grey hair away from his face.

'I've been a fool,' he said. 'You were right, Charlotte, you were right. The tree was nothing but trouble. A curse and the bane of my life.'

'What did you do?'

'I was greedy, I ... I couldn't help myself.'

'Oh, Thomas, you didn't?' Charlotte closed her eyes and pressed her fingers against her forehead.

'He didn't what?' Faye asked. 'What didn't he do? And which Lord Aston is he? The one from the Great Game, or the one I saw this morning that looked fit as a butcher's dog?'

'They are one and the same,' Charlotte said, tipping the cup to Lord Aston's mouth.

'That can't be right. How can he be ...?' Faye trailed off as she figured it out. 'The Ur-Tree. You said he found it. He found it and used it. Bloody hell, how old is he?'

'We discovered the tree in the foothills of the Tien Shan mountains in 1885,' Charlotte said. 'I used a ritual very similar to the one we used in the orchard overnight, on a much bigger scale, as you can imagine. One of the most ambitious rituals I had ever attempted. The tree was guarded by two sisters who looked as old as the mountains. They were helpless in the face of Lord Aston's soldiers, and they held each other and wept as we stole their tree. I spoke to them via one of the local trackers we had hired and they gave a warning. The power of the Ur-Tree, its gift of youth, lasts only one year.'

'That's not much use, is it?' Mrs Teach said, remaining outside the cell and keeping watch. 'A bit of cold cream every day will do much the same.'

Charlotte ignored her and continued, 'If you take a bite from the apple of the Ur-Tree, you remain perfectly preserved for a year. When the sun rises one year later, your age catches up with you at sunset—'

'Unless you take a bite from another apple on the Ur-Tree,' Faye said, catching on. 'Take an apple every year on the same day and you stay young and healthy. But someone locked Lord Aston in a cell, and he missed his apple and now ... Oh, blimey.'

'Today ... was the day,' Lord Aston said, starting to sob.

'Oh, Thomas.' Charlotte held him closer.

'What does he mean?' Mrs Teach asked.

'We discovered the tree on the 19th of July, 1885,' Charlotte said. 'Today is the 19th of July.'

'Actually we're past midnight, so it's the 20th,' Faye said, getting a glare from Charlotte. 'But I can see how you can lose track of time down here. You're saying because he didn't take a bite of the apple before sunset yesterday, he ... he ended up like this. All those years caught up with him at once.'

Charlotte nodded. 'Imagine ageing a year in a day,' she said. 'Now imagine ageing fifty-five years, like Thomas just did. It's more painful than you can possibly imagine.'

'Fifty-five?' Faye frowned.

'That's how long he's been taking apples from the Ur-Tree,' Mrs Teach observed.

Lord Aston, wheezing and coughing, reached for the water and Charlotte gave him some more.

'Crikey, if it's that important then put a note on your calendar,' Faye said. 'Or take one every day.'

'That's what he means by being greedy,' Charlotte said. 'If you bite an apple from the Ur-Tree too soon, the branch that you plucked it from will wither and die. Take too many apples and the tree will die altogether.' She squeezed Lord Aston's hand. 'How many branches are left, Thomas?'

The old man couldn't bring himself to look at her. He stared into his lap in shame.

'Not many, then,' Mrs Teach said.

'He ... he drugged me.' Lord Aston coughed, and Charlotte gave him more water. 'Then he brought me here and locked me up, the little ...' Lord Aston's body convulsed as he coughed again and again.

'Harry?' Faye said. 'Harry did this?'

Lord Aston nodded. Charlotte sat him upright.

'Why would he do this?' Faye asked.

'The Ur-Tree,' Charlotte said. 'He wants the Ur-Tree.'

Lord Aston shook his head. 'He has ...' He gasped for breath. 'He has ...'

'He has it already,' Faye said. 'We saw it, in the circle of candles. Does that mean Harry can do magic?'

'No, it means he can follow instructions sent to him by Otto,' Charlotte said. 'But that's no less worrying. Otto knows where the tree is and he's coming for it.'

Lord Aston's body spasmed with convulsions. He began thrashing about and both Faye and Charlotte had to hold him down to stop him from hurting himself even more. Spots of blood flecked his lips. Faye wondered what kind of monster could do this to their own father.

'Mrs Teach,' Faye called. 'Do you have a hankie?'

Mrs Teach hesitated, looking around the cellar before ducking inside the cell. Faye wondered why she was so reluctant to enter. Faye didn't think she was claustrophobic.

'Mrs Teach, hurry!'

Keeping one foot outside the cell, Mrs Teach extended her arm to pass the handkerchief to Faye.

'Come closer,' Faye said, trying to hold down the flailing form of Lord Aston.

'I can't,' Mrs Teach said. 'I think there's someone else—'

'Mrs Teach, look out!' Faye pointed at a shadow rushing in the darkness.

It shoved Mrs Teach into the cell and she tumbled to the floor. The figure yanked the cell door shut and, with a rusty grind of a key turning tumblers, locked them in.

Harry stepped into the candlelight.

Lord Aston shuddered, reaching out to his son. 'No, Harry, please don't do this, I beg of you.'

'Oh, dear Father, finally you deign to show me a scintilla of respect,' Harry said, tossing the cell key away into the darkness of the cellar where it landed with a distant *clink*. 'Perhaps if you and Mother had bothered a little sooner you wouldn't be in this mess, but it's too late now. I simply can't have you interfering with things this late in the day. I've worked jolly hard to get this far.'

'You? Harry Aston? Work hard?' Mrs Teach said as Faye helped her to her feet. 'You've never worked a day in your life.'

'Up till recently, I would have agreed with you,' Harry said, leaning casually against the bars. 'But when one finds one's calling, work ceases to be a drag and becomes something of a joy.'

'And just what is your calling, boy?' Charlotte asked.

'Why, changing the world, of course,' he said with genuine glee. 'My eyes have been opened by a mutual friend of ours, Otto Kopp. He sends his regards, by the way. Yes, we met in Munich in '36. He saw the war coming and has spent the last ten years honing his already incredible powers. He explained to me how Mr Hitler and his rather splendid National Socialist Party had all the answers. I began working for them in a sort of messenger-boy capacity and worked my way up.'

'You're a spy,' Faye said, sneering at him. 'You're spying on your own country to pay off your gambling debts, you lousy little—'

'You make it sound so tawdry.' Harry grimaced. 'The money is an added bonus, but getting more cash was never a problem for someone like me. Oh no, I'm working for the Nazis because I want to be on the winning side. Look what they've achieved already. And with Otto's power they'll be unstoppable. Very soon, they'll cross the Channel and be running things here, and about time, too. And when they arrive, I shall welcome them as allies and I will be suitably rewarded. Sadly, you won't be around to see my triumph, as I'm afraid ...' Harry drew a Luger from within his sports jacket and aimed it through the bars. 'You will all be dead.'

A roar echoed off the walls as Lord Aston hurled himself at his son, reaching through the bars and grabbing his hair. A gunshot rang out, followed by a wail as Harry clasped his head in his hands.

'He pulled my hair! What sort of man—?' Harry stopped, realising he had dropped the Luger inside the cell.

Charlotte snatched the weapon up, aimed and fired.

Harry was a blur as the first bullet whizzed past his ear and ricocheted off a distant wall with a spark. His footsteps echoed as he ran away.

Charlotte dashed to the bars, stretched her arm through them and fired blindly again and again into the darkness until she was out of bullets.

'Ha ha! Missed me!' Harry snorted a laugh, his footsteps fading into the distance.

Charlotte, grimacing, smashed the gun like a hammer on the cell door's lock.

'Charlotte, stop, please,' Faye begged her. 'Help us, he's hurt.'

Charlotte turned to find Faye and Mrs Teach cradling Lord Aston's head as he lay on the cell floor, blood pooling around him from the wound in his chest.

CHARLOTTE EASES HIS PAIN

'There's a house full of doctors and nurses upstairs,' Faye said.

'It's past midnight, Faye,' Mrs Teach said. 'Most of them will have gone home. And don't forget, we're locked in a cell. Let's solve that little problem first, shall we?'

'Is there a spare key?' Faye asked the wounded Lord Aston. 'A secret passage? Anything we can use to—'

'No.' Lord Aston spoke between gasps of pain. 'I've lived long enough. My time has come. Tell my darling Elizabeth I'm sorry.'

'Don't be a bloody fool, Thomas.' Charlotte knelt by his side, pressing Mrs Teach's handkerchief on his wound to stem the flow of blood.

'Get the tree back ... before he can ...' Lord Aston grimaced, shutting his eyes as pain seared through his body.

'Press down here. Hard,' Charlotte told Faye, taking her hand and placing it on the bloody hankie on Lord

Aston's chest. Faye could feel his warm blood seeping through her fingers. Charlotte tapped her pipe on the flagstones to empty it. 'Thomas.' Charlotte raised her voice as she took out her pouch and selected another blend. 'Thomas, stay with us.'

Lord Aston's eyes opened again, drifting as they tried to focus. 'He has to be stopped.'

'Harry?' Faye asked, and he nodded. 'Where's he going? Who's he meeting?'

Lord Aston's head jerked and he began to kick his legs, screaming with pain.

'Hold him down,' Charlotte said, her pipe lit. Faye and Mrs Teach gripped Lord Aston's arms as he flailed in agony. Charlotte leaned close to his face and gently exhaled the smoke over his nose and mouth. Almost immediately his pain subsided and he calmed down.

'Will that make him better?' Faye asked.

Charlotte never took her eyes from Thomas's as she gently shook her head. 'It will ease the pain, that's all.'

Lord Aston grasped Charlotte's hand, forced it open and pressed something into her palm. 'Use this,' he said. 'Stop him before it's too late.' He shuddered as the last breath left his body. He died in Faye's arms.

A silence filled the cell. Faye felt a damp chill in her bones.

Mrs Teach gently pressed a finger to Lord Aston's neck and then to his wrist. She shook her head and Faye lowered his head to the flagstones.

Charlotte said nothing. She clenched her jaw, slumped against the cell wall, then stared at the floor.

'Oh, Charlotte, I'm sorry,' Faye said.

Charlotte took a puff from the pipe. She inhaled deeply, her chest rising. She held it there for a long time before letting it all out. The blue-tinged smoke formed a little halo around her.

Charlotte twitched a smile. 'I outlive all my friends,' she said. 'You get used to it after the first hundred years.'

Faye thought about asking what magic Miss Charlotte used to stay young, if not an apple, but reflected that now was probably not the best time.

'I thought he would be different.' Charlotte puffed out her cheeks, wiped each eye and sniffed. 'Right, let's get on with it. We have to stop Harry. Can't languish in here all night, can we?'

Faye, wondering if that was the extent of Charlotte's grief, glanced at Mrs Teach who gave a tiny shrug.

Charlotte opened her hand to reveal what Lord Aston had given her.

Faye leaned over for a closer look. A clump of sandy hair rested in Charlotte's bloody palm. 'That's Harry's,' Faye said. 'Lord Aston must've took it when he grabbed him.'

'We can use it to hex Harry,' Mrs Teach said.

'Not in here.' Charlotte clasped her hand shut again. 'But get me to those beeswax candles and the pentagram and he's ours.'

'Can either of you pick a lock?' Mrs Teach asked.

'I can,' Miss Charlotte said, 'but I don't have any of my tools.'

'Who else knows about this place?' Mrs Teach asked. 'One of the staff?'

'I doubt it. You saw Harry's radio and the candles,' Faye said. 'They'd been there for ages. This is his cosy little black magic Nazi shelter. He's probably been working down here for months.' She stood and rattled the bars of the door. They were cold and solid. 'Anyone know any lock magic?'

Charlotte shook her head. 'Locks are maddeningly resistant to magic.'

'We could shout for help?'

'No one's hearing us through all this.' Charlotte rapped a knuckle on the stone wall. 'What have we got? Empty your pockets.'

Faye produced Rudolf's drawing of the trees. Mrs Teach had some tools in the front pocket of her bee-keeping suit: a small brush and a scraper.

'Is that it?' Charlotte asked.

'Not quite.' Mrs Teach got to her feet, moved to the bars and reached around. 'We have these,' she said, plucking one of the candles from its sconce outside the cell. It was still flickering.

'Excellent,' Charlotte said, taking it from her.

Mrs Teach grabbed the second candle and they placed them on the floor.

'Candle magic?' Faye said. 'What can we do with that?'

'We can summon someone to help us,' Mrs Teach said.

'Not another demon,' Faye said. 'You know what happened last time.'

248

'Don't be silly.' Mrs Teach gestured at Rudolf's drawing. 'We'll use that little keepsake to make a psychic connection with the boy and he can help us.'

'Rudolf?' Faye shook her head in disbelief. 'You want me to use magic to wake up that poor, traumatised little lad in the middle of the night, make him come down a secret passage to a Nazi radio room decorated by the devil himself, and then what? Pick the lock?'

'He merely has to raise the alarm,' Mrs Teach said.

'Oh, so you want everyone upstairs to know about this mess, do you?' Faye gestured around her.

'She has a point,' Charlotte said. 'If he raises the alarm, then how are we going to explain to Lady Aston why we're locked in a cell with the body of her dead husband and a smoking gun? We need the boy to come here as quietly as possible and then find the key. It's out there in the cellar somewhere.'

'You've met Rudolf,' Faye said. 'He's about as quiet as a Panzer tank in a china shop, and you can't order him to go looking in the dark. He'll be petrified. Besides which, it's Shabbat. He's not supposed to do any work.'

'This is an emergency,' Charlotte said. 'Jews can break Shabbat to save a life in an emergency.'

'He's the only one we can contact, Faye,' Mrs Teach said. 'It's him, or we rot in this cell for who knows how long.'

Faye chewed her lip. 'All of them,' she said, eventually. 'Magda, Max and Rudolf, we'll have all of them come down together, safety in numbers. And Nelson the dog. He can sniff out the key.'

'Good enough,' Charlotte said. 'Place his drawing between the candles and everyone join hands. Oh, and Faye ... we'll need your specs.'

RUDOLF

Rudolf could not sleep. He fidgeted and shuffled, trying to find a comfortable position. When he lay on his front, he felt like he was suffocating. When he lay on his back, he snored and Magda told him to be quiet. When he lay on his side, Nelson came and licked his nose. Rudolf didn't mind that so much, but it made him giggle and the others shouted at him to be quiet and go to sleep.

The few times he did nod off, the nightmares came.

The night they had to pack everything into one bag, the storm troopers herding them into the street, the oily smell of their machine guns, getting in strangers' cars, hurrying onto trains, the rumble of tanks, the howl of the Stuka bombers as they waved their mother and father farewell at the dock.

He was beginning to forget what they looked like. Every time he closed his eyes he tried to see them, but their faces were fuzzy, their voices ever fainter.

And now Klaus was gone, too. Rudolf's heart twisted

to think of him. He thought Klaus was asleep when he and Nelson found him in the orchard, but when he touched his hand to wake him it was cold and stiff. At first, Rudolf didn't understand. How could Klaus be gone after everything they had been through? It wasn't right. It wasn't fair.

Tears came, and Rudolf's cheeks burned. He buried his head under the pillow. Magda got cross when he cried, because she would cry, too. Nelson hopped up onto the bed and rested a paw on Rudolf's arm. The boy rolled over, snuggled tight to the dog and felt safe again.

'Rudolf!'

He heard the voice but pretended not to. On top of everything else, there was at least one witch in the house and a monster in the basement. Magda said he was silly, but Rudolf knew she was a witch because she had told him she was. She claimed to be a good witch, but that is exactly what a wicked witch would say. Rudolf was no fool.

'Rudy!'

Nelson sat up and barked.

Nelson barking would also make Magda cross, so Rudolf had to sit up to silence him and that's when he saw the faces in the mirror. The witch, Faye, and her two friends – the big bee lady and the nanny with the white hair and red lips – were all crowded in the mirror's glass and staring straight at him.

Faye looked a little different. She wasn't wearing her spectacles. She beckoned Rudolf to the mirror and spoke in words he did not understand. His feet turned to lead. The woman with the white hair nudged Faye out of sight and spoke German.

'Little boy,' she said in a voice that was almost as stern as those of the soldiers who had thrown his family into the streets. 'Wake your brother and sister and come and find us in the cellar. And be quick, we need your help.'

Rudolf shook his head. The cellar. Where the monster lived. It had trapped the witches and would probably gobble them up and him, too, if he was stupid enough to go down there. It would take an army to drag him out of the safety of his bed. So long as he stayed under the sheets they could not get him.

'Little boy—' the white-haired witch started again, but the others seemed to tell her off and she rolled her eyes. 'Rudolf.' She now spoke sweetly and smiled, revealing white teeth behind those red lips. 'Wake Magda and Max, please. There's nothing to be scared of.'

Rudolf half-expected her to offer him a poisoned apple. He ducked under the sheets with Nelson and tried not to think of how much he needed to pee. There was a pot under his bed, but what with witches in his mirror and a monster in the basement, Rudolf was certain there would be monsters under his bed, too. He would just have to hold it in, or pee the bed, which made Magda angrier than anything.

Magda. Yes. She was the eldest. She could deal with this. Rudolf clung on to Nelson, hollering Magda's name over again and again.

How Not to Hide a Body

Faye held her specs at arm's length so they could all see into the children's bedroom. It was the only reflective surface they had to hand in the locked cell and the image was ghostly at best, but she tingled with the thrill of doing real magic.

The thrill vanished as Rudolf ducked under the sheets, screaming his sister's name over and over.

'Rudolf! Come back here, you idiot!' Charlotte commanded, but the boy only burrowed further under the sheets.

'And you were going to be their nanny?' Mrs Teach tutted and shook her head. 'As if the poor tykes haven't suffered enough.'

'He's calling for Magda,' Faye said. 'That's good. She's the grown-up one and she doesn't believe in witches, so we're more likely to get some sense out of her.'

They watched Magda, bleary-eyed, hop out of her bed and hurry to reassure her youngest brother.

Rudolf still would not come out from under the sheets and Nelson kept barking at the mirror. Magda blinked her eyes wide, saw what Nelson could see and froze.

'*Hexe!*' she cried, before rushing to the wardrobe, ducking inside and shutting herself in.

'She's the grown-up one?' Charlotte wrinkled her lips.

'I told you, didn't I?' Faye said. 'They're only kids and magic scares the willies out of them.'

'Who's left?' Mrs Teach asked.

'Max,' Faye said. 'Though he's barely said two words since he got here. I'm not sure he's going to be any help. We should—'

Max's face appeared in Faye's spectacles. He looked into the mirror, then prodded it with a finger. 'Hallo?' he said.

'Max, Max!' Faye waved at him, then nudged Charlotte. 'Tell him ... tell him there's a chessboard down here.'

Charlotte frowned. 'What?'

'Harry's little Viking chessboard and all the pieces are down here. Go on. Tell him.'

Charlotte did so and Max's eyes widened. He blurted something very fast in German, then dragged Rudolf out from under his sheets, yanked Magda out of the wardrobe and they all went dashing from the room with Nelson yapping after them.

Charlotte and Mrs Teach turned to Faye.

'That boy really likes his chess,' she said.

'Indeed,' Mrs Teach said. 'That gives us

approximately five minutes to decide what to do with his lordship here.'

Lord Aston's bloodstained body was still lying in the centre of the cell.

'Oh, Lordy, we can't let the children see that,' Faye said. 'They'll go barmy.'

'Hide him in the shadows,' Charlotte said.

'Hide him in the ...?' Faye spluttered. 'This ain't exactly a big cell. They're bound to notice a dead body covered in blood sooner or later. And look.' She held her hands up. The palms were red and sticky. 'We look like we done him in. We'll be lucky if they don't run off screaming and call a copper. Can't we, y'know, *glamour* him into looking fuzzy, like what you did to yourselves?'

'That takes considerable preparation,' Mrs Teach said.

'Hallo! Hallo?' Voices and footsteps echoed in the distance. The children were already coming down the spiral steps to the cellar.

'In the shadows it is, then,' Faye said. 'I'll get his legs, you take his arms.'

Once Lord Aston was stowed away in the darkest corner, Faye, Charlotte and Mrs Teach all pressed themselves against the bars of their cell, calling out and beckoning the children.

'Three witches in a cell trying to lure innocent kiddies towards them,' Faye said. 'If this ain't something out of a Grimm fairy tale, then I don't know what is.'

Mrs Teach held both candles out, gently waving them to attract the children's attention and calling to them in a sing-song voice. 'Here, my little darlings, follow the light, follow the light.'

'Mrs Teach, don't take this the wrong way,' Faye said, 'but that's probably scarier than if you were threatening to gobble them up.'

'How dare you.' Mrs Teach stiffened. 'I'm very popular with the children in the village. They adore me.'

'These are three terrified kids who've lost all their family and are in a strange land,' Faye said. 'Just try to be less ... witchy.'

'There they are,' Charlotte said.

The trio were edging their way along from the radio room, silhouetted by the light from the thirteen candles. Nelson belted around their ankles, barked and zipped towards the cell. Immediately, he sniffed the floor, darted between the cell bars and made straight for Lord Aston's body. The dog whined and barked at the corpse.

'Oh, bloody hell,' Faye whispered. 'He'll give us away.'

'Ignore him,' said Charlotte, then called out to the children.

Max replied.

'What did he say?' Faye asked.

'He wants the chess set.'

'If we tell him,' Mrs Teach said, 'will he take it and abandon us?'

'I don't think so,' Faye said. 'He's a good lad and we have to prove he can trust us. Tell him it's in one of the drawers in the desk where the radio was.'

'But tell him we need the key, too,' Mrs Teach added.

Charlotte did so. The children huddled to confer, then Max dashed back to the radio desk. He called to confirm that the chess box was there, then ran to rejoin his siblings, gripping it like treasure.

Charlotte pointed into the darkness of the cellar where Harry had tossed the key. She offered the candles to the children.

Rudolf stepped forwards to take them, but Magda stretched her arm out to block his way.

'What's she doing?' Mrs Teach asked.

Magda spoke in stern German and Charlotte translated in brief bursts. 'Shabbat,' she said. 'Once lit, candles can't be touched till Shabbat is over.' Charlotte immediately responded in even sterner German.

'What are you telling her?' Faye asked.

Whatever Charlotte said, it made Magda pout and fold her arms in defiance.

'Jews can break Shabbat in life-or-death situations,' Charlotte said. 'I told her that helping us will save lives.'

'Will it?'

'Eventually.'

Max was arguing with Magda and rattling the chess box. Magda stood her ground, so Max barged past her and took a candle from Charlotte. He waited for his sister to do the same, but she wouldn't budge.

'Magda, please,' Faye said.

Rudolf stepped forward, gently took the remaining candle from Charlotte and stood by his brother.

Magda and Max began arguing again.

'Something about being good Jews,' Charlotte said,

struggling to keep up. 'Max says a good Jew would never stand by when lives are at risk. Magda doesn't want to be lectured on being a good Jew by her stupid little brother and, oh, it's just insults now ...'

As Magda and Max raged, Rudolf quietly walked away from them and began to move methodically between the brick columns of the cellar, the candle throwing long, swooping shadows as he shuffled about.

'The little one's doing it,' Charlotte said. 'He's looking for the key.'

Magda and Max started shoving one another.

Nelson resumed barking at the late Lord Aston.

'Will you give it a rest?' Faye snapped at him.

Mrs Teach crouched down and made kissy noises. Nelson padded over to her and she gently brushed back the hair around his head and neck. 'You're a good boy, aren't you? Leave that poor chap alone and go and help your big brothers and sister. They're looking for a key. Go on, off you pop.'

Nelson looked at her and barked all the harder.

'I think he's saying, "Are you mad, woman? There's a dead body in here,"' Faye said.

Mrs Teach took the pup in her arms and they rubbed noses. 'I know, sweetie, but it wasn't us. No, it wasn't, was it?'

There were cries of excitement from Rudolf in the darkness. Magda and Max stopped their shoving match and only now realised their little brother had wandered off.

'He's found it,' Charlotte said. 'He's found the key.'

Rudolf's candle bobbed towards the witches out of the darkness as the boy hurried closer. He held the key to the cell ahead of him, like a Crusader with a cross. Magda and Max made excited chatter – a mix of praise and disapproval – as Charlotte reached out for the key.

Then Rudolf's candle illuminated the corner of the cell, and Lord Aston's dead body was visible to all.

Rudolf started screaming first and the others soon joined him. Max dropped the chess set, the little Vikings scattering across the flagstones.

'*Ruhe!*' Charlotte shouted so loudly, Faye could feel the cell bars vibrate.

The children shut up instantly and clutched one another.

As Charlotte explained, she pointed first at the body, then at the Luger on the ground and finally towards the candles and the radio. Faye heard the name Harry mentioned a few times. She saw the children's eyes move back and forth, following Charlotte's finger as they began to decide if they believed her or not.

Max and Magda glanced at one another and Faye's heart sank as they snatched the key from Rudolf and walked back the way they came.

Rudolf called after them and began his own speech.

'What's he saying?' Faye asked.

'He's . . . he's reminding them you rescued them from the car, that you comforted them when Klaus died and that you've always believed him when no one else did.'

'Oh, bless,' Faye said, feeling a little flutter in her heart.

'Then there's something about …' Charlotte frowned. 'I can't make it out … Harry is a big, smelly pile of … oh.'

Magda and Max stopped walking away. Magda made a decision, marched back to the cell and stood before Faye.

'*Hexe?*' Magda asked, pointing to Mrs Teach and Miss Charlotte.

Faye nodded. 'Yes. We all are,' she said. 'We're all good *hexe*.'

Magda took a moment to look them up and down. Mrs Teach was cradling Nelson and the pup was licking her face.

Then he farted.

Rudolf began to giggle, Max followed and soon all of them were chuckling along, even Charlotte.

Magda raised her chin and handed Faye the key.

Faye said a quiet, '*Danke*,' before gently taking it and unlocking the door.

The three witches stepped out, slow and calm so as not to set off any frayed nerves.

'I believe this chap is yours.' Mrs Teach handed Nelson to Rudolf, who gave the pup a squeeze.

Faye started picking up the chess pieces. Max brought her the box, though he kept his distance. She placed a knight and a few pawns inside. '*Danke*,' she said again, and he smiled before helping her to gather the remaining pieces.

'Stand aside,' Charlotte said, breezing past them and through the cellar to the circle of candles. They looked just as tall as when they had come in and showed no sign of dimming. If anything, the distortion of the light was stronger. Faye couldn't make out the shape in the centre at all now.

The children watched in fascination as Charlotte stood before the candles and extended her arm. She muttered quietly as she sprinkled a few of Harry's hairs over the flickering flames, one candle at a time. This was going to take a while.

'Stand back,' Charlotte said, releasing the last few hairs over the thirteenth candle.

Faye felt a wave of heat wash over her as the flames burst up then extinguished instantly, leaving spirals of black smoke twisting slowly in the air. Now they would get to see what all the fuss was about. The mythical Ur-Tree.

Everyone nudged closer, but there was no Ur-Tree, no mystical totem, no ancient relic.

There was only a handwritten note. Charlotte snatched it up.

'What does it say?' Mrs Teach asked.

Charlotte's lips twisted as she scrunched the paper into a ball and tossed it onto the desk.

Faye un-scrunched the paper and read aloud. 'Missing: one Ur-Tree, answers to the name of Ur-nie. If found, please return to Harry Aston. Oh no, wait. That's me, and I already have it. Haw haw haw. By the time you read this I will be halfway to Berlin. Heil Hitler and Churchill is an ass. Yah boo sucks, Harry.' Faye handed the note to Mrs Teach. 'What a berk.'

'Then it's gone?' Mrs Teach quivered. 'We're too late?'

'Not if I have anything to do with it,' Charlotte said. 'First, we need to—'

'What the hell is going on here?' A figure stood at the bottom of the spiral steps to the cellar.

It was Lady Aston.

TRY TO LOOK INNOCENT

It wasn't a good look. Smoking candles, a pentagram, three witches with bloody hands, three innocent children and a puppy all crammed into a dank cellar.

Faye's pang of guilt twisted tighter as she realised that not long from now she would also have to explain to Lady Aston that her husband had been shot dead by their son in a frankly barely believable scenario.

'Oh, hello,' Faye said, trying to sound like Lady Aston's arrival was not only expected, but she was, if anything, a little late. Faye was stalling, of course, because how do you explain magic to someone who has never—

'Someone's been hiding something,' Lady Aston said, walking straight to the snuffed candles surrounding the pentagram. 'And they've been using magic. Protective magic.'

'Er, yes,' Faye started, slightly baffled that Lady Aston of all people would know what a pentagram was used for. 'But—'

'Is this your work?' Lady Aston turned to Charlotte.

'Your ladyship,' Mrs Teach interrupted before Charlotte could reply. 'We were imprisoned here by your—'

'Mrs Teach, I'm surprised to see a respectable woman like you in the company of a witch of such low reputation.' Lady Aston sneered at Charlotte. There was no love lost between these two. 'And Faye, I cannot begin to describe how disappointed I am in you. Take the children to their rooms immediately and leave. Your services are no longer required.'

'Give us a chance to explain,' Faye pleaded. 'It's Harry, he—'

'I do not wish to hear any more of your lies.'

'Harry did this, he has the Ur-Tree, and he—'

'Silence. Out. Get out.'

'And he killed Lord Aston!' Faye hadn't meant for it to come out this way, but she had to shout to make herself heard over Lady Aston's denials.

The woman trembled as if she had been slapped. 'I beg your pardon?' The words came as a thin whisper.

Mrs Teach lowered her eyes. The children did likewise. Charlotte was the only one who could bring herself to look at Lady Aston and confirm the worst with a small nod.

'My husband,' Lady Aston said. 'Take me to him.'

℘

Bertie stamped his feet to keep warm. He looked out along the coastline dotted with barrage balloons every few hundred yards. It was nearly two in the morning and there was a chilly breeze coming in from the sea. His roadblock stood on an exposed country road with the cliffs dropping away on one side, a field of corn on the other. There was a concrete pillbox for shelter, but it was so dark and damp inside that he was better off facing the chill.

'Roadblock' was perhaps too grand a word for what Bertie had created with Mr Gilbert and Mr Brewer. A few jerrycans and sandbags topped-off with a long branch he had found on the ground was hardly the Maginot Line, but it would do for now.

Bertie, Mr Gilbert and Mr Brewer were on Local Defence Volunteer duties. Captain Marshall had tasked them with setting up the roadblock before sunset, taking turns to make routine patrols along the coast, then to dismantle the roadblock when the sun came up. This was all part of their militia training in case the Nazis were fool enough to invade. Though Bertie had got into trouble when he pointed out that it was all very well setting up a roadblock, but he had seen Panzer tanks on the newsreels and he reckoned they would just go straight over it without so much as a bump and carry on through the fields. Captain Marshall had told him to be quiet, or he wouldn't get a go on the Sten gun.

Mr Gilbert and Mr Brewer had just returned in their motorcycle and sidecar from their patrol along the coast. It would be Bertie's turn to go with one of them soon – the Local Defence Volunteers always patrolled in pairs – but first they insisted on tea and a smoke. With Mr Gilbert and Mr Brewer, the conversation always got around to artsy-fartsy stuff, which Bertie wasn't much up on, though he was keen to learn. However, Bertie seemed to have upset Mr Brewer by declaring that all art had to be, in his words, 'pretty'.

'No, no, no,' Mr Brewer said before taking a drag on his cigarette. 'Who's to say what is beautiful and what is ugly? Take this, for example.' Mr Brewer gestured to the pillbox by the roadblock.

It was a squat, square structure with grass on its roof. It had just been built as a defensive post in the event of invasion and was quite possibly the ugliest building Bertie had ever seen.

'You're saying the pillbox is beautiful art?' Bertie frowned.

'Let's not get carried away,' Mr Gilbert said, raising his impressive nose.

'Not now, perhaps,' Mr Brewer persevered. 'But when all this ghastly war business is over, we may choose to preserve this structure to remind us of these trying times, and that in itself will lend the thing its own brand of artistic value.'

'Like my Uncle Nick's foot?' Bertie said, brightening up.

Mr Brewer allowed Bertie's words some time to sink in before replying, 'I'm afraid you'll have to elaborate on that, Bertie.'

'My Uncle Nick got frostbite and his foot had to be lopped off, and he went and put it in a jar of vinegar or something, and he has it on the mantel for all to see and to remind him of better times when he had two feet.'

Mr Gilbert and Mr Brewer shared a look and shrugged.

'Yes,' Mr Brewer said. 'Yes, I suppose it is in its own peculiar way very much like your Uncle Nick's foot.'

'That's a nice thought,' Bertie said. 'That we'll look back on this ugly old pillbox and think of when times were hard. It's good to know that this war will end.'

'This too shall pass, Bertie,' said Mr Gilbert. 'All pain and joy are fleeting. Savour the joy and endure the pain, for both will soon be gone, one supplanted by the other.'

'That's beautiful, Mr Gilbert,' Bertie said. 'That's like poetry, or something.'

'Oh, hardly,' Mr Brewer said with a grin.

'Well, I reckon it's art,' Bertie said. 'I think I'm getting the hang of this.'

'There's nothing more endearing in a chap than an enquiring mind, Bertie,' Mr Gilbert said. 'Keep it up and you shall be as wise as Solomon.'

'Can I ask you another question, then?' Bertie asked.

Mr Gilbert stiffened, but smiled. 'Of course.'

'This too shall pass,' Bertie mused. 'Does that count for, like, heartache?'

Mr Brewer and Mr Gilbert shared a look.

'Are you entangled in the throes of romance, young Bertie?' asked Mr Brewer.

'I dunno about getting tangled or nothing.' Bertie gave a shrug and even in the pale moonlight his cheeks turned red. 'There is someone, and I've asked her to step out, but she's a busy lass, and I don't want to bother her with anything beyond that, and I reckoned if I did then she might tell me to sling my hook and then I wouldn't know what to do after that.'

'Aah, I see,' Mr Gilbert said. Bertie offered him more tea, which he accepted gladly. He took a sip before continuing. 'All I can say is that based on my own experience, Bertie, fortune favours the bold. Most of the time. Getting your heart broken is rotten, let me tell you, but letting love pass by without so much as a wave is much, much worse. Be brave, lad. What's the worst that can happen?'

'I could ruin a friendship.'

'Good point,' said Mr Brewer, glancing at Mr Gilbert and smiling. 'Though you might get something much more rewarding in return.'

Bertie cocked his head at some distant noise. 'Car coming,' he said, screwing the lid back on his flask and shouldering his rifle.

Mr Gilbert and Mr Brewer put out their cigarettes, and the three of them took their positions at the road-block. Bertie clicked on his torch and swung it from side to side to draw the attention of the driver. There were no street lights in the blackout, and the car's head-lights were hooded so the driver might not see them until they rounded the corner. If the pitch of the engine was anything to go by, it was coming at some speed. Bertie tensed, ready to leap out of the way if necessary.

A red MG Midget came haring around the bend,

trailing dust behind it. The top was down, and it appeared to be giving a lift to some sort of tree in the passenger seat. The driver's view was obscured by branches and leaves and he only just saw the roadblock in time, coming to a skidding halt just a few feet away.

'I say, what's the to-do?' a familiar voice called from the car.

'Roadblock, sir. Routine stuff. Nothing to worry about.' Bertie shone his torch at the driver and Harry Aston winced and shielded his eyes.

'Well, well, Harry,' Mr Gilbert said, approaching the car. 'We must stop bumping into one another in peculiar places. People will talk.'

'You must be used to that,' Harry said with a smile, though there was more than a little venom in his tone. 'The whole village talks about you two.'

'Indeed, though if there's anything worse than being talked about, it's *not* being talked about.' Mr Gilbert stood by the driver's door of the MG and gestured at the tree. 'Taking your new fiancée for a drive?'

'I see spending your days stuck inside a dusty antiques shop with no customers has not dulled your wit,' Harry said, drumming his fingers on the steering wheel. 'I say, do you mind?' he snapped at Bertie, who was resting one hand on the bonnet of the MG. Bertie jerked his hand away. 'Oh, you blithering idiot. You've left a smudge.'

Bertie took a hankie from his pocket, spat on it and moved to rub out the mark.

'Don't you dare!' Harry's voice tightened into a

screech. 'Step away. Do not touch. Bloody oaf. Let me pass. I'm in a hurry.'

'Of course, express tree deliveries are no laughing matter,' Mr Gilbert said. 'Might I ask what you're doing with a tree in your car at this time of night?'

'As you so expertly deduced, I am delivering a tree. To a friend. Have I broken some law?'

'Almost certainly,' Mr Gilbert said. 'Though I cannot imagine what. Bertie, will you do the honours?'

Bertie hurried to shift a few of the sandbags and jerrycans out of the way and made a point of raising the tree branch they were using as a barrier arm.

'Drive safely,' Mr Gilbert said.

Harry clunked his MG into gear and sped away.

'Toffs,' Bertie said as he lowered the roadblock bar. 'Odd lot.'

'You have no idea,' Mr Gilbert said. 'You know what, Bertie, I think it's time you and I went on patrol.'

Problem Child

Harry knew this road like the back of his hand, which was just as well as it was pitch black and his hooded headlights were less than useless. His passenger, the tree, didn't help. The blasted thing kept shifting over to his side of the car whenever he veered left, its leaves obscuring his view. But it would all be worth it. Soon he would be on his way to the Fatherland, a hero of the conquering Reich. What a day. What an extraordinary few days, in fact. It had all started with Otto Kopp's coded radio message last week. Otto had his feathers ruffled by something or other, and suddenly wanted to take possession of the tree and ordered Harry to bring it to him. Harry had been trying to pin the blasted thing down since Otto first told him of its importance back in Munich, but when your parents own an orchard crammed full of the bally things, it was never going to be an easy task.

He had a stroke of luck, however, when he discovered a map of the orchard in his father's observatory.

It didn't take Harry long to crack the feeble code and discover precisely where the Ur-Tree was hidden in plain sight with all the other apple trees. He radioed Otto to tell him the good news and that he would have the thing uprooted in no time.

'You cannot merely dig up the Ur-Tree,' Otto snapped at him, going on to outline a convoluted excavation ritual that was to culminate in Harry soaking the tree with water heavily spiked with hemlock.

So, there was Harry, halfway through the magical shenanigans, when that impudent thug Klaus came stumbling into the orchard and demanded to know what Harry was doing with a jug, a goblet, an axe, a pestle and mortar, a shovel and a garden fork in the middle of the night.

Harry turned on the charm, explaining that moonlit gardening was a thing in England and Klaus was just in time to help douse the apple trees. The lad looked tipsy and was only too eager to take a gulp of the water Harry offered him. Water prepared especially for the ritual and, of course, laced rather heavily with hemlock.

Klaus took quite some to die, what with the convulsions and all, but Harry kept busy digging up the Ur-Tree, hacking at its deep roots with the axe. By the time Klaus was still, Harry had replaced the Ur-Tree with a look-alike – it really did resemble an ordinary apple tree – and stowed it safely in the cellar, protected with a little black magic. All instructions provided by Otto, of course.

Otto really was the most magnificent man. A

paragon of the Aryan race. Wise, witty and so power-ful. He had introduced Harry to magic not long after they first met, and Harry was delighted to discover he had something of a talent for preparing rituals. Which was a new feeling for Harry, as he had never shown the slightest aptitude for anything other than eating, drinking good scotch and burping 'God Save the King'. It was simply a matter of following Otto's instructions and allowing the power to flow through him. And *what* power. Surrendering to Otto's control started with a sensation of warmth that flushed through Harry, leaving him energised and feeling invincible. It was blissful, but more importantly Harry's taste of Otto's power convinced him that the man was unstop-pable. Who could possibly counter such pure, raw evil? Not the British Armed Forces, still licking their wounds from Dunkirk, not the grim Russians, nor the reluctant Yanks, definitely not three pathetic witches from a tawdry little village in Kent and certainly not Harry's father.

Otto was the attentive, formidable father that Harry had always yearned for.

Of course, he did have a father, but Lord Aston was a selfish ass and over a hundred years old. Only yesterday, he had called Harry to his office in the observatory for 'a talk'. Harry hated the observatory. It was like Kew Gardens in miniature, stuffed with palms and fronds and as stuffy as a greenhouse. His father's glass-domed retreat had been the location for many of their little chats over the years, be it to avoid

Harry's expulsion from Eton, or paying off debtors, angry husbands and the like. But yesterday Father finally confessed all. Harry had to play dumb as his father filled him in on the story of the Ur-Tree and how it had kept him forever young. Harry had to bite his lip to avoid sniggering. Little did his father know that there would be no more Ur-Tree for him. Harry had already slipped a mickey into Father's whiskey and the old man would be unconscious by the end of their tedious conversation. It was as Father revealed that he was considering destroying the Ur-Tree that he became drowsy. Harry knew then he had done the right thing. What made this man think he had the right to destroy something so monumentally useful? Something, let us not forget, that he had stolen in the first place. The sheer arrogance of the man.

Well, he was dead now.

And Harry had pulled the trigger.

It was a moment of madness. The surge of white-hot anger that flooded Harry as the gun went off had felt good at the time, it still felt good now. The gut-twisting pangs he was experiencing now were nothing but nervousness at meeting Otto for the first time since war was declared. It had been so long since he had seen his old friend and mentor and he didn't want to disappoint him.

Harry slowed the MG as he took a tight turn down to the beach for a rendezvous with destiny.

Faye left Lady Aston with her husband's body and sat by the radio desk. Her sobs reverberated off the walls of the cellar. The children huddled together, taking turns to pet Nelson.

Mrs Teach sat upright in deep thought. Charlotte bounced her knee impatiently.

'Where do you think he's gone?' Faye asked in a whisper. 'I mean, where would you take a magic tree if you had one?'

'He's taking it to Otto,' Charlotte said. 'But without the rendezvous point, we have no idea.'

'We don't have any of Harry's hair left, do we?' Faye asked.

Charlotte shook her head. 'Used it all to undo his glamour on the pentagram.'

'There might be something we can use in the house,' Mrs Teach said. 'A hairbrush perhaps?'

Charlotte nodded. 'That's not a bad idea,' she said and got to her feet. The sudden move made the children huddle closer together.

'Where are you going?' Mrs Teach asked.

'I'm going to stop a Nazi spy from delivering a powerful magical object to the enemy,' Charlotte said. 'With a hairbrush. Why, what are you planning?'

'There is a woman in mourning.' Mrs Teach gestured to the cell in the darkness. 'We cannot just abandon her.'

'She'll understand,' Charlotte said. 'We have a job to do.'

'You can be a callous soul.' Mrs Teach bristled.

'If we delay, lives will be lost.' Charlotte said. 'We have to go. Now.'

'Yes, you must.' Lady Aston stepped from the darkness.

Nelson scurried to her side and the children followed him, hand in hand. Lady Aston gave them a wan smile, but her eyes were puffy from crying. Her usual verve was gone.

'My husband and I became aware that Harry had fallen in with a bad crowd. And we knew he had pieced together that his parents were ... somewhat older than he was led to believe.'

'You, too?' Faye said with a gasp. 'Apart from the littl'uns and the dog, am I the only one here who's not over a hundred years old?'

'No,' Mrs Teach snapped. 'You most certainly are not.'

'We met when he first returned from Kazakhstan,' Lady Aston said, dabbing her eyes dry. 'We were very much in love. He told me everything. Said he wanted us to be together for ever. And so I took a bite from the apple of the Ur-Tree, too. We had a splendid life, travelling the world, keeping out of the public eye. No functions, no balls. But people become suspicious of those who do not age. We returned when the Great War began, posting an obituary in *The Times* that the Second Lord Aston had died, trampled by stampeding elephants in India – Thomas always did have a perverse sense of humour – and we arrived as the new incumbents. The war was keeping everyone distracted, so no one took much notice of us, nor asked where we came from. We had Harry soon after. That was something of a surprise. Neither of us wanted children, of course. You will think me heartless to say it, but what use is an heir if one lives for ever? We did our best to love the boy and we swore that we would live normal lives from then on. But once you've tasted the apple, you want more. So we kept our annual ritual and we stayed forever young. Harry began to add two and two when he returned from Eton. We never told him, but he wasn't completely stupid. He became obsessed with finding the tree, and we harboured suspicions that he was consorting with the enemy, so we left him a false trail with maps of the orchard and he became convinced the tree was within its walls.'

'If you thought he was a spy, why didn't you turn him in?' Charlotte said.

'Oh, Charlotte, you never did understand.' Lady Aston shook her head. 'Thomas thought you were extraordinary, did you know that? I was quite jealous of you, early on, but he told me how distant you were. That your own long life had made you cold as stone. Harry is my son.' She looked down at the children gathered around her. 'You think I could report my own flesh and blood to the authorities? Condemn my boy to a firing squad? No, I thought I could talk to him and change his mind. He is a fool and difficult to love, but I do love him. I think that makes us both fools.'

'He killed your husband,' Charlotte said. 'He's more than a fool.'

Lady Aston nodded, and Faye saw a flicker of rage in the older woman's face. For all her protestations of motherly love, Lady Aston looked like she was ready to wring her son's neck. 'He will face justice. I will see to that. But he's no danger to anyone else. He has the wrong tree, and that concerns me more. If he's delivering it to the Nazis ... they will surely kill him for it.'

DAS BOOT

Mr Gilbert slowed the motorcycle, keeping his distance as they followed Harry in his MG Midget. Bertie sat in the sidecar, gripping his rifle and his helmet and trying not to whimper as they left the road and turned onto the bumpy path along the clifftops. Mr Gilbert brought the motorbike to a stop on a byway close to the cliff's edge and shut it off.

'Follow me, Bertie, and keep low,' Mr Gilbert said, shouldering his Sten gun and running in a crouch to a promontory overlooking the sea. There they both lay on their bellies, looking through the sleeping wildflowers to the beach below. The tide was out, revealing a small sandy bay where Harry could be seen pulling a sack-barrow with an apple tree tied to it towards the lapping waves.

'What on earth is that idiot doing?' Mr Gilbert muttered as he peered through his binoculars.

'Can I have a go on the binoculars please, Mr Gilbert?' Bertie asked, mindful that 'a go on the binoculars' had been part of the arrangement when he volunteered to help with the roadblock. It had been something of a deal breaker for Bertie.

'One moment, Bertie,' Mr Gilbert said. 'I just need to fathom what he's—'

'Mr Gilbert, Mr Gilbert!' Bertie patted him on the shoulder with the rhythm of an excited rabbit's foot and pointed out to sea.

The sky was a predawn indigo and the full moon was bright on the still water. A shadow emerged from the depths. A conning-tower, similar to one Bertie had seen at the pictures just the other day, broke the languid sea.

'It's a blimming U-boat!' Bertie squeaked.

Mr Gilbert shushed him and turned the binoculars to the sea. The German Navy submarine surfaced with a chilling silence. A hatch opened on the top of the conning-tower and two figures hurried out. Moments later, a signal was flashing in code from sea to shore.

'He's signalling back,' Bertie said, steering Mr Gilbert's binoculars to where Harry was clicking his torch on and off in response to the U-boat's signals. 'What do we do, Mr Gilbert? Is this it? Is this the invasion?'

'Calm down, Bertie,' Mr Gilbert replied, staying cool and in command, though Bertie did detect the teeniest wobble in the man's voice. 'I think if the Germans were going to invade they would send more than one U-boat. But they're clearly up to something with our friend Harry. Do you know how to handle a motorcycle?'

Bertie's heart raced. This was all a bit too much. A

real U-boat off the coast, so close he could actually see the crew heaving a dinghy off its deck into the sea.

'Bertie, are you with me?' Mr Gilbert's voice broke through Bertie's thoughts.

'Yessir,' he said.

'Good, can you ride a motorbike?'

'That I can, sir. I had a go on my cousin's last summer. I drove into a fence on my first attempt, but soon got the hang of it.'

Mr Gilbert released a shuddery sigh. He glanced over at where the motorcycle and sidecar combination was parked as if it was the last time he was going to see it in one piece.

'Good enough, I suppose,' he said, handing Bertie the key. 'Push her to the road – don't start her up here as the sound will carry – then ride back to Mr Brewer and tell him what we've seen. We need Captain Marshall to send immediate reinforcements and to alert regional command. Understand?'

'Ride to Mr Brewer, tell him to contact Captain Marshall, alert regional command. Roger that.'

'Good lad, now off you—'

A blue light flared off the bow of the U-boat. It formed a bright ball that settled in the raised hand of a dark figure standing in the dinghy.

'What the blazes was that?' Mr Gilbert said, raising his binoculars again.

Bertie didn't quite know what it meant, but he was sure he had just seen some magic, and that meant Captain Marshall and the Local Defence Volunteers would need their own reinforcements. Magical reinforcements.

ℒ

Harry stood on the beach as Otto's dinghy made its way from the U-boat to the shore. Otto stood at the prow, dressed in the deathly black of an SS uniform and holding a magical blue light aloft to show the way. The sky was clear and the dawn light was close by, so Harry wasn't sure the light was entirely necessary, but dear old Otto did like to make an entrance.

Harry didn't mind. He had waited so long for this moment, a few more minutes on a chilly beach wouldn't matter. After a lifetime of being dismissed as a wastrel and a fool he was finally getting the recognition he deserved. And he had worked hard for this, too. Henceforth, anyone who dared to call him lazy would be getting an earful and then some. He had followed every instruction, pursued every lead and clue, and he had delivered, by Jove. It had cost him. Oh yes, he had paid a terrible price. He hadn't intended to actually kill his father, and every so often it made him sick to think of it, but now he chose to reconcile it as an added bonus. Occasionally he felt tugs of what might be perceived as guilt and shame for pulling the trigger, but these were soon swept away by the thrill of knowing that he was a killer. Wherever he went now, folk in bars around the world would nudge one another and mutter, 'He's the one. Murdered his own father for the cause.' Bally right. Harry Aston was a man to be feared and respected.

Otto's dinghy scraped onto the shingle shore. Six grim-faced Kriegsmarine soldiers leapt off the craft, bringing it to a halt. They spread out, forming a semi-circle around Harry and training their rifles on the clifftops. Harry could smell the funk of U-boat life on them; sweat, engine oil and something that might have been boiled cabbage. He was happy to note that none of their rifles were pointed at him.

Otto seemed to float from the dinghy to the shore. He made a twisting gesture with his hand and the blue light vanished, making Harry's ears pop.

It suddenly occurred to Harry that he had no idea how to address the leader of the Thule Society in person. When they first met in Munich four years ago, Otto had started the conversation and all their radio communiques since had been in code and stuck to a strict format. This wasn't exactly the sort of thing they covered in *Debrett's Guide to Etiquette*. Harry went with a jolly, 'Good evening,' and was delighted when he wasn't struck down by a bolt of lightning.

Otto Kopp strode towards Harry, crossing the line from crunching shingle to silent sand. Otto was bald, and his eyebrows shaved. His skin was post-mortem white. He sported a little moustache that wasn't quite as narrow as the Führer's but was close enough for the comparison. He was only five feet tall, but no one ever brought that up and lived to tell the tale. Harry reasoned that Napoleon and Alexander the Great were short-arses and that never did them any harm, so why mock the fellow?

Otto came to a stop before Harry and the tree. His face was still and he didn't appear to be breathing. There were rumours that he was born at the end of the fifteenth century, though he didn't look a day over seventy. Up close, his skin looked as thin as Bible paper, his fingers tapered into nails like talons, and his eyes were dark and pitiless.

'This is the tree?' Otto intoned. His voice had the breathy chill of a tomb.

'As requested.' Harry gestured at the apple tree still tethered to the barrow-sack. 'One legendary Ur-Tree from Kazakhstan, complete with apples at no extra cost.' He ended with a smile. His gap-toothed grin had won him lots of favours over the years. Harry had found it was always good to be jolly in the face of adversity, however big or small. You could smile on the outside and downright despise someone on the inside.

'You followed the extraction ritual?' Otto asked.

'To the letter, dear boy,' Harry said with a nod. He hadn't mentioned Klaus and the hemlock poisoning. And Harry certainly wasn't about to let on that he had left an axe behind for all to see. There were so many tools, and it was all such a rush, he was hardly to blame. No, Otto didn't come across as the sort of chap who needed to be burdened with unnecessary frippery.

Otto stepped closer to inspect the tree, slowly looking from the hessian sack where Harry had stuffed its roots to the highest branches. Harry felt a cold and clammy breeze blow in from the sea. He had been tempted to try a bite from one of the apples before coming here, but there really hadn't been time what with the patricide and all, and besides, it seemed like bad form to get in on the act before handing it over to the client. Harry's time would come, and a long and lustrous life in the Thousand-Year Reich beckoned.

Otto plucked an apple from one of the branches, turned it over in his hand and sniffed it. He looked at Harry from under hooded eyelids before squeezing the apple and taking a small bite. He chewed precisely three times before spitting it out. He tossed the apple to the sand.

'This is not the Ur-Tree,' Otto said.

Something happened inside Harry. His stomach seemed to fall through his body at the same time as his testes shot up into his belly.

'I-I say, w-what?' he managed to stammer.

Otto barked an order and his men all moved at once, turning their rifles on Harry.

IMPERTINENCE

No one had ever pointed a gun at Harry before, let alone six of the things all with their barrels aimed directly at his ticker, which was in danger of conking out any moment now. He couldn't be quite sure what he'd heard. Did Otto really think this wasn't the Ur-Tree?

'I say, old chap, I believe you're mistaken,' Harry said, his hands raised for all the good it did. 'My own father confirmed that this is indeed the almighty Ur-Tree from the foothills of jolly old Kazakhstan. I would ask him to sign something to that effect, but I offed the old chap in order to take it. You see – and this is the thing, Otto, so do pay attention – I murdered my own father tonight to bring this tree to you. So before you start accusing me of any backstabbing or betrayal or trickery, you should know that I have done some dastardly deeds to get to this point. So what say you? Shall we lower the guns and speak like gentlemen? Hmm?' Harry tried his grin again, but Otto wasn't having any of it.

'Your father told you this was the tree?' Otto said, his deathly voice taking a sarcastic turn for the worst. 'Has it occurred to you that he might have been lying?'

'Of course. I'm not a complete blithering idiot,' Harry said, noting that the guns were still pointing at him. He decided to tone it down a bit. 'He did all he could to hide it from me. But I found a map of the orchard. It was hidden away in his observatory, locked in the safe. But I found it and I decoded it and I used it and here we are.'

Otto narrowed his eyes at Harry.

'Otto, my dear chap, I'm on your side. I swear to you this is the genuine article.'

'You're not lying,' Otto said. 'But that does not mean you have not been fooled.' Otto raised his hand and another blue ball of magical energy crackled in his palm. 'We shall test it.'

ॐ

The children were asleep in their beds, exhausted from a day and a night they would never forget. Faye had volunteered to stay with them in case they had any nightmares, but Pinder had come to the room with a request for Faye to join Miss Charlotte, Mrs Teach and Lady Aston in the observatory.

'I don't think I should leave them alone again, Mr Pinder. They ain't out of danger yet.'

'I can ask Doreen to keep an eye on them, if that would help?' Mr Pinder said. 'Miss Charlotte was quite insistent that you join them.'

'Makes a nice change,' Faye said, checking one last

time to make sure the children were in a deep sleep, leaving Nelson on guard before following Pinder down the hall.

He looked as sanguine as ever, his chin held high and his back ramrod straight, despite the earliness of the hour. Faye wondered if he ever went off duty.

Faye dodged over to Pinder as they walked. 'Did you know?' she asked.

'Miss Bright, I have been in his lordship's employ since my fifteenth birthday, and my father served him before me,' he replied, brimming with pride. 'We were sworn to secrecy, of course.'

'Did he ... did he never offer you a bite?' Faye asked as they arrived at the bottom of the spiral iron staircase that led up to the observatory.

Mr Pinder rested a hand on the banister and thought before speaking. 'His lordship was kind enough to offer me the opportunity to partake in the ritual of the apple. More than once, in fact. I refused every time.'

'Why?'

Pinder's eyes darted about, then he leaned in close to Faye. His plummy accent vanished and was replaced by something you might hear in the saloon bar of a pub in Whitechapel on a Friday night. 'Would you wanna wait hand and foot on those two for all bloody eternity? Not ruddy likely. I plan to cash in me savings this August. Me and Doreen have found a lovely bed and breakfast for sale in Herne Bay. We'll run that for as long as we've got our marbles, get married and wear the bedsprings out, if you know what I mean.'

Faye did indeed, but she was so gobsmacked she didn't have the breath to reply.

'Now, get yer backside up there, girl, and then I'll fetch Doreen to keep an eye on the nippers.' Pinder straightened his back and gestured to the stairs. 'After you, miss,' he said, plum firmly back in place.

'Er, yeah, ta,' Faye said, still agog at Mr Pinder's transformation as she began the climb.

They came to a cramped landing. Pinder squeezed past Faye, opened the door to the observatory and they stepped through into its muggy air. Exotic plants filled the circular room, standing in pots or hanging from baskets, their heads drooping down, waiting for the sun to rise. A telescope pointed at the awakening sky, next to an old wooden desk littered with plant pots, twine, secateurs and the like. Lady Aston stood in conversation with Mrs Teach and Miss Charlotte. They were studying a map, trying to deduce the where-abouts of Harry. All heads turned to Faye and Pinder as they entered.

'Thank you, Pinder,' Lady Aston said. As her old retainer made to leave, she added, 'No, please stay. This concerns you, too.'

Mr Pinder inclined his head in a deferential nod, closed the door to the observatory and stood guard, hands behind his back. Faye tensed. Mr Pinder wouldn't be able to fetch Doreen to watch over the children while he was stuck here.

'Faye, Pinder, ladies,' Lady Aston said, leaning back on the desk. 'I've come to an important decision. My day for taking a bite of the apple from the Ur-Tree is today.'

'Today?' Faye's mind scrambled to recall what day of the week it was. 'Saturday? It's the village fair today.'

'Indeed, though of course I will not be making a public show of it. According to the ritual, I must take a bite between sunrise and sunset,' Lady Aston said, then paused for a breath. 'I have decided to honour the decision that my husband and I made and that it will be my last.'

'Oh.' Faye looked to Mrs Teach and Charlotte. 'Does that mean you'll—?'

'I will age somewhat when I miss my appointment with the tree in a year's time.' Lady Aston gave a sad smile. 'It might even finish me off, who knows? Nevertheless, I shall spend my time between now and then making arrangements for the house and my charities and the welfare of the staff and the wounded men here. I will also alert the authorities to what has ...' She faltered for a moment. 'To what has happened to my beloved Thomas. All that aside, I have asked you here, along with Miss Charlotte and Mrs Teach, to take care of a very important task once I am done with the Ur-Tree.' She paused for a moment, folding her arms. 'I want you all to destroy it.'

Faye nodded. 'Right. We're good at destroying things.' She glanced at Mrs Teach and Miss Charlotte. 'We'll have a bonfire.'

'If we burn it,' Charlotte said, 'anyone benefitting from the power of the Ur-Tree will burn with it.'

'Really?' Faye wrinkled her nose in disbelief. 'How do you know this? Did it come with a set of instructions?'

'The two sisters who were guarding the tree in Kazakhstan were very clear. It is protected by their magic.' Charlotte gestured at Lady Aston. 'For a start, we cannot destroy the tree until Lady Aston has passed. If we destroy the tree before then ...'

'She ... she dies?' Faye ventured.

'Correct.'

'Has anyone thought of giving it back to the sisters you pinched it from?' Faye said with a shrug. 'I reckon they'll do a better job of looking after it than we have.'

'Wouldn't they be long dead?' Mrs Teach asked.

Charlotte shook her head. 'They were guardians of the tree, but they had their own magic to keep them alive.'

'That's settled it,' Faye said. 'Back to the sisters it goes.'

'It might have escaped your attention, Faye, but there is a war on. Kazakhstan is controlled by the Soviets and they do not take kindly to foreign invaders. Even if it is just a handful of witches with a tree.'

'We must keep it safe,' Mrs Teach said. 'And then when the time is right we will use a ritual I know of to safely dispose of it. No one will ever use it again.'

'That don't seem right to me,' Faye said. 'You pinch a magical tree from these sisters in Kazakhstan – who, by the way, warned you that it would all end in tears. And now, when it's all gone wrong just like they said it would, you reckon the best thing is to get rid of it so no one else can use it? Has it occurred to you that p'raps the problem ain't the tree, but what you done with it?'

'Is she always this impertinent?' Lady Aston asked.

Mrs Teach, Miss Charlotte and Mr Pinder all nodded.

'Call it what you want,' Faye said. 'I like to think I know right from wrong, and I vote for giving it back to the sisters.'

'Very well,' Charlotte said. 'You can take it to them. It's over there.' Charlotte gestured to the door where Faye came in.

A tiny tree sat in a terracotta pot by the door. Faye hadn't even noticed it among all the lush flora in the observatory. Barely reaching waist height, the tree's bark was a rusty brown and cracked all along its spindly trunk. Five wrinkled and unripe apples dangled from a branch.

'This?' Faye jabbed a thumb at the pathetic plant. 'This ratty little thing is the mythical, magical Ur-Tree that gives eternal youth?'

'Looks aren't everything, Faye,' Lady Aston said.

'One bite from those apples and I'd be on the lavvy for a week, never mind living for ever,' Faye said.

'It wasn't always like that,' Charlotte said. 'Once upon a time it was the tallest tree in the orchard.'

'Is that what Lord Aston meant when he said he got greedy?' Faye asked, and Lady Aston nodded. 'So every time you and him took a bite too soon, the tree lost a branch and now that's all that's left of it.'

'Don't be too hard on them, Faye,' Mrs Teach said. 'Many of us would have done the same.'

'I reckon you're being too kind, Mrs Teach. I don't think I would've done what they did. And I know you, you're a stickler for the rules and you ain't a greedy woman, neither, so—'

'Faye, give it a rest,' Mrs Teach snapped. 'The poor woman's husband was murdered tonight, by her son, who also happens to be a Nazi spy. She's had a day of it already without you laying into her.'

Faye blushed and took a step back. 'All right, p'raps now is not the time, so I'll get off me high horse, but I ain't happy about none of this.'

There was a knock on the door.

'Come,' Lady Aston called. Pinder opened the door and a young woman in riding gear strode in with a folded sheet of paper. She had brown curls and wore jodhpurs and Faye recognised her as one of the girls in Lady Aston's Woodville Mounted Patrol. She handed the paper to Lady Aston. 'Thank you, Grace.'

'We intercepted this on the radio, ma'am,' Grace said. 'Urgent transmission from an LDV radio at a roadblock on the coast road. I heard the young chap and he sounded quite hysterical. Something about a U-boat and Harry.'

Lady Aston scanned the note. 'Private Butterworth. Do we know him?'

'Bertie,' Faye said, her heart suddenly racing. She was surprised by the intensity of her concern for the lad. 'That's Bertie. Where is he?'

The Battle of the
Bramley Apple Tree

Bertie could not have been more relieved when he saw the silhouette of a truck pull up on the coast road and a dozen of his fellow Local Defence Volunteer patrol come pouring out of the back. Captain Marshall led the way, followed closely by Faye's dad Terrence. They hurried to where Bertie, Mr Gilbert and Mr Brewer were crouched on the cliff edge.

'Good Lord,' Captain Marshall said, taking in the U-boat, dinghy, soldiers, Otto and Harry in the bay below. 'Report.'

'They're having some sort of ding-dong over a tree,' Bertie said, then got a shove in the ribs from Mr Brewer.

'Six Kriegsmarine men in total,' Mr Gilbert said. 'One unidentified enemy – the bald chap in the SS uniform – and yes, he does appear to be having a ... disagreement over a tree with Harry Aston down there.'

Captain Marshall raised his binoculars. 'That

really is Lord Aston's lad down there. I knew he was a wrong'un, but I never took him for a Nazi. And what's that blue light all about?'

Bertie wanted to tell them all that it was some kind of magic, but he knew he'd get another dig in the ribs for that. To be honest, Bertie wouldn't have been able to explain it much beyond that. The short, bald man had circled around the tree in the sack-barrow several times, shining the blue light on it. Bertie might have ventured that it was a ritual, but he didn't reckon his captain wanted to hear any such nonsense.

'What do we do, Captain?' Bertie asked.

'They're Nazis.' Captain Marshall lowered his binoculars. 'We shoot 'em, Bertie.'

∅

Harry somehow knew Otto's test would come up blank. Now that he looked again at the tree on the sack-barrow, it did appear to be rather ordinary. But this was entirely Otto's fault. The bald old coot had insisted on rushing the search for the tree. If Harry had just been given a little more time he knew he would have come up trumps. There was no way that Harry was going to take the blame for this, and he would be telling Otto as much any moment now when the ancient wizard confirmed the worst. Oh yes. Otto would soon be apologising and offering Harry sufficient time and resources to do the job properly.

'Bramley,' Otto finally said.

'Beg pardon?'

298

'This is a Bramley apple tree. Quite ordinary. You are a fool, Harry.' Otto gestured to his men. 'Kill him.'

Harry was at first miffed that he wouldn't be able to give Otto an ear-bashing, but as the Germans raised their rifles, he found himself flushed with relief when someone started taking potshots at them from the clifftops.

The men of the Kriegsmarine ran and ducked for cover, and Harry did the same.

⌘

'Fire at will!' Captain Marshall gave the command, and the ranks of the Woodville Village Local Defence Volunteers opened fire with ear-shattering enthusiasm, sending the Nazis below dodging bullets as they rushed to the rocks.

Bertie knew he could not serve on the front lines of the war, what with having one leg shorter than the other, and he'd watched with envy as lads from the village had marched off in their uniforms. One of his pals, Bobby Watts, served on a Destroyer in the Navy, fighting around Norway, and he sent Bertie letters when he could. 'Here's the truth, Bertie, mate,' Bobby had written recently, 'half the time I'm bored out of my tiny little brain, and the other half I can't think for blind terror.' Bertie had wondered what Bobby meant by that, but this evening with the earlier boredom of the roadblock and the present terror of a firefight with highly trained soldiers of the Kriegsmarine, Bertie thought he had a better handle on it.

Bertie hadn't fired a shot yet. He loved Westerns and had often dreamed of being the sheriff of a frontier town, sending no-good varmints packing with a spin of his six-gun. But now that he had the opportunity to open fire on real flesh-and-blood Nazis that had invaded his doorstep, he found it very difficult to actually shoot at anyone. Not that any of his brothers in arms were much cop, either. They were firing like mad, but their aim was pretty poor. Shingle and sand were being kicked up all over the beach below, but not a single enemy soldier had been hit. They were hidden behind boulders, occasionally popping up to return fire which thudded into the chalky cliffs with increasing accuracy.

A few of Bertie's comrades took aim at the bald chap, who strolled to his dinghy like he had all the time in the world, but the bullets swerved around him, crashing into the shingle.

Bertie caught a movement in the shadows. Harry. He was running to where his red MG Midget was parked at the edge of the beach. Bertie took aim. He had the man in his sights. All he had to do was squeeze the trigger. Bertie had encountered Harry a few times. He was a bit of a berk, to be honest, though Bertie couldn't bring himself to kill him, but he had to stop him. Bertie shifted position and fired.

The MG Midget jerked like it had the hiccups, then exploded in a ball of smoke and flame, rising two feet in the air before crashing down again and falling to pieces. Harry's wail of anguish could be heard over the continuing gunfire.

Captain Marshall patted Bertie on the back. 'Excellent shot, Private.'

Bertie didn't want to tell him he had been aiming at the tyres.

'Two explosions in a week,' Bertie found himself muttering. 'First Dougie Allen's garage and now this. I'm a bloody jinx.'

⚹

Harry's beloved MG Midget was no more. He had worked so hard for that car. Begging his father to lend him the money. Now both of them were dead and gone and Harry was having to rethink his immediate future plans in something of a hurry.

He was on his knees when a bright light filled the tiny bay. Harry turned to see Otto raising his hand and generating a ball of light more dazzling than the sun between them and the enemy above. The shots from the clifftop ceased and cries of, 'Can't see a bloody thing!' echoed off the rocks.

Otto's men dashed to the dinghy.

Harry had half a mind to chase after them but reminded himself they'd been rather keen to execute him just a few minutes ago. He would take his chances with the Local Defence Volunteers. Surrender peacefully, tell them he was a double agent and skip town at the first opportunity. Actually, scrap that. Surrendering to a rabble of over-the-hill infantry rejects was too humiliating to contemplate. Harry remembered he had twenty quid in his pocket; that would get him to

London where he could check in with his few remaining fellow fascists. After all his good work, they would surely set him up with a new identity and an allowance and perhaps a new car. Nothing too fancy, though he did have his eye on a lovely Alta Sports Supercharged two-litre Sports two-seater. Not as pretty as the MG, but it went like the clappers.

Harry kept to the shadows. The tide was out, so he could sneak around the bottom of the cliffs and head east to somewhere faintly civilised like Herne Bay or Whitstable and catch the first train to London.

The rattle of an outboard motor came from the dinghy and Harry watched as Otto and his men sped back to the U-boat. The Bramley apple tree remained on the sack-barrow, untouched by the melee. Harry heard voices from above. The Local Defence Volunteers were getting their night vision back and taking potshots at the dinghy, but it was already out of range. Between cracks of rifle fire, Harry heard a new sound. A low rumble like thunder. He didn't much fancy getting soaked tonight, so hurried around the corner of the cliffs to the beach, only to discover the rumble wasn't thunder but the galloping of hooves. Harry curled into a ball as eight horses of his mother's Woodville Mounted Patrol bore down on him.

Captured by a bunch of vigilante jolly-hockey-sticks Girl Guides on ponies was even worse than surrendering to the Local Defence Volunteers. Harry spat sand from his mouth and dusted down his jacket as his mother dismounted her steed.

'Hello, Mater,' he said, grinning that gap-toothed smile. 'You simply won't believe the day I've had.'

He noticed that she wasn't just accompanied by her usual riders. They had three pillion passengers who dismounted and strode towards him. That nosey old bat, Mrs Teach, the common-as-muck landlord's daughter, Faye Bright, and that ghastly witch, Charlotte Southill. They all had the most ungracious look of victory about them. He was about to lay into them when Charlotte took some black powder from a pocket and flung it in his eyes. Harry fell into a deep, dark slumber and, frankly, was grateful for it.

A Warning from Harry

Constable Muldoon was more than a little put out. Not only had he been dragged from his bed at the crack of dawn by reports of gunfire on the coast road, but this incident and the subsequent revelations had generated a mountain of paperwork that would take up most of his weekend. He'd been hoping to take Mrs Muldoon and the little'uns to the Woodville Village Summer Fair later today – he quite fancied himself with the guess the weight of the cake competition (weight assessment was a little-appreciated skill in a police officer) – but the chances of any wholesome family fun had shrunk to nil.

To start with, there really had been a shoot-out on the coast road. Lady Aston handed Harry over to Constable Muldoon to be arrested. Not only had he conspired with the enemy, but he had shot dead his own father.

Lady Aston was accompanied by her Mounted Patrol and Mrs Teach, Miss Charlotte and Faye

Bright, who all claimed they could provide evidence for Harry's crimes.

Captain Marshall and his Local Defence Volunteer rabble could barely contain their excitement as they descended from the clifftop. Even though they hadn't captured the invaders, they had engaged the enemy and sent them packing back to the North Sea. A victory on a par with Trafalgar if their recollections were to be believed.

Miss Charlotte dampened their enthusiasm by making them all sign copies of the Official Secrets Act when they arrived at the Woodville police station. Constable Muldoon supplied the forms from the cabinet in his office. After that, the LDV heroes shuffled off home, saddened that they were unable to share their war story with anyone else in the village. Bertie hung around for a while, wanting to talk to Faye Bright, but she was inside with the other women – all witnesses to be questioned – so Constable Muldoon told him to sling his hook and the boy moped away.

Constable Muldoon officially cautioned Harry, locked him in a cell and had started taking a statement from Lady Aston when a chap from the Secret Service turned up. He didn't say much other than he was here for Harry. Once he had checked the man's identity card, Constable Muldoon sent him down to the interrogation room.

Now he had a new arrival to deal with. A lady from the Caribbean, of all places. She looked oddly familiar to Constable Muldoon, though he couldn't quite place where he had seen her before. She certainly seemed to know him.

'Constable Muldoon, I wonder if you could kindly point me in the direction of Harry Aston, please?' she said when she arrived at the desk. She wore a bright red dress with a matching handbag and looked as if she had popped in on her way to church.

'Might I ask what your business is with Mr Aston?' the constable asked.

'She's with me,' a voice called from down the hall. It was the Secret Service chap. He opened the door to the interrogation room and beckoned the woman towards him.

She took a perfume atomiser from her handbag and sprayed something in Constable Muldoon's face. It had the same comforting aroma as freshly picked tomatoes from his allotment.

'Constable,' the lady said, her voice swirling around inside his mind. 'I don't want to see any paperwork on this. Go home and have a lovely day with your family.'

ȣ

Faye found it odd that they were all crammed in the interrogation room with Harry and no one was saying anything. Faye also found it odd that she was in here at all. She should have been at home with her dad making breakfast and a brew, not stuck in a room with spies and a murderer, but Miss Charlotte had insisted that Faye stay.

The man from the Secret Service was dressed in a dark blue pinstriped suit. He smoked American cigarettes and Faye was sure she saw a gun holstered inside the jacket of his suit. Charlotte had made a few calls as soon as they got to the police station and he had arrived within the hour. He introduced himself with murmurs and handshakes, but that was as far as the small talk went. Since then, he had sat here with Faye, Charlotte, Mrs Teach, Lady Aston and Harry waiting for something, but Faye didn't dare ask what.

All eyes were glaring at Harry who sat handcuffed behind a table. Faye thought he might be in a foul mood, especially after someone blew up his beloved MG Midget, but Harry was remarkably calm. He was still groggy after Charlotte's powder had knocked him out, and he did little more than stare into the corner and occasionally chuckle to himself.

Then Vera Fivetrees strode into the room and Faye realised just who they had been waiting for.

'Good morning, ladies,' Vera said to Faye, Mrs Teach, Charlotte and Lady Aston. The Secret Service man held a chair for her to sit in. 'Thank you, Ian. Good to see you again.'

'Ma'am,' Ian said with a little nod.

'And a good morning to you, Harry,' Vera said, sitting opposite him. 'Though I suspect you've had better.'

'Who the blazes are you?' Harry glared at her through puffy eyes. Faye wondered if Charlotte's powder had stung when she blew it in his face. His usual jolly demeanour was gone. His head bobbed and his words slurred like he'd had a few too many.

'I am Vera Fivetrees, High Witch of the British Empire. What did Otto Kopp promise you, Harry? For handing over the Ur-Tree?'

'He warned me about you,' Harry said, curling his lips into a grin. 'Said you are a housewife with ideas above her station. Said your magic is nothing but crude savagery. If you think he's frightened of you, you're quite mistaken.'

'I have known Otto for many years,' Vera said, smiling. 'He has made his opinion of me very clear on a number of occasions. It's a little game we play.'

Vera's smile vanished, and Faye saw a tiny tremble on the witch's lips. Vera was scared of Otto. Faye noticed that the Secret Service man, Ian, wasn't watching Harry but Vera. Faye wondered who Vera was answerable to, and what would happen if she failed to stop Otto.

'Did he promise to pay off your debts, Harry?' Vera continued. 'Did he offer you a rank of note in the Thule Society?'

Harry twitched.

'It's just as well you had the wrong tree,' Vera continued. 'He would have killed you the moment he had it in his possession.'

'That's where you're wrong. You're all wrong. All of you.' Harry jabbed an accusing finger at everyone in the room rattling his handcuffs. 'Of course, yes, he was trying to kill me, but we all have our little off moments and I was just bringing him round to reason when you lot blundered onto the scene. Otto Kopp is a visionary.' Harry raised his chin like a gap-toothed Mussolini. 'This war isn't about countries and borders and flags. It's about the very future of the human race. We have this one opportunity to scourge humanity of its dregs, to purify and perfect our race and lead us into the future. A glorious empire that will last a thousand years and more, purged of the filth of—'

A slap shut him up. Vera's hand was a blur as she whacked Harry across the cheek.

She glanced at Lady Aston. 'Forgive me, but he was getting out of hand.'

'Quite all right,' Lady Aston replied. 'I was moments away from delivering one myself.'

'This isn't over,' Harry said, dabbing his tender cheek with his fingers.

'I beg your pardon?' Vera asked.

'Otto. He's not done. He knows you won't destroy the tree. That would be bad news for you, wouldn't it, Mother?' Harry grinned and winked at Lady Aston. 'He wants that tree and he will do whatever it takes to get it. He made a promise, you see. That tree is to be a gift. An offering to the only man who matters. Adolf Hitler will take possession of the Ur-Tree and rule for a thousand years or more.' Harry leaned forwards and Faye saw Ian the Secret Service man reach for the gun hidden in his jacket. 'Otto is coming back,' Harry continued. 'When you least expect it, he will return and take what is rightfully his.'

❧

The sun was up by the time Harry was bundled into the back of the Secret Service agent's Austin Sixteen. It was parked around the back of the police station, away from the main road and the sight of any passers-by.

'What will you do with him?' Faye asked.

'We have a safe house nearby,' Vera said. 'We'll continue the interrogation there. He's our problem now. Thank you for your good work, ladies.'

'We should give the tree back,' Faye blurted, getting glares from Charlotte and Mrs Teach. 'Well, who better to look after it than those sisters? They kept it safe for years until you lot came along. Give it back to them and then Lady Aston can stay young for another year, at least. That gives her time to get used to the idea.'

'A noble thought,' Vera said. 'But you don't know Otto the way I do. He really is the most obstinate, pig-headed, arrogant man you will ever meet – and he's up against some pretty stiff competition, let me tell you. He will not stop until he gets what he wants. I'm sorry, Lady Aston. The tree must be destroyed.'

Her ladyship parted her lips and Faye wondered if she was about to object, but all that came was the gentle shudder of a sigh. Lady Aston, tears glistening, nodded with acceptance.

'Give her one day, at least,' Faye said. 'It's the village fair today. She organised the whole thing. Let her have one last day where she can be with her friends and we'll destroy the tree. I promise.'

311

Vera Fivetrees looked to Mrs Teach and Charlotte who nodded in agreement.

'Very well,' Vera said, and Faye felt Lady Aston's hand in hers. She squeezed it in gratitude. 'I will come for the tree at sunset. I will destroy it myself.'

LADY ASTON'S FINAL BITE

The morning sun shone over Hayward Lodge, casting a marmalade glow on the tents and gazebos arranged in the grounds of the great house. Birds gathered on the bunting as if queueing up to gain early entry to the Summer Fair. It wouldn't start till noon, so plenty of time yet.

Lady Elizabeth Aston looked down from the observatory. She'd tried to sleep, but as soon as she nodded off she had a dream where she overslept and woke after dark, and this jolted her awake again. Today would be very busy. No time for napping.

First order of the day: eat an apple. A very special apple. One that would keep her young for another year. Or not. If the tree was to be destroyed today, then what was the point? There was always a slim chance that she would remain the same. No one had ever tried to destroy the tree before, so how did those sisters know what they were on about? Who were they to make the rules?

Lady Aston plucked one of the apples from the tree. Only four remained. One of which was supposed to be for her darling Thomas. He should have been here with her today, holding her hand. Every 19th July, Thomas would take his apple. Every 20th July, Elizabeth would eat hers as the sun rose. Her date was supposed to be 19th – the same as Thomas's. He'd revealed the secret to her on that day, but she had asked to think about it. She recalled Thomas being a little miffed at the time. He wanted them to share the day, so they could enjoy taking the apples together, but she told him that having a day for her and a day for him would make it doubly special.

But for his apple day this year, Thomas had been locked in a cell by his own son, missed his opportunity and left to rot. Harry was her own flesh and blood, but she could never forgive him for this. It was inevitable that his treachery would lead to prison, perhaps even the firing squad or the noose, such was the punishment for treason in wartime. Part of her wanted to campaign for clemency, to allow him to see out the rest of his days in jail to contemplate his crimes. Another part of her yearned for vengeance. Harry had been a rotter from the off. Biting other children, screaming at every nanny who came through the door, always on the verge of expulsion from boarding school for stealing, cheating and lying. They spanked the boy and punished him constantly, but Harry had been heading for a disaster like this his whole life, so perhaps his ending was inevitable. Then again, Lady Aston couldn't help but wonder if she and her husband had spent more time with the boy, they might have got him back on the straight and narrow. Perhaps if they had been a little more trusting then he would have come to understand the power of the tree and the responsibilities that being its custodian entailed.

Oh, who was she fooling? Even her beloved couldn't help himself. Always taking early bites if he saw so much as a wrinkle around his eyes. And every time he did, a branch wilted and fell from the tree. She warned him time and time again, but he just couldn't resist the temptation. And now this was all that remained. An apple tree that any gardener with an ounce of credibility would have put out of its misery years ago, and a few shrivelled apples.

She held the apple in her hand, running her fingers over its wrinkled skin.

She had always known that this day would come, of course, but they had both hoped they could put off the inevitable for a few more years. She was ninety-three, though she looked the same as she did fifty-five years ago when they first made their pact. Together for ever.

Lady Aston bit down on the apple. Despite its looks, it tasted delicious. Crisp and fresh and bursting with flavour, its juices filled her mouth. She chewed some more before swallowing. Despite the incredible magical power of the apple, all she ever felt was a slight warming in her belly, followed by a flush of giddiness. She shook her head clear. Lady Elizabeth Aston would retain her youth for one more year. She raised her face to the rising sun. One important call to make before breakfast, then the preparations for the day's festivities could begin.

THE WOODVILLE
VILLAGE SUMMER FAIR

Woodville had a busy calendar of annual events, start-ing with wassailing on Twelfth Night in January, hen racing and Pancake Day in February, followed by the wife-carrying race in March. Easter often coincided with bun day or worm charming in April. Maypoles and morris dancing were synonymous with May Day. Gurning competitions and bog-snorkelling came every June, and bottom-slapping day was of course always the first Tuesday in August. The nettle-eating contest brightened every September, and All Hallows' Eve concluded October in an appropriately ghoulish fash-ion. Guy Fawkes Night and tar-barrel racing were the highlights on November 5th, and December brought Christmas, clock-burning and much, much more.

The first Woodville Village Summer Fair was organised in July 1919 as a means of raising funds for those soldiers wounded in the Great War. It was a modest affair on the village green – a beer tent, horticultural displays, a ducking stool and a coconut shy were the highlights – but it had raised over two hundred pounds and all agreed that it should become an annual event. Lady Aston took over its organisation in 1935 and it had become something of a spectacular occasion, with fairground attractions and the beginning of the Miss Woodville Pageant. Girls between the ages of sixteen and twenty-one were invited to enter and they had to face three challenges. First was to carry a sack of hops for one furlong in under a minute. Then they had to scythe ten square feet of corn stalks and bind them into sheaves. Finally, they had to pull a pint of stout with a good head and down it before the others.

Faye had won last year, beating the favourite Milly Baxter, but that girl had no clue how to pull a pint and was a danger to herself when it came to using a scythe. Word was, however, that her sister Dotty – an altogether more practical girl – had put extra practice in, egged on by her father, and she was odds-on favourite for this year's title.

Today, retired champion Faye Bright was helping her dad in the beer tent, though she could have done with more than the few hours of fitful sleep she had managed since Harry had been taken to a safe house for interrogation. Luckily for her, Dougie Allen was on hand and had more than enough energy to heft barrels and tankards from the cart to the tent. He happily chatted away to anyone who would listen as he bustled back and forth, but Faye and her father were finding it awkward to come up with a subject of conversation that wasn't covered by the Official Secrets Act.

Lady Aston passed through the grounds as everyone was setting up. She hadn't asked Faye to come back to the house to look after the children, which had saddened Faye. She wanted to reassure them that everything was fine now that Harry was safely locked away. Though she had to wonder what would happen to them when her ladyship was gone. Not to mention a house full of wounded soldiers and staff suddenly without someone to pay their wages.

Faye made an offhand comment about how cheerful Lady Aston looked, all things considered.

Terrence shushed her immediately.

'What did I say?' Faye asked.

'"All things considered"?' Terrence repeated her words back at her, as if that explained everything.

'Wot?'

Terrence lowered his voice to a hush. 'Have you forgotten last night's shoot-out? The arrest of Harry? What if someone heard that and asked you what you meant?'

'She's been through a lot, that's all I'm saying. It's public knowledge that poor Klaus died here a few days ago.'

'And what about the not-so-public knowledge?'

'People will start asking about Harry and Lord Aston sooner or later, Dad. If she doesn't set the record straight then rumours will do the job for her, and they'll do it badly.'

Terrence was frowning at her. 'What about Lord Aston?'

'Oh.' Faye shuffled on her feet. 'Of course, you wouldn't know about that, would ya?' She leaned closer and whispered, 'He's dead.'

'What?'

'Murdered by Harry.'

'When? And what over?' Terrence stopped himself. 'Should you be telling me this?'

'Probably not. They're keeping it quiet till after the fair.'

'Oh, my good Gawd.'

'What are you getting so worked up about?'

'I don't like keeping secrets.'

'Then maybe you shouldn't have signed the Official Secrets Act.'

'I didn't have much of a choice.'

'It's fine. Just keep it under your hat.'

'Keep what under your hat?' Dougie Allen asked as he returned with more barrels on a barrow.

'Dotty Baxter is odds-on favourite to win Miss Woodville this year,' Faye said before she'd even realised it. She tapped the side of her nose and gave Dougie a wink. 'I'd stick a few bob on, if I were you.'

'Ooh, thanks very much,' Dougie said, hurrying off to get more barrels.

'I reckon I'm good at this secrets malarkey.' Faye smiled, shoving her hands in her pockets. 'I might have a go at being a spy. I mean, if George Formby can do it ... What do you think?'

'Do what you like, just leave me out of it.'

'You kept Mum's secret from me all those years.'

'I've told you before, it wasn't a secret. I forgot.'

'You forgot Mum was a witch?'

'She told me to tell you when you was old enough to understand. First off, I had no idea when that was, and by the time I remembered, you'd found out anyway.'

'You ain't cut out for this, are you, Dad?'

'I just want to run my pub. You, on the other hand ...' Terrence gently grasped Faye's shoulder. 'I don't expect you to stay behind the bar for ever, Faye. I've got Dougie and all sorts who can help me out. I know you want to do good and if you can do that with the sort of witchery your mother had, then fine. Just ... promise me you'll stay safe.'

Faye tried to speak, but found her breath kept catching in her throat, so she gave her dad a hug instead.

❧

The fair was opened at noon with a short speech from Lady Aston, followed by the first of many tedious displays from the Woodville Morris Men prancing about with their sticks, bells and handkerchiefs like a bunch of idiots. They had a long-standing and bitter rivalry with the bell-ringers. No one on either side could recall how it started, but Faye resented that they got to do their ridiculous cavorting whenever they wanted, but bell-ringing was banned for the duration of the war. As far as Faye was concerned, they should be let out on May Day for one display and that was it.

Even Bertie – the friendliest chap anyone could ever hope to meet – cast a scowl their way as he skirted around them. He spotted Faye, gave her a wave and limped over to the pub tent.

Faye's heart began to play a jazzy paradiddle and her lips began to tingle. Bertie for his part had eyes like an owl's and was dressed in his Sunday best of a slightly baggy blazer, trousers with a crease sharp as a steak knife and shoes shined to perfection.

'Bertie, my lad,' Terrence said, a little too loudly for comfort, 'you do scrub up something neat, don't you?'

Bertie made a nervous noise somewhere between a giggle and a whimper.

'I think ...' Faye started, suddenly unsure of what she really did think. Then a word came to her. One from a conversation she had with Bertie the other morning in the bell tower. 'I think you're smashing,' she said, and Bertie's face broke into a smile. 'Bertie and I are going for a little wander round,' she told her father. 'I'm sure you can cope.'

'I'll manage,' Terrence said, then wagged a warning finger. 'You two behave yourselves.'

'I refuse to dignify that comment with a reply,' Faye said as she and Bertie strode away towards the heart of the fair, her father's cheeky cackle fading into the crowd.

'Should we ... y'know ... hold hands?' Faye surprised herself by asking this, and immediately regretted it as Bertie's smile vanished.

'Oh, er, I, uhm. If you want to?' he said, looking at the villagers milling around them.

Faye took in the face of every passer-by, waiting for a glance of disapproval or mocking laughter. 'Oh, who cares what they think.' Faye reached out and took Bertie's hand. The skin was dry and rough from working on his dad's farm. She gave it a little squeeze.

'We promised ourselves a jolly old time, Bertie, so where shall we start?'

A Jolly Old Time

They started at the coconut shy, where Mr Paine had indeed painted little Hitler moustaches on each of the hairy husks. Despite such an irresistible target, Bertie and Faye missed every one of them. After that they entered the three-legged race, tumbling into last place. Faye bought them a lemonade each as a consolation prize, but someone bumped into her and she spilled some on Bertie's trousers, making it look like he'd had an intimate accident.

And they laughed through every joyous moment.

'How do you do it, Bertie?'

'Do what?'

'Remain so cheerful when it all goes wrong?'

Bertie took a sip of lemonade as he thought about Faye's question. 'Mr Gilbert said something last night that rang true—'

Faye leaned closer. 'You're not about to break the Official Secrets Act, are you, Bertie? I know you were made to sign it, too.'

Bertie went wide-eyed at the very thought. 'Oh no, I'd never do nothing like that.'

Faye leaned closer and winked. 'I heard you blew up Harry's car.'

Bertie blushed and gripped his lemonade, neither confirming nor denying.

'Good lad.' Faye gave his hand a squeeze. 'So, what did Mr Gilbert say that rang so true, Bertie?'

Bertie composed himself and cleared his throat before proclaiming, '*This too shall pass.*'

'Eh?'

'It's what Mr Gilbert told me. You'll have bad days, and then you'll have good days. It all evens out in the end. Yes, I look like I've wet meself, but on the other hand, I get to be with you and have a laugh.'

'That sounds very wise,' she said.

'Makes sense to me,' Bertie said. 'It reminds me of my uncle Nick's foot—'

'I think I've heard this one, Bertie—'

'Preserved in vinegar, it was, and he kept it on the mantel for all to see. If you gave him thruppence, he would take the lid off and let you see the bone—'

Faye stood on her tiptoes and kissed Bertie on the cheek.

'What ... what was that for?'

'To shut you up.'

And it worked. They wandered around the stalls admiring the floral displays and baked goods and all Bertie could manage was an occasional stunned whimper.

They found Mr Gilbert and Mr Brewer by the hook-a-duck game. A dozen bright yellow wooden ducks bobbed in a barrel with little hooks screwed into their heads. Mr Gilbert and Mr Brewer, dressed in matching white-and-red-striped suits topped with straw boaters, held little fishing rods, trying to snare a duck and win a prize.

'Afternoon, gents.' Faye gave them a wave.

'Faye, darling, how are you?' Mr Brewer said, then looked the still-gormless Bertie up and down. 'What's wrong with him?'

'He's having a jolly old time,' Faye said, giving Bertie's hand a squeeze.

'Excuse me, gents,' Bertie said in a dry whisper. 'I quite fancy another one of those lemonades. Can I get anyone else one?'

'Ooh, yes please,' Faye said, letting his hand slip from hers and noticing Mr Gilbert's smile as she did.

'How did your digging on the Höch sale go?' she asked the gents as Bertie meandered off to the lemonade stand.

'I'm sorry to say it all turned out to be a bit dull,' Mr Gilbert said.

'Yes, we were hoping for smugglers and skulduggery,' Mr Brewer added, 'but in the end it was a simple auction. Nothing scandalous to report.'

'Oh, that's a shame,' Faye said.

'Höch, as we knew, disowned the piece,' Mr Gilbert continued, 'and was ready to throw it out when a friend suggested she donate it to a school.'

'Can you imagine that thing in a school?' Mr Brewer grimaced. 'Poor darlings would have suffered the most dreadful nightmares.'

'Which they did, by all accounts,' Mr Gilbert said, 'because the school sold it off to some gentlemen's club or society or something in Berlin and after a year or two the owner put it up for auction.'

'And that's when Lady Aston bought it.' Mr Brewer shrugged and took a sip of his pint. 'Dull as dishwater, sadly.'

'Well, the chap she bought it off was something of an eccentric,' Mr Gilbert said. 'Bit of a magician or something.'

Mr Brewer wrinkled his nose. 'What was the name of that odd little society?'

'The Thule Society?'

Faye's mouth turned dry. 'The fella who auctioned it,' she began, 'was he called Otto?'

'Uncanny.' Mr Brewer narrowed his eyes. 'Otto, yes, Otto ... Kopp. Do you know him? Faye, are you all right?'

'How does an auction work, gents? Would Lady Aston have met Otto?'

'Oh, probably not,' Mr Gilbert said. 'It would all have been done through the auction house. Are you sure you're all right, Faye?'

'Yeah, I'm fine.' Faye's mind whirled. If Lady Aston had bought the Höch from Otto, and Harry had been turned by Otto – did that make Lady Aston an accomplice?

'Is it anything we can help with?' Mr Brewer asked.

'I'm not sure,' Faye said. 'Sorry, gents. Go and enjoy the fair. Don't worry about me.'

Mr Gilbert and Mr Brewer bade her farewell and strode off to enjoy the fair's attractions.

'RAVVEL TIGGIT, GUV'NOR?'

Faye's train of thought was derailed by Rudolf's voice. She looked up and spotted Magda, Max and Rudolf moving around the bustling crowd selling raffle tickets. They were accompanied by Mr Pinder, who shadowed them like Churchill's bodyguard, and Nelson who barked at anyone who didn't buy a ticket.

'RAVVEL TIGGIT, GUV'NOR?' Rudolf cried, and they were doing a roaring trade as folk gathered around them, buying whole strips of tickets.

Max spotted Faye and waved. She waved back and beckoned them over. Max nudged Magda and Rudolf and the little lad came running over with a book of raffle tickets.

'RAVVEL TIGGIT, GUV'NOR?' He thrust the book at her.

'Ooh, what are the prizes?' she asked.

'We are fortunate enough to have an abundance of home-made jams, ciders, chutneys and knitwear,' Mr Pinder said, and Faye wondered how much he knew about Lady Aston's connections to Otto Kopp, though it wasn't the sort of thing you could just crowbar into a conversation about raffle tickets. 'Though we have discovered that the prize that most tantalises is the bunch of bananas kindly donated by Mr Castle the village grocer.'

'*Yes-we-have-some-bananas*,' Faye sang, handing over a shilling and getting a strip of numbers in return. 'Mr Pinder,' Faye began, speaking in a confidential voice, 'has Lady Aston ever mentioned the name Otto Kopp?'

Mr Pinder's eyes looked up as he thought. 'Not that I recall.'

'He's … he's an art dealer. She might have bought some stuff from him in Germany.'

'Oh, I never joined her ladyship on any of her sojourns to the continent,' Mr Pinder said. 'But she met countless art dealers, Miss Faye. That world is a mystery to me. May I ask your interest?'

'It's nothing. Never mind.' She was being silly. Mr Pinder was right. People bought and sold art all the time and never met. It was just a coincidence. What mattered was the children were happy.

'How are you all?' she asked them, unsure if they understood her exact words, but Magda nodded.

'Good,' the girl replied. 'We are good.'

Faye's heart fluttered to see them smiling again. After all they had been through, no one deserved a lovely summer day at the fair more than these three. And now, with Harry whisked away by Vera Fivetrees and the Secret Service, they were safe. Finally, Faye could offer them the hug she had longed to give them.

Faye crouched down and held her arms wide, and they all bunched together for a hug.

Faye's world swayed around her.

The children's bodies lie in the leaves in the moonlit wood. Their eyes stare at nothing. No breath passes their lips.

HARRY HEARS A VOICE

They wanted to know about Otto. Where they had met, where he was now, what he wanted. They had tried everything, but Harry remained silent. That Charlotte woman had suggested interrogating him at a safe house – hers, to be precise – and it sounded anything but. The car took them to the edge of the wood, and they proceeded to her cobwood cottage by foot. Harry was tied to a chair by Ian the Secret Service man, and Charlotte blew smoke in his face, but the only effect it had on Harry was to make him giggle. This annoyed the woman in charge, Vera Fivetrees or whatever her ridiculous name was. Their magic wasn't working.

Otto was protecting Harry.

Harry knew this because Otto was talking to him. At least, he hoped it was Otto and not just the voices of insanity. This voice was able to curse in fluent German and kept using Harry's name. It had to be Otto. That, and the overwhelming magical power that paralysed Harry to the point where he could barely blink, convinced him it was the man himself. Once Otto stopped ranting at Harry for his blunders, he calmed down.

Give them nothing, Harry. Concentrate on your breathing, and this will soon be over. Stare at the wall, and I will have you out of there before you know it.

This so-called safe house had to be Charlotte's cottage. The pentagram and runes on the wall were a dead giveaway. Harry had heard the rumours that she lived out here in the wood, but he had no idea it would be so grim and dingy. No wonder she was always scowling.

Mrs Teach and Faye Bright had been left at the police station. It was just Charlotte, Ian and Vera trying and failing to interrogate him. Ian spoke of magic with familiarity. He and Vera Fivetrees appeared to be old colleagues and debated the next-best way to extract information from Harry. Ian favoured magical torture. Vera Fivetrees was set against it. Good for her.

I know where the Ur-Tree is, Harry.

It was all Harry could do to stop himself blurting out, 'How?'

It doesn't matter how I know. I just do. You can redeem yourself, Harry. You want to do that, don't you?

Harry nodded. Charlotte narrowed her eyes at him while the others bickered. She suspected something.

It's in your father's observatory, Harry. It was right in front of you all the time.

Otto then ranted at some length about Harry's ineptitude. Thankfully, most of it was in German. He calmed down once more.

I need you to get it for me.

Harry said nothing, but pulled at the rope that bound him. How was he supposed to do anything tied to a chair?

I understand, but be patient and I will free you from your restraints.

Vera and Ian came to some form of agreement. She stood and took what looked like a ceremonial knife from her handbag. Whatever Otto was thinking of doing, he had better do it now.

Very well, Harry. It is time.

Harry felt a familiar blissful warmth. Otto's power was building inside him.

I am going to need to borrow your mind for a while. And your body.

⁊

Charlotte tried to block the sound of Vera and Ian squabbling over their preferred method of interrogation as she watched Harry. Since they'd arrived at her cottage he had changed. His eyelids were heavy, his jaw hung slack and he slouched in the chair. Charlotte had given him a little something to subdue him when they arrived, but it should have kept him lucid. He looked like he was ready for the funny farm.

'Your methods are too crude, Ian,' Vera Fivetrees said, standing and opening her bright red handbag. 'I prefer something a little more subtle.' She took a cere-monial knife with an opal handle from the bag.

'That's subtle?' Ian's eyes bulged at the glinting blade.

'I just need a prick of blood,' Vera reassured him. 'I have a little recipe for a broth that will soon have him talking.'

Harry spasmed and his chair rocked.

'Vera.' Charlotte stood and took a step back.

Harry began to shake all over and his eyes looked to Charlotte, pleading with her before they rolled back. Little bubbles of spittle gathered at the corners of his mouth.

'Is this ... magic?' Ian asked, reaching for the gun holstered beneath his jacket.

'Not mine,' Vera said. 'Charlotte. Do you have any—?'

Harry's chair cracked and he fell to the floor. With an inhuman howl, he raised his arms, breaking free of the rope binding him.

Charlotte reached for the powder in her pockets but was shoved aside by Harry before she even saw him move. As Vera's knife was smacked across the room, Ian managed to draw his gun but had a chair-leg crack down on his skull for his troubles. Ian fell to the ground in a heap.

Harry crashed out of the cottage door and into the wood.

SAFE AS HOUSES

Faye was awoken by the distant sound of cheers.

She struggled to open gummy eyes and found herself on a bed in one of Hayward Lodge's great halls. This was becoming a habit, and not one she liked. Through the windows the sky was a dusky lilac. The clock said ten past eight. All the beds around her were empty while their occupants enjoyed the fair.

Bertie sat beside the bed, every bit of him clenched with worry, but it melted away as Faye stirred.

'Faye, what happened to you?' He leapt from his chair to help her sit up, then gave her a glass of water.

'Long story,' Faye said, taking a sip. There came more cheers and applause from outside. 'What's going on?'

'I think Dotty Baxter's just been crowned Miss Woodville,' Bertie said. 'She played a blinder with the corn-sheaving.'

Faye recalled her own win last summer. Miss Woodville was one of the last big events of the fair, topped only by the raffle. How long had she been out?

'The children,' she said, seeing their still bodies lying in the wood in her mind's eye.

'Faye?' Bertie took her hand. There was no self-consciousness this time, just real concern.

'Magda, Max and Rudolf. The German kids. Where are they?'

'After you conked out, Mr Pinder took them away. The little one was really upset.'

'I have to find them.' Faye swung her legs off the bed, planted her bare feet on the varnished woodblock floor and nearly collapsed as her knees gave way. Bertie was fast, grabbing her under the arms and helping her back onto the bed. 'Blimey, I'm more wobbly than I thought.'

Matron looked up from her desk. 'Ah, you're awake, lassie.' She stood and strode over to Faye and Bertie.

Faye pulled Bertie close to her. 'Find those kids, Bertie. Bring them to me. They're not safe.'

'What about you?'

'I've got Matron. They need you. Now, go!'

Bertie gave Faye one longing look before dashing out of the hall and back to the fair.

Matron took Faye's pulse and checked the watch pinned to her tabard. 'Spinach,' she said.

'Wossat?'

'If a wee girl finds herself fainting on a regular basis, I recommend spinach to raise the iron levels. And seeing as this is the second time I have attended to you in a week, I see a spinach-heavy diet for you in the future, young lady.'

Faye grimaced at the thought.

338

Matron released Faye's wrist. 'You look well enough. How do you feel?'

Faye's head was still swirling a little, but her mind was gently slotting back into place. The vision of the children, lifeless and cold, made her shiver. 'I've been better,' she replied.

'RAVVEL TIGGIT, GUV'NOR?' Rudolf's voice echoed from another hall, followed by a bark from Nelson.

'I have to go,' Faye said, hopping off the bed and finding her legs to be a lot less wobbly than before. The hall tilted to one side a little, but she could remain upright. She sat down again briefly to wriggle on her socks and shoes.

'Spinach, lassie,' Matron said, handing Faye her specs. 'Spinach, nuts and liver. All good sources of iron.'

'Thanks, Matron. I'll go and find some now,' Faye said, getting to her feet and swaying slightly. 'If my friend Bertie comes back, tell him to wait by the beer tent with my dad,' she said as she dashed out of the hall.

She found herself by the nook with the telephone at the bottom of the stairs.

'Rudolf?' she called.

'*Ja?*' came the distant reply from above.

'Wait there.'

Faye took the stairs two at a time and was quite out of breath when she found Mr Pinder, Nelson and the children about to go up the spiral steps to the observatory. Rudolf was carrying a tin box with a lock and was flanked by his siblings. Mr Pinder was holding a ring of keys and he took a step back when he saw Faye come panting towards them.

'Miss Bright, are you well enough to move about?' he enquired, genuinely concerned. 'We were most distraught at your sudden collapse. Your friend Bertie and I carried you directly to Matron.'

Faye's giddiness returned and she reflected that she might have got out of bed a little too quickly for her own good. She rested her hands on her thighs and took a few breaths.

'I'm fine, thank you,' she managed between gasps. 'The children ... I don't think they're safe, Mr Pinder. I can't explain why, but—'

'Lady Aston was kind enough to fill me in on the traumatic events of the last twenty-four hours, Miss Bright. I can assure you that the safety of the children is of the utmost importance. I have been by their side this whole day.'

'Good, good,' Faye said, getting her breath back. 'Mind if I stay with you?'

'Not at all.' Mr Pinder gestured up the iron steps. 'We're about to lock today's takings in the safe. You're more than welcome to join us.'

'Ta.'

Mr Pinder led the way, followed by Rudolf. Both Magda and Max looked at Faye with concern. Nelson sniffed her boots. She gave the children a smile, which she hoped would reassure them, scratched Nelson behind the ear and brought up the rear.

When Mr Pinder reached the door to the observatory he gave a *shave-and-a-haircut* knock and waited.

'What's the password?' came a familiar voice from the other side.

Mr Pinder cleared his throat and glanced at Faye. 'At your request, Mrs Teach, the password is "knockers".'

Locks and latches clicked and the door swung open. 'Enter, friends,' Mrs Teach said, welcoming them into the observatory. Once they were all inside, she locked the door once more.

The air under the glass dome was as thick and tropical as ever and Faye fanned herself. 'Fancy seeing you here, Mrs Teach,' she said. 'Any chance you could open a window? It's like the Devil's own sweat-box in here.'

'I'm looking after that thing.' Mrs Teach gestured to the Ur-Tree sitting in a pot in the corner. 'Vera Fivetrees told me to keep it safe at all costs. An open window is an invitation to burglars.'

'Ain't you hot?'

'My dear, when you get to my age, sudden warm flashes are a daily hazard. This greenhouse fug is nothing, I can assure you.'

Faye inspected the Ur-Tree. Four apples. One fewer than yesterday. Nelson gave the Ur-Tree a quick sniff, deciding that it wasn't even worth peeing on.

'Her ladyship had her apple, then,' Faye said.

'It would seem so.'

'If we left it to grow, do you think it would sprout more apples?' Faye asked.

'Apples hardly *sprout*, but yes, I think it would,'

Mrs Teach replied. 'I find that nature tends to work perfectly well when left to its own devices.'

Mr Pinder placed the takings from the village fair in the safe, closed it with a heavy clunk and attached the ring of keys to his belt. 'Our business here is done, Mrs Teach,' he said. 'If you could kindly do the honours.' He gestured to the door to the observatory.

'I would be delighted,' Mrs Teach said, taking the large iron key and slotting it into the lock. Nelson began barking at the door and Faye's ears tingled. With a couple of swift turns of Mrs Teach's wrist, the door was unlocked and swung open to reveal Harry Aston waiting on the other side, his eyes glowing like the moon.

HERE'S HARRY!

Faye kicked the door shut before the children began screaming. Mrs Teach was quick to slide the key back in the lock. The door jerked as Harry rammed into it. All of them – children included – leaned against the door to keep him out while Mrs Teach turned the key. Nelson growled.

'Where the bloody hell did he come from?' Faye said as Harry began pounding the door. 'Did you see his eyes?'

'He's possessed,' Mrs Teach said. 'I suspect his friend Otto is playing him like a puppet.'

'Can he do that?' Faye asked.

'If half the stories I've heard about him are true, then yes.'

'We should rush him,' Faye said. 'There's six of us and one of him.'

'And there's only one Ur-Tree. That's what he's after.'

The door rocked again and again as Harry threw himself against it with superhuman strength. Nelson barked with every thump.

'We should destroy it,' Mrs Teach said.

'We cannot.' Pinder waved in the direction of the grounds. 'Lady Aston's drawing the raffle prizes.'

'He's right,' Faye said. 'We can't have her dropping dead or turning into an old biddy in front of the whole village. Wouldn't be good for morale.'

'Or her ladyship,' Pinder insisted.

'That an' all.'

'Then we stay put,' Mrs Teach said.

Rudolf cried out in fear as one of the panels in the door cracked.

'Doesn't that hurt him?' Faye asked.

'Otto is using Harry as a battering ram,' Mrs Teach said. 'I don't think the man's physical welfare is his top priority.'

Another panel cracked and Harry gave an agonised groan. Magda and Max held each other tight.

'Hold on a mo'.' Faye dashed away from the door, jumped up onto the desk, clambered onto the top of a bookcase and reached to open one of the glass dome's windows. It was sticky – someone had painted over the window and its frame – but Faye kicked the handle with her boots and it swung open in a shower of paint flakes. The fresh air was a relief after the stuffiness of the observatory.

Faye reached out below. 'Someone hand me the tree.'

'What are you doing?' Mr Pinder asked, jolted away from the door by another of Harry's blows.

'I'll use the tree to draw him away from here.'

'Take the children with you,' Mrs Teach said as one

344

of the door panels splintered and fell away. Harry's crazed face could be seen through the crack. 'Put them somewhere safe, then go. I'll hold him off.'

'Magda, Max, Rudolf!' Faye beckoned them to her. 'Get the tree and come with me. Nelson, you too, boy.'

Rudolf was the first to scramble up the desk and the bookcase. Faye took his hand to help him through the window and onto the roof.

Rudolf lies pale in the moonlight, eyes fixed and devoid of life. A creature growls in the darkness.

Faye gritted her teeth and shook the vision away. Nelson was next, and he wagged his tail as Faye handed him to Rudolf.

Another panel on the door cracked and Harry's arms reached through, grabbing Mr Pinder around the neck.

Magda and Max climbed on the desk and tossed the tree up to Faye. She caught it by one of its feeble branches, which snapped, and the Ur-Tree fell back to the carpet.

'Oh, sod it.'

Max leapt off the table. The tree's pot rolled by Mr Pinder's feet, which were kicking as Harry tried to throttle the poor man.

'Here you are, love.' Mrs Teach handed Max the tree, then stood back. She took a box of matches from her handbag. 'Don't dawdle, boy. Go!'

Max gave Magda the tree and clambered up onto the table then the bookcase.

Mrs Teach lit a match. Closing her eyes, she muttered a few words, holding the match to her palm. The flame brushed against her skin, but she did not even flinch.

Harry screamed in surprised agony, releasing Mr Pinder and shaking his hand.

Magda tossed the tree in its pot to Max, who was able to hand it to Faye. She passed it through the window to Rudolf, the apples on its branches bobbing excitedly. Max helped Magda onto the bookcase. Faye squeezed through the window, then reached back to help the siblings, bracing herself for another vision as she took their hands.

Max and Magda huddle together in the roots of an oak and the shadow of a terrible beast looms over them.

Faye puffed her cheeks out as she cleared her head. The beast was an unwelcome addition to the visions, but she couldn't worry about that now.

As she reached for the window to close it, she saw Harry crash through the door, his face a bloody pulp, the skin on his hand burned red. He threw Mr Pinder into a yucca plant and knocked Mrs Teach to the ground.

Faye slammed the window shut, gripped the Ur-Tree's bulky pot under her arm like a rugby ball and slid down the tiles to the crenellations that lined the perimeter of Hayward Lodge's roof.

'Follow me,' she called to Nelson and the children

and they didn't need telling twice. Behind the crenellations was a narrow walkway, and Faye didn't want to
think about what would happen if she were to trip and
fly head-first over the edge.

They ran to the furthest corner of the house, away
from the hurly-burly of the fair, though a few wounded
soldiers and nurses were wandering about.

'There,' Faye said.

Three storeys below them, a row of hospital beds
were arranged facing the orangery. All but one was
unoccupied. Faye recognised the chap in the last bed.
It was the fellow who had played chess with Max, but
she couldn't for the life of her remember his name.

'Bingo!' Max called, accompanied by Nelson barking. The soldier looked left and right.

'Bingo, up here!' Faye cried, and the man craned his
neck and shielded his eyes from the setting sun.

'Max,' Bingo said. 'What are you doing up there?'

The sound of breaking glass came from the observatory dome, and Faye glanced back to see a figure
tumble onto the roof. Harry. He had a shard of glass
stuck in his leg and was howling in pain.

'Harry's after us, he's been conspiring with the
Nazis,' Faye said.

'Is this a joke?' Bingo scrunched his face in confusion.

'No, it bloody isn't,' Faye said as Harry cried out
again. She and Bingo looked over to see Harry pulling
the shard of glass from his leg. 'It's life and death,' Faye
said. 'We need to get down. Is there a ladder?'

'Jump,' Bingo suggested.

'Are you mad? We'll break our necks.'

'Onto the beds. Wait.' Bingo shifted off his bed, grabbed his crutches and made his way to the next bed. 'I'll pile up the mattresses.'

Faye glanced over her shoulder. Harry was limping towards them, foaming at the mouth and waving his arms. Nelson growled a warning at him.

'There ain't time,' she said.

Bingo looked up at Harry closing in on them. 'Make time. Do a few laps,' Bingo said, then cried, 'Help, help!' to the few people gathered by the orangery.

'Go, leg it,' Faye told the children. Led by Nelson, they sprinted off along the walkway that ran around the whole house.

If it wasn't so terrifying, it would have been farcical. Faye, carrying a little apple tree in a big pot, trailing three children and a dog as they were chased by a limping posh English gent possessed by a Nazi occultist.

At the first corner, Faye nearly lost her balance and had to bounce off one of the crenellations to right herself. At the corner that overlooked the grounds they could see the whole of the fair. Lady Aston was indeed still picking raffle tickets from a drum being turned by Captain Marshall. As Faye came to the next corner, she noticed a few people looking up at them in curiosity, but no one said anything.

They were on the home straight and Faye saw that Bingo and a handful of others had piled the mattresses high and were propping them up.

Bertie was with them, too. 'You found them, then?' he called with a smile.

Faye also spotted Dotty Baxter with her Miss Woodville crown of summer flowers, and Mr Gilbert and Mr Brewer who beckoned at them to jump. Magda was first, leaping into the air without hesitation, landing with all the poise of a girl who excelled at gymnastics. Max was next, less graceful as his legs kicked in the empty air. He landed on his back and rolled off the mattress into his sister's arms.

Rudolf stood trembling, tearful, shaking his head. Nelson dipped his head and tail.

'I know, matey, it's scary, but ...' Faye looked back to see Harry turning the final corner, his every breath accompanied by a groan of pain. He would be on them in seconds. 'Incoming!' Faye hollered, dropping the Ur-Tree and its pot onto the pile of mattresses. It landed dead centre. Clods of soil flew about, but it remained in one piece. Bertie grabbed it and held it close.

'Rudy, gimme a hug.' Faye held her arms out and the little boy ran into them.

Rudolf screams as a beast pounces on him in a flash of fangs.

Faye was not enjoying these new visions in the slightest, but she did seem to be able to shake them off more quickly. Nelson nuzzled up to her and she held boy and dog tightly.

'Do you trust me?' she asked as Harry's uneven foot-steps limped closer.

'*Ja*,' Rudolf's voice whispered in her ear.

Heart thumping, Faye put one foot on the crenella-tions, preparing to push herself, Nelson and Rudolf off before Harry could get them.

But Harry didn't want them. He wanted the Ur-Tree. Without breaking his stride, he ran off the edge of the roof of Hayward Lodge, legs kicking and arms reach-ing out for the tree in Bertie's grip. He fell short of the pile of mattresses, landing face-first on the grass next to them with all the grace of a sack of spuds.

Those gathered winced, turned away and mut-tered phrases along the lines of, 'Bloody hell, I bet that smarts.'

Faye released Rudolf and Nelson and peered over the edge. Harry remained still.

'Oh, blimey,' Faye mumbled to herself before calling down, 'Someone check his vitals. There's a house full of nurses right in front of you. Get some help ... and a ladder.'

Mr Gilbert crouched by Harry and rolled him over. Harry's face was an unhealthy lilac, marbled with burst blood vessels. The gap in his teeth was much wider now.

Mr Gilbert placed his ear close to Harry's mouth. 'He's still breathing,' he said, sounding astonished.

Matron came hurrying out from Hayward Lodge, followed by a nurse. They rushed to Harry's side and started checking his vital signs.

Mr Brewer arrived with a ladder, which he extended and propped up against the side of the house for Faye and Rudolf to descend. Faye clambered down with Rudolf clinging to her back and Nelson tucked under one arm.

As they reached the ground, Max and Magda rushed to hug them. Faye braced herself for another vision, but surely it was all over now? Harry was done for. They were safe.

The ground swayed beneath her feet.

All three children lie in the moonlight. Faces pale. Eyes dead and staring. Their throats ripped out by the beast.

Faye shook her head clear. There was something else this time. As if someone was trying to get inside her mind. *Not ruddy likely, mate.* She pushed it away. It came again, like smoke through a window. She concentrated harder, finding the power within her to create a psychic bubble around herself, Nelson and the children. Faye thought she heard someone cursing in German, then the smoke cleared and her mind was her own again.

She blinked her eyes open. The children were looking up at her in concern. Nelson was whimpering.

'Sorry about that,' she told them, trying to smile it off. 'Another funny turn. Let's thank our friends, shall we? Bingo, Mr Gilbert and Mr Brewer, we can't thank you enough for—'

Faye froze. Harry was sitting upright and staring at them with glowing white eyes. Matron and the nurse stood on either side of him, also staring with glowing white eyes.

Mr Gilbert, Mr Brewer, Bingo, Bertie – not Bertie! – everyone was the same. All standing stock-still, eyes white like the full moon, staring at Faye, Magda, Max and Rudolf. As one, they slowly marched towards them.

VILLAGE FAIR OF THE DAMNED

Faye was about to tell the children that they should run like the clappers, but they were already halfway to the drive, Nelson taking the lead, by the time she opened her mouth.

'Good idea,' she said, picking up the Ur-Tree in its pot and racing after them.

This had to be Otto. His control of Harry had failed, so why not turn the whole village against them instead? That foggy feeling in Faye's head was Otto trying to take over her mind, but she was able to push him away, and the children's close proximity to her must have saved them, too.

One of the walking-wounded soldiers came hobbling out of a side door, his eyes glowing white. The children dodged around him and Faye did the same. Was everyone at the fair under Otto's control? Everyone in the village? Dad? Mrs Teach? Charlotte? She hoped her fellow witches had been able to fend him off. Faye had half a mind to seek out Mrs Teach, who might still be in the observatory, but the idea of entering a house full of these human puppets held little appeal to Faye. They had to get as far away from here as possible.

She rounded the corner to the house's grand gravel drive. Her bicycle was propped against the fountain, but that wasn't big enough for all of them. There were a couple of vans parked side by side. Faye ran to open their doors, but they were locked.

Faye heard the *scrunch-scrunch* noise of feet on gravel and spun to find dozens of possessed villagers slowly closing in on them, arms reaching out.

Then she saw it.

Mr Gilbert's motorcycle-and-sidecar combination. It was a peculiar thing. Black with gold trim, the sidecar had comfy padded seats and was shaped like the upturned prow of a canoe. And it was their way out of here.

'Get in!' Faye ordered the children, who clambered in while Nelson watched. It was a tight fit, with Magda and Max flanking Rudolf whose little head popped up between them. Faye handed the pot with the Ur-Tree to Magda, who tried to shove it deep into the footwell of the sidecar, but Rudolf was in the way and made it clear that he didn't appreciate being squashed by a pot.

'That won't work,' Faye said. 'Out, everybody out.'

They all had to clamber out again, then Faye put the pot with the Ur-Tree in first.

'Back in, that's it, squeeze yourselves around it. Stop complaining.' Nelson was last. He jumped up into Rudolf's lap. Faye closed the sidecar's little door on them, then ran around to the motorbike part of the contraption, aware that the possessed villagers were just a few yards away. She noticed that all their legs moved at the same time at the same slow pace. Faye couldn't begin to imagine how much power Otto had to control so many people at once.

'Hold tight,' Faye said, gripping the handlebars and swinging her leg over the saddle, trying not to think about how she'd crashed Mrs Pritchett's motorcycle just the other day. This one was different. It needed an ignition key for a start, and there wasn't one in the key slot.

'Oh, bumcakes,' Faye muttered as the children began to ask questions in German. She didn't understand the words, but got the gist of, 'Why aren't we moving?' and, 'Are those people going to eat us?'

Faye caught sight of Mr Gilbert in his white-and-red-striped suit and straw boater among the throng. Such a lovely man, now a mindless goon controlled by magic. He must have the bike's ignition key on him. It was too late for them to get out and run. Rudolf's little legs would be worn out by the time they got to the end of the drive. They needed that key and soon.

'Wait there, I'll be right back,' Faye said, hopping off the bike.

The children wailed and begged her to come back, not understanding what she was doing. To test the advancing crowd, Faye move to the left and then to the right, but they all ignored her. All they wanted was the tree.

Faye dashed into the shuffling mob, skipping

between them, careful not touch anyone. That's when she noticed Mrs Teach among them with her eyes glowing white. *Otto got her, too!* Faye saw Dougie Allen, Dotty Baxter, Milly Baxter, Mr Paine, Doreen.

'Dad.'

There he was at the back. Terrence Bright, the life and soul of the Green Man pub, moving as mindlessly as the rest of them. Faye's heart broke a little.

Pushing aside her fear and sadness, Faye came to Mr Gilbert, who looked straight through her towards the tree in the sidecar. She reached into his right pocket. There was a pair of riding goggles, which she decided to keep and left them hanging from her wrist for now. In his left pocket was a packet of cigarettes and a box of matches. Filthy habit. She tossed them away and tried his inside jacket pockets. Bingo. Two keys on a ring. She took them out and twirled them around her finger. Mr Gilbert's hand snapped up and grabbed her by the wrist. Faye winced and tried to prise his fingers off her, but he gripped all the tighter.

'Sorry, Mr Gilbert, I do like you an' all, but—' She stamped the heel of her boot on his toes. Mr Gilbert opened his mouth in shock. No scream came, only a hiss of air from the back of his throat, but he released his hold on her.

Faye dashed to the motorbike as the children beckoned her to hurry up.

She got back on the saddle, wriggled the goggles over her eyes, put the key in the ignition, turned it then put all her weight on the kick-starter.

The engine coughed, then died.

'Oh, no, no, no, no, no.'

Faye took a breath and tried again. It growled for a little longer before dying again.

The villagers were just feet away now, their grasping hands getting closer and closer.

'*Faye.*'

They all spoke at once, like a drowsy church congregation reciting a prayer.

'*Give us the tree, Faye. Give us the tree and they will all return to normal. This can be over in moments. Give us the tree.*'

Faye wasn't the praying type, so she swore under her breath, turned the ignition key and gave it one more kick. The exhaust popped and a puff of black smoke coughed out of the back, but the engine kept firing. Faye nudged the accelerator tentatively a couple of times – not wanting to repeat her mistake on Mrs Pritchett's Douglas – released the brakes and let her rip.

The motorcycle hurtled down the drive, leaving the village horde far behind.

HARRY BECOMES USEFUL

Little more than a glimmer in his own mind, a squatter in his own body, Harry was suffering. His thoughts kept fading to darkness, his hearing was reduced to an incessant whistling and his vision was nothing but grey shadows.

Harry ...

Otto's voice came to him, crackling like a faint radio signal.

Harry, I have some very bad news.

Oddly, this didn't perturb Harry. He was getting quite used to the recent string of flops and failures from Otto's camp.

You have been very foolish, Harry.

Of all the rotten things to say. If that didn't just take the biscuit. After all Harry had done for the blighter.

I thought I could trust you to do one simple job, but even that was beyond you.

This was the last straw. Harry had just flung himself off a rooftop for this utter cad, breaking several ribs and his nose in the process, and if this was all the thanks he was going to get—

I'm afraid you have outlived your usefulness.

Harry wanted to protest, but his mouth would not move. His mind kept blinking like a broken filament in a light bulb.

I have one final task for you.

Something stirred in Harry. A final spit of defiance. The synapses in his brain sent signals to roar and rage and smash, but all that came out was pitiful groan.

I need you as a host.

Just as Harry was wondering what that might mean, his shins snapped in two. Pain came to him in blinding white flashes. His thighs bent backwards with a crack like falling timber, his hips fractured, his spine twisted into a hunch. Heat filled Harry's body as new bones grew and stronger muscles twisted around them. His skin boiled red – the same red as his beloved MG Midget – pustules forming in every folli-cle. He spat loose teeth from his mouth as razor-sharp fangs scythed up through his gums. His jaw jutted out and the first nubs of horns split his scalp. His coccyx spasmed and broke then sprouted a forked tail.

The last thought Harry had before the demon consumed him was that at least he had been on the winning side. Jolly good, what.

⚥

Faye drove at full throttle, eyes on the road, leaning into the bends, not daring to look back. The children huddled together with Nelson as they hurtled past the church.

There was some light in the sky, but sun was gone. The Green Man was closed, as were all the shops. The village's cobbled streets were dark and empty. Everyone was at the fair.

Faye slowed the motorbike as they trundled down the Wode Road. They couldn't stay here, but she didn't want to go into the wood, the vision of the dead children and some kind of terrible beast ripping their throats out still fresh in her mind. Faye needed to find Charlotte and Vera Fivetrees. Even if Harry had somehow escaped their debriefing at Charlotte's cottage-cum-safe house, they had to be alive. Only they would be strong enough to resist Otto's control. Faye reasoned that if Harry had escaped, then they would come to the village and perhaps the police station, where they could lock themselves safely away.

She brought the motorcycle and sidecar to a stop at the bottom of the road by the police station. The engine had been coughing since they left Hayward Lodge and she feared they were running low on petrol. There was no gauge on the bike, so she twisted the petrol cap off, wincing at the eye-watering whiff of gasoline. She shook the whole bike from side to side. In the moonlight, she could just about see the last few liquid ounces of petrol slosh about in the bottom of the tank. This wouldn't get them out of the village, let alone to another town. She would have to fill up at Dougie Allen's ... Oh no. Can't do that, silly girl. It was still warm from exploding earlier in the week. Where else could they go?

The silence in the village was total and eerie. Only one thing for it.

'CHARLOTTE!' Faye called at the top of her voice as she replaced the petrol cap.

The children started shushing her.

'MISS CHARLOTTE! VERA FIVETREES!' Faye called their names over and over, and the children became more and more upset. Faye waved them into silence. 'Wait, I heard something.'

Footsteps echoed off the cobbles. Someone was approaching from Unthank Street.

'Charlotte?' Faye called. 'Is that you?'

Nelson barked as Mr Paine, tall and broad in his ARP helmet, lumbered around the corner. His eyes glowed white.

'*Do not run, Faye.*' Otto's voice came from her friend's mouth. '*Wherever you go, we will find you. I have eyes everywhere.*'

Faye felt a cold chill in her belly.

More footsteps. The door to the police station creaked open. Charlotte, Vera Fivetrees and Ian the Secret Service chap shuffled down the steps, their eyes white as Charlotte's hair.

'*Give us the tree,*' Charlotte said with Otto's voice. '*Give us the tree and this will all be over.*'

'*I have something coming for you, Faye,*' Vera-Otto said. '*Something very special.*'

Nelson was barking incessantly now, and Rudolf

patted Faye's arm then pointed towards Saint Irene's Church. The sound of padding feet was getting closer and closer. Faye wondered if Otto had worked out how to make all the villagers run at once and a horde of possessed friends were about to surround them, but what she saw was much, much worse.

A four-legged creature pounced onto the roof of the church's lychgate. Its skin was a scalded red, covered in blisters. Fangs jutted from its jaws, horns curved from its head and a forked tail swung lazily. It had the same white eyes as the villagers and it looked straight at Faye with an ancient and evil glare.

Faye twisted the bike's throttle, turned in a circle and hurtled down Gibbet Lane.

'*Oh, your little motorbike might be fast,*' Charlotte-Otto called after her. '*But the Jäger can hear your heartbeat a mile away. It can smell the blood in your veins. The Jäger is a hunter, Faye. There is no hiding place.*'

But there was one place they could hide. Faye knew exactly where to go, but it was deep in the heart of the wood.

HIDE AND SEEK WITH A DEMON

The motorcycle ran out of petrol just short of where Gibbet Lane met the path leading into the woods. Faye brought them to a juddering halt, swung herself off the saddle and opened the sidecar's door.

'Move your arses, we haven't got much time,' she told the children, but they remained firmly ensconced in the sidecar.

Max began complaining and pointing further down the road. He wanted to get as far away from here as possible, which Faye completely understood, but she didn't know the German for, 'We're out of petrol and that demon dog thing is going to eat us soon if we don't get a move on,' so she hauled the children out one by one. Nelson and the Ur-Tree were out last. Faye held it under her arm, its few remaining apples swinging about, and pointed to the wood.

'I know a safe place. I need you to trust me. Do you trust me?'

Nelson sniffed at her boots and nuzzled against her

leg. Rudolf seemed to understand and nodded with vigour. '*Ja,*' he said.

A demonic howl came from the village. It was far too close for comfort, but it helped put a little vim into the children's pace as they entered the wood.

Faye tripped as the ferns grew thick around her ankles. Nelson kept dashing ahead and then hurrying back as if to check that he was going in the right direction. Magda, Max and Rudolf all held hands, walking quickly but carefully in a single-file crocodile.

The Ur-Tree felt heavy in its pot, and as Faye got back to her feet she wondered if she shouldn't just destroy it now. For all she knew, Lady Aston was already possessed by Otto or worse. She might even be dead already. Or why not just hand it over in exchange for the safety of the children?

Otto Kopp, that's why. Call Faye prejudiced, but she just couldn't bring herself to trust a Nazi occultist. If she gave him the tree, he would surely kill them. If she destroyed the tree, he would kill them out of revenge. Her priority was the children's safety and the preservation of the tree.

Another howl. Faye dared to glance back the way they had come. Above the wood swifts darted about, feeding on insects. In the gloom of the forest, she could see eyes glowing. The villagers were closing in. She realised that if Charlotte had seen which direction Faye had driven off in, she would know where they were going, which meant that Otto and his demon dog might know, too.

Rudolf squealed. The corpse of a badger was slumped against a tree, animated by the maggots writhing inside it. The boy kept wailing, giving away their position to any predators in the wood.

The Jäger howled again, closer now.

'It's in the trees,' Faye said. 'It's coming.'

She took Rudolf by the scruff of the neck and yanked him away from the dead badger. The path was narrow and steep, lined by waist-high brambles. They were nearly there.

'Faster, children, faster,' she said between breaths.

Faye caught glimpses of the horizon where the sky was still pale and ghostly, but above them it was a deep-sea blue, streaked with clouds dyed pink. The moon was out, too. Full and bright. The strangeness of a midsummer evening's twilight.

They stumbled into the clearing with the standing stones. The children instinctively knew this was their destination and huddled together, Nelson at their feet, standing guard.

They were asking Faye questions, but she couldn't understand what they were saying and had to ignore them. She moved to the head of the slaughter stone and looked for the moon.

She could see its light behind a purple cloud. A very slow-moving cloud. Would this even work if she couldn't see the light of the moon?

The Jäger howled again, much closer now. She could hear Otto's voice calling for them. *'Faye. Children. We promise not to hurt you. All we want is the tree.'*

Faye raised her hand to the sky, closing her eyes.

The children's voices rose in pitch as they heard the rapidly padding feet of the Jäger. She wished they would be quiet while she tried to concentrate. As the cloud passed by, she could feel the energy of the moon in the palm of her hand. She swiped her hand but lost it. Faye spat a curse, took a breath and started again.

Ferns shook as the Jäger drew closer and closer. Faye could feel the children's eyes on her. She could not let them down. Not after everything they had been through. Not after everything she had promised. It could not end like this.

She felt the energy of the moon once more and tried not to panic. She thought of what Bertie had told her.

This too shall pass.

Was he wrong? If the Jäger found them, the pain would not pass.

But the sun would still rise tomorrow, and the moon ...

The moon was never late.

The moon was everything.

The moon was in Faye's hand.

Gently, she brushed it aside, and it disappeared.

THE STANDING STONES

The stones shone the same white as the vanished moon. Everything outside the circle of stones was a void of endless black.

'What happened?' Magda said.

'Where did the moon go?' Max looked at the darkness around them. 'The wood? Where is it all?'

Faye gawped at them. 'You can speak English?'

The siblings shared a look.

'You're speaking German,' Magda told Faye.

'No.' Faye shook her head and gestured at the glowing stones. 'I think there's a little bit of magic happening here.'

Magda turned to her youngest brother. 'Rudolf, do you understand Faye, too?'

'I need to go pee-pee,' Rudolf said, crossing his legs.

'You'll have to do it here, Rudolf,' Faye told the boy, and he nodded with a big smile, delighted to finally understand her. 'Turn your back if you're shy, but do not step outside the stones. That's a big no-no. Understand?'

Rudolf nodded and shuffled over to the smallest standing stone. Nelson joined him and raised a leg in sympathy, peeing on the Ur-Tree.

'I'm not sure that's entirely respectful . . .' Faye raised a finger to object, but boy and pup were already piddling. 'Never mind.'

'Why did you bring us here?' Max asked.

'And what has happened to the moon and the sky and the wood?' Magda craned her head up. 'Where are we?'

'This is a safe place,' Faye said. 'As long as we stay in here, we can't be seen or heard by anyone else.'

A snuffling noise came from outside the stones and Faye's heart almost stopped. A shadow on all fours slowly padded into the circle of stones. The same black as the void around them, its nose swept across the ground like a dog seeking a scent. The Jäger moved from stone to stone, getting closer and closer to Rudolf and Nelson. The boy buttoned his shorts up, wiped his hands on his trousers, and whimpered. The dog barked.

The Jäger carried on sniffing.

'You see?' Faye pointed at the thing as it moved out of the circle of stones and melted into the blackness. 'It can't even smell Rudolf having a widdle. We'll be all right, so long as we stay in here.'

'How long will that be?' Magda asked.

'Till the moon is gone, I suppose,' Faye said. 'A good few hours yet.'

'Then we will live,' Max said, sitting and crossing his legs.

Magda joined him. 'How can you be so sure?'

'To win at chess, you must be patient. That demon dog is not patient. I can be patient.'

'The dog isn't the only thing after us,' Faye said, sitting with them. Rudolf and Nelson snuggled together. 'The whole village is. They're being controlled by a man called Otto Kopp, a ...' Faye faltered, wondering how you describe a Nazi occultist to children.

'He is a very bad man,' Magda said. 'Bald head. Piggy eyes.'

Faye blinked. 'You know him?'

'He bought art from our mother,' Max said. 'She told us he cheated her.'

'He owes us many marks,' Magda added.

'He stinks of sauerkraut,' Rudolf declared.

'Sounds charming,' Faye said, thoughts coalescing in her head. 'He knew your mother, he moved in artsy-fartsy circles, he turned Harry and he sold the Höch to Lady Aston. I'm beginning to join a few dots here.'

Two more shadows stepped into the circle of stones and Faye felt a cold chill in the pit of her stomach. One of the shadows was tall and elegant, the other pear-shaped and moved daintily. Miss Charlotte and Mrs Teach.

'Faye.' Magda's voice was a whisper. 'They are your friends.'

'They are witches, too?' Rudolf held Faye tighter.

'Yes.' Faye nodded as the two shadows moved to the head of the slaughter stone. 'But they ain't themselves, if you know what I mean.' She got to her feet. 'Stay here,' she told the children as she placed herself between Miss Charlotte and Mrs Teach and the tallest stone in the circle.

'What are they doing?' Magda asked.

Charlotte raised her hand, as did Mrs Teach.

'They're trying to bring the moon back,' Faye said, her heart racing as she also raised a hand. 'Now be quiet, I need to concentrate.'

She closed her eyes and felt for that tickling sensation in her palm. She had to find it before Miss Charlotte or Mrs Teach did. Faye put aside all fears and distractions, stayed calm and found it in moments. She held it in her hand.

Faye dared to open her eyes. Charlotte's head jerked about as she tried to understand why she couldn't move the moon. Mrs Teach took a step back, dropped her arm and raised it again. They did this over and over, and each time the shadows became more and more agitated until they lowered their arms and slumped away, their heads bowed in shame.

Faye allowed herself a smile. She kept the moon in her hand until she was sure they were gone, their footsteps fading into the long ferns.

More shadows came and went, passing through the stones as they searched for the children and the Ur-Tree.

Faye sat with Magda, Max, Rudolf and Nelson, leaning up against the tallest stone. They talked to stay awake, swapping tales of friends and family, some long-gone. Faye told them about her mother, her book and the strange events with the crow folk last month.

The children's stories were all about running away

from danger. It was all they had known since they left Berlin. Faye asked them about before the war. Max and Magda remembered school and their friends, but those memories came with tears. Rudolf said he could not remember anything before they were thrown into the street. He held Nelson closer. The day caught up with them eventually. Faye felt her eyes growing heavy, and they slept.

⌀

'Faye? I say, Faye.'

The voice cut through Faye's slumber and she jerked awake. Nelson was licking her hand. The children began to fidget as they awoke.

'Faye? Are you there, dear?' It was Lady Aston. Her voice came from the darkness, accompanied by the occasional movement of a horse's hooves in the ferns. 'It's me, Lady Aston. Do please tell me that you and the children are unharmed.'

Faye checked her wristwatch. 5am. The sun would be rising soon. But when would the moon disappear? She wasn't sure, but knew they didn't have long.

'I've come to a decision, Faye,' Lady Aston said. 'We must destroy the Ur-Tree. We cannot let it fall into enemy hands. Give it to me, Faye, and we will destroy it together.'

'That's Lady Aston,' Magda whispered.

'She doesn't sound like the others,' Max said. 'She's not being controlled by Otto.'

'We can go home,' Rudolf said, getting excited.

'Hang on, let's think about this,' Faye said, a knot of sadness twisting in her belly as she realised something dreadful. 'Max is right. She's not like the others. Why has Lady Aston been spared? And how did Harry know that the Ur-Tree was in the observatory? You were there with me. He escaped from Charlotte and Vera Fivetrees and came straight to the observatory. He'd been looking for that tree for ages, and suddenly he knew exactly where to find it. Who told him?'

'Otto?' Magda shrugged.

'And who told Otto?' Max said, catching on.

Faye pointed to where Lady Aston's voice continued to call to her from the darkness outside the stones. 'She did,' Faye said, feeling sick with betrayal. 'She bought art from Otto and she probably met him – he's the one who turned Harry, after all – and she had the means to contact him. The radio in the cellar. They both want the same thing, don't they? They want the Ur-Tree to stay in one piece. Otto wants it as a gift for Adolf, and Lady Aston wants to live for ever.' Faye took a breath, a wave of sadness washing over her. 'And after Harry failed Otto, who better to try and tempt us out of hiding than our friend and guardian Lady Aston?'

'Why would she do that?' Magda asked in an appalled whisper.

'That thing.' Faye gestured at the Ur-Tree. 'We've got her life in our hands, and she's desperate.'

'She could have just given it to Otto, so why—'

'She sacrificed a pawn,' Max said. 'If Harry stole the

tree, no one would blame her. She can still be a lady in her big house and ride her horses.'

Lady Aston's voice came trilling through the darkness. 'Faye? Children? Are you there? Let's destroy the tree and we can all go home and have some of Doreen's spotted dick and custard, hm?'

Faye's belly gurgled. As tempting as another portion of Doreen's splendid pudding sounded, she wasn't falling for it. 'My dad told me something the other night,' Faye said. 'How some folks are all smiles and sunshine when they want something from you, then toss you away when they're done. I think Lady Aston is giving us the smiles and sunshine bit here.'

'Lady Aston is a bad witch,' Rudolf said, and Nelson growled in agreement.

'No, Rudolf,' Magda said, resting a hand on her little brother's shoulder. 'She's a bad person. Witches, I trust more than her.'

The shadow of a woman on horseback moved into the centre of the stones.

'Is it my imagination or is it not as dark around us as before?' Max said.

'The sun will rise and the moon will be gone soon. Up, stand up,' Faye said, getting to her feet. The children followed. 'We're not safe here any more.'

Lady Aston's shadow dismounted the horse. She was joined by the shadows of the Jäger, Miss Charlotte and Mrs Teach.

'They're not here,' Lady Aston said.

'*They are.*' It was Otto's voice. It came from the

mouths of Charlotte and Mrs Teach. *'This is the only place they can be. We must be patient. In a few minutes, the power of the moon will be gone, and they will be ours.'*

'Where can we go?' Magda asked.

'Out there,' Faye said, pointing to the darkness around them.

'You said we should never do that,' Max said, and Faye recalled Charlotte's warning about it being a place for only the most advanced practitioners. Faye could barely manage basic candle magic.

'We can't stay here,' Faye said.

'You don't even know what's out there,' Magda added.

'Only one way to find out.' Faye hefted the Ur-Tree in its pot with one hand. She looked to Magda. 'You said you trusted me?'

Magda nodded.

'Then follow me,' Faye said.

They stepped out of the circle of stones into the darkness.

A LITTLE KINDNESS . . .

Every step was like standing on a springy mattress. The dark was endless and there was no way of telling up from down apart from knowing your feet were below and your head was on top. The children held hands. Faye gripped the Ur-Tree in its pot. Nelson sniffed around their feet.

The moon was here. Lonely and bright, drifting like a child's balloon. Faye could feel its cold and infinite stillness.

Sitting cross-legged under its light was a slight, bald man dressed in a purple cloak. Eyes closed, his arms were outstretched like a puppeteer's. His eyebrows were missing and he had an almost Hitler-like moustache.

Faye's heart nearly popped from her chest. After all their running and hiding, she had led the children straight to him. They edged closer to her.

'You must be Otto Kopp,' Faye called to him, her voice oddly muted in the void.

'Faye Bright, you have come to me,' he replied in his

high, breathy voice. He opened his eyes and lowered his arms. 'You have saved me much effort. I thank you.'

''Salright,' she said with a sniff, trying to sound like this had been her plan all along.

'I have many questions.' Otto floated to his feet and a tendril of moonlight drifted with him. A tether between him and the moon. He noticed Faye staring at it. 'Its power enables me to control everyone in your little village. From simple folk to your witch friends,' he explained. 'Yet you and these children evaded me. You must be most powerful indeed.'

'You've got no idea, sunshine,' she told him, trying to disguise the wobble in her voice. She jabbed a thumb towards the children. 'I was hugging this lot when you made your move. I think you'll find a little kindness can be a lot stronger than hate.'

'Oh, please. You make me nauseous,' Otto said with a grimace. 'No, you have an innate talent for magic, Faye Bright. Much like your mother. You are far more powerful than your friends realise.'

'I doubt that very much.' Faye's belly tightened at the mention of her mother and she wondered how he knew her.

'When they finally discover this, when your friends see you for what you really are, they will resent you, Faye Bright. They will become afraid of you, and they will turn on you.'

'We're not all like you.' She glanced down at the children who were watching Otto wide-eyed, like mice cornered by a cat.

'Not all, no.' Otto walked in a wide circle around them, a delicate thread of light connecting him to the moon. 'Though plenty are. This world, my country, your village have just enough petty hate and vindictiveness to feed my dog, and it is very, very hungry.' A smile crept across Otto's face.

Faye's stomach turned. She had met enough folk who were happy to get by on hostility alone. People who loved nothing more than a fight and someone to blame for their woes.

'I've seen what happens to people like that,' Faye said. 'They turn out twisted and bitter.'

'Yes, how marvellous.'

'Well, if that's how you want to end up, that's down to you.' Faye recalled what Mrs Pritchett had told her on the roof of Saint Irene's bell tower. 'Me, I prefer to bring a little goodness and light into the world, if you know what I mean. There's plenty more good folk than bad. We just don't make as big a stink as people like you. Your time has come, but you won't be around for ever.' She was reminded of what Bertie had told her. 'All things must pass, and all that.'

'Here, that does not apply,' Otto said. 'Here, everything ends and nothing begins. Eternal darkness. For you, Faye Bright, the darkness will never pass, and you will never find your way home.'

As he spoke, she realised her mistake. While she was arguing with this idiot, she should have been destroying the Ur-Tree. She shifted it from under her arm and reached to snap it in two.

Otto flicked his wrist and the sliver of moonlight that snaked around him and the moon cracked like a whip. It snatched the Ur-Tree from Faye and delivered it into his grasp.

'I see you brought me a gift. Thank you.' Otto held the pot at arm's length.

The children stepped back from Faye, eyes darting between her and Otto. Faye felt sick to her stomach. How was she supposed to protect them from that sort of power?

'Only four apples. How pitiful.' Otto placed the pot at his feet and admired it. 'Nevertheless, the Führer will be delighted.' He glanced at Faye and turned his nose up at her. 'Perhaps you are not as powerful as I had imagined. Farewell, Faye Bright. Children. When I leave, I will take the moon with me and you will be left in total darkness for all eternity. Don't worry, the first few centuries are the worst. After that, you'll—' Otto gave a sudden whelp of pain. Nelson had clamped his teeth around the little bald man's Achilles tendon. Something snapped and Otto fell to his knees by the Ur-Tree.

Magda dashed to snatch it up, running in a circle around Otto. He reached for her, but the girl was fast, tossing the tree – pot and all – to her brother. Faye held her breath, hoping that Max would remember how to catch. He reached out, clamping his hands around the pot and bringing it in to his body like a slip fielder catching a good outside edge. He staggered a bit but kept it safe and hurried behind Faye.

'Nice catch, Max,' she told him. 'Excellent throw, Magda.'

Rudolf whistled and Nelson stopped gnashing at Otto and scampered back to the boy's side.

Faye felt a swell of pride. While she had been exchanging pointless banter with the Nazi nut job, the children had concocted their own plan *and* put their burgeoning cricketing skills to good use.

They gathered around Faye as Otto writhed, clutching his heel.

'If you've done your Achilles tendon, you need to see a doctor, mate,' Faye told him. 'And be quick about it. You'll be in a cast for weeks. Happened to poor old Tommy Anderson in the football team at school. He was limping about for months.'

Any hope that Otto might take Faye's anecdotal medical advice was dashed when he turned his hand in the darkness. Faye felt a breeze and a presence behind her.

Nelson began to bark. The children wailed.

Faye spun to find the Jäger slowly padding towards them, glaring at her with bloodshot eyes from under its brow.

'Harry, so good of you to join us,' Otto said between pained gasps.

Faye frowned. 'That's ... that's Harry?'

Otto bared his teeth in a mockery of a smile and nodded.

'What did you do to him?' she asked.

'A simple transformation,' Otto said.

Faye crouched down. She was eye level with the

creature as it circled them. She noticed its legs tremble with every step.

'He's in pain,' she said.

'It is always in pain, and always will be for as long as I allow it to live,' Otto said, licking his lips. 'Echoes of the agony of metamorphosis. Its suffering makes it angry, which feeds its hunger. Hate makes it powerful, as you will see when it devours you.'

'Harry.' Faye reached out to the horned beast, looking for some glimmer of humanity in its eyes. 'I'm sorry, Harry. I promise to do what I can to help you. Maybe we can change you back? Maybe Vera Fivetrees knows a way to—'

'Oh, don't be ridiculous, child,' Otto sputtered, then snapped his fingers. 'Harry, start with the children. I want their cries to haunt her before she dies.'

The Jäger bared its teeth and its back legs tensed.

Faye slowly rose from her crouch and placed herself between the Jäger and the children. 'Harry, listen to me,' she said.

The creature snarled, its top lip curling.

'Let me help you, Harry,' Faye said.

'Harry, what are you waiting for?' Otto cried.

The Jäger was trembling, its red eyes darting from Faye to Otto.

Faye kept her voice as calm as possible. 'I might be able to help with the pain, Harry.'

'She lies. Obey me!' Otto screeched. 'Kill them now.'

'Harry, I'm sorry for all that's happened, but it wasn't because of us.'

'Kill them, or I will do it myself and then turn you inside out, you miserable wretch. You think you're in pain now? I haven't even started—'

'If it weren't for Otto . . .' Faye's mind ran dry. How do you appeal to a mindless creature fixated on causing pain and misery? She had to reach out to Harry if he was still in there. What did he love more than anything? 'If it weren't for Otto, you would still have your lovely MG Midget. What about that, eh?'

The Jäger launched itself into the air with incredible strength.

Faye grabbed the children, wrapping her arms around them. She expected a terrible vision before they died, but none came.

The creature bounded directly over them, landing on Otto and biting down on his neck. Otto drew a dagger and stabbed it into the Jäger's side. The creature whimpered and fell onto its back, legs kicking.

Otto took an orb from his cloak. It glowed blue and the void hummed. Bolts of energy lashed at the Jäger, which howled in pain.

The bolts had the same light as the moon.

Faye knew what she had to do.

She closed her eyes, raised her hand at the floating moon and felt for its energy. She expected the same tickle on her palm that she got when she'd first tried this in the standing stones with Mrs Teach and Miss Charlotte. This time, it was like a heavyweight boxer's knockout punch. She gasped at the sheer power thudding into her hand.

'Children, hold on to me. Rudolf, grab Nelson!' she yelled.

The children threw their arms around her. She could feel Nelson wriggling in Rudolf's arms. Still no vision from their touch. Good.

Faye carefully rotated her hand.

The moon vanished.

The light in Otto's orb dimmed like a dead light bulb. His source of power was gone.

'No!' he cried as the Jäger pounced on him.

A roaring wind came and twisted into a vortex around Otto and the beast. They both rolled over into darkness and were consumed by the abyss.

There followed an ear-numbing silence.

Faye and the children huddled together. Nelson barked at where Otto had just been.

Faye could feel the moon inside her. A force older than the Earth itself coursing through her veins. Faye sighed as the atoms in her body sparkled like stars. Her fingertips tingled, her skin glimmered in moonlight. She could change the world with this. Stop wars. Stop everything. Stop time. The power made her giddy and she cackled.

'A witch.' Rudolf's voice came to her through the void.

Faye gasped and opened her eyes. The boy cowered before her, frightened. They all did and started backing away.

Faye moved her hand and the moon returned to its rightful place.

'What the blinkin' flip was that?' she whispered. Her

head was light, her feet felt like they were floating, but she was shrinking back to her usual self.

The children were all staring at her as if she was a ticking bomb.

'I'm all right,' Faye said, only half-believing herself. Her heart slowed to something like normal. 'Just had a bit of a funny turn. Sorry if I scared ya.'

She turned to where Otto and the Jäger had been just a moment ago. The moon floated by trying to look innocent.

'Where are they?' Magda asked.

Faye adjusted her specs and took a breath. 'Back where they came from? Maybe, somewhere in a U-boat in the North Sea, Otto and that creature have just popped out of thin air and are creating all sorts of havoc.'

'Will they come back?' Max asked.

'I reckon Otto will have enough on his plate to keep him away for a while. Even if he doesn't sink to the bottom of the sea, he'll have to explain to his beloved Führer why he doesn't have this.' Faye patted the Ur-Tree's pot.

'We should destroy this now,' Max said. 'Checkmate.'

'I've been thinking about that,' Faye said. 'There's more than one way to end this game, but we need to get back.'

Magda gestured at the eternal void. 'How do we do that?'

'Same way we came in, I suppose,' Faye said with a confidence she didn't entirely feel. How could they retrace their steps in this void? She thought about tapping into the moon's immense power again but, like Doreen's spotted dick and custard, there could be too much of a good thing.

'Nelson,' Rudolf called to the pup, who scurried to the boy's feet. 'Pee-pee.' Rudolf, who hadn't had the opportunity to wash his hands after peeing against the standing stones, dangled his fingers under the dog's nose. Nelson barked, sniffed the air then darted like an arrow into the darkness.

'Follow that dog!' Faye cried.

... Can Go a Long Way

They stumbled back into the circle of stones, which still glowed. The void surrounded the stones, but the sun was rising and the moon was nowhere to be seen. The shadows of Miss Charlotte, Mrs Teach, Lady Aston and her horse were here, too, though there was something different about Charlotte and Mrs Teach. They were more upright, more themselves.

'I need to find the moon,' Faye said, moving to the head of the slaughter stone. 'I need to find it and put it back.' She raised her hand, trying to feel the cold satellite's pulse. 'Where is it? It has to be here. Where can it be?'

The sun was brighter now, the stones thin silhouettes, her friends' shadows gone. Panic clouded Faye's mind.

'It's here,' said a voice next to her ear. It wasn't Miss Charlotte and it wasn't Mrs Teach. It was a woman's voice and Faye dared to wonder who it might be.

Faye felt a hand guide her. She closed her eyes and the moon's familiar faint energy tingled on the palm of her hand. With a slight movement, she put it back.

She heard birdsong. A breeze ruffled her hair. A hand gently squeezed her shoulder.

'Mum?' Faye was giddy, as if waking from a nap. She looked around in every direction, but her mother, if it was her, was gone now. Faye felt faint at the thought of how close she had been to speaking with her again.

'Well done.' Miss Charlotte's voice snapped Faye back to the real world. 'That could have gone very badly for all concerned.'

Faye opened her eyes and hugged Charlotte tight. She needed a cuddle and if her mother wasn't around, then Miss Charlotte would have to do.

'Oh. No. Please don't.' Charlotte stiffened as Faye gripped her more tightly. The children joined in, forming a circle of hugs. 'This is completely unnecessary.'

'*Danke*, Faye,' Rudolf said, and Magda and Max said the same.

'You're talking German again.' Faye released her hold on Charlotte and stepped back. The sun was low, still rising, but its light filtered through the wood's canopy and birds chattered their dawn chorus. Mrs Teach was holding Lady Aston by the arm in a gentle arrest.

Faye smiled and took a breath. 'Miss Charlotte, Mrs Teach, back to normal, then?'

'I feel like someone's had a rummage through my drawers,' Mrs Teach said with a grimace. 'That was a most unpleasant experience, having that awful man's mucky fingers in my brain.'

'Not something I ever want to repeat,' Charlotte

said. 'Like the worst kind of pawing and fumbling from a man.'

Faye grimaced. 'But you're all back to normal,' she said. 'You *are* back to normal, right?'

'There's a very strong argument that Woodville is far from normal at the best of times,' Mrs Teach said. 'But if there is some level of regularity for this village, then I sense we have returned to it.'

'Otto?' Charlotte asked.

'He won't be bothering us for a while,' Faye said. She turned to Lady Aston. 'And neither will Harry, I'm afraid.'

Her ladyship lowered her head. 'I never meant for any of this to happen,' she muttered.

'You radioed Otto, didn't you?' Faye stood before her, arms folded. 'You told him where Harry could find the Ur-Tree. What did you think would happen?'

'I didn't want it destroyed.' Lady Aston raised her chin. 'I wouldn't expect you to understand.'

'No, I don't,' Faye said. 'I don't understand how you could do that to your own son.'

Lady Aston looked at Faye with heavy-lidded eyes. 'When he killed my beloved Thomas, he was no longer my son.'

Faye didn't know what to say to that. She turned to Miss Charlotte and Mrs Teach instead. 'I have an idea of what to do,' she started.

'So do I,' Charlotte said, moving to the tree and producing a box of matches. 'And we can finish this right now.'

'No,' Faye said and was surprised to see Charlotte stop on command. 'That's what someone like Otto would do. I've just learned that a little bit of kindness can go a long way. I have a solution to your problem, Lady Aston. I don't reckon you'll like it, but it's all I've got.'

※

It was a little after nine when Faye found Bertie with her dad at the Green Man. They were drinking tea in silence, both too baffled by the night's strange events to speak. Faye said nothing as she sat on a stool next to Bertie. Terrence poured her some tea. Faye took Bertie's hand.

'How are the children?' Bertie asked.

'Wonderful,' she told him. 'They're wonderful.'

Terrence looked up from his tea. 'They're safe, yes?'

Faye nodded and cradled her mug. She took a breath. She knew what she had to do but wasn't sure how to do it. She gulped at her tea and slammed the mug back on the table, making Bertie jump.

'Dad, I don't want to run the pub.' The words tumbled out faster than she wanted them to. 'Sorry.'

Terrence nodded slowly. 'I know.'

'I'll still help out.' Faye glanced at Bertie who was stuck between them and looked like he wanted to leave but was too polite or terrified to ask. 'But after what's happened these last few days, I think . . . I think I have to be a witch.'

'Have to?' Terrence frowned.

'It's what I am. It's what I'm good at. I think.'

'Are you?'

'She is,' Bertie confirmed.

'I know this isn't what you wanted, Dad, especially after all that Mum went through, but I think I can make a difference to the war effort. I can do my bit.'

'I don't want you putting yourself in danger, Faye. One of the blessings of having a girl is she doesn't go off and fight.'

'Dad, a bloomin' great plane fell out of the sky the other day. There's a war going on right over our heads. I know the sun is shining and the birds are singing, but the war is already here, and it'll get worse before it gets better, and if I can do something to help bring it to an end, I will.'

Terrence placed his hands flat on the table and puffed out his cheeks. 'I've seen some strange stuff these past few weeks, I don't mind telling you. Knowing your mother the way I did and what she could do, I knew she had a gift. I knew there was such a thing as magic, but I chose to pretend it weren't nothing to do with me. And then you came along.' He smiled at Faye. 'I've done all right, haven't I, Faye? I've been a good father?'

'Of course. What are you saying?'

'You ain't a child no more. I can't tell you what to do with your life. I know your mother would have wanted you to be yourself. If this is what you want to do, then you should do it.'

Faye reached across the table and took his hand. 'Thanks, Dad.'

'Just promise me you won't do anything stupid.'

'I could, but you know that would be a lie,' she said with a smile. 'And I'm sorry to leave you in the lurch with the pub. I'll still help out, like I said, and Dougie's always—'

'He's going back to Glasgow,' Terrence said. 'His mother's ill and he reckons a garage up there is less likely to have flaming aircraft come crashing down on it.'

'What about Bertie?'

Bertie choked on his tea.

'He practically lives here anyway,' Faye said, patting the lad's back. 'He's a grafter and knows the punters. What do you say, Bertie?'

Bertie couldn't say anything as he continued to cough away the tea caught in his oesophagus.

Terrence thought it over. 'What about your dad's farm, Bertie?'

Bertie cleared his throat and got his breath back. 'Actually, Mr Bright, Dad has all these land girls working for him. He hardly needs me these days.'

'The girls are taking over,' Terrence said.

'About time,' Bertie replied. 'I can put me feet up.'

'Not if you're working for me, you can't.' Terrence jabbed a thumb at the bar. 'Start cleaning the glasses and get the chairs out. I reckon folk around here will be in need of a drink or two today.'

∅

The following week there was a funeral for Klaus. His body had been taken to a Jewish cemetery in London after his death, but the children never had an opportunity to grieve or mourn him. Magda had written to a rabbi and asked to sit shiva. Seven days of mourning for the children. The rabbi had replied and said it wasn't necessary. They were not close relatives and besides, they were too young. Only adults were obliged to sit shiva. Magda replied immediately, all but demanding that the rabbi come to Woodville to perform a service and allow them to sit shiva. *We have lost our mother and father, our home and our cousin*, she wrote. *All we have is this. Please, let us say goodbye to the boy who saved us.*

The rabbi came and performed the service in the grounds of Hayward Lodge. All were welcome, and everyone came. Villagers, soldiers and staff. It began with a eulogy read by the rabbi. He had spoken with the children beforehand and relayed their memories of Klaus and how he had shepherded them from danger to this village. Prayers, psalms and hymns followed, some in Hebrew. The rabbi explained that shiva would now begin. Magda lit the candle. It was placed in the window of their bedroom at Hayward Lodge. Faye came to visit them every day.

On the final day, the rabbi was there, too. He had news.

'I have found a home for them. A family in Cambridge. They are good people.'

'I thought they might be able to live here?' Faye said, feeling the sadness rise within her. All week, she had been fooling herself that they could stay. She made lists of people who might be able to put them up. She kept suggesting to Mr Pinder that Hayward Lodge was their home now, but since Lady Aston left with Ian, the man from the Secret Service, the house had been handed over to the government who were running it as a full-time hospital. The soldiers, pilots and sailors kept coming from the front lines and still screamed for their mothers at night. That was no place for children.

'Faye, your heart is in the right place, but these children need a home with a family who can care for them all day,' the rabbi told her. 'After everything they have endured, they deserve some peace.'

Faye nodded and asked to say goodbye.

She found them in their room. Cases packed, they sat at the ends of their beds, dressed neatly in clothes donated by villagers, their hair brushed and shoes shined. Nelson barked, and Magda, Max and Rudolf rushed to Faye the moment they saw her.

She threw her arms wide, ready for a final embrace. At the back of her mind, she was worried that she might see another terrible vision, but they were safe now. The worst was over with. No more—

The world swayed around Faye.

Someone lights a candle on a menorah. An elderly man. His remaining tufts of hair are grey. He stands back and blows out the match. He is joined by a woman a few years older who takes his hand, and a younger man who takes hers. They are joined by children, grandchildren, nieces and nephews, brothers and sisters. A family saved by the kindness of strangers and their own determination to survive. Magda, Max and Rudolf weep for all they have lost, and give thanks for all they have.

EPILOGUE

As punishing as the journey had been, Elizabeth Aston – no longer a lady – knew this was only the beginning, and it was better than the alternative which was a firing squad for treason. Faye's solution was indeed the best that Elizabeth could hope for.

As her truck trundled into the foothills of the Tien Shan mountains, she looked around at the place she would have to learn to call home. The snow-capped peaks that rose ghostlike on the horizon were beautiful enough, but here on the streets of the town, peasant children ran alongside the truck laughing and calling at her.

'I don't have any money,' she hollered through the window. 'Go away and pester someone else.'

'I suggest you look again,' Ian said. He had been her constant and tiresome companion through the three weeks of their journey. From the moment they were waved off at Therfield train station by Faye, Miss Charlotte and Mrs Teach, through seasickness on a naval vessel, hiding in coal trucks on trains, freezing in aircraft seemingly made of tin and finally three days of bumping through the bleak Kazakh landscape in a rickety truck, dodging Soviet patrols. Whenever she complained, Ian didn't hesitate to remind her of the firing squad.

Elizabeth gave the children another glance. They weren't begging, they were offering her purple flowers as some sort of gift. She grimaced to think of what she had become since Harry murdered his father. A stranger to compassion.

Ian told Elizabeth he had some experience working here, though he wouldn't elaborate any further than that. He was dressed in khaki military fatigues with no insignia or rank. He had grown a dark and scruffy beard on their journey and wore a traditional Kazakh fur-lined borik hat that sat on his head like a pie. He had sent word ahead of their arrival and followed precise directions to the hills where the sisters were waiting for them.

Their home was a yurt by a stream, and Elizabeth had to concede that it looked quite cosy. Around them, the hills were covered with apple trees, rolling away as far as the eye could see.

The two women stepped outside when they heard the rattle of the truck. Elizabeth had expected cadaverous, weather-beaten hags, but the sisters looked much as they did in her late husband's photograph. Rounded cheekbones and bright green eyes greeted Elizabeth's arrival.

The truck jiggered to a halt and Elizabeth stepped out. She wore a long-sleeved camisole she had picked up in a market in Aktau. Bright red and trimmed with a floral pattern in silver, she had hoped it would make her look imperious, but the two sisters wore more impressive traditional Kazakh shapan velvet robes, deep blue with gold embroidery.

Ian spoke a greeting in Kazakh, but the sisters said nothing. Elizabeth had a feeling that these two would get on with Miss Charlotte and Mrs Teach like a house on fire.

Ian opened the rear of the truck. The Ur-Tree had toppled over, but it was still in one piece with the four remaining apples clinging on to their branches. Elizabeth pulled the pot towards her, stood it upright and patted some of the loose soil back into place. Taking a breath, she heaved it out of the truck and carried it to the sisters as ceremonially as possible.

As soon as they saw it they started wailing, clutching their hair and waving fists. Elizabeth didn't need a translation to understand the emotion, but she asked Ian all the same, just in case their grief came with death threats.

'It's a little tricky to make an exact translation,' Ian said. 'But, roughly speaking, they're saying, "What the bloody hell have you done to our tree?" And there are some general insults, but you don't need to hear those.'

'No threats of disembowelment?'

'Not yet.'

'Good. Remind them of our deal.'

'They know what the deal is—'

'That's as maybe, but it can't hurt to remind them.' Elizabeth placed the tree before the sisters and stepped back. She spoke, and Ian translated. 'Sisters, I return the Ur-Tree, which was taken from you by my late husband. I apologise for the poor condition of the tree and promise to care for it and nurture it for as long as I live.'

The sisters replied, and Ian translated. 'Too bloody right, or something along those lines,' he said. 'Their vernacular is quite colourful.'

'Good. We'll get along just fine. One more thing,' she said to the sisters and Ian continued to translate. 'I would ask that we dedicate the tree to a man of courage. He passed away recently, and I feel it is only right that we celebrate his spirit with this extraordinary tree in this wonderful landscape.'

One of the sisters asked a question.

'Was he a warrior?' Ian said.

'He was certainly brave,' Elizabeth said, and she handed one of the sisters a brass plaque that Faye had given her as a farewell gift. The girl had it made with this moment in mind.

The sister looked at it. Elizabeth doubted the woman could read it but was astounded when she spoke in clear English.

'Klaus Schneider. Yes. It will be done,' she said.

'Thank you,' Elizabeth said, but the sisters were already walking away up the hill towards their orchard with their sacred tree.

Clouds rolled in over the tops of the mountains and

the sunlight caught their edges in silver. Somewhere an eagle screeched, and the sound echoed around them.

A horse, golden-brown with a blaze of white on its face and white stockings on its legs, rounded the yurt and munched on one of the more fruitful apple trees.

'Oh my. Hello.' Elizabeth's heart fluttered to see the beautiful creature. 'Yes. Yes, I think I could quite like it here.'

THE WITCHES OF WOODVILLE
WILL RETURN ...

Acknowledgements

On behalf of the Woodville Village Council, the author should like to offer thanks to ...

All at Simon & Schuster, not least Bethan Jones for her patience and wisdom.

Lisa Rogers for once again saving me from looking like a complete loon.

Ed Wilson for his excellent cricket advice.

Julian Barr, Ian W Sainsbury and Sage Gordon-Davis for their early and insightful feedback.

Victoria Goldman for her feedback on Jewish customs. Any mistakes are mine alone.

Sinead Hering for checking my German.

Duncan Moyse for tips on barrage balloons, which was supposed to be for the next book, but a bit of his feedback ended up in this book, too.

The Hannah Höch collage *Babes in the Wood* does not exist, so don't go googling it, but she was an amazing artist who created mesmeric photomontage work.

JOIN THE WOODVILLE VILLAGE LIBRARY AND GET FREE STORIES

If you're wondering how Charlotte has managed to live such a long life, you can discover more in The Miss Charlotte Quartet, a series of free short stories. Simply sign-up to the Woodville Village Library Newsletter for these and more free and exclusive goodies, including recipes for Jam Roly Poly and Spotted Dick and Custard.

The Head Librarian, Miss Araminta Cranberry awaits your application. Join now at . . .

https://witchesofwoodville.com/#library